BLOOD SCION

BLOOD SCION

DEBORAH FALAYE

An Imprint of HarperCollinsPublishers

HarperTeen is an imprint of HarperCollins Publishers.

Blood Scion
www.epicreads.com

Library of Congress Control Number: 2021942747
ISBN 978-0-06-295404-6 — ISBN 978-0-06-325210-3 (special edition)
ISBN 978-0-06-322645-6 (special edition)

Typography by Corina Lupp
22 23 24 25 26   PC/LSCH   10 9 8 7 6 5 4 3 2 1

First Edition

To Matthew, who planted the seed long before I knew it would bloom.
Thank you for walking this path with me.

THIS BOOK IS INSPIRED BY THE REAL-LIFE HORRORS
ENDURED BY CHILD SOLDIERS AND THE WAR ON
CHILDREN IN PARTICULAR AND THEREFORE TACKLES
THEMES OF WAR, VIOLENCE, AND SEXUAL ASSAULT.
PLEASE READ WITH CARE.

PART I

THE DRAFT

Omo iná là ń rán síná.
It is the child of fire one sends on an errand to fire.
—PROVERB FROM THE ANCIENT KINGDOM OF OYO

ONE

Another night, another dead body that isn't Mama.

I stop digging and stare at the young woman crumpled in the hole. Small, pale, and fragile-looking, a porcelain doll even in death. She hasn't been dead long. A few hours perhaps, a day at most. The bullet hole in her forehead still shines with blood, dried crimson against a purple-tinged face.

May your spirit find rest in òrun rere. I mumble a quick prayer to Olodumarè as I take in the rest of her innocent features. The Nightwalkers must have gotten to her, just like they did Mama. Despite what villagers whisper about her and Felipe, I know those skull-faced monsters are responsible for both of their disappearances.

And I'm going to prove it.

I stab the ground with my shovel, grip tight around its rusteaten handle. Beads of sweat trickle down my face, widening the wet patch on my shirt. After hours of shoveling, I can barely pick my way through the growing pile of debris. The Agbajé foothills have become a labyrinth of skulls and bones, some old enough to crunch underfoot, others crawling with maggots and rot.

It takes three bleeding hours to dig through the hard-packed earth, only to find the next hole empty. With a grunt, I toss the shovel, letting it clatter against the mound of dirt gathered to my right.

There, beneath the rubble of turned soil and uprooted moss, a bud of fabric blooms, petals of golden thread winking in the night.

"Gods above."

For a moment, I can only stare at the àdìre scarf, the shifting sunburst patterns dotting the length of the fabric. With a shaking hand, I reach for it, letting my mud-stained fingers trace the letters stitched along the hem: *A.S.*

Adeline Shade.

Memories I struggled so long to push away come rushing back: rusted needles breaking between calloused fingers, threadbare stitches unraveling after hours of struggle. Mama's beaming face as I draped the scarf around her neck. The crack in her voice when she said, *I'll be back soon.*

But Mama never returned. Worse, they never even found her body.

The ache in my chest swells, and tears gather in my eyes. I clench my jaw against the sob threatening to break free. One by one, I shove each memory away, turning my focus back to the present, to the scarf clutched in my hand.

A hot mountain breeze sweeps across the brush of the hills, swaying the light from my lantern. The darkness is thick now, a black void pressing in on all sides. Somewhere in the distance, the village bell tolls eleven. An hour left to curfew.

I don't have much time.

If I leave now, I could make it back to the village well before the Nightwalkers arrive. The queen's patrol guards are never late, pouring into the village at midnight like rats on a deadly mission. My eyes flick to the corpse a few yards away, and a shudder skitters down my spine. I *should* leave now.

Yet, the scarf in my hand roots me in place, and I can't help but wonder what else might lie beneath the dirt. I only dug four feet deep. *Two more feet.* Two more and perhaps I'd find Felipe's bloody dashiki, Mama's battered sandals, maybe even their remains. Anything to quell the rumors that Mama ran off with my best friend's father. Anything to finally put her memory to rest.

I set a brisk pace. Scoop. Toss. Repeat. But even with the sun long gone, the heat is still a terrible companion, making it harder and harder to keep up my speed. Stifling a groan, I gather another clump of dirt and hurl it to the side.

I spot two brilliant lights on the horizon, and my stomach clenches.

A roar splits the air. Two airships slash across the sky, tendrils of light trailing behind their wings.

Nightwalkers. They're early.

Move, Sloane. Now!

I drop the shovel, panic lancing through me. One second is all I have to douse the flame from my lantern, hoping to gods I'm not too late. Surrounded by the darkness of the foothills, even a light this dim is like waving a flag and screaming, *Here I am. Come kill me!*

Two columns of white light stream down from the airships, basking the hills in a ghostly glow. The beams dart from slope to slope as they search for sudden movements. I scramble down the hill and head straight for the trail. Swarms of fireflies chase me down the rocky terrain. Their low buzz rends the humid air. Beneath the canopy of trees, I can only make out tiny slants of the airships' lights, each one fighting to cut through the dense boughs. Low-hanging branches snag the ends of my braids. The thorny ones prickle my bare skin. But my only thought is of the patrol guards. Anyone foolish enough to be caught by them is executed on sight.

No questions. No pardon. No mercy.

I'm going to die.

A flash of light streaks across my vision as the beams descend on me, trapping me in their glare. In that instant, I'm seized with a paralyzing terror, and I can't bring myself to move. Then the airships come swooping down on a nearby hill, the sound of engines rattling the ground. My survival instinct returns, and I dash through a stream snaking along the foot of the hills. Water sloshes against the rocks lining the creek, drenching my boots, but I don't stop running.

Through the thicket of baobab trees, I spot a small clearing. I veer right. Acres of grassland lie beyond, dotted with thorny shrubs and acacias, their silhouettes menacing in the dark, open space. But my eyes are on the flame flickering beyond the plains.

Agbajé village. *Home.*

I look over my shoulder, listening for the guards over the sighing of warm wind. Behind me, the Agbajé Range rises and falls like a sea of jagged fangs gnawing at the full moon. They could be anywhere on those damned hills. My breath echoes raggedly as I steal another glance around.

Something flickers at the edge of my vision. I reach for my dagger, ready to stab my way free if need be. Instead, a firefly twirls out of the darkness, flapping just above my head. With a sigh, I start toward the plains.

A strong hand yanks me back by my shirt and slams my body to the ground. The dagger slips free. I gasp as air rushes from my lungs. My shoulders burn, the skin scraped raw from the impact. A burly figure straddles me, pinning both knees on my arms. The acrid blend of palm wine and taba on his breath sends my head spinning. One hand clamps tight around my throat while the other holds a gun to my head.

"Going somewhere?"

The voice is cold, colder than the harmattan trade winds, and edged with equal menace. A metal skull clings so tight to the man's face, his head may very well be carved in black iron.

Nightwalker.

On his uniform, the royal crest of the Lucis gleams—a gilded flaming torch with golden-feathered wings spread wide, as if readying for flight.

I stare at him wide-eyed. Never in my life have I seen a Nightwalker. Now, cowering under such a fearsome thing, it's easy to see why villagers call them the horrors of our night.

I thrash in his grasp, but it does no good. His fingers dig deeper into my neck, squeezing until all I can think is *breathe, breathe,*

breathe, and I'm gasping for air, hacking up spit as my vision starts to blur.

"Please—" I'm struggling for words, choking from his iron grip. "I ha-haven't done anything wrong."

He frees my neck and leans over, his masked face close enough I can see the hunger growing in those two slits. They creep over my body and linger on my heaving chest. I don't need an oracle to tell me what he's thinking. It's right there in his predatory gaze, like I'm his first meal after a harsh dry season. A cry escapes my lips. The Lucis guard shoves a gag in my mouth.

His thumb grazes my cheek. "I haven't had a dark skin before." I shudder from the touch. "Such beauty. Hard to believe from a scrawny little thing like you," he murmurs, fingers tracing the edges of my lips.

The shudders grow until I'm a trembling mess. He smiles, satisfied with my reaction, and busies himself with a small black box fastened to his waist. When he brings the strange thing to his mouth, a low buzzing sound breaks out.

"Caught a good one," he says into it, regarding me the way a vulture would a carcass. "Told you flying here early would be worth our time. Over."

The second soldier's voice spills out of the box. Such fear roars through every inch of my being that I don't even hear him. But I'm sure it won't be long now before he, too, arrives, hoping for a piece of the captured prey.

The Nightwalker's hand roams freely until he finds the ìlèkè Mama strung around my hips years ago. Oblivious to their meaning, he hooks his fingers around the tangle of beads and tugs, letting them rattle.

My belly churns, and I wish I could somehow reach for my dagger, wish I could put up a real fight, wish I could do much more than groan and wriggle pathetically. But no matter how hard I squirm beneath him, his knees only sink deeper into my arms, his grip tighter around my neck, his weight heavier on my body.

He's going to have his way with me. Then he's going to kill me. The way the Lucis do all their victims. A show of power. To remind us just how vulnerable we are. It doesn't matter if they capture a young child or an old maid. We are all targets, all prey to these skull-faced monsters.

They say just before death, life flashes before your eyes. They are wrong. I see nothing but the reality of this moment, the drumming of my heart inside my chest, spurring my body to act, to move. Even in the face of horror, Mama taught me not to give up.

Her scarf flutters in the wind, and an image wrestles its way into my mind. The fall of Mama's brown locks, the spark behind her golden eyes. Each memory cuts deep, like the machete she always carried in her pack, a painful reminder of what the Lucis took from me. What they're *still* taking from me. These bastards ruined my search. Because of them, I may never have another chance to make things right. And for that, I will fight. For that, I will make them pay.

Blood rushes to my face, bringing with it warmth and courage. When two fingers snake inside my mouth, I don't hesitate to clamp my teeth down on them. Hard enough to slice through calloused skin. Hard enough to feel the tangy taste of blood on my tongue. Even when the Nightwalker points his gun at my face, I don't stop biting. I'd rather die. I'd rather die now than be raped and killed later.

Do it. Shoot me.

He doesn't. Instead, he strikes the butt of the gun on my head, sending sharp bolts of pain through my skull. I loosen my teeth's grip on his finger and spit blood in his face.

"Bitch!" His hand comes down hard on my cheek, drawing tears to my eyes. Blood oozes from the cut on my lips. "I'll enjoy making you scream, girl."

Another hit. This time, a fist right to my head.

A scream erupts from my throat, and I bite the insides of my cheeks to keep from crying. My head rings, a loud buzzing sound that drowns out the Nightwalker's brassy voice. White spots dance across my vision, and I see two of him: two skull masks moving above my face, two iron hands hurling blows at me, two mouths coughing up phlegm and spitting on me.

My eyes close.

The slimy blob running down my cheek stirs a burning sensation deep within. Time slows. I hear the Nightwalker's heavy breathing mingling with my own. The roar of my heartbeat in my ears. An echoing clamor in my skull. The heat, wretched as it always is, closes in around me, coating my skin and setting every nerve on fire. A familiar rush of life and power thrums through my veins, begging me to set it free.

No, no, no. Not here. Not in front of him.

With every bit of strength I can gather, I push back against the àse already flowing through my blood, tamp down the magic humming in the deepest parts of me, knowing what the consequences will be if he finds out what I truly am. But the more I fight it, the worse the pressure in my head flares, sending daggers of pain across my body.

My àse swells. It unfurls, a dormant beast awakening from its slumber. Within seconds, my entire body is drenched in a sick sweat. Heat, pure and raw, blazes in me like wildfire, consuming every inch until it becomes impossible to contain.

Flames crackle to life on my arms, flickering in and out of sight, but not before the Nightwalker notices. The blood drains from his face at the tracery of fiery veins bulging against my dark skin.

His eyes flash. He rolls off my arms at once, fumbling for his gun.

Fear ripples through me. *Run,* my mind screams. *Run!*

I push off the ground and slap my hands hard against his uniform, taking what little chance I have at freedom. Red sparks burst from my fingers into his chest.

A shrill cry spills from the Nightwalker's lips. He tumbles to his side, releasing me. I push myself backward as fast as I can. A cloud of dust kicks up into the air as he thrashes around in the sand, calling for help, reaching for me. I scramble farther away.

The metal skull on his face reddens, a deep scarlet that glistens like liquid fire in the darkness. The Nightwalker howls in agony, clawing at the flaming mask. It stays put, melting onto his face.

"Make it stop," he cries. "Make it stop."

Even if I could, I don't know how. Years of suppressing my àse, hiding my power from those who would easily kill me if they knew who I was, have made me just as much a stranger to the beast as he is. I can't stop this.

And why should I?

Even if I could, I wouldn't.

Something else snags the Nightwalker's attention. With maddening haste, he tears through layers of his uniform, revealing bare, pallid skin.

I gasp in horror at the fire spreading beneath his flesh in a growing mass of red. I've never seen it like this before, and I can only watch as ten quick fingers chase the spider veins of heat fanning out across his chest.

The Nightwalker's skin starts to blacken. The smell of copper and burnt flesh sears my nose. The air is thick with it. *With him.* It clings to me like a second layer of skin I want nothing more than to peel off.

My heart hammers against my ribs. *Leave,* the voice in my head warns. *Get out of here.* But shock grips me with desperate claws, and I'm powerless against its hold.

The screams come to a halt. My gaze fixes on what's left of the man before me. His scorched face moves, twitching where his lips once were.

"I know what you are." His garbled voice barely rises above a whisper. "Scion."

For a second, the word hovers in the fiery space between us.

Scion. A descendant of the ancient Orisha gods.

Scion. The same people the Lucis have hunted and killed for over three centuries.

Scion. Scion. SCION. The word echoes over and over in my brain. I grasp my head, wanting to claw away the thought, his voice, all of it. I don't need to hear it to know what I am. *Who I am.* It's written in the àse raging inside me, a fire born of Olodumarè's divine energy, flaming bones and blood underneath my skin.

I am a descendant of Shango, the god of heat and fire. I am a living inferno.

I am a dead girl walking.

"You will die for this," the Nightwalker growls with the last of his strength, a deep, guttural sound that's more animal than man. "Your family, your friends, every last one of them. They will bleed for—"

He crumbles before my eyes, leaving behind dark plumes of smoke and ash. The flakes hit the ground like a downpour, coating my face with soot. I scream, a wretched sound twisting into the night until my throat gives out.

I'm a quivering mess, too weak to do anything but stare. For a second, I almost want to believe this is all a dream, a horrible nightmare. I will wake to the mud-caked walls of my hut, the morning sound of axes biting into wood, the strong aroma of Baba's ègúsí soup. But the churning of hot, seething embers floods my senses like a ruptured dam, drowning me in a pool of heat and pride and fury, and I know this isn't a dream.

My breaths come in sharp, ragged gasps. Tears I didn't know had gathered trickle down my cheeks. I wipe them away quickly. Now isn't the time to cry. I have to get out of here. I have to make it home.

Bushes rustle in the shadows of the clearing. Amid the chaos, I'd almost forgotten about the second Nightwalker. If he catches me, he'll discover who I am and realize what I've done. The punishment for killing an officer of the crown is death.

Cold fear bleeds through me at the thought of being carted off to Avalon, the capital island, to face the Lucis and their royal bloodlines as they scream for my execution. I'm sure it won't be a quick bullet to the head. It will be planned, torturous. A slow death. I'm a Scion who killed one of their own, and they will rip me apart for it.

No. I shake my head, refusing to accept my fate. I won't die tonight. Not here, not in Avalon, not after everything.

I snatch my dagger off the ground and push myself up, stifling a moan. My body aches, my muscles throb, every part of me over-wrought from the horror that just took place.

The Nightwalker's charred face swims into my mind. With one final glance at his scattered ashes, I do the only thing left for me to do:

I run.

TWO

By the time I arrive at the village square, I'm stumbling over myself, but I don't dare stop to rest. Merchants' stalls blur past, their display stands long abandoned. Usually, in the heat of the day, the square buzzes with the boisterous energy of vendors screaming out prices for their wares, hoping to draw the eyes and silver keddi of lowly shoppers. But with only a few minutes to twelfth bell, the villagers of Agbajé have fled into the shadows of their huts, behind strong latches and bars meant to shield them from the Nightwalkers' frequent invasions.

Families killed in their homes. Wives raped as their husbands are forced to watch. Children yanked from sleep and shot dead before parents who dared rebel against the Lucis monarchy. Day after day, new stories replace old ones, but the horror remains the same.

My mind flashes to the Nightwalker I incinerated minutes ago. The taste of soot still lingers on my tongue. All my life, I've been told to hide my magic, suppress my àse. To protect myself from the wrath of the Lucis; keep my family safe. What will the royals do to me once they learn the truth? Who will save Baba from their guards' bullets? Fear curls through me, along with the àse still churning in my blood.

By gods, what have I done?

Pain gnaws at my limbs, making every bleeding step a torment. Despite the ache, I push forward, terrified the second Nightwalker may have tracked me down to the village. I sprint from one alley to another, as though his booted steps are an echo behind me. The stars are my light, guiding me through a village that's known darkness for so long, even the smallest stars shine bright.

Sweat rolls down my neck, soaking through the collar of my shirt. The fire clings to me still, a miserable leech pulling warmth into every crevice of my body. I draw deep, shuddering breaths, hoping to release some of it. But it only worsens when my finger grazes one of the sconces flanking the alleyways. A flaming tendril spills from my fingertips into the wrought iron holder. Unlit torches blaze to life along the hardened clay walls. I force myself to look away, rounding a narrow bend I know too well.

The bell tolls just as I reach my hut. Stained mud bricks rise before me, with scalloped whorls and stepped patterns arching from the base up to the thatches crowning the roof. I was only a child when Mama painted the elaborate frescoes using wet soot and charcoal. Years later, the very sight of them still warms my heart.

I dart past Baba's favorite kola nut tree and tumble onto the makeshift porch. My legs wobble over the stacked stones he and I set into the ground when I was barely old enough to lift them. A dim glow of light streams through the cracks beneath the door. I crumple in a broken heap before it, no longer able to stand. I can only hope my grandfather finds me in time.

"Sloane?" His strained voice flutters out. Loud, frantic shuffles echo behind the door. Seconds later, Baba yanks open the wooden frame.

"Gods above!" He presses both hands to his heart when his eyes land on my bruised face. His breath stutters until I fear he might collapse.

I reach out a shaking hand to steady him. "Baba—"

"Come, come." Like a Nagean cheetah rescuing his cub, he lowers himself to the ground and swoops me up. I can't bring myself to look him in the eyes—or do much else, for that matter. I can only surrender to the wave of exhaustion sweeping over me as he carries me inside and kicks the door closed.

The second my body hits our thinned cushions, my vision starts to blur. I'm overwhelmed by the sudden urge to fall asleep.

Baba has the sense to smack my cheek gently, whispering, "Stay awake, dear," as he rushes to collect crushed Siam weed and lemongrass salve from the drawer at his feet. After wiping my face with a wet rag that quickly turns brown with blood, he spreads the Siam weed over my cheeks, ignoring the tremors in his fingers.

I hiss as the crushed leaves sink into my wounds, the sting settling once Baba applies the lemongrass salve. This isn't the first time he's seen to my injuries after so many street scuffles, but there's a difference between a few measly scrapes and the Nightwalker's brutal blows. The memory rouses the last remnants of àse in my core. The clamor in my head swells, always, always inaudible. Still, heat seethes inside me, bubbling dangerously close to the surface. Try as I might to push back against it, my skin pricks with a sharp pain, and I'm no match for the cursed thing.

I was only five when the first buzz of àse sang through my veins. A sacred life force bestowed onto every Scion by Olodumarè, the supreme creator, àse connects me to Shango, my blood deity. It allows me to invoke the god of fire's spiritual energy on earth. Yet, Mama and Baba have done everything to crush its presence ever since.

Flames slither through my veins, branches of red across obsidian skin. Sweat breaks out on my face.

"You—should—get the—tea—" I shudder.

Baba's eyes flash when realization strikes him. Then he's on his feet, dashing into the corridor, leaving me with pain and heat as my clinging companions.

Control it, I tell myself, trying to grab onto my power before it flares into something much stronger. But my years of fear—fear of who I am and what I'm capable of, fear of the Lucis and what they'll do to me if I'm discovered—have made it impossible. So I'm not surprised when, instead of control, I do the opposite: I unleash. Fire leeches from the table lantern across from me and settles onto my arms. I throw myself off the couch, determined not to burn the threadbare sofa like I did its twin.

As flames spit and crackle up my arms, I cringe, remembering the first time I ever felt the heat of my magic. Though I don't want to think about it, my mind takes me back to the village inferno from years ago. I hear the screams of the wounded, the never-ending cries of terror. The images scar and burn, a sickening reminder of the cost of my àse.

"Sloane." Baba's voice is a ladder in the horrible well of memories, and I latch onto it, climbing out into reality.

He appears before me, a steaming flask clasped between his hands. I snatch the cup of àgbo from him and guzzle the home-brewed herb down to its last drop. Ten years spent drinking the tea doesn't stop me from flinching against the taste, willing it to pass. It doesn't, and I could almost retch from the bitter tang of neem leaves and iyerosun crystals on my tongue, the stench filling my nose. Almost immediately, the relief I've longed to feel all night washes over me, dulling the flames and the clamor in my head. The calm that comes after is merciful and familiar as heat recedes slowly beneath my skin, a tamed beast retreating to its cage.

"It's okay. You're okay." Baba's voice barely rises above a murmur as he guides me back to the couch as though I am a broken child. When he takes up the space beside me, I press myself into him, a trembling little girl craving only the comfort of her grandfather.

He leans back, and I do the same, meeting his worried eyes. "Where did they find you?"

Of course he knows who did this to me. From the ragged strips of fabric hanging off my body to the swollen bruises marring my face, I'm a barely breathing Nightwalker victim. For a village that mourns a death or two every morning, I'm a bleeding miracle. And I have this damned magic to thank for it.

So here in the safety of our hut, with nothing but inches between us, I tell Baba everything. Everything but the rape I almost suffered at the hands of the first Nightwalker. I don't know why I choose to keep it to myself. Why I feel my silence is better than the truth. Even when I plead with myself to say something, do something, *anything*, to reveal what my mouth can't speak, I taste the Nightwalker's fingers on my tongue and the only thing that rises in my throat is bile. With great effort, I force it down.

Baba listens as I stumble through the last of my tale. His gaze falls on me, and in his eyes, I see the desperation and fear I've felt since I slapped my hands on the Nightwalker. He tries to recover quickly, to mask his emotions with a quick breath, but nothing can erase what I did.

Tonight, I almost doomed us both. If that monster had survived the attack, if the second Nightwalker had found me in the clearing, our lives would be different now.

In Nagea, to harbor a Scion is to suffer the same fate as one. The Lucis don't only kill us; they make sure to slaughter anyone who dares protect us. How many days has it been since a mother and her eight-year-old boy were peppered with bullet holes in the village square? How many weeks since the last Cleansing, when ten Scions were burned to death in the distant city of Ilé-Ifè?

A new wave of heat rises in me with each painful memory, simmering just beneath my skin like it always does when news of another Scion execution spreads through the village.

Long ago, Nagea was home to the sixteen kingdoms of the Yoruba people, each land ruled by Scions descended from a different Orisha god. Ilé-Ifè once thrived in the hands of the descendants of Obatala, the god of mind and body. And the dynasty of Shango reigned over the vast empire of Oyo, the flaming kingdom. Those days, Scions were alive and free, revered even. There were shrines dedicated to children whose àse had just awakened, sages who taught them how to harness, mold, and nurture their deity's divine power until they became alaàse.

But all of that ended 342 years ago, when the Lucis arrived from the ruins of the old world and invaded Nagea, conquering the Yorubas and every last Scion among them.

Now, even though I'm sure there are other Yorubas and Scions in the village, you wouldn't know it if you went looking. We have no choice but to hide with our tails tucked—growing without an identity, living without a culture, and taking on names that embody nothing of who we are.

Mama once told me her real name is Adelina Folashadé, but to claim it is to die like the other Yorubas before her. So she dropped a few letters and became Adeline Shade, another villager eking out a living in the slums. When she named me Sloane, she gave me a name without burden, without any ties to my past, and I grew up a girl with little knowledge of her culture.

I am Yoruba but I am not. This is Nagea, but it is not. My world is only half of what it should be, and I am only half of what I really am.

I cannot afford to be whole.

On instinct, I feel for the strings of ìlèkè around my waist, the red and white Shango beads Mama gave me the night my àse manifested. A token of my connection to the Orisha we are descended from, a small reminder of who I am in a world that wishes to make me forget.

Baba takes my hands, his fingers still trembling. I squeeze hard, wanting to give him the strength I know he needs. But I fear I have nothing more to give.

"Your mother and I have spent fifteen years keeping you safe." His brown eyes darken with determination. "That won't change now."

I want so badly to believe him, to trust his words, but fear wraps me in a cocoon so tight, I cannot see past it. Still, for him, I nod.

As we sit in the silence of our dingy hut, my eyes wander the room, forcing me to see the things I couldn't when I first arrived. Colorful paper streamers dangle from the thatched roof, and I don't doubt both Luna and Teo had a hand in it. A calabash bowl full of fried periwinkles lies on a stool in the corner, close enough to smell the scented thyme and dash of Maggi cube Baba seasoned them with.

My stomach growls in response. I pretend not to hear it as my eyes settle on the slab of raisin fruitcake spread next to the bowl, its fifteen candles blown out. Just the sight of it makes my insides ache.

All my grandfather wanted was to give me the same kind of celebration Mama used to when she was still around. But how do you celebrate the day you were born when it is also rooted in pain? On this day two years ago, Mama left the hut and never came back. On this day two years ago, my world fell apart.

Yet, despite the lump heavy in my throat, I imagine Baba limping around the marketplace, trading what little keddi we have for a bowl of periwinkles and a slab of fruitcake. Guilt ripples through me.

"Happy birthday, Sloane," he says, even though I don't deserve it.

I drop my gaze to the floor in shame. "I should have been here. I'm sorry."

"You think I don't see, but I've watched you leave this hut with a shovel every day." When he speaks, I expect to find a hint of bitterness in his voice, but all I hear is pity. He rests his fingers under my chin, tipping my head up to meet his eyes. The dim lantern on the table casts jagged shadows across his worn face, making him look far older than he is.

"I know where you go, what you're searching for. Yes, the village speaks, but not every noise is worthy of your ears, Sloane."

"How can you even say that?" I shoot him a glare. "How much damage has their noise done to this family? There are baskets of cassava roots from last harvest rotting in the kitchen because no one is buying them. We can barely afford a week's meals. How long before we're standing in an alleyway begging for some silver keddi?"

Before Mama's disappearance, our cassava field was among the few thriving ones in the village. Harvested tubers were in such high demand, even merchants from the city traveled the long, arduous journey from Ilé-Ifè to Agbajé for their very own bushels. The profit after every harvest was enough to feed our bellies and put some savings away for drought season. But all of that changed when Mama and Felipe didn't return.

Once the rumor that they'd run off together began to spread, every trader in the village avoided our field as if the crops were infected with a poisonous blight. Even merchants from Ilé-Ifè stopped visiting for more bushels. No one is willing to trade with families of runaways. They think it's only a matter of time before Mama and Felipe are caught, and anyone associated with them thrown in prison. So to protect their heads, they shun us instead.

Even when I fought and cursed and pleaded, no one would listen to the foolish claims of a desperate child. Not without proof.

"I was so close tonight." I shake my head, hating myself for not digging fast enough, hating the Nightwalkers even more for arriving before midnight.

It's only then I realize Mama's scarf is no longer in my possession. The only piece of a clue I've found since she disappeared and I lost it. It's all I can do not to scream. I clench my fists and close my eyes. I just want to make things right. Gods, why does it have to be this hard?

"It is not up to you to save this family." The pain in Baba's voice is unmistakable. "You're still a child. You are my granddaughter, and you're all I have left. I won't lose you."

My eyes snap open when he dissolves into tears, his quiet sobs echoing in the emptiness of our hut. I frown at him. Baba doesn't cry. If he does, it's never around me.

I give his shoulder a gentle squeeze. "What is it?"

Veins web on his forehead, protruding with every clench of his jaw. At the sight of it, a ribbon of dread coils itself around my heart.

"Has something happened?" I press further. "Baba, tell me. Please."

"Officers caught three child soldiers trying to flee earlier." He can barely force the words out. "Nicolai was amongst them."

"By gods . . . ," I gasp, picturing the tanned face of the boy I grew up with. The boy I once played and fought with. Memories of our time wooden wheeling in the village park flit through my head, and a deep ache settles in my chest.

This can't be real.

In two days, Nicolai was set to be transported to the capital island to be trained as a child soldier. From there, he would have been sent to the desert up north to join more soldiers like himself in the Lucis' decades-long war against the Shadow Rebels. It's why many children try to run after getting drafted. Though no deserter has ever made it past the city borders. They always get caught. And they always get killed.

Nicolai knew this. So many of us do. Even though no one wants to be forced into a life of war, we only risk so much more by attempting to flee.

"Did they come for them?" I try to ignore the tightness in my throat. "His parents? Talia?"

Baba nods. "Around seventh bell. One airship and six soldiers."

Of course. It's not enough for the Lucis to kill anyone who tries to desert; they have to destroy their families too. Nicolai's parents will most likely die in Cliff Row prison while his little sister wastes away in the Itakpe mines. All for a crime they didn't commit, a punishment they don't deserve.

"Sloane . . ." Baba pauses, as if trying to figure out the right way to tell me what he must. He clenches and unclenches his fists, his well-kept anger threatening to unravel. "They will try to replace those boys."

I realize then the meaning behind his pain, what he's been wanting to say all along. Despite the heat from the table lantern, that realization alone sends a chill across my skin.

"Gods above," I whisper, my teeth chattering.

Nicolai's death burns through my mind, and now more than ever, I wish he hadn't tried to run. I wish he and the other children could have at least made it to Avalon—all so I won't have to dread what's surely coming.

When the Lucis issued a royal order for the Draft fifteen years ago, they also decreed that for every dead conscript, another able-bodied child would take their place. As long as they weren't Yorubas, as long as they weren't Scions, any young, innocent Nagean could just as easily be recruited.

Sharp nails dig into my palms as Baba's voice rises around me, offering words of hope, words meant to calm my racing heart. But it becomes harder to hear him over the dooming word echoing in my head.

Redraft.

Five days ago, when Lucis messengers roamed about the village serving draft letters, I knew not to worry. At least not for another year.

I wasn't fifteen then. I wasn't of age.

I glance across the room, at the slab of fruitcake in the corner.

But now? Now I am.

THREE

I wake to the spicy aroma of pepper soup.

Across from me, Luna perches at the edge of the bed, a calabash bowl balanced between her freckled brown hands. Wisps of hot steam curl up from the rim before fading into the air, and I can already imagine the chunks of smoked goat meat and dried stockfish swimming in the bowl. A growl rumbles in the pit of my stomach. It's what I get for missing out on last night's meal.

"Are you all right?" Luna asks the second her eyes meet mine.

I manage a nod and pretend not to notice the black long-sleeved sweater she's wearing, even in the blistering heat. With a grunt, I force myself up on the bed, squinting against the light slanting through the wooden shutters of my window, casting golden stripes across the carpet of woven rushes. My only pair of boots lies in the middle, grass stained and ripped from my time on the foothills mere hours ago. Day-old memories cascade through my mind. I clench my jaw as my gaze settles on my best friend's slumped shoulders, her disheveled curls, her shaky limbs. I can only imagine what she and Teo must have felt all night, wondering if I was lying in some dingy alleyway with a bullet buried in my head. On instinct, I reach for Luna's hand and squeeze.

"I'm fine," I tell her with more conviction than I feel.

With a sigh, she offers me the bowl. "Here. We both know nothing cures like—"

"Pepper soup," we say at the same time.

I grin, staring down at the dish and the heap of mouth-watering delicacies floating in the brown broth. A more generous helping than I know she can afford.

"Lu," I breathe, "this must have cost some keddi."

"Not really. I may have promised Alhaja I'd weave her a new straw mat."

Her sweet, dimpled smile is enough to force one onto my lips, despite the bruises stinging the corners of my mouth.

I gulp down the soup in no time, relishing the fiery taste of the broth and the tenderness of the fine goat meat. When I'm done, Luna takes the bowl and tosses it at the foot of my bed. Then she crawls up the tiny cot and flings her slender arms around me. I almost yelp from the pain shooting down my sides. But I hug her tighter, damning any pain I feel to hell.

"You frighten me, hermana," she whispers in the native tongue of her old-world ancestors, and the strain in her voice twists my insides.

I've never seen her this rattled, even though we've practically been attached at the hip since our crawling days. Ever since our mothers first met during our mandatory lessons at the institution. I don't have a sibling of my own, so she's easily the closest thing I have to a sister, though we're nothing alike. Luna isn't Yoruba, for one. Her ancestors, like many others, were brought to Nagea during the Lucis migration. But more than that, Luna is warm, gentle, and sweet—and I'd sooner take a beating than allow anything to happen to her.

I plant a kiss on the top of her head. "I think I frighten myself too."

She untangles herself from me carefully and sits up. Relief floods me when she doesn't bring up the redraft. It's the last thing I'd want right now. Ever since Baba gave news about the boys' deaths, I can already feel my hope burning away, like wax trickling down a melting candle. Even now, my skin prickles, dreading what's to come. I take little comfort in knowing that no matter what happens, at least Luna won't have to worry about conscription. She's still fourteen, her birthday a few months away. She's safe—*for now*.

I drop my head onto her lap. She grabs the ends of my braids and starts unraveling them. With every cornrow she takes out, the tension on my roots fades, and I sigh with relief. When she's done, she works her fingers through the kinks with care, and gods bless her, she proceeds to massage my scalp for a full, glorious minute before weaving each wiry strand back into place.

We are quiet for some time after, the only sound in the room my crunching hair and her practiced fingers. The silence is uncomfortable now. Almost immediately, I know what thoughts are occupying her mind, and for once, I pray she won't speak of them. She does anyway.

"Why didn't you tell me you were headed to the foothills?"

I work to keep my voice low and steady. "Because I knew you'd try to stop me."

When her fingers tense around the ends of my braids, I know I've said the wrong thing. Luna doesn't lie, and she only demands the same from me in return. A simple request, as one should expect from a friend, a sister. But we've lived different lives. Truly, my secrets and lies are what keep me safe, and she couldn't begin to understand the weight of such a burden.

"This is becoming too dangerous, Sloane." She smooths down the stray wisps of hair between the braids and rests a hand on my shoulder. I shrug it away, my irritation rising. "Night after night, you risk your life searching the Agbajé hills. And for what? To almost get killed by Nightwalkers? When does it end?"

"Ha! I could ask you the same." I sit up, ignoring the way my limbs tremble even at the slightest motion. I nod at the sleeves stretching down her arms. "You think I don't know why you're wearing that? You told me you'd stop. What happened?"

Her honey-brown eyes flash, and for a moment, she watches me quietly. Then she glances down at her sleeves, as if she can see right through the braided wools, see the rows of scars darkening her wrists.

The sight hurts more than any village rumor could. A reminder that Baba and I are not the only ones suffering from Mama and

Felipe's disappearance. My best friend hurts, too, if not more, and my heart breaks for the girl who needs a razor to manage her pain.

A thorny silence spreads between us. With each passing second, I'm forced to relive old, painful memories I wish I could forget—finding Luna alone in her bath chamber, wrestling the blade from her grip, wiping every speckle of blood on the floor with a wet rag. Two years since she's been struggling with this illness. Two years of praying to Olodumarè I don't walk into the bath chamber someday and find my best friend at death's door. Her gaze falls on me. I wince at the tears filling her eyes.

"Talk to me," I say, softening my tone. "Please."

"You wouldn't understand" is all she whispers.

Her words give me pause. For a moment, I think she will say more, reveal more, but she only draws a breath, reining her memories and grief inward like she always does.

"All of this is because of the rumors," I hiss through gritted teeth. "Because of what the villagers are saying."

Before the disappearance, Luna Herrera was the sun that warmed many people's hearts. Shoppers who bought her woven wares always left her stall with wide grins and joyous laughter. She was especially popular among the merchants, able to charm her way into lesser deals with nothing more than an easy smile. But all of that ended the night her father promised to return and never did. The night that changed our lives and turned our fates. The night that broke my best friend.

"You see why I have to prove these idiots wrong." I search her eyes for a glimmer of understanding. "If I can show them the Nightwalkers are the ones behind what happened, things can start to get better. I can fix this, Lu. I can make it right."

A disapproving frown twists her face. "That won't change the past."

"No, but it will end this pain." When she shakes her head, my jaw tightens. I bite back my growing frustration. "By gods, Luna. You can start to heal. Don't you want that?"

She doesn't speak for some time after. While she does her best to avoid my gaze, pulling at some loose thread on her sweater, I fix mine on her, anticipating a glance sooner or later. Finally, she looks at me.

"Someday, I worry you will go too far." She twines her fingers with mine and squeezes. "If the Lucis are behind this like you say, then maybe you should stop digging for answers. You got lucky last night, Sloane. Luck like that doesn't come around twice."

"No," I growl, and force myself off the bed. After throwing on my boots, I rummage through the scattered heaps of clothes littering my floor, searching for a clean shirt. When I'm all dressed, I whip around and glare at her. Why can't she see that I'm trying here, trying for us, trying for her. *Gods!*

"I don't care how risky it is." I shove a few daggers into the sheath around my waist. "Hell, I could give two dungs what happens to me. I'm not giving up until I prove the Nightwalkers are responsible for what happened."

I'm halfway across the room when she calls after me. "Where are you going?"

"To Teo's." I don't bother turning around. "At least he understands what I'm doing . . . and is willing to help."

Before she can try to stop me or ask more questions, I yank the door open and set off down the corridor, boots scraping against the earthen floor.

The second I step outside the hut, I inhale deeply, trying to gather my ragged breath. Instead, I'm greeted by the stink of dried sweat and elephant dung. Down the dirt road, a rather hefty pair lumbers past, each with a grinning child perched atop its slate-colored skin. I'm still staring when the sight of a uniformed Lucis messenger stops me short.

A tremor begins in my chest and quickly spreads to my limbs. They tremble as I wait for the messenger to make it up the last stone step, fighting against every ounce of instinct urging me to flee.

Fear hums beneath my skin as I fix my gaze on his pale face, half hidden beneath the visor pulled low over his head. From the moment Baba told me about Nicolai's and those other boys' deaths, I knew what it would mean for every fifteen-year-old across the nation. What it would mean for me. Still, some foolish part of me had hoped—even prayed to Olodumarè—that no Lucis would show up at my door. That my life doesn't end with a single envelope.

I should have known better. After all, hope is a dying ember in Nagea, and not even the gods can bring back the flame.

I can barely breathe as the messenger stops before me.

"Sloane Shade of One Hundred and Nine Agbajé village?" His voice is sharp, like the edge of a razor, and equally menacing.

"Y-yes?"

A bead of sweat crawls its way down my neck as his hand slithers inside the bag strapped across his shoulder. Seconds later, he slaps a white envelope lined in gold foil into my hands, and just like that, the last shred of hope I held on to disappears.

My eyes are on the Lucis' winged-torch crest stamped right into the paper. I don't need the messenger to tell me what this is. I already know.

It is my draft letter.

FOUR

ORDER TO REPORT FOR CONSCRIPTION

Her Royal Highness,
Queen Olympia of the Turais Bloodline
To Sloane Shade of 109 Agbajé Village
Born April 18, 327 PME

By order of the queen, you are hereby notified that you were, on April 19, 342 PME, legally drafted for training and service to the Avalon Defense Forces for the period of three years. You will report to your city dome on April 20, 342 PME, for assessment before departure. If you are not accounted for, you will be deemed a runaway, committing treason against the royal crown and the Lucis, and will thereby face execution, as stipulated in Article 138 of the updated 327 PME Penal Code.

Signed,
Thelma Craft
Secretary of the Avalon Defense Forces
Long Live the Bloodlines.

I read the bleeding letter again and again. My eyes run over every inked word on the page, wishing for the world they'd fade, yet knowing how foolish a wish it is. I am a child soldier now, bound in service to the Lucis and their terrifying army.

Dear gods. My limbs give way. I sink to the ground, collapsing against the cracked clay walls of my hut.

Three years. Three years without my home, without Luna and

Teo and Baba. Tears sting my eyes at the thought of never seeing my grandfather again. The only family I have left, and they wish to tear us apart. Since Mama disappeared, I've protected Baba just as much as he has me. When the tremors began in his right leg, it was me who carved a walking stick for him from the heartwood of an iroko tree. Me who spoon-fed him for a month when he came down with a horrible fever and couldn't lift a finger. I've stolen from the marketplace so we both could eat. How will Baba live without me? How will I survive without him?

My whole body shakes. With a scream, I snatch the draft letter off the ground and rip it to shreds. But even without the paper, the knowledge of what awaits me in a few hours gnaws at my core.

Avalon. The capital island. That's the last place any child should be, much less a Scion. If the Lucis discover what I am, I doubt they'd hesitate to kill me. Even if I manage to keep my identity a secret, becoming a child soldier means fighting the Shadow Rebels. I don't know which is worse—dying for who I am, or being forced to kill other Scions and Yorubas. Being forced to kill my own people.

Tears spill down my cheeks. I gasp for air. *Breathe, Sloane. Breathe.* Mama's voice is in my head, the ghost of her hand on my chest. What I would give now to be wrapped in her arms. If Mama were here, she'd wipe away my tears and tell me I was greater than my fears. She'd tell me I was made of heart and fire, and not even the Lucis can take that from me. She'd tell me no matter what, I can survive this.

I try to hold on to that thought, try to channel the strength of the woman who once fought her way out of a Nagean leopard's mouth with nothing but her bare hands. I try, desperately, to believe. But I am not my mother.

At the sound of sandals scraping against the rushes in my hut, I force myself up. I can't face Luna or Baba right now. To see the pain and fear in their eyes, knowing I'm the one who put it there, is far more than I can bear. So I head into the streets, past the stand of baobabs stretching along the winding path, and make for Teo's hut.

At Ireyomi crossing, the dusty road twists downward, dragging me toward the Oba River. Teo's hut is perched on a hill beside it like a malimbe bird on a raised wire. A year ago, he'd gutted the whole thing and rebuilt it using strong bamboo from his master's shop. Now, the house is one of the few fine ones in the village, a marvel made not of mud and thatch, but real, polished wood.

I pause at the entrance. A few feet away, Teo crouches before a fenced coop where Fat Daisy, the village's largest chicken, plucks grains of corn right out of his hand. Once, she had been a scrawny little chick, the last of her brood, before Teo saved her from the mouth of a vulture. He's raised her since, plumping her up with gods know what.

My heart thuds at the familiar sight of his warm chestnut face, his slow-growing buzzed hair, and the thin coat of sawdust perpetually stuck to his right lobe. Another day, another moment, I'd reach for his ear and scratch off the powdery flakes of wood. In turn, he'd shove me away gently. But today, I can't bring myself to do it. Not when I have to say goodbye.

Just a few nights ago, we made a plan to travel to the neighboring city of Oyo at week's end. We'd heard that a Lucis defector was selling information on missing victims. Victims like Mama and Felipe. But everything has a price, and for the informant to talk, word on the street was he demanded one gold nagi. A hundred silver keddi. A fortune I couldn't afford. Until Teo offered to scrape up every last silver himself.

Now I have to tell him none of it matters. Even if he managed to get the money, I won't be able to go to Oyo with him. I'll never get to prove the Nightwalkers are responsible for what happened to Mama and Felipe. I'll never get to save Baba and Luna from their pain. It's over.

"Teo."

When he looks up at me, I frown at the tears drowning his eyes.

Immediately, dread crawls up my spine. He stands, and my gaze trails down to his clenched fists, the skin purple and swollen. For a moment, I don't understand—until I see the torn envelope at his feet and the letter crumpled right next to it.

"Please tell me that's not what I think it is."

"My draft letter," he mumbles. "Signed by the one and only Thelma Craft."

No. No, no. Not him too.

He kicks at the paper with his boots, sending a ripple of dust into the air. "Long live the bloodlines."

My throat tightens as I try to grasp the horrible meaning of his words. Like me, Teo is a soldier now. Another child soon to be forced into a life of war and death. Gods, he was just barely a boy when he lost his parents to the river hippos and his older brothers to the war. Now this? It takes everything in me not to let out another scream.

"I can't believe this." Somehow, I find the strength to move my feet until I'm standing in front of him. "That bastard must have come here right after he left my place."

"What?" Teo's head jerks up, his river-brown eyes wide with panic.

I can only nod, choking on my words. His gaze darkens, and he spits out a slew of curses—at the messenger who delivered our letters, at the Lucis who began the Draft fifteen years ago, and at Thelma Craft, the bitch whose signing hand I'd give anything to shove a dagger through.

"Hundreds of fifteen-year-olds in Ilé-Ifè and we're the doomed ones." I set my jaw. "How the hell did this happen?"

Beside me, Teo glares at the distant horizon, where jagged peaks jut out above low-hanging clouds as they yawn across the length of the village.

"We're not going anywhere," he says as he continues to look straight ahead. He sounds so certain; I almost want to believe him. But I know not even my best friend can change our fates.

"What other choice do we have?"

A flash of defiance crosses his face. When he whirls, his eyes lock on mine, dark and steely. "There's something I have to show you."

Moments later, Teo and I slink down the pathway behind his hut. An eerie silence looms over us, enough to keep me vigilant. Teo's steps are calculated, careful, as he marches down the riverbank—away from mothers collecting water from the river and children darting in and out of its murky shallows. Neither of them goes as far as the deep end, careful to keep the stories of the deadly hippos close to their hearts.

Beyond the mangroves, we are surrounded by beds of wilted grass and the sprawling haze of greenery that cuts Nagea in half.

Irúnmolè Forest. Or as the Lucis would call it—*the Wild*.

I shudder at Teo's side as we draw nearer and nearer to the sacred ground.

Some don't believe the legends surrounding Irúnmolè Forest, of Iwin, Ebora, and Egbére—the mythical spirits of the shadows. It's easier to feign ignorance than admit to a fear of the unknown. But we've all lived through nights of the Spirit Song, when the wind screams and howls as it carries whispers from the forest into the village, into our homes and uninformed ears. They sound real at first, like a throng of people deep in a distant chatter. Until you hear your name in the wind and the hairs on your nape rise and cold shivers snake through your skin. Some don't believe, but all know—there is something alive in the forest, a twisted world of spirits just beyond our own.

Before, villagers would venture into the tangled fold to forage. Others stumbled in as a dare. All of that stopped when the fools never returned.

My pace slows, knowing even Teo isn't stupid enough to wander too close to the forest. I'm grateful when he comes to a stop underneath the green awnings of a banana tree, though the look on his face sets my body on edge.

"What are we doing here?"

When he starts kicking a heap of fallen leaves and rotten fruits with his feet, I don't understand. Until I see a layer of àdìre fabric beneath the scattered pile. What it's hiding, I don't want to know. But Teo takes away my choice when he yanks the fabric away, revealing what must have been a long-planned secret.

"Royal heads on a pike," I breathe aloud, unable to tear my eyes away from the object at my feet. "That's a—"

"Canoe," he finishes. "I've been working on it for some time. When I wasn't drafted last week, I thought I'd no longer have use for it. But now . . ."

"You want to run." I draw my eyes away from the wooden boat and stare at him.

"Tonight," he blurts out. Desperation coats his next words, almost making them impossible to comprehend. "I have the money. One hundred keddi. We can row to Oyo, find the informant like we'd planned, and pay him. Once you have your answers, we leave. Escape into Naine through the Okpara River and never come back."

Naine. One of the five free nations. A sprawling kingdom that sits to the west, with a monarch protected by an army of female warriors, warriors even rumored to be just as deadly as the Lucis army.

That is where Teo wishes us to flee to. I can barely breathe. So many dangers; my mind races with them.

"Are you mad?" I snatch the fabric from the ground and spread it back over the boat. "After what happened to Nicolai, how could you possibly think running is a good idea?"

Teo and I have made many mistakes over the years, most of them on the playgrounds of our old institution, but nothing compares with this. *Oloshi!* I curse him the way Mama used to whenever another villager came yelling that I'd bruised her son. I can only hope no one else knows about this. If word gets back to the officers, Teo is done for. And so am I, if they find us together. With haste, I kick leaves and rotten bananas into a heap I pray looks natural enough to ward off prying eyes.

"Nicolai's death is tragic," Teo fires back, "but he left on foot. He was never going to get far. We have the canoe. It will be a few weeks' journey to Okpara River. We'll need some more keddi to bribe the Naine border officials. But I can get the money. I can get it before sundown."

"Stop talking." I try to block out his words, but even I can't deny the thread of desire tugging at me, taunting me with a life without the Lucis, without child soldiers, without war. A life with Teo.

It's impossible, I tell myself. *It can never be.*

Because unlike me, Teo is neither Yoruba nor a Scion. Even if we were to make it into Naine, the free nations are bound by treaty to arrest and return any Yoruba or Scion caught fleeing into their territories. Teo might be able to find refuge out there, but I'm not safe anywhere.

"We can do this, Sloane," he urges behind me. "Forget the Draft; forget Avalon. You and I, we can make it out alive. We can be free."

"That's nothing but a fool's thought." I take a step back from the freshly concealed boat, examining my own hasty work. Satisfied, I toss him a glare. "And you of all people know how I feel about fools."

"Sloane—"

"No!" Something snaps inside me. Every ounce of anger and fear I've kept bottled up since the messenger handed me my draft letter comes spilling out, a poison without a cure. I shove his shoulder, hard, pressing him into the very tree that hides his deadly secret. Overhead, a disgruntled pair of olive baboons swing off their resting branch and scurry farther up the tree.

"There's no freedom in running, only death. Yours, mine, Luna's, and Baba's."

I picture Baba shackled and imprisoned in Cliff Row, Luna sent off to work in the Gbomosho plantations, harvesting cashew, cassava, maize, and tobacco for the Lucis for the rest of her life. The images pierce like a dagger to my heart, and I swear I almost punch Teo in the face for it. *What in gods' names was he thinking?*

"What freedom is there in going to Avalon?" he growls. "How many of us are drafted each year? How many return?"

"I know the risk," I say. "But Baba and Luna—they are all I have left. I'd rather die than let anything happen to them."

"I thought you, more than anyone else, would want this." His voice is small and pained. "I have the silvers, Sloane. Just like I promised. We can pay that brute. You can finally have your answers. If you go to Avalon, you'll be throwing all of that away."

He's right. The second I leave for the capital island, my chances of finding out what happened to Mama leave with me. Without Oyo, without the informant, I'll have no way of putting an end to those bleeding rumors. No way of making things right for Baba and Luna.

With a sigh, I lean against the bark of the tree. Silence falls over us, and with it a blanket of doubt cloaks me. But even though I want nothing more than to prove the Nightwalkers are behind Mama and Felipe's disappearance, I know I can't risk Baba's life.

There has to be another way.

A way to protect Baba and learn the truth about Mama.

A strange thought blooms inside my head, a flimsy idea born of my desperation. But an idea nonetheless.

I push off the tree trunk and straighten my spine. "Maybe I don't have to throw anything away."

"What?" Teo furrows his brows.

"The defector *is* from Avalon, isn't he? This Book of Records, the one he claims to have, he got *from* Avalon too."

Realization dawns on his face, and already, he's shaking his head back and forth.

"If some brute can get his hands on a book, then so can I," I continue, my heart suddenly set on the new plan. "If I must go to that pissing island, it sure as hell won't be for nothing."

I've never been to the Lucis military base. Even with our teachings back at the institution, I have no idea what the fortress looks like, what information lies within it. But the defector was a soldier once. He fled from the base. Which means, he'd stolen the book from somewhere inside those bleeding walls. Once I'm in Avalon, all I have to do is find out where the Lucis keep such records and break in. A dangerous mission, if not impossible—especially on a base teeming with an army of deadly soldiers. But what choice do I have? This is the only way I can think of to keep Baba and Luna safe and still uncover the truth about Mama and Felipe's disappearance. I have to see it through.

When Teo meets my gaze, I think he sees my decision reflected in it. He bridges the gap between us and, slowly, touches a hand to my face. Despite the hard calluses marring his palm, his touch is surprisingly tender, like warm water soothing an aching limb. Without thinking, I close my eyes and press my face into it, craving the relief it provides. A familiar yearning pulls at me. Even though my first thought is to back away, this time I allow myself to remain still, not quite ready to sever the strange link between us.

"Sloane." His warm breath brushes against my skin. I know what he will say, and more than anything, I wish he wouldn't. I can't buy into his dreams of hope, of freedom, of a whole new life. I can't give him what he wants. "Don't do this. Please."

I force my eyes open and work to keep my voice from shaking. "I'm sorry, Teo. I have no choice."

A dark, hollow look crosses his face. "I've already lost two brothers to the Scion War. I won't be the third."

Teo was only four when his brother Antwone died at war. He was thirteen when his other brother, Basil, was conscripted. Now he's fifteen, a boy of age who has also fallen into the shackles of the Draft.

Fifteen years ago, when the Shadow Rebels stormed through the Sahl desert, it was to reclaim everything the Lucis had stolen from them. Centuries after the invasion, my people have returned to take back their birthright, and they won't stop until the Lucis are destroyed.

But those bastards are not the ones dying. We are.

"Luna believes Bas is still alive," I tell him, even though I know it's not what he wants to hear. "His third year is coming up. Maybe he'll—"

"He's not," Teo snaps, veins bulging on his temple. "Luna can't see past her love for him, so she tells herself what she wants to believe. He's not coming back, Sloane, and I'm not going."

Despite the sun beating down on my skin, cold fear bites away at me. I don't want my best friend to run. I don't want him to suffer the same terrible fate as the children who have tried, only to fail. I wish I could somehow take this all away.

And in truth, I could.

Ever since the Lucis introduced the pardon clause, anyone drafted can be pardoned from war if—and only *if*—they capture a Yoruba or Scion alive. Every day, Nageans betray one another to save their own skin. With one spoken word, I could save Teo from running. Keep him away from Avalon.

But at the cost of my own life.

Even with my life already at stake, I can't make such a sacrifice.

Still, I know I must say something, anything, to stop my best friend from following through with his mad plan. I have a quick mouth; I've been threatening people my whole life. But never my friends, never my family. The words are wrong, so wrong, but I have no choice. *It's for his own good.*

"Teo, if you run, I *will* report you."

For a moment, he stands frozen, grimacing as if I've just kicked him in the gut. "You wouldn't."

I cross my arms in front of me, ignoring the way my heart slams against them. "Try me."

He backs away from me slowly, his entire body growing stiff. "I—I can't believe you," he stutters. "After everything we've been through. You'd seriously . . . have me killed for wanting to be free?"

A flash of betrayal pokes through his stony face. I pale at the sight of it, afraid I may have gone too far. But what kind of friend would I be if I didn't try to steer him off this terrible path? Gods, if only he could see that I'm just trying to save him from a plan doomed to fail.

"I'm doing this to protect you." I soften my words, hoping my new approach will make him understand. "I know you're afraid. So am I. But after what they did to Nicolai, to his family . . . I can't let that happen to you."

I edge forward, desperate to close the growing distance, desperate to feel that yearning again. "I can't lose yo—"

Just as I reach out a hand to touch his shoulder, he shrugs me off with a hard turn.

"Don't." His voice is a jagged edge of rage.

I wince at the harshness in his tone. For as long as I've known him, Teo's never treated me like this before. Not even when I stole from his master's shop and he took the whipping that was meant for me. Now I find myself grasping for words, grasping for a way to clean up the mess I've made. Perhaps threatening him wasn't such a good idea after all.

"Teo—"

"No, Sloane," he barks, already storming off. "We're done here."

The look in his eyes is one I never want to see again.

FIVE

After Teo leaves me standing in the bushes of the riverbank, I swallow my guilt and head back into the village. I should return to the hut, find Baba, and break the news of my conscription to him. But after my fight with Teo, the last thing I want to do is cause the ones I love any more pain. So I find myself at the west-end corner of the market-place instead, tailing a mob of drunken fools as they enter the village's palm-wine tavern.

Inside, raucous energy rends the air, a mingling of old-world languages and muddled accents carrying through the crowd's chatter. Famed kutibeat swells through the dry stone walls. The sweet aroma of freshly tapped sap from the palm trees of the Itsekiri rainforest fogs my senses, laced with the spicy tang of taba smoke wafting over the room.

Usually, Teo and I would come to the tavern together, making quick work of what little keddi we earned that day. But that was before Mama disappeared. Before Baba and I started struggling to make ends meet and every single keddi I got went to our starving bellies. Now, with only a few hours remaining before I leave for Avalon, I don't feel as bad dropping twelve silvers for a small calabash of the milky white beverage.

Tonight might be the last time I ever taste palm wine.

When the tavern keeper slides the calabash toward me, I raise the bowl to my lips, savoring my first sip of the bubbly drink in almost two years. As it froths in my mouth, my mind goes back to Teo and the canoe hidden beneath a pile of banana leaves and àdìre fabric. I thought I knew what Teo was thinking at all times, his reckless acts that came and went, even the most vulnerable moments he keeps tucked away. But the boy who led me down that riverbank is someone else entirely, and I don't know what to make of him. *Will he run like the other children? Or stay?*

A boisterous noise pulls me from my thoughts. A few feet away, a group of young players argue around a bar table, lit taba rolls in hand, making bets over the strategy game of Ayo. The carved wooden box that sits between them is one I recognize, and I can only watch as Valeria, the tavern keeper's daughter, scatters a handful of seeds across all twelve of the box's holes. Judging by the rowdy crowd, she's favored to win this round. Not that I'm the least bit surprised. Valeria has been emptying the wallets of everyone and their mama since the girl could crawl. Though she's barely ten years old, she's the best Ayo player in the village, losing only to Teo twice last year. Behind her, silver keddi jangle in the hands of betting spectators. It occurs to me then that Teo must have scraped all hundred silvers needed for the Oyo informant over multiple winning hands. The ache in my chest unfurls, but I try not to dwell too much on our old plans. None of it matters now.

As Valeria's hearty laughter blankets the entire tavern, the smallest pang of jealousy stirs in my belly. I take another swig of my palm wine and turn away from the merriment of it all.

My gaze settles on a giant map of the old world sprawled across the back wall, a stained replica of the one back at the institution. Despite the map's well-worn state, its intricate mass of oceans and lands are still clearly visible, all marked within their own jagged borders. Towers rise within the confines of each continent, animals roam the green jungles twisting across a faded equator, and vast bodies of water spread far and beyond, into the coasts and mountains of many forgotten nations. This was the world before the Lucis' invasion, centuries ago, when old empires and great continents still stood. Now Nagea brims with the remnants of that ancient civilization, an amalgam of cultures and tribes all under the Lucis' military rule.

A cluster of names spills down the length of the map, each one scribbled by villagers trying to cling to any reminder of their lost ancestral lineage. I remember the day Luna dragged me and Teo inside the tavern to scratch *Herrera* across what she called De Minécas, another ruined nation in a sunken archipelago.

It's strange to think that of the multitudes of nations that existed back then, only six remain now. My eyes find Kasau, the desert nation that borders us to the north, well known for its blooming cotton fields and tie-dyed garments traded all over the continent. The kingdom of Umuchi lies to the east, a tribe of people with sun-glazed skin and sacred ùlì art painted along their bodies. And then there's Naine, Togus, and Ganne—all of them free from the tyranny of the Lucis. All because they traded resources for liberty. All because they cowered when Nagea cried for help. All because they let my people die.

Nagea itself squats along the western fringes of the only remaining continent, a nation once forged by culture, now reduced to the Lucis' bloody playground. I follow its city boundaries and river lines all the way up to the north, until I see the sloping borders of the Sahl desert, a barren swath of land wrought by heat and decades of a brutal war.

The same war the Lucis have now forced me into.

I'm still scowling at the map when the air shifts. One second is all I have to duck before a knife whizzes past my face, the sharp end of the blade stabbing the calabash in my hands. The force of it cracks the bowl in half, and palm wine drains between my fingers, with most of the cold beverage spilling onto my shirt.

Malachi.

I whirl slowly, cursing myself and this bleeding day as the brown-skinned brute moves toward me with Shahid at his side. Knotted gray scarves hang loosely around their necks, marking them as members of the local Mamba clan. Today, Malachi wears the gang's familiar colors, green and silvery gray, his coal-dark hair tied neatly at the back of his head. As they approach, I grab the daggers tucked in my belt and set each blade on the table, the threat plain as day. History has taught me not to trust either of these boys. After many years of being Malachi's punching bag, around him, I know to keep my eyes open and my daggers close.

"Back begging for scraps, Sloane?" Malachi says as they coast to a stop before me, a little too close for comfort.

"At least I know how to aim, bastard," I spit back, squeezing the liquid from my shirt.

His jab is obvious, the meaning even more. The first six months after Mama's disappearance were the worst for me and Baba. There were days when I turned to the tavern keeper for his table crumbs and the last dregs of palm wine left in his gourds—if only to fend off starvation for another night. Malachi knows this and, of course, throws it in my face every chance he gets. But I won't give him the satisfaction of seeing me wounded. Not today.

"If I wanted to make you bleed, it wouldn't be the first time." Malachi's hazel eyes are steady on mine, taunting, trying to draw a reaction from me.

Next to him, Shahid bores into me with an equally predatory look, as if ready to pounce should his friend give the order. Despite the boy's tall, bull-necked frame and arms the size of baobab branches, I can't find it in me to see him as anything more than Malachi's favorite puppet.

"Try it," I growl at the both of them.

Any other day, I'd have a dagger pressed against Malachi's face and another aimed at Shahid's chest. Neither of these idiots is truly skilled with a blade, so the warning is always enough to keep the two of them at bay. Of course, if Teo were here, the circumstances would be far worse.

We were, all of us, friends once. Long ago, back when our biggest threats weren't each other, but rather the steep slope of a village half-pipe. But that was ten years ago. Before a fire burned through the entire village and Malachi lost the only family he'd ever known.

The hanging lanterns flicker along the right side of his face, illuminating the thick ridges of flesh marring his otherwise smooth features. Though I try not to think of it, the sight of the scar is still a torment on my mind. I remember the way the boy's face lit up from the flames of his hut. His screams as his mother tossed him from the windows of their burning home, moments before the blaze swallowed his entire world whole. My hands tremble at the memory. For a second, I can't bring myself to meet Malachi's gaze, gripping one of the handles of my daggers as guilt bites away at me.

It was an accident. But even when I repeat the words Mama and Baba whispered to me that night, it does nothing to lessen my shame.

It was my àse that took his parents. My fire that ruined half his face. Every day, I wrestle with the bitter truth. But I know if Malachi should ever discover who I am and what I've done, the boy won't hesitate to hand me over to the Lucis. So to save myself, I clamp my mouth shut and pretend the bad blood between us is rooted in typical village rivalry.

Malachi takes a step forward until we're face-to-face. Unlike Shahid, he's rather lean and spindly, and his towering height casts a shadow over me. I force myself to look up at him, ignoring the familiar rage he wears as armor.

"You know, you tried to kill me once," he murmurs, referring to the day I stabbed my way through one of our bloody scuffles. I didn't regret it then, and I don't regret it now. It was the day I stopped being a bully's punching bag. But Malachi hasn't forgotten, and his hatred for me has multiplied since. With a slight shuffle, he leans even closer. A dark smile crawls onto his lips as he says, "I'll make you regret ever doing that."

I flinch in spite of myself, and I can only watch as he and Shahid turn on their heels, heading in the direction of the Ayo players across the room. It isn't the first time I've sat through many of Malachi's threats, but something about this one makes my stomach churn.

Then halfway through the tavern, he glances back at me and winks. "See you in Avalon."

It only takes a second for me to understand.

Malachi was drafted today too.

SIX

The sunset comes and goes, leaving a bruised sky in its wake. I file out of the tavern then, knowing Baba and Luna must be expecting me back, though I'm still not prepared to face them. I doubt I'll ever be.

Malachi's words trail my every step, echoing along behind me until his voice is the only thing I hear. Now that I know the bastard will also be heading to Avalon tomorrow, I imagine his presence on the military base will only make life far worse for me. But whatever it is he's planned, I'll be ready.

Eight bell tolls by the time I emerge from the alleyway next to my hut. There, a flock of children sprint up and down the narrow path in a frenzy, searching for the perfect hiding spot as some scrawny kid chants, "Boju Boju."

I squeeze my way through the pack and trudge up the stone steps of my porch.

The second I shove the door open, three pairs of eyes fly straight to me. Teo and Luna huddle together on the beat-up sofa while Baba slumps alone at the head of the dining table, lips set in a narrow, quivering line. I'm still wondering what Teo is doing here, how long he's been waiting, and if he's forgiven me at all for our stupid quarrel when Luna leaps off the couch and springs forward. She crushes me in a tight embrace, her sobs echoing in the silence of the hut.

"Don't go," she whispers. "Please, don't go."

The crack in her voice hits me like a blow to the chest.

They know.

My gaze falls on Baba as I brush a hand down Luna's back. He does his best to keep still, but he can't hide the tremors racking through his entire body. At the sight of the walking stick perched next to his chair, I swallow around the painful reminder of his sickness. It's been months since Baba's had any need for that cane. Even on days when the tremors return, I've never seen him shake this much. I close my eyes and grip Luna tighter.

I'm not gone yet, and already, everything is falling apart.

"Sloane." My name trembles on Baba's lips. Despite the sinking feeling in my stomach, I force my eyes open.

Teo is at my side, prying Luna away from me. He regards me with an even stare, the two of us locked in a silent battle that began the moment I threatened him into staying. But the last thing I want to do is fight him. Not tonight, not when I need him most. So as he wraps an arm around Luna, I mouth the words *I'm sorry*, hoping it's enough of an apology. He manages a slight nod before guiding her down the corridor that leads to my room. I can only watch them go, wishing I could do the same. But I can't escape this. Whether Baba and I wish to or not, we must say our goodbyes. Even if neither of us is truly ready.

I shuffle over to where he sits and flop down on the chair beside him. Neither of us speaks. The knowledge of what awaits me in a few hours says a lot more than we ever could. That bitter understanding sweeps through the hut now, drowning us in a pool of fear we can't escape.

"Baba, I—"

"You're not leaving with Teo, are you?" When he meets my eyes, I'm sure he sees the answer in them. I steel my nerves and prepare myself for an argument I know will surely come.

"The boy only wishes to protect you," he tries, even though he knows the promise of Teo's protection isn't enough to change my mind.

"Who will protect you?" I whisper. "Who will fight for you when the soldiers come for you and Luna?"

"Everything has a cost, Sloane. I'd lay down my life if it meant saving yours."

His words are like a knife in my heart, bringing with it a great swell of pain. *I know. I've always known.* After all, I'm the grand-daughter he swore to protect, the child he's raised as his own since Mama disappeared. I'm all Baba has left and he won't let me die. It's what makes it so hard to say goodbye. Because if I decided, right now, to run off with Teo, Baba would fill a willow basket with all my belongings and shove me toward the Oba River without hesitation. He'd walk right into the soldiers' chains tomorrow if it meant giving me a small chance at freedom tonight.

It would be too easy to say the words. But what would freedom be if the only reason I'm alive is because I traded my grandfather's life for my own?

"I won't allow you to make such a sacrifice." My voice dips, and what comes out is a brittle, hoarse sound.

"This isn't just about the Draft," Baba says. "It's about you. Who you are and what you're capable of. What happens if your àse flares and your power decides to show during a training drill? What happens if another soldier attacks and you have to defend yourself by burning him alive? A Scion in Avalon is a sheep in a lion's den. There's no surviving this."

"Then I'll bring the iyerosun tea. It won't last three years, but it will be enough to suppress my àse for the training period."

It has to be.

Baba holds my gaze for a long moment. The tears shining in his eyes are enough to unravel my entire being. My nerves respond in kind, replacing hope with dread, courage with fear, and what little bravery I might feel with a growing sense of cowardice. *What if I fail to keep my identity a secret and I die in Avalon? What if I never make it out of the Sahl alive? What if I never get to see Baba again?*

"The Lucis have taken so much from this family." He bows his head, ten dark fingers sinking into his gray hair. Then he starts to cry, his shoulders trembling as he tries but fails to collect himself.

In that moment, something cracks inside me, and it's all I can do not to burst into tears. A lump sits heavy in my throat, but I manage to push it back down. It's harrowing enough seeing my grandfather cry. I won't do the same. I won't add to his pain. Not in these last few moments we have together.

"How can I stand by and watch them take you too? How can you ask me to do nothing?" He lifts his head, and in the darkness of his eyes, I see the pain of his past laid bare. Though he barely speaks of it, I know the ghost that haunts him every day.

Isaiah.

Baba's son. My father. He died months before I was born. A black market trader whose obsession with steel from the Itakpe mines condemned him to the bullets of the firing squad. We would have been executed, too, if they'd known Isaiah had a family to his name. It's the Lucis' well-used method of punishment. Why kill a single man when his entire family could perish with him? But when my father died, he died alone. And I spent my childhood longing for the man I never knew.

Though I'm sure Baba didn't mean to, his silent memory of my father only serves to strengthen my decision. I won't condemn Baba to the same fate as his son. The Lucis can have me, but they won't have my grandfather too.

In the silence, my gaze runs over his slightly bent frame, the sprinkle of liver spots on his timeworn face, and an ember of determination sparks within me. I can't go down without a fight. No matter how difficult it may be, how impossible it may seem, I have to fight to come home.

For Baba, I must surely try.

"You've always been headstrong, like your grandmother." Baba struggles to keep his voice steady. "I have to accept no one can turn you off this course. Not even me."

For fear of weakening my already fragile resolve, I remain silent. But when his hands close around mine, I squeeze them like they are the last remaining thing left of a vanishing world.

He digs around in his pocket for something. Seconds later, he pulls out a beaded choker made of white cowrie shells strung together. "This belonged to her."

Yeye Celeste. Baba doesn't speak much of his dead wife and the life they once had together. Still, I remember the first time he told me she was a Scion. *Iyánífá*, he'd called her then. A descendant of Orunmila, high priestess of the sacred practice of Ifá divination. *Celeste could see anything, predict anything. The future was hers to read, and she died for it.*

I remember the strain of emotions in his voice, the sheer amount of anger behind those final words. Even then, I didn't need to ask how she'd died.

The choker sits delicately in his palm, the pearly white shells free of any blotches and scratches. It's obvious how much care Baba has given to the jewelry—the only precious thing he owns of his wife. But then he turns the choker around, revealing an intricate web of lines, ancient symbols, and strange letterings—all of them carved into the smooth, shiny surface of each egg-shaped shell.

I frown at the elaborate design. Despite all the maps of the old world I've caught Baba and Mama poring over, this one is strangely unfamiliar, its thin borders too foreign for me to discern.

"Is that a map?"

"Yes," Baba confirms. "To Ilè-Orisha."

The words steal the breath from my lungs. Immediately, my gaze darts up to him.

Ilè-Orisha. The Shadow Rebels' hidden fortress. I search his eyes for signs of a joke, but Baba only fixes me with a grave, solemn look. Can he truly own a map to the rebels' sacred sanctuary, the same place the Lucis have spent almost two decades searching for?

Even with their advanced weaponry and endless voyages of exploration, the royals have yet to find their enemies' hidden lair. Some say it's because Ilè-Orisha is a magical land cloaked with Scion power.

Others argue the fortress is nothing but horse dung. But even those fools can't deny the Shadow Rebels come from a place far beyond the Sahl desert. Yet, where that is remains a mystery to all—all except for Baba, it seems.

I gawk at the carvings once more. It's impossible.

"You're a fighter, like your mother," Baba says, a sudden edge to his voice. "And that is what I need you to be now, Sloane. Go out there. Get through their damned training. Be their finest soldier. Do whatever you must to survive. But the second you get to the Sahl, I want you to run."

"What?"

He holds out the map in front of me. In the flickering light of the table lantern, the shells glow a brilliant orange, every carved line and letter illuminated enough to pick out a few words: *odò-ìbejì, iyanrìn-iná, ihò-egungun.* Inscriptions written in the ancient Yoruba language of my people, a forbidden dialect I barely understand. My heart thuds faster as Baba speaks.

"This—this will lead you to Ilè-Orisha. It will be a long journey. The desert isn't without its own horrors. You must prepare yourself and stay alert. But once you reach the fortress, you'll know. Tell the rebels who you are, tell them everything, and they'll grant you refuge. Do you hear me? Sloane, I need you to hear me."

For a moment, I can barely make sense of what Baba is asking of me. When I finally understand, I shake my head, despairing of his words.

No, no, no!

"I'll never be able to return to the village." I turn my wide eyes on him, flinching when he doesn't deny it. A wave of nausea passes through me, and I feel bile coating the walls of my throat. "I'll—I'll never get to see you again."

"But you'll be free"—Baba clasps my face in his hands—"and that is the life Adeline and I have always wanted for you. You're a child, Sloane, not a soldier. You deserve the chance to live as a child.

To dream and hope and find some semblance of peace. You don't deserve this life of war."

My vision blurs as tears spring to my eyes. "Is this because I don't want to run with Teo? Is that why you're sending me away?"

"Oh, Sloane." Baba manages the barest smile, though it doesn't reach his eyes. "I just want better for you than what this world has given. You're my granddaughter, and I'll do anything to keep you safe, even if it means never seeing you again."

"You're going to need me." The words tumble out in an attempt to change his mind. "The cassava field. Who will ready the soil for next harvest?"

"I'll take care of it. It won't be much. Just enough roots to test the market so nothing goes to waste."

"And what about the hut?" I breathe through the ache in my chest, a wound growing by the second. "Who will lay the new thatches before raining season starts? You can't do that alone. Your leg—"

"I'll be all right, Sloane," he says softly. "I'll be fine."

Like water flowing over a broken dam, the tears leak from my eyes, tracking a wild, hungry path down my face. Every bit of strength I've struggled to latch onto falls and crumbles. I'm a little girl again, sobbing into my grandfather's arms.

"I can't say goodbye to you forever. I won't." I bury my head into his chest to muffle the sound of my sobs. "Please don't make me."

"You can and you must." Baba pulls away gently. Even though I don't want to let go, even though I wish he'd fight to hold on, I wriggle out of his arms and lift my gaze up to him.

He leans forward and gathers my braids to the side. Àse courses through my skin, a flimsy fire aching for release, as he fastens the string around my neck. The shells lie flush at the base of my throat, the deadly secret they carry concealed from plain sight. I run a finger along their smooth surface, wishing they'd disappear, wishing none of this was real.

"Promise me, Sloane." Baba's eyes beseech mine. Though swollen and red—they are the eyes of my grandfather, my friend, my salvation. The eyes I look to when I bite down a scream and prepare myself for the sting of bitter leaf on my wounds. They plead with me now, asking me to do the impossible. "Promise me."

I don't want to. I don't want to. Yet, through my tears, I force the words out.

"I promise."

With nothing left to say, I leave Baba alone in the living room and stumble into my bedchamber. Inside, Luna and Teo are on my bed. A Ludo board sits between them, a few colorful tokens scattered from their squares along the worn track. An easy distraction. To keep their minds away from the coming storm. But the second they turn their gazes on me, their smiles fade, and tension crackles in the air like kindled flame.

Though Teo may have forgiven me for threatening him earlier, there's still so much left unsaid between us, so many of his decisions I don't know.

"You're not staying," Luna says in a hushed tone, as if speaking louder could make the truth so much worse.

When I don't answer, she looks between me and Teo, her eyes heavy. Then the tears start to fall, and pain clamps a fist around my heart. More than Baba, she's the one I fear for the most. I know what losing Felipe did to her, the marks she carved to show her pain, the scars that remained long after. Now, with only a few hours left between us, the razor I fought from her grasp flashes in my head. The bloodstained floor, the dampened rag—all memories of a night seared into my mind.

Since that night, I've kept every blade out of her reach. I've shielded her from the rumors swirling around the village. I've kept her safe the only way I know how.

I can't protect her if I'm away. With me gone, who will Luna turn to—her mother, Baba, or the sharp edge of a razor blade? I shut my eyes and grind my jaw, haunted by the thought. No matter what happens to me, even if I can never return to the village, I have to know Luna will fight to live. I have to make sure she'll survive.

"Really, three years isn't that long." I force hope into my voice, even though I feel everything but. "And Bas—you know he'll be home any month now."

At the mention of Bas's name, I glance at Teo. He meets me with a frown. My skin grows hot, simmering only when he looks away and starts gathering the Ludo tokens into a black canister.

Beside him, Luna mutters, "No one ever returns from the Sahl, Sloane."

"But Bas will." Despite the truth wrapped in her words, I lower myself onto the edge of the bed and reach for her hands. "You've always believed it, and I need you to continue to believe. Teo and I will be back before you know it too"—I fight the urge to cast another glance in his direction—"then it will be the four of us, like it used to be."

My cheeks flame as another wave of heat sings through me, knowing I'm feeding her nothing but false hope. But I'd rather keep her alive with lies than bury her with the truth.

When I stand and head toward my dresser, I think I hear Teo say my name. I ignore him, ignore the slamming of my heart against my ribs, as I comb through the contents inside the wooden chest. Seconds later, I return to the bed with two notebooks in my hands.

"Here." I flop down on the thinning mattress and drop one of the books in the space between Luna's crossed legs. "I got this for you weeks ago. I was going to wait until your birthday, but . . ."

With a shaking hand, she picks up the book and flips it open, staring at the blank pages.

"Remember when we were little and we'd write everything we did while the other wasn't around?" I say hastily. "I'm not sure why we stopped, but I want us to start again."

"Us?" Luna's voice is small, smaller even than the mice creeping through the hut.

"Yes. Look, here's mine." I hold out the second notebook in front of her. "I'll bring it with me to Avalon and jot down whatever happens every day. I'll even include drawings of the island so you can picture it all."

"Your drawings look like Fat Daisy's scratches."

"Then you'll love them even more."

For the first time since she found out about the Draft, she laughs. Even Teo lets out a gruff bark. I try to match their blooming sound, I really try, but the only thing I can manage is a withered smile.

Luna throws her arms around me and pulls me close. I breathe in the familiar scent of marula oil and shea butter in her hair, allowing myself a moment to memorize the small comfort it brings.

"I'll miss you, hermana," she whispers, and my grip tightens around her like a lifeline. "But I'll see you again, won't I? In three years and not a day later."

The words stick in my throat. I can't squeeze out another lie. Nor can I tell her that I'm never coming back, that I'm never going to see her again. For the second time that night, my tears fall.

"In three years," I breathe, "and not a day later."

That night, I don't know when sleep finally comes for us. When it does, we drift off with our limbs braided together, a constellation of bodies sprawled across the poor, unforgiving bed.

Footsteps echo down the corridor.

I bolt awake, searching the room for signs of a Nightwalker. Night invasions are not uncommon, and with the Draft at an end, I don't doubt those monsters are on the prowl, a pack of sharp-eyed cheetahs ready to spill innocent blood.

In a matter of seconds, I have two daggers in hand as I tiptoe out of my chamber. Even with the darkness swallowing the hut whole,

I manage to navigate my way to the living room, where Baba keeps a dim lantern burning. Only then do I see the silhouette of a boy crouched low across the room, quietly undoing the bottom latches of the front door. A willow basket perches on the stool beside him, brimming with all the things he'd stashed and stored away for this very moment.

My stomach twists at the sight. "Teo?"

He whirls, face blanching the moment he sets his eyes on me. "Sloane."

"What are you doing?" I drop my daggers on the dining table and stride over to him, glancing back and forth between his face and the willow basket.

His silence is all the confirmation I need.

"You're running," I say, my voice heavy with the truth. "Even after everything, you're still going to leave."

His gaze drops to the floor, and he kicks at the woven rushes with his boots. "I can't go to Avalon, Sloane."

"Not even for me?" I step closer to him, my legs shaking as I take his face into my hands, needing him to look at me. Really look at me. We can't avoid each other any longer. He tries to fight off my grip, but even with my sweaty palms and trembling fingers, I hold tight. "Why is fleeing more important to you than the two of us staying together?"

"I wouldn't last a night on that island." His ragged breath brushes against my face, and something strange glints behind his eyes.

Eleven years I've known this boy, I've never seen him like this: raw, desperate, and vulnerable. I try to gulp down the bitter taste of dread on my tongue, but I can't shake the feeling there's more Teo isn't saying.

"I've watched you fight every boy in this damned village," I tell him. "If there's anyone capable of surviving Avalon, it's you. Why are you so afraid?"

"I'm not."

"Then stay. Stay and fight with me," I plead, tossing aside Mama's old vows to never beg a boy for anything. But Teo isn't just any boy. He's my friend. He's—*he's something more.* "We can survive this, you and I. I know we can."

Teo is quiet. In that silence, Baba's and Luna's heavy snoring drifts up to my ears. The familiar sounds only distract for so long as I wait for Teo's response. With every second that passes by, hope and despair wage war inside me, each one fighting for control. *You and I . . . It's always been you and I. Please, stay.*

"I can't."

My clammy hands slip down his face. Through a haze of numbness, I stumble backward, no longer able to stand so close to him. Teo watches the distance stretch between us. His mouth opens, as if to say something, but he clamps it shut and swallows hard, burying the words in his throat.

It would be too easy to give up on him, to let him go, but I'm too stubborn for my own good. There's more left to say, and by gods, he will hear it. Despite the ache strangling my chest, I start to speak.

"Three years ago, we were at your master's shop cutting bamboo. A gust of wind blew in and sawdust scattered all over our faces, and I laughed and you did, too, and somewhere between a cackle and a snort, you whispered, 'I love you.' I heard it, yet I pretended not to. Not because I didn't want to. Not because I didn't feel the same. But because I was afraid. I was so afraid, I ran. But not tonight." My voice is low and fragile, like glass teetering on a knife's edge. Any moment now, it may fall and I may shatter. I take a deep breath before narrowing the space between us once more. Another step, and the yearning I felt by the riverbank returns, pulling and tugging and wrenching at the corners of my heart. It exposes something deep inside, a truth I've kept caged for too long. I set it free.

"I love you, Teo."

A glimmer of hope sparks in his eyes. He pulls me closer and seizes my hands, locking our fingers in a tight embrace. I've seen that look before, earlier, beneath the awnings of a banana tree. I know where that hope leads. *Please, don't do it. Please, don't say those words.*

"Come with me." He lifts our clasped hands to his lips and kisses them. "Just think what we could have together. We can be free, Sloane. Free to live our lives whatever way we want."

"Teo! I can't run."

He sighs. "And I can't stay."

I pull my hands away and squeeze a fist against my forehead, wishing I could ignore the swell of bitterness stirring inside me.

"I don't understand. I thought . . . I thought you loved me."

"I swear I do." His chest heaves as the words rush past his lips. "You have no idea how long I've waited for the words you said tonight."

"Yet it isn't enough to change your mind."

What more could I do to make him stay? My thoughts are as desperate as I feel: so jumbled, frantic, without sense and caution, that for a moment, I even consider telling Teo the truth about my identity. That I'm a Scion. As much prey as he is, if not more so. But I doubt even that will be enough to turn his mind.

I've tried. Olodumarè knows I've tried.

"I'm sorry," Teo whispers.

"So am I," I say, because in that moment, I realize there's no convincing him off this path. Nothing will stop him, and I see it clearly in his haunted gaze.

I have to give up on him. I have to let him go. Everything inside me breaks, scattered pieces of my heart left at Teo's feet. Àse burns through my body, from my scalp down to my toes. The fire sears behind my eyes, flaming my tears, so when they fall, they sizzle on my cheeks. Gods, I hate crying. If this is what it means to love, then I want no part in it. I only want my heart whole again. I only want to forget this pain.

Teo's fingers graze my cheeks as he wipes off the tears. Then his large hands are on my face, cradling both sides as he presses his forehead to mine. The last time we stood together like this, we were four, mourning the death of his older brother, Antwone. Then, I promised him he would never have to feel that kind of pain again. He would never have to say goodbye. Now he's the one breaking that promise, leaving me with nothing but heartbreak and the ghost of the memories we once shared.

I think back to the days we spent wooden wheeling at the village park, picking periwinkles off wet leaves and muddy walls, jumping into each other's scuffles to lend a blow, a scratch, even a dagger to some poor, unsuspecting foe. More often than not, we are, both of us, two reckless fools who would do anything to keep each other alive. Without him by my side, how will I survive Avalon?

"I do love you, Sloane." His voice is tender, yet firm, like the touch of his hands still cradling my cheeks. "I truly do."

We are silent for some time after. Our eyes rove each other's faces, capturing all that we can for the last time. Because truly, we both know that after tonight, we will never see each other again. Our worlds will be different, our fates no longer dancing on twined strings.

"Stay safe, Teo," I whisper. "I hope you find the freedom you've been longing for. I hope it brings you peace."

In the dim light, tears drip from his glossy brown eyes. When he wraps his arms around my waist and lifts me right off the ground, I fold myself around him and bury my head in the warmth of his shoulder. If it were up to me, we would remain this way for as long as the world still turns. Let it crackle and burn, I wouldn't care, if it meant keeping Teo here. *With me.*

But the boy wants something else for himself, and I no longer have the strength to fight him.

I'm tired.

He plants me back on shaky limbs, his warm hands lingering on my face. I allow myself to be pulled by that yearning one last time, giving in to the storm of desire that's loomed over us since that day inside his master's shop.

Teo leans down in the same moment, his pillowy breath teasing my lips. A rush of heat, unlike any magic I've ever known, floods through my veins, igniting even the quieter parts of me. Tender hands snake down the small of my back, drawing more fire to my skin. But this is no fire born of ordinary magic. It is his desire and my heart-break kindled into a wild flame. Teo brands me with his kiss, searing me with every taste, every caress, every breath. It's the worst thing he could do. Yet, I never want it to end.

When we finally stop, it's only because I force myself to pull away. Our breaths echo in the silence, ragged and strained, as we fight to meet each other's gaze. There's nothing left to say. Nothing at all.

Teo picks up the willow basket and clutches it close to his heart. I wrestle with the knot surging up my throat, trying to shove it back down.

"I'm sorry" is all he says.

I can only nod, too afraid to speak.

Then he's out the door, moving as nimbly and quietly as he can. The night is dark beyond my porch, a world of horrors gathering in the shadows, waiting for easy prey. But if Teo is afraid for his life, he doesn't show it. The last memory I have of him is the small, bitter smile he flashes me over his shoulder.

SEVEN

Dawn breaks, and still Teo remains on my mind. I picture him as he was last night, a desperate boy who would risk anything and everything to set himself free, even if it meant leaving me behind.

Now, as I ride into the belly of Ilé-Ifè, I try to make myself forget. Forget the hollow words that fell from his lips. The crocodile tears that drained from his eyes. Even the ghost of a kiss that refuses to let me go. Yet, try as I might to forget the boy who broke my heart, I remember the friend who knocked out Malachi's teeth for me, the friend who scraped up a hundred keddi so I could learn the truth about Mama. Like the Oba River during a bitter drought, the pain I've felt all night starts to ebb, giving way to dread.

Is Teo safe? Did the Nightwalkers get to him before he made it out? Where is he now? Every question begets another, each one with no answer. *No. There's nothing to worry about. Where others have failed, Teo won't.*

With that, I steer my mind away from the doubts already sprouting thorns in my heart and turn my eyes on the orange tide sweeping across the eastern horizon, dragging me toward whatever horror awaits me at my assessment.

The ox wagon itself is a nightmare, jostling me side to side as it rattles along the dirt road of the crowded city. After an hour-long journey from the village, squeezed between some old hag and her bleating lamb, I sigh in relief when the wagon coasts to a stop and the driver lets me off.

Ilé-Ifè rises before me, a dust-blown city flooded with a sea of people. Eight bell hasn't tolled yet, and already merchants swarm the market square in a frenzy—men and women coated with dirt and a thick sheen of sweat, bustling beneath the wide awnings of their labyrinthine stalls. Their shouts fill the air as they bargain over fresh bunches of plantains, uncut slabs of goat meat, and yards of ankara fabric. Silver keddi jingle in exchange for bought goods. The cacophony makes my head ache. When the pungent smell of smoked panla fish and fresh locust beans assaults my nostrils, I immediately remember why I hate coming into the city at all.

I curse under my breath as I weave through the crammed streets teeming with damp bodies and not enough air. But at the sight of the bronze statue floating in the middle of the square, my pace slows.

Down the road, a vandalized sculpture of Obatala pokes at the morning sky. A chain dangles from his left hand. In his right, a bird figurine perches beside a snail shell tarnished with age. The word *Scum* is painted across the white aso-òkè draped around the Orisha's body.

I was eight when I first laid eyes on the ancient monument. That day, Mama and I had just arrived in Ilé-Ifè with a sack of fresh tubers when a mob of hagglers rushed the street, shoving me into the gap beneath the god's feet. Before then, I'd only heard rumors of the floating statues left standing all over Nagea and how the Lucis couldn't destroy them like they did our shrines. So, as Mama pulled me to my feet, I summoned the courage to ask about the statues.

"They are a symbol of the Yoruba creation myth," she said hesitantly as she dragged me toward the marketplace.

"Creation myth?" I tugged back. Even though she swore keeping our heritage a secret was her way of protecting me, my curiosity was an itch I desperately wanted to scratch. And the older I got, the worse it spread.

"Mama—" I tried again, but as always, she silenced me with a look.

"Let's go, Sloane. These tubers won't sell themselves."

The monument disappeared from view as she wrenched me farther away. But the creation myth remained a mystery on my mind.

So as we finished up the day's trade, I caught myself prodding Mama with more and more questions, until finally, she gave in.

"All right, all right." She sighed. "But after today, we'll speak of it no more, understood?"

I squealed as she led us into the shade of a nearby guava tree. Her well-trained eyes darted, making sure there were no prying ears. And then, she began.

"In the beginning, Olodumarè looked down from òrun rere and saw that the earth was nothing but water and marsh." Her voice was a careful whisper despite the drowning babel of the square. I pressed my body against the tree and held still, determined not to miss a single syllable. "He desired a world filled with all the great wonders of his creation, and so he tasked Obatala, one of his greatest emissaries, with a mission. To complete it, Olodumarè gave him a golden chain, a white hen, and a snail shell full of sand."

My eyes widened as I glanced at the sculpted pieces held in the Orisha's bronzed hands. Sure enough, the braided links of the chain bore traces of its golden past, and a layer of red paint coated the once-white hen.

"On that day, Obatala did as he was told and lowered himself on the chain, far enough to glimpse the earth below. He poured sand from the shell across the vast ocean and threw down the hen. As the bird scattered sand across the rolling seas, Obatala marveled in awe as dry land formed and valleys and hills rose and the sixteen kingdoms of Nagea were born."

Lost in the tale, the wariness behind Mama's gaze dissolved, and her voice rose in a sweet crescendo. Her eyes sparkled and danced with high exuberance. I beamed before her, hungry for more of her words, more of my history, more of our beginning, *more*.

"Upon seeing what Obatala had achieved, Olodumarè molded humans out of dust and clay. To his creation, he gave èmí, the breath of life, and on that day, the first Yorubas were born. But Olodumarè knew his children needed guidance, and so he sent forth his emissaries to lead.

"Before they could rule, the Orishas desired full control of their divine power. Thus, Olodumarè bequeathed to them a portion of his àse, allowing the gods and goddesses to harness his sacred life force on earth. Obatala was first to descend, and where he landed, he called Ilé-Ifè, the cradle of the Yorubas. Yemoja came upon the Èkó Islands, where she reigned as goddess of the high seas. Third was Aganju, who ruled the northern savanna of Shaki as the god of wilderness and land. While Shango, the mighty warrior, laid claim to the kingdom of Oyo as the god of heat and fire."

At the mention of our blood deity and his ancestral land, I gasped aloud. I was always told Oyo was where Mama's family had once lived, but until that day, I never knew it held a spiritual connection to Shango and his descendants.

"Have you ever been to Oyo, Mama?"

"A long, long time ago." Her lids fluttered shut as an old memory swept through her. When she finally opened them, a deep yearning swam in the depths of her eyes. "Perhaps one day, we'll go to visit."

I grinned, already drawing up images of the old kingdom in my mind. Oyo was the land of our ancestors, and soon, Mama was going to take me there. She smiled a warm smile as she pinched my cheek between her calloused fingers.

"One by one," she said, carrying on with the tale, "the Orishas fell from the skies. As they did, towering statues made of the finest bronze rose above the earth. When the Yorubas witnessed this, they knew Olodumarè had sent guardians to protect them. And so for centuries, the Orishas were revered as gods and goddesses of the sixteen kingdoms.

"Soon, they began to marry, and the first Scions were born, each with the same magic as their blood deity. They were known throughout the land as Iran Orisha; omo àse mímó."

I creased my brows at Mama. "What does that mean?"

"It means Descendants of the Orishas; children of the sacred power. They were revered in full measure as the gods. And when it came time for the Orishas to return to òrun rere, it was the Scions who ruled as kings and queens of the Ancient Kingdoms."

When Mama finished the story, a long beat of silence stretched between us. The weight of our history pressed down upon me. Before that day, I'd barely known who the gods were or where my magic came from. I barely knew about Olodumarè, about the Orishas' kingdoms, and how much the Lucis had robbed us, *robbed me*, of the life we were truly meant to have.

We were rulers, not subjects. Kings and queens. Descendants of light and magic.

We were free.

With a sigh, my gaze lingered on Obatala's statue. This wasn't the world the gods left behind.

Yet, there was still so much I didn't understand. Questions pricked at my mind, the thorns of a cactus I couldn't pluck away.

"What, dear?" Mama asked, sensing my unease. "What is it?"

"If all of this belongs to us, if we are the rulers of the land, then why do we have to hide?"

She nodded. The silence lengthened. I could almost hear the wheels turning in her head as she searched for a way to make me understand. In the end, she crouched low before me and took my hands in hers, locking them together.

"Because, Sloane, there are people—horrible people—who have stolen what belongs to you. People so threatened by your magic that they'd sooner destroy you for fear of what they do not understand." Her gaze was a cloak beaded with pain, her voice a tapestry woven with sorrow.

"Do you see that word?" She pointed to the insult scribbled in bloodred paint across Obatala's statue. *Scum.* "The Lucis did that because despite the many weapons they possess, no blade is sharp enough to crack the bronze. No bomb or bullet strong enough to bring down those statues."

I blinked up at her, confused. "Why?"

"It is said that when the Orishas returned to Olodumarè, they left fragments of their souls in those monuments." Despite the blazing afternoon heat, she rubbed my bare arms, drawing a different kind of warmth to my body. "But the Lucis have no understanding of our gods, no belief in our spirituality. Thus, they've taken to defacing the statues the only way they can."

My eyes ran over the slur once more. I shifted my gaze back to Mama. "Will Olodumarè ever send them back down? To save us? Take back what was stolen from us?"

"I don't know," she admitted, and the tiniest spark of hope in my belly dulled away. Tears stung my eyes, but I fought the urge to let them fall. "Listen to me, Sloane." She gripped my shoulders with firm hands. "No matter where you go, what path you find yourself upon, you must never tell a soul who you are. Guard your secret with your life, Ìfé mi. It is the only thing that will keep you alive."

Ever since that day, I've kept the promise I made to Mama. I've remained within the safety of my hut, never strayed too far from the confines of Agbajé. I've done all I could to shield myself from the Lucis' brutality. Yet, here I am, seven years later, moments away from being thrown into their lair.

A Scion in Avalon is a sheep in a lion's den. Baba's warning from yesterday slips into my mind. I mull over those words until I'm nearly overwhelmed by the impulse to flee from the city. But what little chance I had of deserting died the moment Teo walked out of my hut and I stayed behind. There's no turning back now.

O tóbi ju ìbèrù re lo.

You are greater than your fears, Sloane.

Another image of Mama flashes in my head. I try to draw courage from her familiar words. Words that strengthened me on days I stumbled home from a heavy beating. Words that calmed me on nights I woke screaming from a bleeding nightmare. The words are as vivid now as the last time she whispered them, filling me with a new rush of determination.

"You can do this," I breathe.

For Mama. For Baba and Luna.

Clutching my notebook to my chest, I shove past Obatala's statue and head for the dome.

The building itself squats like a giant toad at the top of the square. With its gleaming steel walls, the monstrosity is a pariah in a world of wood shacks, mud huts, and bamboo stalls. Long before the dome existed at all, a shrine stood right there on that land. Now altars that once held ancient relics and feast offerings have become an evaluation point for the new soldiers drafted every year, with one in every city across the nation.

Within seconds, I'm standing outside the dome's entrance with a multitude of conscripts from varying villages and towns. The children try to appear confident, to shield their nerves from sight, but I don't miss the gloom in their eyes, a shadow of my own.

Lucis officers surround us on all sides, many of them with skin tones at odds with the searing Nagean sun, blue uniforms and glass helmets shielding their pale features. The airships streaking through the sky are a testament to how much more there is to come.

I'm wary to see so many soldiers in such close quarters, especially with their long rifles and pistols at the ready. Just the sight of them makes my stomach clench. If any of these men should find out who I am, I already know where those guns will aim. I'm trapped in a world of monsters who will eat me alive once they realize I'm their enemy.

It's all I can do to straighten my face, focus on the line thinning ahead as each child is granted entry inside the dome. But with each step I take toward the looming steel doors, the energy I felt moments ago starts to dwindle. I can barely stop my legs from shaking.

Keep it together, Sloane. I recover just in time, coming to a halt before the two potbellied officers guarding the door.

"Name?" barks the one with a logbook in his hands.

"Sloane Shade," I answer, careful to keep my voice low and level.

While the first officer barely looks up at me, his gaze fixed on the log, the other man reaches for my notebook and snatches it out of my hands.

"It's only a book." I frown when he tosses it into a plastic bin at his feet.

His glare is murderous as he points to the sign scribbled in tiny block letters above his head. "Nothing allowed inside the dome."

I stiffen and bite my tongue. But even the sharp sting doesn't erase the fact that I'll never get back that damned book. The only real promise I made to Luna, and I've now broken it.

"Carrying any weapons, little girl?" The officer's grunt draws me away from my thoughts.

Reluctantly, I pull out the daggers I tucked into my belt before leaving the hut that morning and dump them into the bin.

"Is that all?" The guard's brows knit with suspicion.

I stifle a curse and reach for the last set of knives sheathed into my boots. My hands tremble as I'm forced to turn Mama's blades over to him, and I don't care to hide my bitterness when my gaze falls on both men again.

I expect them to wave me off—in fact, I hope they do—and while the first one almost does, his partner only leers, not quite ready to let me go.

In one step, he swoops forward and starts patting me down. I cringe away from his touch, remembering the feel of the Nightwalker's assaulting hands on my skin. My throat burns with the memory of a night that insists on holding me prisoner. With one shuddering breath, I try to set myself free. But this is a captivity I can't seem to escape. Especially not with the way the officer palms every inch of my skin, from my heaving chest down to the round of my ass, invading, as if I'm a tool to be handled as he sees fit. As if I'm nothing at all.

I dig my nails into the skin on my palms, wishing the torture would end. A new horror descends on me when the officer finds the herbs Baba stashed into my inner thigh pocket earlier that morning.

He holds it up to my face. "Hoping to sneak this in, were you?"

"I—I wasn't—"

"What is it?" he asks, puzzling over the tiny pouch of green-white powder.

"Tea," I mutter. But when the brute turns his glare on me, I immediately add, "I had no idea it was even in there."

His eyes smolder in silent scrutiny. Yet despite the threat of punishment, the only thing I can think about is the bag of neem leaves and iyerosun powder dangling between his slimy fingers. All he has to do is seize the herbs, and my chance of surviving Avalon disappears. Without Baba's àgbo, I'll have no way of hiding my power, no way of keeping my identity a secret, no way of protecting others from magic I can't control.

Before I can shove it back down, Malachi's scarred face bursts into my mind, shadowed by those of his family. Faces I try not to remember but can't forget. I've killed more people with this fire than I wish to admit. Not just the Nightwalker, not just these monsters, but people I once cared for. And now, without the safety of Baba's àgbo, I fear I will only kill more in Avalon. Then I'll be exposed for what I am and destroyed like the many Scions before me.

Moments pass and my pulse quickens. When the officer crushes the tea bag in his fist, puffs of deep green cloud before my eyes as he scatters the herbs into the wind. I bite the insides of my bottom lip until I taste blood on my tongue. He watches me all the while, sneering with his teeth. I have to remind myself that now isn't the time to fall apart—not in front of some pudgy old bastard trying to find the cracks in my armor. Finally, he backs away.

"Move along," he says, waving me off.

When the double doors open, I force my feet forward, one leaden weight at a time. Away from the officer's shrewd gaze, I release a ragged breath and try to convince myself I'll find another way to hide my àse. Tea or no tea, I can survive Avalon. I *will* survive.

Inside is a hall like I've never seen before, with tall columns of white light erected at every corner. Lights powered by the Kainji Dam up in the north. I remember when Baba first told me about the dam and its ability to generate enough electricity for all of Nagea. Yet, this supply of energy remains limited to the capital island and other Lucis establishments across the nation, while the rest of us simply rely on candles and kerosene lanterns.

Overhead, interlaced steel poles rise in perfect arches toward a glass-paned roof. With the sun filtering through, the world seems brighter than it should be, especially the carpet of well-trimmed grass rolled out beneath my feet. The turf makes me sick, knowing what a withering mess the dry season made of our plants and crops back in the village. Another tragedy we suffer alone.

I cut through the crowd of unfamiliar children, my gaze darting between their blank faces. Shoulders square and bodies straight, no one utters a sound as they stare toward the empty podium. Already acting like soldiers, and we're not even at the base yet.

I'm halfway across the chamber when the doors slide open and a line of men file in briskly. Their charcoal military garb is an intimidating sight, emblazoned with gold buttons and the Lucis' winged-torch crest. Rows and rows of medals gleam across their breasts, and I swear the last soldier almost seems to dazzle, a wretched star come to burn us all to the ground.

I can't tear my gaze away from the black swirls of ink curling around his left eye, making him appear more fearsome than he already is.

He must be the commander, judging by the way every officer salutes him in passing. A brawny beast with more power and control in his gloved fingers than I'll ever know. The closer he comes, the more I wonder how many Scions and Yorubas have fallen to his bullets, how much of my people's blood stains this savage's hands.

A dead silence settles over the entire dome as he climbs the dais, taking center stage while the other soldiers flank him from behind. His fierce, predatory eyes skim the hall, scrutinizing every child trembling before him.

For a second, I forget to breathe. Even all thoughts of past gods and dead Scions flee my mind. It's impossible to think about anything but the leader's stifling presence.

Assessment day has begun.

EIGHT

"Greetings, new recruits," the Lucis roars, his voice humming with enough authority to make me shiver. "My name is Faas Bakker, High Commander of the Avalon Defense Forces, Juvenile Division. You are all here today because you have been called to a duty, to join your fellow brothers and sisters in arms in our war against the Shadow Rebels. It is a privilege and honor bestowed onto each one of you, to become part of an army dedicated to destroying the Scion *scum*."

I bristle, hating the way he spits out the insult like poison on his tongue. It sends a faint ripple of àse beneath my skin, curbed only by the two cups of àgbo I drank earlier that morning. Even after years of enduring such a hateful, cruel slur, hearing it again doesn't ease the humiliation worming its way into my gut. All because the Lucis loathe us so much, they see us as nothing but dirt. A stain only their bullets can cleanse.

But you are more than what they say you are, Sloane, Mama told me once. *You are a gift from the gods, a light born of Shango's divine fire. And no weapon can wipe that away.*

"Scions have always been this continent's greatest tyrants," Faas continues, rewriting history with his words. "Three centuries ago, when our ancestors first arrived in Nagea, it was Scions who fought to keep them from establishing a new settlement on this land. They feared us, feared our advanced weaponry, feared what we could do to their devilish practices and rituals, and so they tried to eliminate us."

Like the teachers back at the institution, the commander doesn't speak of his ancestors' desire for our lands, our resources and prized artifacts, or the millions who died because of it. He doesn't speak of the destruction of the Ancient Kingdoms, of Ira—the once habitable region beyond the Itsekiri rain forest, now ruined by centuries of violence and oil spills. Instead, every word and every syllable is meant to portray my people as what they aren't. Murderers, barbarians. Terrorists who deserve nothing more than death and ruin. He justifies our genocide with unflinching lies, justifies the Lucis' evil with patriotic necessity.

"Only few know about the heroism of the Founding Lucis," he says. "Even fewer know the costs and sacrifices they bore—sacrifices that would one day give you the right to call Nagea home. But I'm here today to remind you of their courage and resilience. Because without those brave men and women, our humanity would be lost, our liberation long forgotten. That is why, today, when you fight, you fight for them!"

The commander's sharp eyes skim the hall, flitting from one recruit to another. When they land on me, I want nothing more than to poke them out with one of Mama's daggers. Hell, if I thought I could get away with it, I'd stab this man, Faas Bakker, a thousand times for his audacity. For his lies.

Despite what he wishes to make us believe, the Founding Lucis were no heroes. They were thieves. They were the real tyrants. Because while it's true that the Lucis did in fact lead survivors of the old world into Nagea, they always fail to mention how they ran every Yoruba and Scion out of their own land.

They didn't give us a chance to leave. They murdered us. Ruined us. The world survived and continued on, but it did so without us.

All around me, the children nod along, silent ducklings forced to listen to the dung coming out of the commander's mouth. It's a pain none of them can begin to understand. After all, the Lucis helped save their ancestors from a doomed world while they slaughtered and exterminated my own. They have no ties to the Ancient Kingdoms. Not like me. They may be Nageans today, but they aren't Yorubas. They aren't Scions. They have no idea what it's like to be erased from your own history.

My heart pounds in my ears. I grind my jaw and try to keep my face blank, emptying it of every trace of emotion as Faas carries on with his wretched speech.

"Your strength in battle will win this war, and your victory will preserve the longevity of this very nation." His voice booms. "In a few hours, you leave for Avalon to begin training. Now the time has come to put your strength to the test. Let this serve not only as an evaluation of your devotion, but of your worth. Do you have what it takes to survive the base? The Force awaits your arrival. Good luck, recruits."

When he finishes, he slams a clenched fist over his heart in salute and jumps off the dais. Icy fingers carve a path along my spine, and I can only stare as the commander and his soldiers exit the dome, disappearing as if they were never here. But his words do linger, a cloud of horror engulfing me and every child in the hall.

For a second, the ground quakes beneath me, rocking me back and forth as it pulls me down. I curl my toes inside my boots, and it takes every ounce of strength I have left to steady myself.

I don't want to be their soldier. A weapon doomed to serve; a killer trained to destroy. I don't want to be like these monsters. But what chance do I have of escaping right now? *Gods, I can't do this.*

The next moments pass in a blur with officers separating us by our last names. My group sits in front of one of the many back chambers now, biding our time to be called in for testing. None of us know what awaits us behind the door, but whatever it is must not be pleasant. The first girl to enter emerges after what feels like an hour, bile coating her lips. She looks about ready to pass out as she staggers off behind an officer. But it's the horror in her eyes that slows my breathing.

What the hell did they do to her? Worse, what did they make her do?

The longer I stare at her retreating frame, the more questions grow inside me like wild, stubborn weeds. Before I can uproot them, images branch out in my mind of all the terrible things possibly taking place inside those chambers. *Flogging. Maiming. Torture.* The worst evil. All to prove ourselves worthy of a uniform stained with the blood of many Yorubas and Scions. All to show them I'm capable of murdering my own kind.

Am I?

When the female officer conducting the test summons another child, I realize it will be a while before I'm called in. I grumble to myself, cursing Faas, cursing the officer and everything about this damned assessment. My skin hums and I jump to my feet, eager to pour my anger into something other than the blades of grass clutched between my fingers.

The target wall in the corner lures me forward, several rows of black rings etched into steel. I'm searching for the weapons' table at once, though what I end up finding aren't even weapons at all. A colorful pile of plastic darts scatter across the table, their usual sharp points replaced with round flattened tips made of dull steel.

Of course, the Lucis won't risk having sharp objects lying around, for fear of what we might do with them. I can't speak for the other children, but it isn't the first time I've imagined what it would be like to bury a dagger inside one of these bastards' skulls. The right moment, the right time, I'd do it. I know I would.

I grab three of the plastic-winged darts and tuck two more inside the back pocket of my pants. I know the punishment for stealing, especially in a room full of Lucis officers. But they not only took my daggers and my notebook; they also seized my herbs. It seems fair now that I take something of theirs in return.

Within seconds, I'm standing a few feet from the wall, spinning the first dart between my fingers. Far from the real thing, it slides awkwardly, the plastic almost too slippery to the touch. Still, I tighten my grip around it, curling my thumb and index finger just above the length of the dart. I home in on the wall across from me. With a quick inhale, I release my grip. My hand stiffens in the same moment, so even before the dart hits the target, I know my aim is wrong. Sure enough, the bleeding thing sinks into the edge of the fourth ring, nowhere near the small black dot in the center.

I curse at myself.

"That's bad form," a cool voice says, almost floating out behind me.

I spin around, ready to face the wrath of some brazen officer. Instead, I'm staring up at the shadow of a boy's face, hidden beneath the hood drawn lazily over his head. With a tilt of his chin, he lets it fall, revealing clean, buzzed hair and ocean-green eyes that stand in stark contrast to his tawny brown skin.

I frown. Nothing about him looks familiar, a random city boy probably seeking idle chatter to take his mind off the assessment. Well, I'm the wrong person for the task, more than content to remain in the torment of my own solitude. I don't spare him any more of my time, wheeling myself back in place.

When he settles in beside me, his shoulder almost brushing mine, my frown deepens until it damn near twists into a scowl. He doesn't seem to notice nor care. His keen eyes are on the target wall, staring at my mistake. The side of his mouth twitches slightly, betraying a hidden smile.

"If you want to survive Avalon, you'll have to do better than that."

My cheeks flame under his scrutiny and criticism, and a slew of curses come to mind. But I clamp my mouth shut. I won't be his escape from his own misery. Impossible as it may seem, I must try to remain calm if I want to survive the rest of this day. I can't fall apart. Not before the assessment.

I tease the second dart between my fingers, readying for another go. Even though the boy keeps his gaze on the wall, I feel him watching my every move. Usually, I can pretend not to notice an unwelcome presence, but I struggle to do the same now. It takes more effort to shut him out, long enough to steady my breath and let the dart fly.

When it lands a hairbreadth away from the dotted mark, I can't resist the faint smile tugging at the edges of my lips. Though nowhere near perfect, I'm sure it's enough to shut the city boy up and send him off on his way. I cast a sidelong glance at him, my eyebrows raised.

"Better," he says, "but not quite."

"You can either try to beat that or shut the hell up," I snap.

I know people like him. Most likely, he's someone whose brother barely made it out of the war alive, and now he thinks he can do the same. Arrogance has made him foolish.

When the boy's eyes rove over me, from my tangled braids to my chewed-up boots, I set my jaw and raise my chin.

"They're going to break you, you know?" His cool, grating voice returns.

"Excuse me?"

"You heard me."

I wish I hadn't. Still, I can't ignore the question already pushing past my lips.

"Why?"

"Because you're useless to them whole." He looks past me, to the mass of seated children still waiting their turn to be assessed. His smug smile disappears, chased away by a dark look I know too well. *Anger.* Though that vanishes just as quickly. "Great soldiers are made from pieces of their broken selves, and the most vulnerable children are always the easiest to use, abuse, and destroy. The base isn't just a training ground. It's where children like you come to die and be reborn as murderers. You will obey, comply, and pledge yourself to the Force as they mold you into a weapon fit for war. They will destroy every last semblance of your humanity, and you cannot fight it, you cannot change it. Because from now on, *they* own you."

"Stop talking." A shiver skitters down my spine. Because in my heart, I know he speaks the truth, a harsh truth I've tried so hard to ignore since the moment I decided to go to Avalon.

The boy presses on, though his words are torture to my ears.

"You are nothing but pawns in a war the Lucis are determined to win," he says. "A thousand fragile pieces with little to no value. A bloody means to a bloody end."

A slight tingle prickles the hair on my neck. Despite the light breeze drifting through the dome, the first sheen of sweat coats my face.

"You know what happens to those pieces one month in?"

"Shut up."

"They break."

"I won't!" I glare up at him. My hands are clenched into two clammy fists, the round tip of the dart digging into my flesh. The pain is a welcome reprieve from the terror and rage the idiot has managed to push into my bones.

He chuckles, looking almost amused. He's taunting me, I realize. A sick, twisted game that only makes me want to shove the dart down his throat.

"You're a little spitfire, aren't you?"

The name takes me back, dragging me through a painful wave of memories: warm nights spent squabbling with Mama, my foolish temper and the nickname it spurred to life.

"Don't call me that."

He grins, flashing even white teeth. "As you wish. Though I should warn you, that fire will be your undoing in Avalon."

With a step, I match his sly, mocking smile with my own. "You keep talking, and it very well could be yours."

When his smile spreads, I'm suddenly overwhelmed by the need to put some distance between me and the boy. Otherwise, I might end up in a torture chamber for stabbing a smug-faced recruit who won't leave me alone. But as the boy's final words ring in my head, I feel myself starting to unravel, pulling apart rapidly at the seams. *What if he's right? What if I can't survive this?*

Baba's tea is scattered to the winds. Without it, I am vulnerable, stripped bare, a frayed wire on the verge of ruin. The strain of it tugs at my magic. A current of àse buzzes through me, the clamor in my head a familiar peal. Even beneath a layer of fabric, I can feel the rush of heat in my veins, sharp and searing, as magic licks a path along my skin. Flames spark to life inside my palms. The urge to burn something—set fire to the grass carpet, the light columns, even the bleeding dome—is too great. For a split second, I consider it.

Then I think of Baba and the string of cowrie shells he tied around my neck. I think of Luna and the notebook I gave her. I even think of Teo, wherever he may be. I've given so much to keep them safe, keep them alive. I can't stop now. I can't destroy their lives. Because if I were to burn this hell to the ground, I know the Lucis would track down my family and friends and make them suffer for my crime. So as àse simmers in my blood, I clench my fists against the fire, snuffing it out before the boy sees.

You are greater than your fears, Sloane. Mama's voice in my head again. *Ìfé mi, breathe.*

Somehow, I find the strength to do as she asks. I draw a breath, shutting out the city boy in the same moment. I don't think twice about it when I take a step forward, then another, and another, until I'm yards away and he's nothing but a looming shadow at my back.

As he stomps off behind me, I train my eyes on the target wall, determined to land one perfect shot before I'm called in for testing. A quick glance at the dwindling pack of children tells me I don't have much time.

You can do this. I narrow in on the center. *Forget the boy, the dome, the assessment. Forget everything.*

I straighten my back and steel myself, tilting my wrist at an angle. My breaths rattle in and out, steadying slowly, until each one is sharp, focused, and controlled. With a snap of my wrist, I release the dart. It whizzes through the air, a straight blur, before stabbing the black dot in the center.

For the first time, I allow myself to laugh, a strange, aching sound I haven't heard in a long while. It feels empty in the vast hollow of the dome, but it eases my lingering tension, if only a little.

It's my foolish need to gloat that makes me whirl, searching for the boy I left behind seconds ago. I'm still smiling when I find him in a conversation down the hall, but every trace of it vanishes at the sight of the person holding his interest. An officer. A bleeding Lucis officer.

I'm suddenly aware of the boy's broad, commanding frame, aging him at least three years older than I thought him to be. His light brown skin is too rich, his ocean eyes too bright and hard at once. Even his clothes are all wrong, and I don't know why I failed to notice such fine wool to begin with.

By gods, how could I have been so stupid?

It's the way those eyes fall on me now that sets my heart racing, every muscle in my body rigid with fear. I'm too stunned to move, and I can only stare as he puts an end to his conversation and strides over, bridging the distance between us. He looks past me, to the wall, where he'll surely find my dart lodged into the heart of the target, but I no longer care. Gloating suddenly seems impossible under the pressing weight of what I know now.

"Not bad." His voice remains casual, but there's something different about it, a brute force that wasn't present before.

"You're not from the city." Despite my nerves, I force the words through clenched teeth.

"I never said I was."

When he shifts, the smell of steel and ocean and death fills my nose, a powerful air that clings to him like a curse. It's both chilling and overwhelming, enough to make my limbs twitch. *Walk away while you still can.*

I would. In fact, I almost do, until the tiniest pressure in my pocket roots me back to the ground.

"You're only allowed to leave with one," the boy whispers against my ear.

My face burns. One of the two darts I stole now dangles from his hand, and I expect him to cuff my wrists and drag me to a torture chamber for whatever punishment he deems appropriate. But he doesn't pull me away. Instead, he holds my gaze for far too long, his eyes steady as he angles his wrist and chucks the dart.

My curiosity betrays me, and I turn in time to see the object buried into the dotted center, right next to mine.

My jaw tightens. It takes great effort to chance a glance around, only to find the city boy gone. *No, not the city boy.* He wasn't raised in the dust of some Nagean village, but on a patch of green paradise in the middle of the Atali Ocean.

Avalon.

He's nothing but an island-devil.

By the time the Lucis officer finally calls me in, fourth bell's come and gone, and I'm one of the few remaining children in the dome. The faces of the other recruits are a blur as I weave past them, yet I feel the weight of their eyes on me, watching, wondering what horror awaits the latest child to enter the chamber. I find myself thinking the same, and my stomach dips and twists as the petite officer nods me inside and shuts the door.

The room itself is incredibly narrow, stretching a good ten yards away from the door. There isn't a single piece of furniture in sight, only a strip of clear plastic laid out on the floor across from me. What it's meant for, I don't know. Still, the slow, familiar creep of dread pools in my stomach.

"Tell me, Recruit," the officer says, idly petting the pistol in her hand. "Have you ever seen a Scion before?"

She speaks the words so casually she may as well be asking me if I've ever come across a damned monkey in an alleyway. But it's the feral look in her eyes, born of a predator that's just ensnared its prey, that makes me want to shrink away.

She knows. By gods, she knows, and now she's going to kill me.

I should have known coming here today would spell my doom.

I glance back at the door, wishing I could make a run for it. Before I can even summon up the courage to try, something screeches a few feet away from the carpet, drawing my attention. If not for the two parallel slits carved into the wall, I wouldn't notice the hidden door at all. It groans open now, and nothing prepares me for what comes next.

A hulking male guard emerges, dragging a young boy forward by his shackles. Metal chains crisscross down the boy's limp frame, and I almost don't recognize him beneath the map of fresh wounds marring his face. But his eyes . . . I'd know those river-brown eyes even from fields away.

A small, strangled gasp rushes past my lips.

"Teo."

NINE

He shouldn't be here.

The boy who chose freedom over his heart should be paddling off in a canoe to Naine.

The boy whose kiss still kindles a flame on my lips should be far, far away from the city dome.

Yet, somehow, Teo stands before me now—though not for long.

My pulse races as the guard drops him onto his knees. He sways from his place on the floor, barely conscious. His muddy shirt is torn through, revealing the giant welts covering his chest. Blood pours from the gash above his left eye, streaking all the way down to his busted lips.

Teo ran. This is what happens to those who run.

I can't tear my gaze away from his swollen brown cheeks, the purple patches marking his arms, each one a horrible brand left behind by the officers. I see their brutal hands in every torn patch of flesh and jutting bone. I'm no stranger to pain, but even I can't imagine the hurt and suffering he must have felt all morning, since the moment he was caught.

Now they are going to kill him. And I'm going to be forced to watch.

With a gasp, Teo raises his bloodshot eyes to mine, the collar around his neck glinting in the sunlight. "Sloane."

Almost immediately, the guard drives the butt of his gun into his skull. I scream as blood sprays from his mouth, staining the drab gray floor.

"Look down," the brute barks, readying his gun for another hit.

Before I can think any better of it, I rush forward. But just as I get within a few inches of him, the guard shoves me back so violently my head smacks the concrete when I fall.

Black dots eat at my vision. I shake it off and scrabble to my feet, my eyes on Teo. Even though it was only hours ago the boy broke my heart, I'd hoped and prayed he would make it to Naine, survive long enough to live out a life of freedom. Perhaps even grow old enough to marry, bear children, do what many have only dreamed. That was the life I wanted for him. Not this.

"Please—please—" My heart hammers against my ribs as I look between the officer and the guard, begging them for mercy I know they won't grant. Still, I try. For Teo's life, I surely try. "Whatever you think he's done, you're wrong. He's my best friend. Please, don't hurt him."

"Oh, but that's exactly why we're here, Recruit," the officer sneers. "Especially when there's Scion scum involved."

The venom with which she speaks makes my blood run cold, and the only thing my mind latches onto is *Scion*.

I was right. She's figured it out. She knows who I am. It's the only reason she's kept Teo alive this long—so I can witness his death before they kill me too.

To harbor a Scion is to suffer the same fate as one. The Lucis' threat from long ago repeats in my head. First Teo, then Luna and Baba. Everyone I know, everyone I love, will die because of me. The pressure in my chest expands, making it harder for me to breathe.

"He didn't know," I choke out. "I swear he—"

My mouth goes dry as the officer slinks toward Teo. She sinks her claws into his bruised cheeks and jerks his head upward, forcing him to meet her reptilian gaze.

"Strange," she says, her nails reddening with his blood. "I always thought his kind knew exactly what freaks they were."

His kind?

Shock barrels down my spine. I'm too numb to do anything but stare.

She spits in his face and shoves him aside. Teo falls to the ground like an unstrung marionette, unable to keep himself upright. Satisfied, the officer whirls on me.

His kind. Freaks.

By gods. She . . . she thinks Teo is a Scion.

No. They are wrong. They must be.

"He's no such thing!" The words are out of my mouth in an instant. "He's not who you think he is. Teo, tell her!"

Instead, it's the officer who speaks. "Earlier this morning, air patrol caught this rat traveling downriver." Her voice hisses and slithers like a snake in my ears, making me shudder. "He turned two Nightwalkers' guns against them. Buried bullets in their skulls with a flick of his hand. If he's no Scion, tell me, Recruit. What is he?"

I shake my head, as if I can keep her words from burrowing deeper into my brain. But they bury deep, so strong they force me to my knees.

"Teo, say something." Desperation leaks through my voice, begging him to protest her lies, do all he can to clear his name. But he doesn't. And the longer he remains silent, the harder it becomes to ignore the truth.

I wouldn't last a night on that island, he told me. I didn't understand him when he said those words to me. The Teo I knew was a carpenter skilled even with the most useless tool, a brawler who could fight his way out of any trouble with nothing but his calloused fists. The Teo I knew was a survivor. Realization turns my body to lead.

"That's why you couldn't stay." I glance beyond the officer to look at him. When he lifts his head, the tears in his eyes are enough to confirm the woman's accusation. "It's why you chose to run. Why you said goodbye."

My breath stutters as images start to cascade through my head, strange memories from our childhood I'd long forgotten and buried away. Like the day I visited him at his master's shop only to find him pulling bent, rusted nails from a piece of iroko wood without even a hammer in hand. That image of him stains now, blotting out all else until only his tugging hands remain.

Gods above. He is a descendant of Ogun. A boy of steel. Teo is a Scion like me. How did I fail to see it before?

His urge to flee, to distance himself from Avalon no matter the cost. He'd rather risk his life as a runaway than die at the hands of those who would kill him for who he is. If only we'd trusted each other enough to reveal our truths. Could I have saved him? Could we have saved each other?

"I wanted to tell you," he slurs after what feels like hours. His voice is small and hoarse as he struggles to get everything out. "I was afraid. I didn't know—"

The guard stabs Teo's head with his gun. He cries out and doubles over, coughing up blood.

"Stop hurting him!" I scream before I can stop myself.

As the brute moves to strike again, I duck past the officer and throw myself over Teo's hunched frame, letting the weapon dig into my back instead. Bone-chilling pain explodes down my spine. I bite back another scream and wrap my arms around Teo's trembling body. It doesn't matter what they do to me, how much they torture me for protecting him. I won't stand by and watch him suffer.

"It's okay." I press my quivering lips to his head, kissing him softly. "It's—"

A hand wrenches me back and flings me across the room, knocking the wind out of my lungs. Before I can recover, the officer is standing above me. She tugs me off the ground and slams me against the wall, her pistol aimed at my head.

"Try that again, and I'll kill you myself, assessment be damned."

"Don't—don't hurt her—" Teo shudders behind the officer.

Through my daze, I meet his eyes, and it's as if I'm looking into a mirror. I see my own future laid bare, a reflection of who I could become if I'm caught too. Trapped beneath the weight of fetters and manacles. Beaten, broken, and left at the mercy of those who wish death upon me. Because no matter what, Scions will always fall to the Lucis' bullets, either in the dome or on the battlefield. *They'd sooner destroy you for fear of what they do not understand.*

Today, it's Teo. Tomorrow, it could be me.

The officer lowers her gun and backs away slowly. The thinnest blade of a smile gleams on her lips.

"This is your test, Recruit. Your chance to prove yourself to the Force. What better way to show loyalty than the sacrifice of a loved one?" When she glances at Teo, a deep, feverish tremor passes through my body. "The bravest amongst you have executed friends, brothers, even mothers, in honor of this nation and the royal bloodlines," she says as she turns on me once again. "Kill him, and you'll join the rank of recruits leaving for Avalon. Fail, and, well . . ."

You die. Her unspoken words echo around me. I sway on my feet, barely breathing, my balance unsteady.

Let this serve not only as an evaluation of your devotion, but of your worth. My skin crawls as the commander's voice rings in my head, and I slowly begin to understand. This is what assessment day is all about. Not a vicious fight, not even the torture of innocent citizens. But murder—bloody murder of our families and friends.

My gaze darts to Teo. His swollen eyes are nearly shut, even as he struggles to keep them open. Just a few hours ago, those eyes had burned into mine, lit with a fire I felt deep in my core. They are the eyes of the boy who whispered *I love you* inside his master's shop. The eyes of the boy I've loved far longer than even he knows. They stare back at me now, the flame in them replaced with an emptiness that chokes my heart like death's noose.

"This isn't right." The officer shifts, but I swallow back my fear. "I'm the one you want. Why must he pay the price?"

"Up until this morning, he wasn't yours to kill, Recruit. We had planned on your grandfather. He was going to be your target—"

"Baba?" All at once, my insides freeze.

"So unless you want the old man to die," she continues, "you will do your duty."

The second I look into the officer's narrowed eyes, I know she means every word. All my life, I've known the royals to be cruel, vicious creatures who see us as nothing but ants beneath their feet. Prey whose days were numbered. But this—this goes far beyond cruelty.

Something withers inside me, the last bloom of a dying flower. When the officer slaps a gun into my hand, I flinch away from it. Steel drops, heavy metal clanging against the dirt floor.

"Pick it up," she snarls.

I reach down to retrieve the weapon, my clammy fingers searching for purchase. Across from me, Teo lets out a cry as the guard forces him onto the clear carpet. *Oh.*

"I can't do this." My words are a broken whisper as true terror coils in the pit of my stomach.

Even though I know I'm trapped, I back away slowly, desperate to put as much distance between myself and the monster they want me to become. Because if I kill Teo, that is what I'll always be known as, what I'll always see myself as. A murderer no better than the demons who forced my hands.

I don't get far. In one stride, the officer closes the gap between us. She slaps me so hard, I taste blood in my mouth. Then her hand is around my throat, squeezing with enough force to draw a choking sound out of me.

"You will kill this scum."

It's impossible for me to breathe, even more impossible to speak. Still, I find the strength to say, "I—will—not."

She frees my neck. I know not to see it as an act of kindness.

"You have a choice," she says, circling me the way a hyena does its prey. I work to keep track of her every move, fearful of what she might do while I'm not looking.

She pauses at my side. "Right here, right now." She leans in close, so close I can see the devil himself in her eyes.

Then her pistol knocks against my skull, and my body goes rigid. I don't know when I start to cry, but tears spill down my cheeks, and I can't stop them.

"Please, no," I whimper. "Gods above, please!"

Through my tears, I offer a silent prayer to Olodumarè. But I know not even the gods can save us right now. Àse lashes through my veins like the crack of a whip, and the fire in me screams for release. Now more than ever, I wish I could set it free. I wish I could show them what I'm capable of. I wish I could burn these savages to the ground. But I can't.

"Sloane." Teo's voice finally forces me to open my eyes. My blurred vision makes it hard to look at him, but I hear him all the same. "Do it," he says.

Despite his misplaced bravery, I see the fear in him too. He is, after all, only fifteen. A boy on the edge of an abyss he doesn't deserve.

"If you don't, you'll die. We both will."

His words draw hot new tears to my eyes. Because like him, I know there's no escaping this. We entered this steel cage, and my key to freedom is to take his life. But how will I live with myself knowing I killed the boy I love? Is such a life even worth living at all?

"Sloane!" he urges. "You. Have. To. Kill. Me."

I shake my head, my throat too tight to form a syllable.

A small smile pulls at his blood-smeared lips, much like the one he flashed me as he walked out of my life the night before. "I love you, Sloane. I love you so much I'd die for you."

I shouldn't listen to him. I shouldn't allow him to sacrifice himself for me. I should choose death over a life of eternal slavery. Because if I do what Teo is asking of me, I know I will always be a slave to my guilt. I know it deep in my soul. Yet, my sobs pierce the gloom of the steel chamber as I utter the words, "I'm sorry. I'm so sorry."

He nods slowly.

My entire body trembles. I bring the weapon forward and aim shakily at his head. Time stretches as a host of memories parade through my mind, tugging at my heart, filling me with sadness and shame and pain and guilt.

"I love you," I breathe.

The words flutter in the space between us like the wings of a dying moth, bruised and broken and barely catching flight. Yet, somehow, they fight their way into Teo's ears.

He smiles, even as tears track down his face. "I know."

My finger finds the trigger. I squeeze.

When I was six, I witnessed my first Cleansing in the village square. Despite Mama's and Baba's warnings to stay away from the execution, I managed to persuade Luna and Teo to sneak off with me. We arrived at the square moments before the Lucis' firing squad began their countdown. Ten armed officers, all for one scrawny old Scion man.

When their guns went off, it crackled like thunder.

This sounds worse.

TEN

The morning after Mama disappeared, it was Teo who stayed with me while Baba headed to the foothills with a few trackers from the village. He held me in his arms as I sobbed and prayed for Olodumarè to bring Mama back to me. Yet, hours later, when Baba and the trackers finally returned, they arrived alone. I crumpled to the ground despite Teo's firm grip, gasping and shaking as everything I was, everything I held on to, became weeping, fleeting ghosts of themselves.

I feel the same way now as the chamber shrinks around me and pain tears my world apart. I'm struggling to breathe, struggling to speak, move, do anything but stare at the boy who lies in a growing puddle of blood. The gunshot echoes in my head, louder this time.

I scream.

A powerful surge rakes through me, a vibration deep in my core. The clamor in my head is harsh, an aching din that throbs against the insides of my skull. Heat prickles my feet, my chest, my limbs. I wrap my arms around myself, grasping and squeezing, hoping to crush the magic within. Pain lashes up my spine the more I struggle to push it down, and my body convulses. Now more than ever, I wish I could reach for my herbs. The only thing that could save me from myself, and it's gone.

My breath strains with every rush of àse flooding my veins. I feel the red tendrils writhing like cobwebs beneath my skin. Just as the heat threatens to consume me from within, the thrum of magic dwindles. The steel walls of the chamber blink back into focus, and the female officer slowly materializes before me.

I'm still panting and shivering from my place on the floor when she yanks me up on my feet and shoves me toward the male guard.

"Get her out of here," she growls.

He barely catches me in time, his fingers tightening around my arm, sharp nails digging into skin. I sway on weakened knees, still too fragile to stand on my own.

Behind him, Teo's splayed corpse remains unmoved, bathed in dark crimson. When I force myself to glance at him, I see the bullet that whizzed toward his head. The blood that sputtered from his mouth when steel found flesh. Every image leaves a painful brand on my mind, marking me as a traitor of my own kind.

My entire body withers beneath a swell of shame. *What have I done?*

The guard whisks me out of the chamber, dragging me toward the back entrance of the now-empty dome. I stumble after him, bile bubbling up my throat.

I should have let them kill me. I should have died rather than sell my soul to the devil.

You and I . . . It's always been you and I.

Teo, I'm sorry. I'm so sorry. I beg for forgiveness I don't deserve, forgiveness I know I'll never find.

Outside, the sun is bright overhead, scorching my bare arms. I squint hard against the glare, straining to see the long stretch of paved road running almost the entire breadth of the city. A massive airship perches at the start of the runway like a crow preparing for flight. Its wings are made of freshly oiled metal, clawed feet replaced with black, rolling tires.

I can only watch as Lucis officers bound in and out of the transport meant to ship the newly assessed recruits to Avalon. We survived the test, pledged our lives to the Force, each one sealing our allegiance by killing a friend, a relative.

Gods, how much blood was spilled inside those chambers? How many loved ones were lost across Nagea today?

The guard leaves me at the rear of the airship, where the ramp inclines gradually toward the maw of a giant beast. Inside, rows of plush chairs line the metal-paneled walls. A few recruits are already belted into their seats, their faces stony. All of them are quiet, save for the one boy whose muffled sobs still manage to punctuate the silence that has fallen over the entire ship.

More soldiers and recruits pour in as I settle into a chair farther away from the cluster of bodies. The airship hums to life. A steady stream of chatter rises, mostly among the Lucis officers eager to return to their precious little island. A paradise I know will be my hell.

I don't spare them even the slightest glance, my face pressed against the small glass window cut into the wall next to me. Ilé-Ifè sprawls beyond, the only place I've called home my entire life. Though I try to keep the memories at bay, Teo haunts my mind like a vengeful ghost. It takes everything I have to steer my thoughts away from him. *Think about Mama. Focus on the mission.*

I draw a ragged breath as the ramp door lifts to a close. Whirring engines swell into a loud roar. I feel the wheels at work, rolling us forward, gaining speed with every passing moment. My hands grip the edges of my seat, holding on for dear life. That's when I notice the boy strapped into the chair beside me, his usually tamed bun unruly for once.

Malachi.

I frown, tensing at the silvery raised scars along the right side of his brown face. A cluster of scratch marks leaves fresh wounds over the ruined flesh. As always, I feel a familiar stab of guilt even as my hand strays to the set of blades tucked into my belt, until I remember the officers seized every bleeding weapon I brought with me. Quietly, I curse them.

"I was wondering when I'd run into you," Malachi says. Though his hazel eyes shine with distaste, he seems rattled, worn, like a used rag that's been wrung out and hung to dry.

Any other day, the mere sound of his voice would have earned him a clever retort. Right now, I can barely manage a simple "Piss off."

But Malachi's like one of the flying cockroaches hissing about the alcoves of Baba's food cabinet, impossible to kill and even more impossible to get rid of.

"Where's Teo?" the bastard asks, and I hear the echo of gunfire. *Where's Teo?* and Malachi forces me to relive every single moment of my best friend's death.

Nausea churns in my stomach. The same guilt I've wrestled with since the moment I pulled that trigger reemerges. But I don't want to feel the pain, the grief, the sorrow. I don't want to feel anything at all. So I turn away from Malachi and return to the window, watching the city blur past as the airship screeches down the runway.

With a thrust, the beast takes flight, soaring higher and higher through the air. The sensation is like nothing I'm used to, and if not for the belts holding me in place, I fear I might have been thrown off my seat. The runway disappears entirely beneath us, replaced by warm skies and drifting clouds.

Across the horizon, the Agbajé Range cuts sharply through the blanket of gray, jagged spires of naked rock stabbing at the setting sun. A few miles away from those mountains lies my village, my hut, *my home.* The place where Luna weeps and Baba laments over steaming pots and soiled dishes, the both of them still grappling with the pain of the friend and grandchild they lost to the Draft. I wonder what they'll think of me once they find out the truth about what I've done and the blood that clings to my hands now because of it.

"You killed him." Malachi's voice jolts me from my thoughts. "You killed Teo, didn't you?"

Shame seeps through my entire body as I round on him.

"I had no choice," I confess, though the lie tastes sour on my tongue. "It was what he wanted. He begged me to do it."

So I did. The ache stabs with unrelenting force. I blink back the tears clinging to my lashes, trying to hide them from Malachi. Even though I don't care what the boy thinks of me, I can't bring myself to meet his eyes.

A ray of sunlight hits his left arm, enough to glimpse the blood smearing his skin. Part of me wonders whose life he was forced to take, whose ghost stalks his mind like Teo does mine.

I glance up at him. He shifts his gaze from the scarlet stain to me. A dark look crosses his face, revealing the pain he fails to numb.

"Shahid's dead," he murmurs with a set of his jaw.

Shahid. I hear myself gasp. The bull-necked boy who stood by and watched as Malachi kicked me bloody in the darkened alleyways of the institution when we were six years old. The same boy who gripped my arms as Malachi dragged me into a cornfield a year later and knocked out three of my baby teeth. I remember him just as he was yesterday, a shadow inside the palm-wine tavern. A puppet ready to dance at the pull of a string. But to Malachi, Shahid was his friend. He was his family.

I don't know what I feel more—pity for the boy who's bullied me for ten years, or rage for the devils who wove this pain into our bones. Because while Malachi and I may have left each other with too many scars to count, even he doesn't deserve this grief. Not after all he's been through.

"He was there, you know?" His coarse voice breaks through the quiet. "The day after Ma and Papa died. Shahid was the only one who came to bury them."

I stiffen at the mention of his parents, though Malachi hardly seems to notice.

"Neither of us knew what to say. So we stood before their burnt bodies, staring, until the sun went down."

When he glances at me, I wince at the pale, knotted ridges taking up half of his face—a reminder. I should look away, but I can't stop myself from staring at the scars.

"Do you remember the fire?" Malachi asks. Something like the ghost of a memory glints behind his cold, haunted gaze. The sight chills my blood.

"Ten years is a long time, Mal," I say a little too quickly, turning my face away. "The memories of a child are a fickle thing."

Baba said the same to me once.

"True." Malachi nods, and for a moment, he remains stoic, silent, long enough for me to hope he won't speak anymore of the past. Then his voice drops into a low, crackling hiss. "But not when you're the child who started the fire."

The words flash through my mind, and memories of a night I wish I could forget swirl before me. I'm inside my hut, surrounded by darkness and the warmth of two bodies. Mama and Baba sit on a couch across the room, deep in an argument I cannot hear. One memory stands out above all else, the one of a little girl, five years of age, glaring out the open window. Somewhere beyond those wooden shutters, an inferno ravages the village. *I couldn't control it*, the little girl whispers, more to herself than anyone else. *I couldn't control it.*

I squeeze my eyes against images I've fought so long to keep out of my head. But as much as I try, I can't stop the onslaught. Many villagers had been terribly wounded in that fire, some more so than others. But all had survived the horrible flames born from the fingers of a frightened little girl. All—except for two.

He knows.

My eyes snap open. I round on Malachi, trying my best to remain calm, a mask to hide the whirl of emotions underneath. Beside me, the boy's face tightens, the only indication that he's still present, even though his eyes and thoughts seem far, far away.

"Mal—"

"You killed my parents," he says hoarsely. With one bloodied finger jabbed at his scars, he adds, "*You* did this."

The airship rattles, bumping me side to side. I focus on the pressure of my nails against the edges of the seat, anything but the fear raging inside me. Still, I hear mothers crying and fathers groaning, children and elders bleeding on the ground. Flames roar all around, making cinders of every hut. Ash drifts in the night, coating the world gray. The little girl's sobs are a piercing echo as she screams at the top of her lungs, *I'm sorry, I didn't mean to. I'm so sorry.*

I am reduced to that same little girl now, trying to make sense of the sins I've kept buried for so long, even as they stare me right in the face.

"Go ahead," Malachi spits out. "Deny it. Tell me I'm wrong."

My heart constricts around the horrible truth. The belts that have kept me safe and secure on this damned airship now feel like restraints, trapping me in a prison of Malachi's making. If I could, I would get up and leave, distance myself from the boy with cold, bloody vengeance on his mind. Because I know he'll surely want it, now that he knows I'm responsible for the death of his parents. Now that he knows I made him an orphan at the early age of five.

"H-how long have you—"

"Does it matter?"

Despite the guilt scraping my mind raw, I turn to look at him head-on. A storm gathers on his face, twisting his features into something dark and cruel.

"Malachi, I'm—"

"Sorry?" His empty eyes are firmly fixed on me. "A little too late for that, don't you think? I have no use for your apology, Sloane. I just want you to pay for what you've done. It's the only way to make it right."

The remark makes my skin prickle. Every bloody fight, every wicked blow I've suffered at his hands, parades before my mind now, an ugly procession that brings with it a bitter understanding of the boy I thought I knew already.

You tried to kill me once, he told me the night before, back inside the palm-wine tavern. *I'll make you regret ever doing that.*

Now I can barely breathe. "Is that why we've spent all these years at each other's throats? You're punishing me for an accident that happened ten years ago?"

I wish I could tell him I understand his pain. The kind of pain that will never fade, no matter how much you wish it would. I stole two lives from him, the same way the Lucis did from me. And for that, I wish I could tell him I'm sorry, I'm sorry, I'm sorry.

To my surprise, Malachi chuckles. It sounds strange coming from him, hollow, an empty noise more menacing than anything else.

"You haven't even begun to know what real punishment feels like." He nods in the direction of the officers, his eyes sliding over a few seated men. "These fools, they have no idea what you are. A Scion, a killer, a dead girl walking. But I do."

I stare at him, too numb to speak. The small shred of pity I felt for him quickly vanishes once I realize what he plans to do. In its place, a seed of terror takes root inside my gut, sprouting thorns.

"So that's it." Somehow, I manage to find my voice. "You're going to hand me over to the Lucis. Summon the pardon clause. Free yourself from the Draft."

I glance at the dozen or so officers scattered throughout the airship, each one with a loaded rifle or pistol in hand. One word and Malachi could unleash every single one of them on me. Trade my life for his freedom. He'll do to me what I did to Teo.

Perhaps that's what I deserve after all the people I've killed. I am a murderer of a mother, a father, even the boy who once held my heart. Perhaps death is a fitting punishment for someone like me. But if I die now, then it means Teo died for nothing. Is that what he wasted his life for? A broken thing willing to accept death so easily? *No.* I can't die now, not yet, not after everything. I owe Teo that much.

Years ago, I swore never to beg Malachi again. Some people don't respond to such things, only violence. But now, with my life in the hands of this vengeful boy, begging might be the only way to save my skin. Before I can even muster enough courage to start, he stops me with his hand.

"I'm not a rat, Sloane. I don't plan on saying anything." His lips curl into a sneer. "Besides, why should I grant you that small mercy?"

At first, I don't understand. Is he sparing my life? I know the boy too well to think he'd do anything without cause. If he thinks death at the hands of the Lucis isn't punishment enough, what is?

He wheels his entire body toward me. His safety belts are gone, dangling from the sides of his seat. Even though I know not to trust him in such close proximity, I don't move. Our bodies are inches apart; I can almost smell the village on him. Dust and mud and rain. It would be too easy to focus on the earthy smell, reminding me of home and Baba and Luna, but something about Malachi's unusual posture, cutting me into a corner far beyond the officers' easy line of sight, keeps me alert.

He pulls out a knife from his pocket and flips it open, letting the blade gleam before our eyes. I don't have the time to wonder how he managed to sneak a knife past the officers. My breath hitches, but I'm quick to remind myself that he won't hurt me. Not here, not with so many officers a few feet away. Still, I keep my muscles taut and ready, primed for any sudden movement.

"My parents cried for help as they burned in that fire. No one came for them." He looks at me with coal-black eyes, his fearsome gaze worse even than the fire burning through my veins. His voice is cold, though, and just as sharp as the knife he wields in his hand. "I want to watch you do the same," he says, "knowing no one will come for you."

The blade scratches against my skin, burrowing deeper as Malachi carves a small slit into my thigh. Pain bites through my entire body, gnawing up my bones. If not for the officers milling about the airship, I would snatch the knife from his scrawny fingers and shove it inside his stomach, next to his old stab wound. Instead, I clench my fists, seething, as Malachi wipes the blade on my pants and tucks it away in his pocket.

"Careful, Sloane," he says before storming off to the other side of the airship.

A small warning, but I know to read the threat between the lines. Malachi will come for me, and when he does, I have to be ready. I know my life depends on it.

I'm still attending to the cut, drying the blood with my sleeves, when a voice blares from the ceiling, echoing down the airship. I can't make out a single word except *Avalon*, but when some of the recruits start pressing their faces to the windows beside them, I understand why. Even I can't help but turn my gaze toward the window now, watching the vast Atali Ocean beneath and the island perched right in the middle.

Avalon sprawls with lush greenery, golden sands, and slate-roofed buildings. A small, separate island dots the edge of the Lucis' capital city, connected only by a long, massive bridge that arches over the wide stretch of vibrant blue water.

King's Isle.

That's what they called it in the large tomes the institution tried to force us to read when we were little. Home to the thirteen founding bloodlines and their royal court, as well as all of the Lucis' other government and administrative buildings. A marvel of crystalline towers gleaming like stars from far, far below.

So much beauty. I can't help but scowl. *It would be a joy to watch it burn.*

For the rest of the airship's slow descent, I force my eyes away from the window and turn my thoughts to the journey ahead. Instead, the words of the boy I met back in the dome prey on my mind until it's impossible to shake the dread knotting around my heart.

It's where children like you come to die and be reborn as murderers.

I barely hear the thud of the airship when it lands, but I feel the dip and lurch of my stomach, making me sick. The urge to retch only worsens as the reality of what awaits me starts to set in. Cold sweat beads on my brow, and I hope I haven't made a mistake by coming here to Avalon. I hope the truth about Mama does lie somewhere inside this base, that I find it well before the Lucis figure out who I am.

The next moments pass in a blur as the airship whistles down the runway, coasting to a stop at the end of the paved road. Officers are the first to rise, flooding the back of the transport like a swarm of giant wasps. The rear door yawns open, and one by one, the beast spits them out, until only the recruits remain.

They march us out in a single file, with me at the tail end of the line. I know to move only because an officer barks out the order.

I force my legs forward. My heart hammers like a bàtá drum, matching the quick, panicked rhythm of my feet. Then it's my turn to descend the ramp.

I'm halfway down the slope when a female officer rounds up the waiting recruits and says, "Welcome to Fort Regulus."

ELEVEN

The walls of Fort Regulus are monstrous, climbing at least fifty feet into the air. Thick coils of steel wire run across its jagged, iron-spiked ledges, a death trap for anyone foolish enough to scale such bleeding heights. The base itself sprawls as though it were a beast claiming territory among its lesser brethren. Domed compounds rise in the open terrain beyond, with fenced fortifications surrounding each giant facility. Long strips of black tarmac loop their way around the meandering grounds, fringed by tall growth of local gmelina and pruned shrubbery. I glare at the expanse of raw concrete and stone, wide-eyed and in utter disbelief.

By gods. Behind these walls, I feel infinitely small, a cornered prey searching for an escape but finding none. With nothing to do but follow, I turn my gaze on the officer's deft form as she hastens us away from the massive airfield.

We weave through a maze of flat, gray stone buildings, each one bustling with too many uniformed soldiers to count. A few yards away, what looks like a thousand more soldiers drill across the scattered training fields, their booted feet stomping the hard-packed earth as one.

It's clear that the Lucis are a highly militarized race, equipped with the deadliest, most advanced weaponry ever known to the continent. But nothing is as feared as the Force—an army of elite soldiers willing to commit even the most unspeakable horrors in the name of the monarchy. To them, serving in the Force is an honor, their brutality a rite of passage. After all, they are the sons of the Lucis' most decorated warlords, daughters of such ruthless political figures, and their status affords them a privilege no Nagean child soldier could ever enjoy.

Even from this distance, they look terrifying—a sea of black ebbing and flowing at their lieutenants' commands. My stomach churns. I'm the very thing these soldiers are training to kill. Yet, here I am, smack-dab in their territory. Gods, what the hell am I doing here?

It takes everything in me to keep my face straight, burying my fear behind a plain gaze. As if Malachi can read my mind, his eyes find me. He tilts his head in the direction of the soldiers and grins, flashing stained, crooked teeth. Anger boils beneath my skin, but I stifle my retort. *Don't let him get to you. Don't give him a reason to talk.*

"What is that?" asks another one of the recruits, drawing our attention to the fire burning on a training field across the base.

"The burning ritual," the officer tells us, stopping briefly to watch. "Illegal artifacts seized from the black market are stored inside the military's storage pit, and every two weeks, the soldiers burn them on the main field."

There are at least eight Lucis gathered around a heap of cobbled scraps, each one feeding hundreds of looted items into the roaring blaze. We look on as pieces of tarnished metal, ivory ceramics, and leather-bound books are tossed into the flame. The soldiers erupt in cheers, howling like a pack of wild jackals. Even the officer before us smiles openly, her lips spreading at their jubilant outburst.

"Entertaining, isn't it?" She meets our gazes, anticipating some sort of response.

Instead, she's only met with silence from the rest of the recruits, while I wrinkle my nose in distaste. Of course an hour of needless destruction would amuse these barbarians.

A deep breath hisses past my lips as the officer takes us around a slight bend. Beyond it, a cluster of three buildings rise ahead, their arching entrances decorated with tall, barrel-shaped columns. Soldiers arrange themselves before the front lobbies. Though the gun-wielding brutes are fearsome enough, it's the blue-eyed Nagean leopards leashed to their hands that make me squirm. The giant beasts sit on high alert at the guards' feet, fangs bared and claws sharpened, ready to pounce on any idiot who comes too close.

As we draw nearer, the names chiseled across each building become large enough to read. *Research Center* sits to the left, and I can only imagine what the Lucis are researching, or worse—who they're experimenting on. I have a mind to caution myself again, knowing if I'm not careful, I could very well end up behind those walls. I set my jaw and force myself to move. But the second I run my gaze across the building to my right, my feet slow.

Archives Hall. The place where the Lucis keep a database of all confidential files—like the Book of Records. The same book the defector in Oyo claimed to have. The one I pray will tell me all I need to know about what happened the night Mama and Felipe disappeared.

For a moment, all I can do is stare at the looming structure. This is it. The reason I'm here. A burst of energy sweeps through me, my own advice long forgotten. If I could, I'd tear up those stairs now and start searching for that damned book. I'd burn my way through that bleeding hall if it meant learning the truth about Mama today. But the faces of the soldiers and those of the snarling leopards come into sharper focus, a grim reminder of where I am and what they can do. My adrenaline wanes with each wasted second, driven away by fear.

Easy, Sloane. You've come too far, sacrificed too much, not to think this through. I can't afford to be foolish about this. I know the only way I'm getting inside that building and getting out alive is with a solid plan. A well-thought-out, calculated—

"Back in formation, Recruit!"

The officer's voice breaks into my thoughts, making me flinch. I'm not sure when I strayed too far from the group, but I look up to see the remaining recruits a few feet ahead.

I rush forward, settling back in line as the officer leads us toward the building that sits in the middle. *Grand Hall* is the largest of the trio, a sweeping architecture of concrete and steel. I squint my eyes against the godsforsaken structure, focusing on the sculpted pillars flanking it. Each one is mounted with a statue of the Lucis' royal bloodlines. Thirteen busts cast in shimmering gold, with crowns of precious stones, beaded pearls, and braids of gilded petals adorning their heads. Colorful flags flutter above the thirteen pillars, displaying the varying heraldries of each royal line. The burning phoenix of the Regulus bloodline; the soaring raven of the Ascellus dynasty. Raised high above the rest, the green banner of the reigning Turais bloodline flaps in the wind.

Strike with Venom, Queen Olympia's flag reads, along with an image of a three-headed hissing viper. How fitting, really, for such a poisonous creature.

Without sparing another glance at the garish display, I march up Grand Hall's long flight of stairs, past the throng of Lucis personnel roving about the entrance. Common workers in plain clothing. Not a single person stops to stare. The ones who do barely cast a glance over their shoulders as they step through the door. They are used to seeing so many child soldiers trudging up and down these darkened halls; the sight of a dozen more means nothing to them. Yet, for all their snobbery, these pompous fools are still living, still breathing, because we make it so. Because we are forced to fight their war while the lot of them carry on with their stupid lives.

Down the hallway, a set of double doors looms ahead, manned by two blue-uniformed guards who yank them open the moment we arrive.

Inside the grand chamber, rows and rows of wooden chairs line every inch of floor space, occupied by scores of blanched-faced recruits. A thousand child soldiers, to be exact. Though we all come from different cities and have lived different lives, one thing remains the same now. We are all threads of a worn fabric, creatures of heat and dust, stitched together by a common fear.

Since we are the last of the recruits to arrive, the only chairs remaining are the ones pushed against the back walls of the hall. The officer directs us toward them, and I settle into the chair at the edge of the row, eager to keep as much distance as possible between myself and Malachi. To my relief, the boy sits farther down the other end, far enough not to be a bother. Then the officer is out the door, leaving us to anticipate what comes next.

Silence pours through the hall like poison, tinging the air, choking every single recruit in the room. Next to me, a red-haired girl trembles in her seat, her eyes glossy with tears yet to fall. The boy beside her is no better, hard veins straining against the brown of his temple. As I stare down the rows of recruits, I start to see the same fear mirrored in each child's gaze. My own nerves scream in solidarity. So much that I'm grateful when a long procession of soldiers march forward into the hall.

I train my eyes on the parade of uniformed men and women, long rifles firmly propped against their plated shoulders. I lose count after eighteen, but more and more follow, slowing to a halt when they reach the front podium.

Commander Faas Bakker is the only familiar one of the pack. The black whorls on his face gleam beneath the chain of crystal lights dangling from the high ceiling. Only then do I notice the shiny white orbs mounted at every corner of the vaulted roof. Security cameras. Though I've never seen one before today, I've heard rumors of the Lucis' *vigilante*, all of them watching with their invisible eyes. I count at least ten inside Grand Hall alone. The entire base must be crawling with these things. Another leash around our necks, to keep us firmly in the Lucis' grasps.

As Faas climbs up the dais, I rub my palms along the fabric of my pants, wiping the sweat that has gathered there.

"Recruits!" Faas's voice bounces off the ivory-painted walls. "Welcome to Fort Regulus. For those of you who don't know, I'm Faas

Bakker, High Commander of the Avalon Defense Forces, Juvenile Division. Hours ago, your loyalty to the Force was put to the test, and of the thousand drafted this year, eight hundred and twenty-five of you survived the assessment. Congratulations on making it this far."

By gods. Nearly two hundred of us chose death over a life of war, over inhumanity. Were they right? Does it even matter now that they're dead? Despite how hard I try not to think of it, the iron scent of Teo's blood wafts up my nose and guilt coats my tongue like ash.

Up on the dais, Faas's mouth moves. I haven't heard a single word. He glances briefly at the ceiling, and to my shock, a flimsy white parchment descends over his head, almost taking up the length of the wall behind him.

"At this time, Queen Olympia Turais wishes to convey a message to you all," he says before stepping off the platform to join the other soldiers standing off to the side.

My pulse quickens at the thought of seeing the royal bloodlines for the first time. Though the queen and her noble court often make scattered visits across Nagea, none have ever deigned to step foot in a slum village like Agbajé.

Overhead, the crystal lights dim. The paper beams to life. The world on the screen is an ornament dipped in white—white stone walls, white arched roofing, white polished marble floors. This must be the throne room. The place where the queen attends to her official councils and grants audiences. Gilded thrones grace the back wall, occupied by twelve of the thirteen royals. They are the most powerful among the Lucis; the founding families who rule over us like gods, controlling our lives and fates without even the slightest remorse. They wear the white and gold colors of the Lucis, each of them drowning in a cape of white damask edged with swirls of gold metallic stitching.

Even from down here, I recognize their faces from years of old classroom teachings. Lord Bharani stares absently into the distance, looking almost bored. Beside him, Lord Wurren fixes a dutiful smile on his lips, though not enough to hide his obvious distaste for this sham of a gathering. Far down the row of seated royals, my gaze lands on Lord Sol, the only brute to show a degree of interest so far. His dark, shadowy eyes seem to bore into the camera, as if searching for a particular face in the crowd. I leave the man to his quest and turn my focus elsewhere.

By the time the queen appears, everyone in the hall is on their feet. Reluctantly, I join them, rising in time to see Olympia gliding toward the last empty throne. Her cadre of masked sentries trails closely behind. She's smaller than I expected, a delicate little thing no more than five feet tall. Yet, despite the inches I have on her, I feel instantly reduced by the queen's cold, unflinching presence.

Olympia Turais has ruled for as long as I can remember, a young general who inherited the throne after the old Ascellus king died and her bloodline was next in the line of succession. As is customary, power rotates only among the thirteen founding bloodlines. It has been that way since the beginning of the post migration era.

While the rest of the royals wear the official Lucis colors, Olympia dazzles in a black floor-length aso-òkè, studded diamonds gleaming vividly against her smooth alabaster skin. The crown on her head shimmers in gold, its sharp spikes adorned with bloodred rubies that match the paint of her pouted lips.

For a moment, I can only stare at the queen, unable to take my eyes off her outfit. Never in my life have I seen an aso-òkè worn openly and with such flair. Even Mama kept hers hidden in drum barrels buried beneath the ground of our hut. The traditional Yoruba attire would doom any brazen wretch caught wearing it. Yet, this vulture has the gall to parade through the throne room in it. That she would even dare wear my people's garb is a testament to just how much the Lucis have stolen from us. How much of our lives they control.

I still remember the stories Mama told me about the Great Cleansing that began after the invasion, when the first Lucis king ordered his soldiers to hunt and kill anyone who dressed, spoke, or even so much as *looked* Yoruba.

Women in printed bùbá blouses and trailing ìró wrappers were gunned down. Men were slain at palm-wine taverns for whispering dialects that sounded strange and unfamiliar. But it was the deaths of the newborn babies that brought the nation to its knees. Babies with skin the color of ebony wood. Babies born too brown, too black.

Some called it desperation. Others said it was madness when mothers began to scrub their babies raw with Dudu-Osun and soak them in lemon-juice water for long hours. To peel their skin, rid their color, preserve their lives. The taboo years lasted over a century before another Lucis king ended the massacre. But history isn't so easily forgotten, especially when it is still the only reality we know.

Anger flares within me the longer I'm forced to stand before them, and there's nothing I can do about it. So I suppose I should feel some semblance of gratitude when Olympia nods sternly at the waiting crowd, granting us permission to take our seats.

The queen remains standing, though, glaring at each and every recruit for a long, heart-pounding moment. Perhaps it's the ghostly blue burn of her eyes or the raven hair framing her sharp features, making her appear like a corpse frozen beneath a layer of ice. But even from a screen, there's something about Olympia that stokes my fear. And when she finally speaks, her voice lashes out like a whip, commanding everyone's attention.

"Nero Regulus, the First Commander, was seventeen when he led the greatest battle of the post migration era," she says. "The most barbaric, most ruthless Scion warriors fell at his blade. By his order, the ancient Yoruba kingdoms were brought to ruin. His strength raised our army. His valor won us Nagea. He was a soldier, a king, a force to be reckoned with. But a child, he was not. And today, neither are you."

Despite the bits of history the institution drilled into my head, the First Commander's age isn't something I remember. Now learning that Oyo and the rest of the Ancient Kingdoms were conquered by some seventeen-year-old brute only makes my skin crawl. If all it took was one boy to lay waste to an entire race, imagine what 825 more could do. I'm sure the Lucis have thought the same, which is why they collect us by the thousands.

Up on the screen, Olympia carries on with her practiced speech. I wonder how many of these she's delivered.

"The deadliest weapon we have at our disposal is our youth. Emboldened, brave, the strongest and most hardened of the chosen. Yours is the path to freedom, to liberty, to life. And it is my hope that you shall see this as a fight, not only for the hands that rule, but for the brothers and sisters who have come before you. For the friends and relatives whose great sacrifices have sustained the very heart of this nation. For yourself."

Like a chameleon, she changes form right before my eyes, becoming everything she needs to be to sell her terrible speech: warm, gentle, sympathetic to a pain she knows nothing of. A human rather than a monster. It doesn't suit her.

"Many amongst you were abandoned as children. Many were left in the mud, without a family, without a home. How many days were you hungry? How many nights were you afraid? No longer will you be doomed to such a fate. Today, we celebrate the end of your misfortune. Today, *you* become one of us." This stirs a buzz from the recruits, and the fervor in their voices sends a brush of bitterness across my skin. "We will feed you, arm you. We will protect you and see to your every need. We will be your home, and you will be our hope. For it is my vow to make you the strongest amongst your peers, the most lethal soldiers yet to march into the Sahl. Because only you can bring about the destruction of the Shadow Rebels and assure our future. A future we will share, together.

"Nagea is your home, your legacy," Olympia says. "No Scion scum shall claim it from you!"

The entire room rumbles with a thunderous clap. Even the recruits have the nerve to slap their hands together. I clench my jaw against the noise. *Idiots. Fools.* How quickly they seem to have turned, so easily seduced by a few sweeping words that mean nothing. After all, the Lucis are the ones who planned this war, bred out of their own greed and prejudice. Now they sit back and watch as we go on to pay the price, sent into battle like cattle raised for slaughter.

Olympia lifts a hand, silencing the roar. "Now the time has come for you to become great crusaders. Warriors of blood and steel who believe, so fervently, that it is better to die for tomorrow's freedom than live to surrender today. And surrender, we will not!

"Blood and valor!" Her small fist punches the air.

A deep chorus rolls through the hall. "To the very end!"

The explosion of cheers is deafening. Through it all, the queen nods with a mix of pride and satisfaction from her throne room. After all, she's convinced 825 child soldiers their lives are meaningful despite the inevitable death that awaits them on the desert front. But I'm not so easily fooled. I see the woman on the screen for what she truly is: a cunning, slithering viper.

"Commanders." She speaks over the noise, addressing the long rank of soldiers taking up the front rows. "Let us begin."

TWELVE

It takes almost an hour to sort us into our respective squads. I'm one of the ten recruits placed in Storm Squad and left to the charge of two fearsome commanders.

One of them happens to be the High Commander himself—Faas Bakker. Next to him, the second commander, Lieutenant Caspian Amin, is equally terrifying. A lean, well-built soldier with sharp gray eyes and even sharper features. He carries a large assault rifle on his body, the gleaming black weapon strapped across his back. At least a hundred ammunition rounds fill the pockets of the bandolier hanging in the lieutenant's leather-gloved hands. With his deep bronze glow and oily black hair, I'm reminded of Malachi, the boy who I've now the misfortune of calling a squad mate.

As we march down the cold tarmac, Malachi ambles closely behind the commanders, probably hoping to pick out pieces of their whispered conversation. I've no doubt he will do anything to get ahead, even if it means sucking up to these monsters.

I expect Faas and Caspian to show us to the barracks after the terribly long day we've had. Instead, they usher us toward the training center a few yards across the way. The two-story building nestles up against the towering back walls of the base, a long chain of ocean cliffs poking out just behind. A gust of salty breeze teases my bare arms. If I strain my ears enough, I can almost hear the waves crashing against the rocky outcrops of the cliffs.

The calming sound is soon replaced by the slamming of doors as we enter one of the many rooms within the facility. The wide block of space likens more to a gathering area than a training hall, especially with the small screen tucked into the far corner wall. A muted broadcast shows footage of Olympia's sweeping palace, followed by the baronial mansions of Castlemore Court, where the rest of the Lucis' royal bloodlines reside. It's no surprise that while many in Nagea are buried up to their necks in poverty, these bastards have somehow managed to build a heaven from our hell. I tear my eyes away from the rolling images of King's Isle, hating the royals and the luxury afforded only to them.

In the middle of the room, a boy dressed in black hooded fatigues awaits, hands deep in both pockets. With his massive height, broad shoulders, and light brown complexion, I recognize him long before the hood slips off his shaved head.

"Storm Squad!" Faas says as he and Caspian come to a stop beside the boy I met back in the city dome. "Meet Dane Gray, one of the Force's finest soldiers." When the commanders clap him on the shoulder, he gives a curt nod. "Officer Gray's just completed his fifth tour of the Sahl and will now be joining us as your squad leader."

Like lightning, an image of the boy—*Dane*—gunning down Shadow Rebels on the desert front streaks across my mind. With five tours to his name, I've no doubt he's killed over a hundred Yorubas and Scions. And he'll surely do the same to me if he finds out who I am.

I can't fight off the clamor in my head as my àse climbs to a steady pulse and heat flares within me. With a shaky gasp, I manage to tamp down the swell of magic in time. But something tells me this will only worsen as Baba's àgbo slowly dwindles in my system.

Across the room, Dane watches me, his green eyes firmly locked with mine. Hours ago, I thought the Lucis boy nothing but a common island-devil. Now I know him to be far worse: a soldier, a Scion killer.

My enemy.

Yet even though I think to look away, I match him with an equally menacing glare of my own. He may be the squad leader, but no Reaper will ever have my respect and submission.

"Starting tomorrow, Dane here will be responsible for making sure each of you is skilled in close combat and ready to be deployed,"

Faas continues. "You will report to him as arranged in your individual schedules, which you will receive at first light. Any missed session will count as a strike for which you will be punished. Is that clear?"

"Yes, sir!" Our shout bounces off the walls of the training hall. The ensuing silence is heavy enough to crush any thoughts I may have. Even Caspian and Dane are quiet, allowing the High Commander to do most of the talking.

"Look around you," Faas says. When none of us move, the commander juts out his chin. "Go ahead. Look."

For the first time since I was sorted into the squad, I regard the other recruits with a little more than a fleeting glance. My gaze tracks down the pack, taking in the lanky frame of the boy a few feet away. A freckle-faced girl stands close to his side, so close I wonder if they know each other. Off in a corner, separate from the rest of the group, another girl with dark brown skin and a head full of tight coils fixes her beady eyes on the commanders, never once breaking contact.

"If you haven't noticed already, there are ten recruits in this room." Faas's voice is strangely calm, bored even, as if his next words shouldn't come as a shock at all. "I only have room for nine."

It takes a few seconds for the meaning to register. When it does, my eyes dart from one recruit to another. One of us is going to die.

The commander lets his haunting words sink in. Then he continues. "The squad is only as strong as its weakest soldier. A dead weight could mean the difference between life and death for the entire team. Since there are ten of you, that means there's at least one recruit in this room who isn't as committed to the cause as the others. So today's decision is yours. Find your weakest link. Get rid of the dead weight. Training begins now."

Furtive glances are cast across the room. A few even come my way. Despite the dread blanketing my entire being, I stand taller and square out my shoulders, hoping it's enough to keep the target off my back. But the second I meet Malachi's eyes, the rat gives a vicious smile and winks.

He's coming for me. I'm sure of it.

I crack my knuckles and steel my nerves, bracing myself for his attack.

Without uttering another word, the commanders and the squad leader exit the room, leaving us confused and full of questions. Outside, what sounds like the scrape of a key throws a bolt into place. We are truly alone.

A hush falls over the squad, the calm before a dark storm. No one moves or speaks. All of us deep in an unspoken battle, waiting for the first poor bastard who makes a move. Back in the village, Teo and I used to play a similar game with Malachi and Shahid. Except we weren't playing to kill.

With one eye on Malachi, I watch the other recruits too. I have no idea who they are or where they come from. Whether they live or die shouldn't be my concern. But after Teo, my chest seizes at the thought of taking another life. I can still hear the voices in my head, whispering, *murderer, murderer, MURDERER!* Now, here I am, set to commit the same evil twice in one day.

A scream tears through the air. Across from me, a scrawny-looking boy hits the floor as a blow to his face knocks him off his feet. Another recruit punches him again, drawing blood from his lips. Crimson stains the gray concrete where he sprawls.

Madness unfolds.

One by one, recruits turn on each other, charging at whoever they've deemed the weakest of the squad. My heart pounds as I weave through the chaos, searching the fray for Malachi. If I attack first, I can get the upper hand on him.

Someone grabs the ends of my braids, dragging me to the ground. *Malachi.*

Pain spreads through my scalp, and I let out a startled yelp.

Despite the throbbing, I reach for his familiar hand, clawing hopelessly at the fingers locked tightly around my hair. He fights me off at every turn. When his large fist strikes my cheek, my head smacks against the cold concrete.

Stars burst across my vision, making it hard for me to see. I blink them away quickly, scrambling to get on my feet before Malachi manages to pin me down. If he succeeds, I know what will come next. This is his way of making me pay for what I did to his parents. He'll kill me right here, right now, just to have his vengeance. But I'll be damned if I let that happen.

Morality vanishes, and all I can think about is killing Malachi before he does the same to me. Fear chases away what guilt I should feel, replacing it with dark, seething rage. I charge at him, aiming for his groin. An offensive ploy Teo taught me long ago. Just before my foot finds its target, Malachi seizes my leg with his hand and twists, knocking me off balance.

My body hits the ground. He doesn't waste a second to pounce, straddling me before I can even think to escape. Then his hands are around my throat, gripping and squeezing.

"Mal—" I choke out, writhing beneath him.

"Say their names." Above me, Malachi's chest rises and falls as his hands strain against my neck. He bares his teeth, though in my current state, they look more like a Nagean leopard's fangs. "I want to hear you say their names!"

White spots dance before my eyes. I reach for his hands again, but I only grasp at thin air.

"Yosef—Fatima—" I force out Malachi's parents' names despite the knot in my throat.

In response, his fingers tighten around my neck, cutting off the last of my air supply.

"Mal, please—" I kick out with my legs. Bend them inward and drive them into his back. Nothing happens.

Until he draws the knife from his pocket. The thin silver blade flashes before my eyes.

My heartbeat slows.

I wheeze.

"That's enough!" Somewhere in the room, Faas's voice cuts through the din, rising above all else. I've never been more relieved than by the commander's timely presence.

Malachi releases his grip on my neck and tucks the knife away. Slowly—painfully slow—he rolls off my chest and rises to his feet.

I blink up at his eyes, bright and red with naked fury. I can't believe he almost succeeded in killing me. If not for the sharp sting blooming up my neck, I would think it all a dream. A nightmare forged from the depths of my guilt.

I'm still on my knees, gulping in as much air as I can, when Faas shouts.

"Kill or be killed. It is the law of the Force. The foundation upon which the base was raised." Beside him, Caspian and Dane nod along. "Over the next one month, you will be tried, challenged, pushed beyond your limits. Physicals. Tactical drills. Conditioning. Combat training. And most importantly, the Phases. These were designed solely to separate the strongest from the weak. I don't care about quantity. If at the end of the month, I only have one recruit standing, it will be the deadliest, most ruthless soldier the base has ever seen."

Even in my daze, the commander's words stab like a dagger. Thirty days. Thirty days of absolute torture. Thirty days to uncover the truth about Mama. I reach for the cowrie shells Baba strung around my neck. With its map hidden flush against my skin, the beaded choker looks ordinary enough not to arouse any suspicion. But to me, it's a promise of the freedom that awaits in Ilè-Orisha if I should survive. It won't be easy, not with Malachi hell-bent on taking my life. But I have to try.

For myself, for Mama, I have to fight to survive.

Across the room, Faas's gaze hardens. "So many recruits have entered Fort Regulus. Only a few make it out alive. Kill or be killed. Live by those words and you might just make the cut. Ignore them and, well, this could be you in the days to come."

The commander kicks at whatever lies at his feet. A boy shudders uncontrollably on the ground, his bloodied face swollen beyond recognition. The girl with the rich brown skin and thick coils of hair stands over him, her ringed knuckles red with his blood.

Faas glances up at her. "You. Did you do this?"

"Yes, sir!" She salutes him with a clenched fist, like we've been taught.

"Impressive." A deep, selfish fervor flickers in the commander's gaze, the kind you get when you come across a rare gold nagi. I realize then Faas has marked her the strongest recruit of his squad. A sting of jealousy creeps up my spine, a leech preying on my senses. *You couldn't even defend yourself against Malachi. How will you make it through the next thirty days?*

Faas takes a step toward the girl, and the squad inches backward, clearing enough space between them.

"What's your name?"

Despite his unnerving closeness, the recruit straightens under the commander's stare, almost adding an inch to her small, willowy frame.

"Izara Makinde, sir!"

The hush that hangs over the room is oppressive, enslaving us all as we wait for Faas's next move. His hand disappears into the pocket of his uniform. Seconds later, he pulls out a silver chain strung with a single white-tipped bullet. He wears his pride like armor as he drapes the chain over her neck.

"A reward," he says. "I believe you'll find use for it in the Sahl."

The implication is clear. A bullet to kill the Shadow Rebels, to destroy every Yoruba and Scion fighting for their rights on the desert front. Once again, àse webs its way through my veins, and heat blankets my entire body. As the clamor rings in my head, I flex my fingers against the visible red tendrils, inhaling deeply in a struggle to quell the fire surging underneath. This time, it takes a few painful seconds for the magic to simmer. When it does, my breath rattles to a somewhat even pace as the commander turns his attention on the rest of us.

"For the duration of your training, Lieutenant Caspian and I will be ranking you based on your performances. In the end, the first amongst you to earn three bullets from me will have the honor of visiting Castlemore to meet the queen and the royal bloodlines before deployment."

I grit my teeth against the low murmurs passing between the recruits. Truly, only a fool would be spellbound by the promise of visiting Olympia's glittering court. A place made not only of stolen jewels but the blood of every child soldier and the souls of every dead Scion. I have no desire to meet those thieves. If that is the reward for being the best, then I have no desire to compete.

While the commanders discuss strategy and the squad leader offers some needless advice on navigating the base, I shut them out and look to the broken boy still lying on the ground.

He doesn't move. He doesn't breathe. He stares with empty bloodshot eyes, his withered skin now reduced to a pale husk.

A mix of pity and disgust stirs in my belly as it slowly dawns on me.

The boy is dead.

Another innocent life bled dry before our eyes.

THIRTEEN

In the wake of the boy's death, the commanders finally retire us to the squad barracks. Night has fallen, and a thick haze now blankets the massive compound along the western edge of the cliffs, obscuring much of the barracks' grounds. Still, a row of adjoining buildings, at least five stories high, peers through the fog like a beast lying in wait.

I eye the towering structures with growing unease as a female barracks officer ushers us past the front gates. She's rather tall, a silver-haired woman with twin scars splitting her cheeks, as though carved with a knife. Even her demeanor is commanding enough, cut with that same familiar Lucis fervor that demands absolute compliance without question.

"You've been assigned to Block F, ground floor," she informs the squad, one finger pointed at the last of the stone buildings facing the ocean. "Recruits will reside in shared sleeping quarters for the duration of their training. All male recruits will be accommodated in one room, while female recruits will be housed in a separate chamber. Under no circumstances are recruits permitted to visit nondesignated quarters without authorization. Is that clear?"

The squad gives a silent nod. But when a thin, reedy boy next to Malachi grumbles back, the officer glances at him over her shoulder, deep blue eyes alight with fury. For a moment, she regards him like one would a gutter rat, until the boy practically shrinks into himself. Without a word, she turns back to the barracks and sets off down the curving pathway, her booted steps echoing in quick, rapid strides. We work to keep up pace behind her, all nine of us stumbling along as she begins to relay the barracks' rules.

"Recruits will remain confined to their quarters during off-duty hours, including all military imposed lockdowns, sanctioned drills, and nightly curfews. Any recruit caught outside the barracks in those hours will face strict disciplinary measures as deemed fit by the High Commander," she says with a firm resolve. "Smuggling of illicit items, stolen goods, unregistered firearms, and personally owned weapons of any kind are banned from the barracks at all times. Any recruit charged with burglary and larceny of any properties belonging to the Avalon Defense Forces will be subject to life imprisonment."

As the officer rattles off the rest of the barracks' standards, a familiar weariness worms its way through the entire squad. I see it in the tightness of everyone's faces, their hunched shoulders and dragging limbs. But no one dares to make a sound, let alone draw breath. Minutes after another recruit was just killed before our eyes, the last thing anyone wants is to risk the officer's wrath and suffer the same.

The boy's corpse flashes in my head, until I'm once again overcome with the sudden urge to flee this hell. I am without my home, my family, and my friends, trapped in the middle of an ocean without an anchor to cling to. Perhaps I was wrong. Out here surrounded by death, perhaps I don't have what it takes to survive in a world like this—a world where children like me are ruined for the glory of a monarchy that cares nothing about whether we live or die.

But even if I were to run now, where would I go?

We're halfway to our assigned block when a clash of deep, startling growls echoes in the darkness of the barracks compound. We jump at the sound, our eyes drawn to the courtyard, where soldiers yank at a circle of leopards straining against the force of their leashes. The beasts snarl and hiss, teeth bared, claws lashing at the ground with wild viciousness. For a moment, I don't understand—until I see what looks like the tiny form of a girl curled up in a fetal position.

Nausea swells in the pit of my stomach when one of the soldiers kicks her hard in the face, spraying rocks and dirt over her head. The recruit collapses backward with a keening wail, writhing and twitching in a terrible spasm. Her sobs rend the air, her desperate pleas cutting like jagged glass. Still, no one moves to stop the soldiers' abuse. Not even the barracks officer who slows to watch the whole thing with a look of pure indifference spread across her face. Behind her, the rest of the squad stands frozen too, their jaws hung wide in horror.

My entire body shakes as the soldiers continue to take turns with their torture, each kick more violent and bloody than the last.

What is this? What the hell is going on?

At last, the barracks officer turns to address us. "*This* brings us to the final standards," she says. I don't miss the wretched glee in her eyes as she adds, "Any recruit caught trying to desert will be executed. On sight."

One look at the open display of savagery unfolding before me and I know she means every word.

There is no escaping this place.

That night, I don't fall asleep.

I lie in my bunk and stare at the cracked ceiling as rain lashes against the windows of the girls' barracks. It's been hours since the barracks officer confined us to these cramped quarters. Now the three other female recruits from my squad spread out in separate cots next to my own, their bodies curled beneath a layer of thin sheets.

They look childlike in sleep, small and innocent, as though one of them hadn't just bludgeoned a boy to death hours ago. Even in her dormant state, the dark-skinned girl sprawls so brazenly across the room, a shadow of frail limbs taking up space in every direction. Her loud snores are a growing rattle in my ears, broken only by the downpour battering the walls of the stone building.

Back home in Agbajé, I slept to the sound of rain as it cascaded off the thatches of my hut. It's hard to do the same here. Even in the darkness, the loneliness of the barracks is a blanket I cannot lift.

With its cold, narrow space—and patches of mold spreading along the sloped roof—the room is a prison both strange and unfamiliar. We sleep on slabs of raised stone inlaid with a slim cushion of foam. The only furniture in sight is a shared dresser pushed up against the far wall, stuffed with new uniforms the commanders provided. I scratch at the fresh fatigues, hating the itchy graze of the fabric against my skin. But hours after the barracks officer took our old clothes, I have only what's left inside those drawers to wear.

Outside, a flash of lightning cuts through the sky, lifting the curtain of darkness for a split second. The clap of thunder that follows rumbles in my chest. The storm does nothing to drown out the sobs reverberating from the quarters on the other side of the wall, where another recruit cries herself to sleep. It's the third one tonight, a weeping ballad that began moments after the bells rang. Now, as the recruit's sobs echo in the silence of the barracks, my own tears prick at the corners of my eyes.

I miss Agbajé. I miss home.

Though it's only been a few hours since I last saw them, my mind wanders back to Baba and Luna—the family I left behind. Their faces swim before my eyes, and I imagine them just as they were that morning. Baba, frail and worn from a night of sleeplessness, a pillar of grief in our living room as he kisses my forehead goodbye. Luna trembles next to him, her fingers tight as they close around my arm, tugging me back a step, refusing to let go.

Stay, Sloane. Please, stay.

The memory burns in my chest, an ache that burrows deep into my heart. What I would give now to be back in their arms, away from the shackles of the Lucis army, surrounded by the comfort of my own hut. But the image of the soldiers torturing the girl spins in a constant loop in my mind, a reminder of how dire my circumstances are, and what little I can do to change them.

My tears fall, one after another, dripping onto the threadbare sheet that clings to my skin. Though my body shakes, I wipe my cheeks and swallow the sobs caught in my throat.

I can't fall apart, not now.

It doesn't matter that I can never return to Agbajé, that I will never see Luna and my grandfather again. The Lucis may have ripped me away from my old life, but I made a promise to Baba, that I'd survive long enough to find Ilè-Orisha. And that is what I must do.

Thirty days of training.

Thirty days to learn the truth about Mama.

Then I'll be free.

The thought loosens a knot in my chest, and a rush of warmth drapes over me. I curl into it and let it wrap me up, a refuge away from the uncertainty that lies ahead. With a deep breath, I close my eyes and shut out the muffled cries of the recruit from the other side of the wall. Even when a distant scream pierces the air around me, I squeeze my lids tighter.

Thirty days.

Outside, the rain sings a soft lullaby that lulls me into a restless sleep.

PART II

THE PHASES

Okàn kìí fó kó pé mó.
A mind once broken is no longer whole.
—PROVERB FROM THE ANCIENT KINGDOM OF ILÉ-IFÈ

FOURTEEN

Recruit Shade,

The schedule below has been reviewed and approved by High Commander Faas Bakker:

0530h—Reveille
0600h—Rifle Marksmanship / 0900h—Culture and Theory
1200h—Mess
1230h—Combat Training / 2030h—Call to Quarters
2100h—Lights Out

Signed,
Thelma Craft
Secretary of the Avalon Defense Forces
Long Live the Bloodlines.

The first shooting drill begins at exactly 0600h, when the sun is still a whisper on the horizon. With Lieutenant Caspian leading the squad, we set out from morning formation toward one of the many training fields scattered around the base. We wear the official charcoal uniform of the army, with splotches of dull gray marking us as fledglings. The pants are spotted the same, tucked into black combat boots squelching through the muddy field. Like the military garb, the shoes are newly made, buffed to a soft polish. The outfit is unlike anything I own back in Agbajé. Still, I long for my plain shirt and threadbare pants, the frayed laces of my chewed-up boots. But my old clothing is gone, seized by the barracks officer and replaced with these bleeding army fatigues.

The morning wind howls like a black-backed jackal, whipping the ends of my cornrows about my face. Sluggishly, I gather each piece into a single braid, groggy from my night of troubled sleep. Despite the scant hours of rest, there isn't a single heavy eye among the other recruits. Even the girls from my barracks look well rested, and it seems I'm the only one fighting to suppress a yawn.

"Storm Squad, form up." Caspian's voice is low and flat, yet the lieutenant's command cuts through the field, sharp as a knife.

The murmurs passing between some of the recruits fade to a hush as we spread out in a single-line formation. Malachi settles in next to me, close enough that I'm painfully unnerved by his presence. I step sideward, suddenly grateful that the barracks officer had the mind to keep the boys in their own separate quarters. Surely, being confined to the same room with Malachi would have only ended in a bloodbath. Even now, the ghost of the boy's grip still lingers around my throat. I grit my teeth as my fingers trace the dark bruises he left behind yesterday. Malachi struck once, and I don't doubt he'll strike again. Except this time, it will be my hands wrapped around his bleeding throat.

"You are now about to begin day two of your training." Caspian fixes us with a cold, stern gaze. Though the lieutenant is ranked Faas's second-in-command, he possesses a similar air of authority.

He marches toward the weapons table alongside the field, setting a brisk pace even at this ungodly hour. Before him, more than a dozen assault rifles fill every square inch of the tabletop. I shrink back at the sight of them, reminded of the horror that took place just yesterday. The image of Teo's bloody corpse is a constant torment. The last thing I want to do is hold another one of the Lucis' weapons in my hand. Though judging by today's drill, it seems inevitable.

A few feet away, Caspian runs one hand down the length of a rifle, head tilted, caressing the weapon as though it were a lover. It's odd that a man should show such affection to an object capable of so much destruction. But he is a Lucis, after all, and the Lucis are nothing if not unhinged.

With his gloved hands, the lieutenant snatches the rifle off the table and slings it around his shoulder. It's the second time I've seen him clad in those same ugly pair of black leather gloves, if only to conceal whatever nightmarish scars he obviously has.

"There are lots of shooting drills, many of which you will be exposed to in the coming weeks," Caspian says. "Marksmanship is a skill honed with repetition and practice. It requires mastery of the fundamentals, which is what you are here to learn today. So that when faced with an enemy combatant, you won't find yourself wondering how to properly handle your weapon, or whether or not you've aligned your sights. By the end of training, all of that should be easy to execute upon contact with your enemy target."

Target. A world of people like me. Like Mama and Teo and every Shadow Rebel now reduced to one hostile word.

"There is no room for errors," the lieutenant continues. "Out there on the front, if you are not prepared and alert, you die. So watch closely."

He wraps his gloved fingers around the rifle, settling into his stance. Shoulders squared, spine straight, and feet a few inches apart. Across the field, a target dummy rises from the dirt, revealing the molded figure of a Yoruba man dressed in battle armor, war paint smeared across his black face.

The sight coils my stomach, and a bitter chill chases up my spine. Suddenly the silhouette twists and morphs, first into Teo. Then its face takes on the familiar angles of Mama's own. Soon I'm the one standing out there, moments away from being gunned down by Caspian. The illusions splash across my mind like dark crimson, and it takes a few moments to convince myself that none of it is real.

Still, my àse is quick to respond. As the clamor rises in my head, thin swirls of fire branch beneath the brown of my hands, curling up to my fingertips. I barely react in time, fisting both hands into the pockets of my uniform before anyone sees. It's the worst possible time for my magic to manifest, with Caspian standing a few feet away, rifle in hand. But without the comfort of Baba's àgbo, the rush of heat has become more difficult to suppress. An ache, worse than the one I felt the day before, pricks behind my skull. I shut my eyes and massage my temple, stifling a low groan until the sensation passes.

"One shot," the lieutenant breathes as I force my eyes open. He doesn't seem to notice a thing, his focus maintained on the rifle. "Line up those sights, and . . . fire."

The gun echoes with a loud bang, and the bullet tears a hole through the target's skull. When the dummy drops and a new one rises in its place, Caspian turns to look at us, a soldier's pride visible on his face. I can't help but recoil, my lips pulled in disgust. Only the devil takes pleasure in death, and the lieutenant is no different. Still, I find his blind prejudice hard to understand. How is it that even though they are the ones with their hands to the guns, somehow *we* are the objects of their fear, the symbol of so much hatred that they must kill us in order to feel safe, in order to feel peace?

"Take position," Caspian says, handing each of us a rifle of our own.

My arms buckle beneath the weight of the gun, and dimly, I wonder whose blood and sweat is forged into this weapon. I imagine the front lines, imagine how many Shadow Rebels have fallen at the squeeze of this very trigger. We will always be at their mercy, either in the mines or on the battlefield. We will always die with our knees buried in the dust.

Across the field, my target rises. Even though I know what is expected of me, it's impossible to think beyond the figure of the Yoruba woman standing hundreds of feet away. Real or not, I struggle to right my aim, fingers numb as I pull the trigger.

The gun goes off, and the force of the blast jerks me backward.

I stumble on my feet, barely catching myself in time. When I glance back up, I find my target still intact, free from any scratches or bullet holes.

"Recruit Shade!" the lieutenant calls over the steady rain of gunfire. "The objective is to hit the targets, not waste my damned bullets."

In two strides, he bounds over to my side. I lower my gaze, heart plunging beneath the weight of his glare. My cowardice is unfamiliar, a stranger in my own body. I don't know when this weakling took over, but her fear consumes me now, threatening to tear my nerves apart.

"Aim," he growls low over my head.

My jaw tightens as I reposition the rifle.

"Steady—"

I steel myself and suck in a hissing breath.

"Fire."

I pull the trigger.

Once again, the bullet misses, landing a wretched distance away from the target. In response, Caspian clucks his tongue and storms off, noting my failure into his logbook.

I wipe the sweat off my forehead and leer at the lieutenant's retreating form. That's when I notice a figure standing at the far end of the field, hands clasped behind him, watching the training with curious interest. It takes a few moments to recognize the dark-skinned man from yesterday's assembly. Even in broad daylight, Lord Sol looms like a shadow, clad in a simple black suit rather than the finely woven damask known to other Lucis lords like him. If not for the old lessons from the institution, I might have mistaken the royal for a common soldier. He doesn't linger long, though, and when he whirls, I wonder if perhaps he, too, has seen enough of my incompetence. A slash of irritation cuts through me.

Halfway through the drill, there are at least twenty empty shell casings spread at my feet. Yet, I'm the only one who hasn't dropped a single target. Izara, the girl who earned a bullet from Faas last night and one of my bunkmates, has barely missed a shot. Next to her, a gangly boy with golden-brown skin and black hair kneels in the mud, eyes locked on his own target.

Jericho Ahmadi is the lieutenant's favorite of the day, and it isn't difficult to see why. The precision with which he shoots his rifle is unmatched, and every bullet he fires collapses a dummy into the dirt.

I stifle a curse when another one of his targets hits the ground. Compared with both of these recruits, I am a girl treading deep water, trying to keep her head above the waves. But I'm drowning, slowly, in this treacherous ocean where no one makes it out alive.

Beside me, Malachi grumbles at his own clumsiness, having managed only two measly shots since the drill started. I find small comfort in his failure.

Far away, the bell rings from the soldiers' tower, and Caspian orders all rifles to be returned before dismissing us. The squad thins as recruits slowly trickle off the field until Malachi and I are the only two remaining.

I fumble with the safety of my rifle, trying to remember the correct way to position the lever. Just when I finally lock it into place and turn to leave, he cuts me off.

"Judging by today's performance, I think the squad's found its new weakest link," he says coolly. The barrel of his rifle impales the ground, cutting a divide between us. "I wonder how long before Faas gives the order to kill you?"

My stomach lurches at the thought. By now, I'm sure news of my failure has reached the commander's ears, and it's only a matter of time before he marks me as the squad's latest victim. He'll do to me what he did to the recruit from yesterday. Still, I don't want to give Malachi the satisfaction the bastard so desperately craves.

"Go to hell," I growl, ready to walk away. But Malachi grabs me by the arm and wrenches me back with brute force.

"Next time, there will be no commanders around to save you, Sloane," he hisses in my ear.

Though it's only been a day since we arrived in Avalon, his voice sounds sharper, stronger, a twisted blade forged from steel. I ignore the shiver of fear and yank my arm free.

"You lay one finger on me again, and it will be the last thing you ever do."

"Are you sure about that?" Malachi grins, but the smile doesn't reach his eyes. Instead, I see the pain behind the mask, his deep, aching thirst for vengeance.

I should feel sorry for him. But then I think back to his calloused hands wrapped tightly around my throat. His narrowed eyes flashing down on me. If the commanders hadn't stopped him when they did, Malachi would have killed me inside that training room. A son seconds away from avenging the death of his parents. Yet, I can't bring myself to feel a shred of sympathy for the boy before me. Not anymore.

With a breath, I take an easy, defiant step toward him. He rips his weapon from the dirt and makes a move of his own, until we're a hairbreadth away from each other's faces.

A dark, violent energy twists and crackles in the small space between us. Malachi's gaze hardens. I clench a fist around the stock of my rifle.

"This isn't a game, Mal." My voice is coated in venom, the words laden by their terrible meaning. "Mess with *fire*, and you too will get burned. Don't try me."

My heart knocks against my chest as I shove past him and start toward the weapons table. But by the time I cross the field, I already regret everything I said. What's to stop Malachi from ratting me out to the commanders now? If he does, my plan to uncover the truth about Mama falls apart before I even get a chance to make my move.

Stupid.

When he brushes past me, I almost expect him to attack. Instead, he tosses his rifle onto the scattered pile and storms off the field without another word. I watch him all the while, knowing deep in my gut there's only one thing left to do.

I have to get rid of him. The boy is a liability, a threat to my survival and the very thing I came here to do. It feels shameful to think this way, and disgust rises in me like vomit. But I've sacrificed too much to risk it all now.

I have to kill Malachi.

An hour after Caspian dismisses us, I wash off the morning grime, change into clean fatigues, and report to a room inside the training center. The entire squad is present by the time I arrive, all of them settled into the small wooden chairs attached to their desks.

The last time I was in a classroom like this was when I was twelve, forced to attend an institution run by Lucis teachers, learning nothing but the lies and hogwash they try to pass off as real history. As is expected, attendance at the institution is mandatory until the age of twelve. But quite honestly, chasing rats around my hut would have been a much better use of my time.

I lower myself into one of the chairs lining the back of the room, making sure to steer clear of Malachi. The boy sits in a corner one row away, his eyes on the black screen in front of the room. As if sensing he's being watched, he turns his head. We lock eyes for a brief moment, the tension between us broken only by the deep rumble of Faas's voice.

"Eyes front," the commander says as he barges into the room with Caspian at his side. Behind them, the door slams shut, and silence falls over us like a heavy blanket.

Faas clicks some tiny device in his hand. Almost immediately, the black screen flashes to life, broadcasting images of war. Even though

I've never been to the Sahl desert, I recognize the dunes of the northern land, the place where thousands of Shadow Rebels are slaughtered every day. My hands sweat, and I feel unease deep in my gut as I prepare for graphic images of dead Yorubas and Scions, their corpses mangled and mutilated at the hands of the Lucis army.

Instead, when the front lines come into sharper focus, I'm greeted by a very different sight on-screen. Shadow Rebels fill every inch of the frame, lethal warriors hacking through a sea of Lucis bodies with their machetes. The Scions in their midst are easy to recognize, and my jaw nearly drops as descendants of Aganju bury a line of screaming soldiers beneath the void of quicksand. The next piece of footage reveals descendants of Oya summoning a deadly storm that quickly swallows up an entire garrison. Each image is worse than the last, depicting the Shadow Rebels as monsters quick to execute child soldiers without mercy. The children lie in heaps across the desert sand, their eyes wide with fear, limbs frozen in death.

"What you're seeing is raw footage from the Sahl," Faas says as the broadcast continues behind him. "These are the Shadow Rebels. The savages killing innocent victims in the name of freedom. Freedom at the cost of civilian lives—civilians like you."

Suddenly Faas's propaganda begins to appear more and more clear to me. Every footage is carefully selected, a ploy to incite rage among the squad. But I've heard stories—stories of children like me being used as human shields, cannon fodder, on the front. Others strapped with hidden explosives and tossed into the company of Shadow Rebels, only to be detonated moments later. Faas's broadcast does not expose any of that. No, these images are calculated, revealing only what he wants us to see, tugging at the exact emotions he wants us to feel.

As I glance down at the other recruits, I see the fire sparking behind their eyes, muscles coiled tight as if readying for a fight. It's precisely what the commander hoped to achieve, and I realize then what Culture and Theory is truly about: an indoctrination of some sort. To force us to conform, exploit our vulnerability, and mold us into war machines ready to carry out commands without erring.

"The days of the Shadow Rebels are over," Faas declares with absolute surety. He paces back and forth between the two rows of chairs, gazing at each recruit in turn. "Our war will not end with the victory of these monsters, but rather the destruction of their race. In twenty-eight days, when you join your fellow comrades on the front, remember this"—he gestures at the screen—"the mass slaughter of your brothers and sisters. Remember who the enemy is. So when you fight, you fight with vengeance. When you kill, you kill with purpose. And when the battle cry is over, and the victor's flag is raised, it will be the white and gold of the Lucis, stark against the desert sand running red with Scion blood."

The squad erupts, hurling insults at the Shadow Rebels. *Scum. Killers. Terrorists.* Malachi is the loudest of them all. Though my blood boils, I have no choice but to echo their outbursts, hating myself as the words pour out.

Traitor. I am a traitor to my people.

Faas lifts his hand, calling for immediate silence as he returns to the front of the room to join Caspian.

"For those of you who make it to the Sahl, your training doesn't end just because you leave Avalon. The same dedication and valor will be expected of you out there. You will be subject to daily evaluations by your unit leaders to determine what roles you are best suited for. Some of you will be relegated to domestic chores—cooks, porters, base keepers. Others may be planted as sleepers within the free nations. Kasau, Umuchi, Naine, Togus, even as far as Ganne."

A few murmurs rise among the recruits, and I know we are all wondering the same thing. Prior to today, I thought I would only be a soldier for the next three years. Spying across the continent? Far away from the Sahl? That complicates things, certainly my plan to escape to Ilè-Orisha. Although I have no means of fleeing the desert once I arrive there, I want to believe there's a way out of that camp. An escape strategy I'll have to figure out when the time comes. It seems impossible right now, a world far beyond my reach. Still, I know I must try.

I've only just begun to catch my breath when the commander's next words send a ripple of gasps through the room.

"As for the select few who don't have what it takes to survive the Sahl"—Faas's eyes turn solemn—"you will soon find that children fetch a hefty price in the bidding market."

At midday, I trudge toward the mess hall, still shaken by the commander's sick threat. Though I don't want to believe in the possibility of an auction market where dead-eyed kids are sold for a few nagi gold, I know only the Lucis could conjure such horror. But I'd sooner die than be doomed to such a cruel fate.

I wear my bitterness like a cloak as I kick my way past the swinging mess doors. Inside the stone-block building, uniformed bodies spill across long wooden benches, and a deep cacophony rises among the Lucis soldiers swarming the hall. The recruits are there as well, confined to the middle section of the room. Unlike the mob of rowdy soldiers, many of the children sit in stiff silence, eyes downcast as they work through their rations.

My stomach grumbles at the sight of their bowls, and I rush toward the canteen line, ready to devour my first food of the day. Since this is the only time allotted for meals, I expect the portions to be somewhat generous. Instead, the Lucis cook sends me off with a small tray of garri and a handful of groundnuts.

I'm no stranger to hunger. After all, there were many days when Baba and I struggled to sell our cassava tubers and all we could afford was a single meal. Worse were the nights we went to bed on empty stomachs, surviving only on tall glasses of cold water. Still, I find it hard to believe that even with the Lucis' large, booming plantations and traded commodities from the free nations, this is all these greedy bastards could afford to feed us.

I swallow my distaste as I leave the cafeteria line and head down the aisle toward Storm Squad's bench. Across the hall, there are over a dozen officers silhouetted against the cracked stone walls, armed and ready to strike if need be. The security cameras are present as well, tiny white orbs dotting every corner like stars strewn across the high ceiling.

A few of my squad mates slide down the bench when I arrive, making enough room for me to sit. Most of them have already disposed of their trays, their attention fixed on some dark-haired recruit busy spewing whatever gossip he's wrangled up.

"My brother told me he once saw the Shadow Rebels bewitch an entire platoon," the boy drawls from his spot farther down the bench. "They attacked one of the desert outposts where he was stationed. Turned every Lucis soldier against each other. He said it was a complete massacre and the only reason he survived is because he ran."

Startled gasps hum through the table. After Faas's broadcast, it seems all anyone can talk about now is the Shadow Rebels—their barbaric tactics and imminent annihilation. Even in the barracks, recruits boast of the day they, too, will finally get a chance to fire their bullets into the heart of a captured Rebel. I try to ignore it as best I can, but their bloodlust only sends a flash of heat through me.

"Is it true the Scions amongst them feed on the blood of their victims?" The barest whisper comes from the girl to my left, Miriam, one of my bunkmates, with a round, moonlike face and a naive gaze that darts out when she speaks. "I heard that's where their magic comes from."

"That's just some stupid rumor." The first boy dismisses her with a wave of his hand. "Have you even seen a Scion before? They look normal, as normal as you and me. It's terrifying."

He shudders on cue. I have to roll my eyes, jaw set in an effort to grind back the words already at the tip of my tongue. One admission is all it would take to rattle these gossip folks and watch them come undone. Though tempted as I am, I know the risk far outweighs my petty desires.

I tune them out, but just as I start to reach for my now soggy bowl, a familiar voice freezes me in place.

"Yes." Malachi rises to his feet slowly, an empty tray in hand. "Normal enough that there could even be one amongst us right now."

He sounds indifferent, borderline sarcastic, as though the discussion itself is beneath him. But the cutting glare he throws at me as he leaves the table tells a different story.

He's taunting me, like a cat does its prey moments before death. Payback for what I said to him earlier out there on the field. A reminder of what the bastard could do if he so wishes.

Well, at least his little tantrum seems to have shut the squad up.

In their stunned silence, I gulp down my food in no time. Though it doesn't sate me, I trick my brain into believing I'm full.

Now, without Malachi's foolish antics or the squad's gossip to distract, I turn my thoughts on Archives Hall. I've been here all of two days, and I've yet to figure out a way to break inside that damned chamber. If I'm ever going to find out what happened the night Mama disappeared, I need a plan, and soon. My mind buzzes, trying to come up with something, anything, that will help me get past the guards and those bleeding leopards prowling its entrance. But with every minute that passes, no good strategy forms in my head. Gods, I don't even know where to begin.

By the time I leave mess, I've run over a dozen failed plans. Somehow, each one manages to be even worse than the last, with the promise of death if I'm caught. Either by the Lucis or the leopards, should they get me first.

Outside, the afternoon sun burns brightly, drying the puddles from last night's storm. I drag my boots along the pocked tarmac, my pace slow as I approach the alleyway leading to the training center. Faced in the same bleak, quarried stone as the other buildings, with its gaunt, windowless walls and the wretched Lucis flag soaring high above its gables, the sight of the facility is enough to darken my already foul mood. It's the last place I want to be.

Now, more than anything, I wish I could retreat to the barracks and sleep off the rest of this pissing day. Instead, I have the misfortune of combat training with none other than the squad leader himself. Dane, the Lucis soldier I foolishly thought was just another recruit from the city. I mutter a long curse at the boy, wincing at the thought of having to breathe the same air as him for the next hour.

I round a bend, and the front steps of the training center come into view. That's when I catch a glimpse of two figures lurking in the shadows of the alleyway. I recognize their faces immediately.

Two recruits. Both members of my squad. The boy is Jericho Ahmadi, the young sharpshooter from today's drill. The girl huddled next to him is another bunkmate of mine. Nazanin Shah, I think. Her skin is the same golden-brown shade as his, though speckled with light brown spots. It isn't the first time I've caught these two together, I realize, remembering how close they seemed when I first saw them at yesterday's impromptu training.

Their low, frantic voices drift down the narrow path, a jumble of obscure words. I have a mind to leave them to whatever it is they are up to. If I'm not at the training center in ten minutes, only gods know what the squad leader will do. Faas already warned that any missed session would result in punishment. I imagine that includes tardiness. Slowly, I edge forward, until the recruits' voices become clearer.

"The tunnels—you're certain of them?" Nazanin asks.

I stumble to a halt, suddenly curious. Neither of them seems to notice me when I slink back behind the wall, hoping to catch the rest of their whispered conversation.

"If it's anything like I saw, they practically run all over the base," Jericho says. "But it's a maze down there. Without the map, we'd be going in blind."

Map . . . tunnels. My brain works quickly, imagining a labyrinth of passages spread just below my feet, all of them abandoned, unguarded, and free of snarling leopards with sharp fangs. If what the boy says is true, and there is in fact a tunnel leading into Archives Hall, then this could be exactly what I've been praying for. A way to break into the chamber and steal the Lucis' Book of Records. Adrenaline bursts through my veins, a thrilling sensation that leaves me almost breathless.

"I know that look." There's a slight tremor in Nazanin's voice, a ghost of fear she tries to chase away. "What exactly are you saying?"

"We steal it and the day is ours."

Unlike hers, Jericho's tone is sharp, laced with equal vigor, as if what he's proposing doesn't come with great risk. If either of these fools is caught stealing, I shudder to think what the barracks officer will do. Or worse—Faas. Again, the image of the female recruit being tortured by the soldiers last night stalks my mind. But even with the threat of punishment, the boy wears a strange confidence, like he's done this many times before.

"I was afraid you'd say that." Nazanin heaves a sigh. "But this isn't another sting in the marketplace, Jer. It's the lieutenant's office. Even if we somehow pull this off, neither of us knows how to read maps."

Oh.

I understand now where the girl's doubt comes from, because only an idiot would attempt to break into Caspian's office, much less steal from him. Though I know better than to consider it, I find myself mulling over Jericho's stupid plan anyway. For a moment, I even imagine a reality where he succeeds in pulling it off.

If Jericho and Nazanin manage to get their hands on that map, I could help them navigate those tunnels. After years of watching Mama and Baba pore over ancient maps from dusty tomes, it's no surprise I picked up a thing or two. It's why Baba gave me Yeye Celeste's cowrie shell necklace, why he trusts me enough to find my way to Ilè-Orisha. With my navigation skills, and Jericho's and Nazanin's talent for theft, accessing Archives Hall would almost be too easy.

Nothing good can come from this. The warning echoes in my head. *Remember the barracks' standards. You're already late for combat training. Walk away.*

Instead of leaving, I step out into the alleyway and clear my throat. Jericho is the first to react, a slingshot drawn deftly in his hands. Beside him, Nazanin jumps back a step, though when she realizes I'm only a recruit and not a guard, her shoulders relax a little. Jericho still has his weapon aimed at my head, the stone pulled taut, waiting to be fired.

I'm a fool, and this is a terrible idea. Yet, the words slip out of my mouth with ease.

"I can read a map."

FIFTEEN

"Who the hell are you?"

Jericho's voice is a low growl, the slingshot in his hands a loud threat. For a second, I forget what I'm meant to say. All I can do is stare at the chain around his neck, silver interlocking links drooping with the weight of a bullet pendant. A gift from the commanders, promised only to the finest recruits. This must be how Jericho caught a glimpse of the map inside Caspian's office. After the way the boy performed earlier, I can see why the lieutenant would reward him with the chain of ammunition, just like the one Faas gave to Izara the day before. So far, they are the only two recruits to show promise.

"You're Sloane." Beside him, Nazanin cocks her head, regarding me with cool interest. It's the first time any of the girls in my quarters have spoken to me since we were lodged together. "I saw you on the field this morning. Your aim is terrible."

With a smirk, she pushes a lock of black hair away from her face and presses close against Jericho's side. He lowers his slingshot, shoving the weapon back into his pocket. The intimacy between the two of them is so familiar, I'm reminded of Teo and the days we spent together in Agbajé. A bitter ache tugs at my heart. I try to ignore it.

"What do you want?" Jericho's brown eyes are firmly fixed on me, the intensity in them burning through my skin.

Though my nerves tingle, my voice never wavers. "You need a map reader. I can help you."

He casts a quick, furtive glance at Nazanin, and I can almost hear him spewing curses in his head. Neither of them expected anyone would be listening in on their conversation. A careless move, one that could have gotten them killed if it had been a soldier or a guard who caught them. Even a recruit could easily turn them in for a prize of some sort—perhaps a more generous helping at tomorrow's mess. Judging by his tightening jaw, I know Jericho's thinking the same.

When he shifts his weight and squares out his shoulders, I wonder if he's going to attack. I plant my feet and brace myself for a fight. But he only folds his arms across his chest.

"Why?" he asks. "What's in it for you?"

I don't hesitate. "I need to get into Archives Hall."

"Not a chance." Nazanin shakes her head and gives me a sharp, pointed look.

I knew this would be the hardest part, convincing two strangers I should be included in their mission. But after failing to come up with a plan of my own, I see no other way.

I swallow the bad taste on my tongue and force the words out. "What do you think the barracks officer will do when she finds out what you two are planning?"

The barracks' standards are clear: any recruit charged with burglary and larceny will be subject to life imprisonment. Jericho and Nazanin are no friends of mine. I don't know them well enough to care what they think of me.

The alleyway is deathly quiet as the two of them pale, and I can almost hear the gasp caught in Nazanin's throat. She does her best to recover from the shock, brown eyes flashing as she takes a bold step forward.

"I don't take too kindly to threats, little girl," she snarls, baring teeth. "Where I come from, others get their throats slit for less."

My brawler's instinct kicks in immediately. "You couldn't touch me even if your life depended on it, *little girl*," I shoot back, sizing her up.

Nazanin is considerably short, a couple inches over five feet, with full, curvy features. She doesn't have the reach for a full swing, so even if she makes a move, I'm certain I could easily take her down. Next to her, Jericho clears his throat, his expression now indifferent.

"There's something inside the hall, something valuable that you want." He tilts his head toward me, a quiet curiosity on his face. "It's the only reason you're still here and not at the commander's office giving us up. So what is it you need?"

"That's not your concern."

"It is if you want to work with us," Nazanin snaps.

We lapse into an uneasy silence as they wait for me to speak again. Nazanin especially takes some comfort in watching me squirm, her face stuck between a scowl and a smirk. I know what I should say, but I can't bring myself to tell them the truth. Such information in the hands of two people I don't know is far too risky. But if I don't give them anything, a bone with enough meat to sink their teeth into, then what chance do I have of getting inside Archives Hall on my own?

"There's a book—" I settle on a response with the least amount of detail possible. "It's very important, and—"

"The Book of Records," Jericho cuts me off.

I blink up at him, the force of his tone arousing my suspicion. "We're after the same thing."

His silence is confirmation enough. I pause, dwelling on the new piece of information. If Jericho wants the Book of Records, then he, too, must be searching for answers. I know nothing of his past, what horror lurks in the deepest parts of his memories. But I'm willing to bet the Lucis are its architect. They are the root of all our pain, the seed from which our grief grows.

A memory of the night Mama left the hut breaks into my thoughts, and a familiar ache squeezes at my chest. She'd promised to return that night, swore whatever business she had on the foothills wouldn't take too long. It was only supposed to be a quick errand. *What went wrong? What could she have done to earn the wrath of the Nightwalkers who took her from me?*

Each memory leaves a deep bruise, but the unanswered questions are worse, a plague on my mind for way too long. I have to know the truth, and this might be my only chance.

"My mother," I say, fighting off the tremor in my voice. "She disappeared from our village two years ago. I've been trying to find out the truth of what happened to her ever since. I know the answer is inside that hall. If I could just get my hands on the book."

Jericho and Nazanin are quiet for some time. In their silence, dread rolls in my stomach, and I can almost feel the pressure squeezing up my chest. Gods, have I made the right decision telling them anything? Now that they know, will they use it against me?

As each second ticks by, my eyes dart back and forth between them, my entire body suddenly on edge.

"*Please*," I add gently.

When Jericho finally opens his mouth to speak, I breathe a silent sigh of relief.

"Eight months ago, my parents were arrested during an uprising in Shaaré." His voice is wooden, hollow, as if any moment now, it will simply splinter and crack. "They were brought here, to Cliff Row. I never thought I'd get a chance to find out what happened to them, to know whether they are alive or . . . or dead. Now that I'm here, I can't leave Avalon without knowing."

Veins web across his temples, each one standing out sharply. Nazanin places a hand on his shoulder and gives him a gentle squeeze, a small but needed gesture of comfort. Even I can't help but feel a pang of sadness for him. As a child, I heard stories of the small uprisings occurring in several parts of Nagea. Most were born from pain, from parents mourning the deaths of their conscripted sons and daughters. Others were dull sparks, so foolishly lit, without enough fuel to truly catch fire. In the end, none of it made a difference. The Lucis crushed them all.

"You can't do this alone," I murmur, if only to convince Jericho he needs me as an ally. Now that we share a common goal, he must know we stand a better chance if we work together. "You get me the map, and I promise I'll guide you through those tunnels. You have my word."

Nazanin scoffs. "How do we know you're not lying and this isn't a setup? You can't just expect us to go around believing every sad story we hear, even if it comes from some pretty face."

My cheeks flush, and a retort rises quick in my throat. I choke it down with gritted teeth. This won't work if I can't get the girl on my side too.

"Look, I'm not a fool. I just told you something that could get me killed should the barracks officer or the commanders ever find out. That's leverage you can use. If you go down, so do I."

She purses her lips, though not quick enough to hide the slight twitch. As expected, she latches onto the small bit of power I've just handed her, like a kitten unable to resist a ball of yarn. When I know I have her, I push on.

"If that isn't enough, then we've wasted enough time, and I'm already late for training. So what's it going to be?"

She and Jericho trade glances. He winks at her and she nods along.

"Fine," Nazanin mutters at last. Something tells me she isn't a girl who likes to concede. We have that in common. "But this is only one mission," she adds with a scowl. "Once it's over, we go our separate ways and never speak a word of it again. Agreed?"

"Agreed."

For the first time since I stepped foot on this damned base, I feel like I can breathe. Finally, finally, I have a plan. Now all we have to do is steal the map from Caspian's office, and possibly break all the standards doing so. The barracks officer's voice rumbles in my head for a few seconds, the bloodied face of the female recruit still too fresh to ignore. To violate these rules is to risk getting thrown into Cliff Row, tortured and killed, or worse. But for a chance to uncover the truth about Mama, anything is worth the risk.

"I hope you aren't one of those girls who will expect some kind of friendship at the end of this." Nazanin wrinkles her freckled nose, studying me once more.

"Don't worry," I say, offering a smile, "I don't befriend bitches."

If the jab stings, Nazanin doesn't show it. "And I hate strays. So we understand each other."

Jericho looks between us both and flashes a sly grin. "This should be fun."

I sprint up the steps of the training center, but by the time I arrive at the practice room, I already know I'm late. The squad leader, Dane Gray, waits for me inside, arms crossed in silent rage.

"Next time you find yourself running late, don't bother showing up." Dane's voice is a smooth whisper, but I flinch all the same. Especially with the way the boy peers low at me beneath his military visor. Unlike the first time I laid eyes on him, he stands in full army attire, broad and imposing, a patriotic soldier in every sense.

"Fine by me," I grumble under my breath.

For a moment, Dane holds my gaze, his expression so intent I have to force myself not to look away.

"Let me guess," he says coolly, "your mother never taught you anything about manners."

"My mother taught me many things, but none of them involved kissing a stranger's ass."

He strides forward then, green eyes ablaze with a fire to match my own. My skin prickles at his sudden closeness, but I manage to keep still, feet locked tightly in place. Judging by the way the squad leader grinds his jaw, I know I've crossed the line. After all, he's an officer of the crown, a Lucis soldier with enough authority to kill me for mouthing off. I should mutter some form of apology, but even with the threat of punishment, my lips won't move. No way I'm letting this brute speak of my mother that way.

"This isn't some slum village in Nagea, Recruit." His response is firm, deliberate. "Words like that have consequences here. Consider this a warning. You won't get another. On the mats." He nods me toward the middle of the room, where a cushion of blue mats spreads out across the concrete floor. Even though my first instinct is to tell him where to shove his order, I do nothing but obey.

Dane wastes no time and unbuttons his uniform jacket, revealing black, form-fitting fatigues and a fine gold medallion that dangles around his neck. His brown skin stands out, a shade darker than I last saw it, but still very much lighter than my own, with the kind of bloom only those who haven't suffered a day of famine would know. I regard him with a vicious scowl, but even that doesn't seem to faze him. With smooth, practiced motions, he wraps a long strip of cloth around the palm of his right hand, working it up to his wrist and back. Then he tosses his jacket off to the corner, next to a leather backpack propped idly against the wall.

"You're on the front lines," he says, joining me on the cushioned floor. "An enemy combatant comes charging at you. There are no bullets left in your rifle. What do you do?"

"Fight."

"No, you kill." He buzzes around me in a slow circle. I have to scratch my palm to keep from swatting him off. "If you go into a battle thinking all you have to do is fight your way out, you're dead before you even get started. This isn't a street brawl. The Shadow Rebels aren't there to spar with you. Kill or be killed, Recruit. Learn it or die."

A chill races up my skin at the mention of the famous military slogan. I detest everything about those four dooming words. Together, they bear the weight of a threat too impossible to ignore. *Kill or be killed.* Become a savage like them or die clinging to humanity. I force a stiff nod.

"Now let's see what you can do."

Across from me, Dane rolls up his sleeves, the lean muscles in his arms pulling against the visibly thin fabric. I set my gaze on his face, even as the sharp lines of his stomach poke at the edge of my vision. He snaps his long, brown fingers, knuckles cracking as he clenches and unclenches his fists. The sound grates my nerves, though I certainly try not to let it get to me. In fact, I welcome the challenge to unleash my rage on him. I feel it now, wild and consuming, a hurricane of every emotion I've felt since the moment I left the city dome. Since I said my goodbyes to Baba and kissed the sister I'll never see again. All because of the Lucis. Because of monsters like Faas Bakker and puppets like Dane Gray.

Just the thought rouses the àse in my blood. My head thrums as magic coils itself around me, scarlet threads of heat unspooling rapidly beneath my skin. I strain against the sensation, ignoring the sudden jolts of pain as my toes curl into the mats. But even when the magic starts to ebb and the pain slows to a dull ache, a different kind of fire clings to me. I draw on the familiar sparks of fury, letting it blaze through my senses as I round on the squad leader. Every bone in my body seems to pulse and vibrate with equal fervor.

I can't fight Faas, but today, I can fight Dane.

"Strike," he commands.

I charge at him, eager to deliver my first punch. Swiftly, he smacks my fist with one hand and palms my face with the other, shoving me backward. His touch burns, worse than my own fire, and heat flares across my cheeks.

"I expected more from you," he taunts. "Again."

This time, I don't wait for him to settle into his stance. I lunge forward, aiming for his chest. Before the strike finds home, he yanks my arm downward and doubles me over. His elbow cuts into the back of my neck. I grunt as a stab of pain brings me to my knees.

"Never trick yourself into believing you have the upper hand." Dane's voice rings in my ears, cutting through the frenzied thud of my heart. "Your enemy has the advantage, always. Your job is to turn that around, find your enemy's weakness, and use it against them."

His words are stern and direct, meant to teach me the error of my ways. I should listen to him. After all, he's managed to survive this world for many years. Yet, the mere sound of his voice pokes at my àse, causing it to simmer beneath the surface. I bite the insides of my cheek, drawing blood to keep the fire at bay.

"Get up," Dane growls low over my head.

I spot a blur of black in front of me and scramble to my feet. *Duck, spin, swing.* I roll out of Dane's range. Throw my fist out when he's within reach.

"Technique, rhythm." He dodges the blow with little effort. "A good soldier possesses mastery over both. Every footwork, every strike, has a specific beat of its own."

He moves with deadly precision, his motion fluid and sure, like the legendary bàtá dancers of the Ancient Kingdoms. This isn't another one of the village rodents I spar with, I realize through my daze. Dane is a soldier trained in the art of war and combat, and a ruthless one at that. Every strike, every kick, he blocks with ease. But when his fist slams against my jaw, I'm not as quick. My face smarts from the violent blow, and I taste more blood on my lips. Around me, the room starts to sway, keeping me in a staggering, dizzying motion. I dig my feet into the mats and blink, trying to clear the stars from my vision.

"Even more important is your ability to identify an opponent's rhythm," he says as my fist once again connects with nothing but air. "Whoever disrupts the rhythm controls the fight. Remember that."

I don't miss the disappointment laced into his words. It seems to taunt me with my failures. A reminder that despite my many years of scuffling back in the village, in this world, my strength isn't enough, my body isn't capable, and I am simply not able.

He stalks me across the mat like a predator, his steps measured. Something dark and violent glints behind his eyes. A twitch dances at the edge of his lips.

"I know you hate me," he says.

You have no idea! I want to scream. Though the words linger on my tongue, unspoken, Dane picks up on them anyway.

His gaze hardens. "Show me how much."

He advances on me, a wall of muscle racing toward me at a terrifying speed. In my desperation, I throw one foot out, hoping to land a kick to his face. Instead, Dane catches my leg and twists, flipping me up in the air. I land on the ground with a loud thud, and a sharp sting shoots up my spine. I gasp in pain, coughing and wheezing as the tendons in my back twist in pure agony.

The boy doesn't relent, and for one brutal hour the beatdown continues. Dane runs me ragged, determined to break my spirit. Every failure, every mistake, is a ruin on my body, and my skin tells the tale.

I'm still kneeling on the mat, struggling to fill my lungs with air, when he bounds over. I can sense the battle rage still coursing beneath his skin as he stares down at my sweat-soaked face. He wields his words like a soldier would a blade, meaning for them to cut.

"I was wrong about you," he says, his voice deep. "You don't have what it takes to survive this place."

The insult wounds more than I'd like to admit, a bitter, poisonous thing that makes my stomach churn. Despite the pain licking up my spine, I rise determinedly on my feet, lips curled into a stinging snarl.

"You're wrong," I fire back at him. "I may not be a monster like you, a glorified killer, but that doesn't make me any less worthy."

With a step, Dane bridges what little gap remains between us, until every quiet rasp of his breath becomes my own. He smells of steel and ocean, blood and terror, and the air suddenly becomes too menacing for me to inhale.

"You don't get it, do you?" He leans even closer toward me, jaw clenched. The look on his face is a cold, jagged glass. "I am a monster," he whispers low. "The same monster you must become if you want to make it out of here alive. Real monsters are not born, Recruit. We are made."

His eyes linger on mine a second longer, an ocean of nothing but dark shadows. I know to breathe only when Dane finally pulls away.

He cuts through the room in quick, even strides, grabs his belongings, and heads straight for the exit. I watch him all the while, rooted to the mats, wincing when the door slams shut behind him. My pulse pounds as his words replay over and over in my head.

I spend the rest of the day sweating through long hours of circuit drills and tactical maneuvers meant to prepare us for the front lines. In a series of hill sprints, we race up and down a steep incline with heavyweight plates strapped to our backs, followed by repeated rounds of lunges and jump squats across the training field. The commander's tactics are far more direct than Dane's, relying only on torture and intimidation to force us to comply. His harsh commands ring out clear and stern, spittle flying from his mouth every time another recruit fails to execute the proper formation sequence. Faas exhausts us far beyond what our bodies can endure, and by the time the punishment ends, my joints ache, my muscles quiver, and all I want is to fall asleep.

With a groan, I limp down the hilly ground beyond the fields, desperate to return to the barracks. Now that training is finally over for the day, I long for the cold concrete I call a bed, with its thin layer of foam and its even thinner blanket. But what little comfort my stone cot promises is soon forgotten the moment Nazanin and Jericho catch up to me outside the barracks' gate.

"Up for a mission tonight?" Nazanin's face is still flushed from the training session, her black hair damp with sweat. Next to her, Jericho looks just as disheveled, his fatigues stained with mud and grass.

I rub the sleep from my eyes and look between them. "What kind?"

"A stakeout," Jericho says, glancing around briefly to make sure there are no officers nearby.

I don't know what a stakeout is, but I'm certain these two wouldn't ask me to join them if it didn't have anything to do with our arrangement. But with curfew less than an hour away, not a single recruit would be caught wandering the base this time of night. Not unless they wish to suffer the commander's wrath. If Jericho and Nazanin are willing to risk being seen by a guard, then it must mean something. Whatever it is, for Mama's sake, I have to know.

"Are you coming?"

The two of them are already pulling away, heading in the direction of the training center. Without any hesitation, I turn from the barracks and hurry on after them.

Curfew can wait.

Minutes later, we creep up behind a thicket running along the northern side of the training center, crouching low against the dense overgrowth. The darkness is thick now, making it hard to see far beyond the surrounding branches. Still, from our vantage point, I can just make out the silhouettes of three patrol guards as they cross the lawn, each with a blue-eyed leopard leashed in hand. After witnessing the beasts' ferocity last night, I freeze, barely breathing, almost waiting for them to sniff us out of our hiding place. Instead, the guards shuffle away without so much as a glance in our direction. Only then do I settle onto my knees, releasing a bit of the tension in my stomach.

Beside me, Nazanin shifts on her feet, cursing as she scratches at her right arm. "How much longer do we have to stay here?" She wedges herself between the bushes to protect against the insects buzzing around her face. "The mosquitoes on this island are bloody vicious."

"Just until the last guard leaves," Jericho murmurs on an awkwardly bent knee.

He keeps his eyes glued to a fenced compound attached to the back of the training center, counting the number of guards emerging from its gate. The same slingshot he had earlier dangles in his hands, a small pebble caught between its straps. When a nightjar *churrs* too close overhead, he raises the weapon skyward, firing at the bird before it alerts the soldiers to our presence.

"You're really good with that," I tell him a second later when a thud echoes nearby.

"Thanks," he says, tucking the slingshot into his pocket. Then he glances my way, and something seems to soften in his eyes. "My grandfather—he, uh—carved it for me when I was six," he adds with an almost sheepish smile. "He loved to hunt, and so every morning before he died, we'd head to the forest and hunt for hours. He taught me everything I know."

Though the memory of his grandfather is a distant one, it's obvious how fondly Jericho remembers it. It makes me think of my own baba, alive but far, living a life we can no longer share. I feel the ache in my heart, cutting with a knife's edge.

"How did you get it past the guards in Shaaré?" I hear myself ask, if only to turn my thoughts away from my grandfather and the home I can no longer return to.

"I sewed it into my shirt." Nazanin, still crouched between the shrubs, offers me a proud smile.

"And no one found it?"

She just shrugs. "The guards can't find what they can't see." With that, she spins away, muttering more curses as she swats at the mosquitoes.

I swallow hard, suddenly wishing I'd done more to save my daggers and herbs from the guard's grasp. Perhaps both would still be within my reach, a balm when I need it most. As if on instinct, a trickle of àse leaks into my body, the warmth of magic chasing away the chill of the night. I bury my arms inside my fatigues, hoping to hide the red veins already bulging beneath my skin. Though the pain doesn't last long, it's a reminder that without my grandfather's àgbo, I'm at the mercy of a magic slowly slipping beyond my control.

"Hey, you all right?" Nazanin gives me a nudge on the shoulder, enough to snap me out of my discomfort.

I inhale slowly and let my hands drop to my sides. When another pair of uniformed officers marches down the field away from us, I turn to face Jericho.

"That must be the last of them," I say, fighting to keep the strain from my voice. "So what exactly is the plan?"

For a moment, the boy remains quiet, watching the compound a little longer to make sure there are no more officers in sight. Then he draws himself up, shaking out his long, lanky limbs. I do the same, and Nazanin especially breathes a sigh of relief as she springs to her feet. Jericho motions us forward, and together, we charge through the trees, our steps light on the thick carpet of grass.

"I counted six entrances to the training center earlier," he says as we come out on the other side of the thicket. "All are heavily guarded except for that one."

He points to the only back door that leads from the building into the fenced compound. With the branches no longer there to obscure our vision, it's easy to make out the tarnished metal bars rising at least twenty feet above our heads. A wide, open space stretches out behind the fence, dotted with clusters of thornbush and patches of elephant grass. At first, I wonder if it's an abandoned training field. Until I catch a flash of movement in the branches of a jackalberry tree alongside the fence.

"Of course the entrance is unguarded." My eyes widen once I realize what it is we're staring at. "That's a bleeding leopards' den."

When I peer out at the cage, I notice two sprawled beneath the canopy of the tree, pale blue eyes shining in the darkness. I shudder, unsettled by the beasts' nearby presence, but Jericho doesn't seem the least bit fazed. He maintains a tall and lazy stance, hands deep in his pockets as he takes in the sight around us.

"The guards take the leopards out on patrol every night after curfew." He turns to me, his voice soft and calm, as if trying to soothe a child. "Which means the den will be practically empty."

"Tell me you're not thinking about—"

"We scale the fence and get through to the training center using the door."

"Are you mad?" In that moment, my gaze cuts to Nazanin, almost expecting her to deny what Jericho is proposing. But she only nods along, mirroring his foolish determination.

"You two can't be serious." I look between them, imagining all the horrible things that could go wrong, all the possible ways we could die. This isn't just about breaking the barracks' standards anymore. "Am I the only one who remembers what happened last night? Only an idiot would willingly step into that cage knowing what lurks inside."

Nazanin scoffs under her breath. "See, I told you she isn't cut out for this."

I do my best to ignore her snide remark, focusing on the looming fence instead. "Have you even seen the height of that thing? How the hell are we supposed to scale that?"

"*That thing* is all the access we have to Caspian's office. Without it, there's no other way in." She folds her arms across her chest, pinning me with a cold, hard glare. "Besides, you heard Jer. The leopards will be out roaming the grounds, so I don't see what the problem is."

I'm silent for a while, once again weighing the risk in my head. After everything I've sacrificed to come here, getting inside the lieutenant's office is all that stands between me and the truth about Mama. I need that tunnel map. I need this plan. But the knowledge that I must somehow scale a den full of monstrous beasts is enough to rattle my nerves, especially if it ends with me caught between their jaws. Even Mama barely survived an attack by one of these things, and I can still trace the crisscross of long, jagged scars that raked down her stomach. When an image of bared fangs and torn flesh flashes in my mind, I gulp around the tightness in my throat. Still, despite the threat of death, I know I must see this through. If this is the only way in, then I have no other choice.

"Even if this works," I murmur, lingering on the silhouettes of the caged leopards, "if we somehow manage to get inside the training center, security cameras will be everywhere."

"Well, we haven't exactly figured out that part yet." Jericho's admission only sends a fresh ripple of dread over me.

If we can't find a way past the Lucis' machine eyes, our plan is doomed before we even get started.

"This isn't going to be easy, is it?" Earlier, when I struck a deal with these two, it felt like progress. Like I was one step closer to discovering what really happened the night Mama disappeared. Now what little hope I had is slowly trickling away, replaced by a gnawing sense of defeat.

"It's a break-in, Sloane." Nazanin's nostrils flare, the annoyance in her voice just as palpable. "If it was easy, everyone would do it. Seriously," she adds, her eyes narrowing, "are you sure you can handle this mission?"

"What the hell is that supposed to mean?"

"Well, you've done nothing but whine all evening," she answers flatly. "And quite frankly, I'd much prefer not to be sharing a cell in Cliff Row at the end of this mission. They don't serve palm wine in prison, you know?"

"Do they serve priorities?" I snap back.

Next to her, Jericho just chuckles, foolishly amused. "I'm guessing this is how all female friendships start," he says with a grin.

But that only earns him a quick punch from Nazanin. "Shut up, Jer," she grumbles, even as she tries to fight off a smile.

I fail to do the same.

Suddenly an alarm blares across the base, a deep, guttural wail that shatters the silence. Twin flashes of light gleam off the soldiers' tower, and within seconds, the overhead beams erected at every corner spark to life, each one a bright white fire to split the darkness.

The three of us jump, startled by the noise and the harsh, glaring lights.

"What's happening?" Nazanin jerks her head around.

"They know we're here," I hiss as my gaze darts to the soldiers' tower, searching for oncoming guards with wide, frantic eyes. If any of them find us now, I already know what the punishment will be.

Beside me, Jericho's face hardens, the same thread of fear weaving through us all. "Get behind the trees."

He grabs Nazanin's wrist and pulls her toward the bushes. I scramble in after them, ignoring the thorned branches poking and scratching at my skin. My pulse pounds as we drop down behind a row of shrubs, our knees digging into the damp earth.

When a shadow sprints across the field, Nazanin jolts on the spot. "What the hell is that?"

At first, I think it's one of the leopards loose on the prowl, and my entire body tenses. I'm up on my feet within seconds, ready to break into a run if need be.

"Wait." Jericho wrenches me back to the ground and gestures toward the den. "Look. I think another recruit's trying to make a run for it."

I track the direction of his finger, until I spot a small figure clambering up the side of the fence, thin, reedy limbs gripping the railings with desperate effort.

Another deserter. The second one in two days. I almost can't believe my eyes. But judging by the boy's panicked steps, it's the only explanation that makes sense. Someone must have seen him escaping the barracks and signaled the alarm.

Any recruit caught trying to desert will be executed on sight.

Footsteps approach in the distance. Voices drift from an alleyway nearby. The guards are on the hunt, and they won't rest until he's been captured.

"We should get out of here," Nazanin urges.

She and Jericho are already backing away. I should too. But the sight of the recruit keeps me in place, and all I can do is watch as he hops from the fence onto the jackalberry tree.

In his haste, he doesn't see the leopard stalking along the shadows of the branches.

Not right away.

Not until the beast leaps forward and seizes him by the throat.

His dying screams burrow into my brain, echoing long after we flee the bushes.

SIXTEEN

All night, I dream of the deserter. I see the sudden lurch of his body as he plunges into the tree, hear the snarls of the leopards as they tear through him. When he collapses into the dirt, his limbs convulse once. But instead of the boy's mangled face, I stare into my own hollow, empty eyes.

The image clings to the corners of my mind, a tightly spun web that grasps at my fears. Last night, when Jericho told me of his plan to scale the den, I knew, deep down, the kind of danger it would put us in. If the deserter couldn't survive those blue-eyed beasts, what chance do we really have?

Even now, my chest tightens at the thought of it as Faas marches us toward the cliffs jutting out behind the base. The jagged crags rise at least seventy feet from the ocean, dull gray stones turned crimson beneath the morning sun. With a breath, I fall in behind the rest of the squad, roots and rocks crunching underfoot as we ascend the steep, winding slope. By the time we reach the top of the cliff, my body drags, my knees shudder, and every gulp of air burns in my lungs.

To my dismay, Dane waits for us on the ledge, black fatigues rippling in the cool, salty breeze. Even with his face turned to the ocean, I recognize the slight lean in his stance, the rise and fall of his broad shoulders, and, of course, the hood drawn low over his head.

He whirls as we approach, his gaze sliding over the recruits struggling to catch their breath. He regards each of them with a single nod, but when his green eyes meet mine, they linger for a second or so, before landing on Faas. Though fleeting, I can see the challenge in them, enough to wonder what the hell he's really doing here. The squad leader hasn't bothered to attend any training drills so far—a welcome respite, especially after the way he stormed out of our combat session the day before. *You don't have what it takes to survive this place.* His words were a slap to the face then, and I hate that they sting just as much now.

I set my jaw as the commander settles in next to him. We snap to attention before the both of them, bodies stiff as rods, arms locked behind our backs, a tense energy pulsing through the entire squad.

"Last night, another recruit was caught trying to escape the base." Faas's voice is cold and stern, a bitter wind that steals through the high bluffs. "This traitor's been firmly dealt with."

Beside me, Nazanin shifts uncomfortably on her feet. But with Dane and the commander mere inches away, I keep my eyes forward and school my features into a careful indifference. The last thing I need is to draw the attention of the commander at a time like this.

"By now, you should already be familiar with the barracks' standards. Deserting is a crime punishable only by death," Faas barks. "So let this serve as a warning to the rest of you. If you run, if you attempt to flee, you will be hunted down and executed. Do you understand?"

"Yes, sir!" Our voices echo out across the cliffs, rising above the roaring waves below.

The commander surveys us a moment longer, his face stony. Then he breaks away from Dane, revealing a deep fissure in the cliffs behind them. A thick braided cord stretches out at least thirty yards across the ocean, a bridge between our cliff and the distant crags.

"In a few minutes," Faas says, "you will attempt to traverse this chasm by means of a rope. There will be no safety harness to prevent your fall. Without proper technique, strength, and balance, you risk plummeting to your death."

Uneasy glances dart among the squad, though none of us dare to speak. Still, I hear the low whoosh of air that escapes their lungs, the rapid inhale of breath that follows. Even Jericho pales a little, the color draining from his golden-brown face. Next to him, Izara looks equally on edge as she clenches and unclenches her fists.

"You will have five minutes to cross the rope, ring the bell, and pull yourself over the ledge," the commander continues. "The first amongst you to complete today's Physical in record time will be rewarded. Whoever finishes last will forfeit their meal ration for the day. Officer Gray will be waiting to receive you on the other side."

In that moment, Dane steps forward, his expression impassive, languid even, as he bounds toward the edge of the cliff. Watching him, a prickly sensation jolts beneath my skin, every nerve in my body pulled taut. When the squad gathers behind him, I chance a look at the massive gorge far below. Naked rocks line the surface of the ocean, with giant, white-capped waves crashing against the cliff face.

My gut drops. Seventy feet is a long way down. Only a fool would choose to dangle like a pig on a spit from such bleeding height. Gods, this is suicide.

Across the ledge, Dane crouches low and grips the rope, yanking it a few times to test its strength. When he's sure the thing won't snap, he lowers his weight on top of it. All I can do is keep my eyes locked on him, trying to memorize his every move, every shift and turn of his long limbs.

He hooks his right leg over the rope and lets the left one hang down his side. The air catches in my throat as he launches forward, until the ledge disappears entirely beneath him. If he falls now, there's nothing but the howling wind and the open waters to guide him to the afterlife. But even with death one wrong move away, Dane maintains his balance on the cord with a feline grace. He glides along swiftly, his movements smooth and controlled, as if drifting on the air. The squad looks on in rapt silence, our concentration focused on the squad leader as he swings the clapper once, letting it chime before hoisting himself over the ledge.

When Dane rises to his feet, a chorus of gasps ripple out in awe of him. But if the squad leader hears them, he doesn't show it. Even from this distance, the boy's demeanor remains remarkably calm for someone who's just completed a lethal obstacle course in less than two minutes.

Satisfied, the commander turns on us. "Recruit Mahrez, you're up," he says, and the knot in my stomach tightens.

At the far end of the line, Malachi strides forward. My gaze moves with him as he heads toward the cliff's edge, knowing all too well the threat he poses to me. Even the mere presence of him is a dagger pressed against my throat, so much that I imagine, for a moment, what it would be like to shove him off this bleeding ledge. An impossible thought, especially with Faas standing so close. But it comforts me all the same.

Malachi drops to the ground, his back flat against the uneven surface. With a grunt, he pulls forward until he's hanging beneath the rope, a swaying monkey suspended only by his hands and heels. I frown at his strange technique, a far cry from the one Dane demonstrated earlier. With his eyes turned skyward, Malachi swings one hand in front of the other, lands one foot ahead at a time. He doesn't even fumble a step, his form sharp and agile as he skitters determinedly down the rope. Unlike the rest of us, his face betrays no hint of terror. In fact, out there in the middle of the ocean, he looks like his usual self: smug, devilish, a rat with the irritating confidence of a river hippo.

A second after the bell tolls, Malachi hauls himself onto the ledge alongside Dane, a foolish grin on his lips. When Faas looks up from the round, ticking device in his hands, I realize why.

"Four minutes and thirty-eight seconds." The commander nods in approval.

Scattered whispers flit between some of the recruits. I set my jaw, annoyed the bastard somehow managed to finish within the time limit. If the rest of the squad performs half as well as he did, there's a chance I might end up at the bottom of the ranks again.

How long before Faas gives the order to kill you? Malachi's jab from yesterday pokes at me, a reminder of everything I stand to lose if I fail another training drill.

I won't fail, I whisper in my head, echoing the words until I can believe them. Yet no matter how hard I try, I see myself plunging seventy feet into the chasm, body splayed and twisted across the unforgiving rocks. I see myself dead.

My legs tremble. I bite my tongue against the dread filling my mouth.

Moments pass. One by one, Faas orders another recruit to the rope. But so far, no one comes close to beating Malachi's record. Not even Izara, who swings onto the other ledge at exactly five minutes.

After almost an hour, the squad dwindles, until only two people remain on the cliff—me and the commander. My pulse gives a sudden throb when he looks down at me, the same cold, unfeeling expression on his face.

"Recruit Shade." He waves me forward. "You may begin."

Steeling myself, I move toward the edge of the cliff and glare out across the chasm, watching the cluster of uniformed bodies in the distance—all of them safe and steady on their feet once again.

Five minutes, and I can join them on that ledge. Survive this bleeding Physical and prove myself capable to Faas and Dane. I won't give either one a reason to label me the weakest link of the squad. Not now. Not when I'm so close to uncovering the truth about Mama. *Five minutes.*

I stoop low, a burst of adrenaline buzzing through me as I close my fists around the cord. Despite the roar of the ocean churning far below, I focus on anchoring my weight onto the rope, letting one of my legs dangle, just like Dane did. The squad leader's movements are familiar enough, every push and pull of his limbs swimming before my eyes. All I have to do is mirror his exact steps.

Be nimble. Be swift.

With a gasp, I wrench myself forward. From this height, the air is thinner, sharper, making it difficult to breathe, much less crawl. I inhale and exhale, struggling to fill my lungs. The wind screams as it bites away at my skin and whips about the ends of my braids. When it rustles the thick cord beneath, I make the mistake of glancing down. My stomach plummets at the slabs of rock strewn like gravestones across the ocean. Harsh waves batter the walls of the cliff on both sides. Even though the fall seems so far, I know death will be instant. It's all I can do to tighten my grip on the rope, clinging to it as hard as I can.

Despite my pounding heartbeat, I heave a breath and tear my eyes away from the tide below. My gaze locks on the ledge still some yards across. Gods, I'm not even halfway through. I don't know how much time has passed, if any at all, but determination drags me farther and farther along.

Inhale. Exhale.

If I could just make it close enough to ring the bell. Close enough to grab the ledge—

An ache starts in my muscles, and my limbs quiver in protest. With every pull, I feel the tension in my fingers down to my toes. *I'm doing this all wrong,* I realize, when the rope starts to jerk back and forth. My balance shifts. I sway for a terrifying second, fighting to keep my body pressed against the cord. A sharp burst of air rakes over my skin. The wind is stronger now, lurching me sideways. My foot slips off the rope, and I'm dangling over the chasm, legs flailing seventy feet in the air.

Horror crawls up my throat, and a scream escapes me. I can't breathe, I can't think. My arms tremble with every second that passes, too weak to hold me up for much longer.

I'm going to fall. I'm going to die.

My chest constricts. Every ragged rush of breath feels like my last. I clench my teeth and fling my foot upward, hoping to secure it around the cord. It doesn't catch. My body swings with the motion, teetering in the air like a strung corpse. This time, I gnash my teeth together to keep from crying out. Something pricks at my eyes, blurring the edge of my vision. Through my tears, I think I see the recruits gathered at the ledge, all of them watching with wide eyes and slack jaws. A few look on with pity. They don't think I'm going to make it. They expect me to fall. Others, like Malachi and Dane, might even crave such a fate for me.

You don't have what it takes to survive this place.

I wonder how long before Faas gives the order to kill you?

Their words are an echo in the wind, taunting. But Baba's cowrie shells rattle around my neck, a familiar *clack* that rises above their doubts and my fears. I made a promise to my grandfather to survive this hell. I will not fail now. Though my heart thuds so fast it hurts, I harden my nerves and try to focus on staying alive.

"You can do this," I growl to myself.

Get back on the rope.

Ring the bell.

Grab the ledge.

The cord slides between my palms, slipping faster and faster. I grasp at what I can, clammy fingers scrabbling for purchase. With every bit of strength I have left, I throw my foot out at an angle, high enough to swing it over the rope. When it locks into place, I waste no time pulling myself up. Every muscle in my body tightens as I sprawl out, adjusting arms and legs into the proper form. The second I catch my balance, I snap into action. The momentum pushes me forward, sending me hurtling toward the ledge looming close ahead. With every step, I focus on the breath wheezing past my lips, not the fist of terror clutching my chest.

I reach the bell within minutes. Sweat drips down my back, soaking through my fatigues as I tug at the clapper. The noise buzzes around me, a hollow sound that mingles with the squad's harried whispers above my head. I ignore their shocked gasps and shove my fingers into a crevice in the cliff, using the handhold to lift myself onto the ledge.

Though some of the recruits scatter from my path, I can feel their gazes on me as I sink to the ground, panting heavily on my knees.

I'm alive is all I can think, and that realization alone almost makes me smile. Then a broad, familiar silhouette cuts across my vision, tall enough to block out the sunrise behind him. Dane looms over me, so close I'm forced to look up into his eyes.

"Seventeen minutes and twenty-one seconds," he says without any trace of sympathy.

His words shouldn't come as a surprise, but my whole body seizes anyway.

I failed the first Physical.

SEVENTEEN

My performance worsens as the day wears on. All around me, the squad whispers of my failures, my weakness, and I can't shake the sense that no matter how hard I try, it seems all I've done is put a target on my back.

At Culture and Theory, Faas instructs us to memorize *Edictus*, the soldier's creed:

> *I am the Force's shield, a warrior of blood and steel.*
> *With my rifle, I swear fealty to the Founding Lucis,*
> *To defend the bloodlines and the crown with life willingly given.*
> *By flesh and by bone, I will raise death unto them who dare defy the will of the throne,*
> *In this, I will not fail.*
> *I swear this creed with my blood and my valor,*
> *To the very end.*

The decree itself is centuries old, yelled by the First Commander, Nero Regulus, as he stood on the field of battle against the Ancient Kingdoms. It is the song of a young tyrant, the ballad of a phoenix that once burned through my world and laid waste to my people. It's why I struggle to repeat it now, even as the rest of the squad chants the words freely.

With every failed attempt, Faas strikes the back of my hands with a wooden stick until my knuckles are raw and bleeding.

Though the commander inflicts as much pain on me as he possibly can, his cruelty doesn't end there. As the remaining recruits prepare to flock to mess, starved and eager for the day's ration, Faas orders me to report to the armory, where some further punishment awaits.

I file out of the classroom behind the others, my hands so badly bruised I can barely clench them. Some of the recruits avoid making eye contact with me as they brush past. Others, like Malachi, even go as far as to deliberately bump my shoulder hard enough to send me sprawling across the floor. My elbows scrape against the cold concrete, and I wince at the sudden bite of pain. The bastard throws his head back and laughs, and it takes every ounce of restraint not to lunge at him. Instead, I'm forced to watch him leave, knowing if I were to go after Malachi now, not even the gods can save him.

Jericho and Nazanin are the last to emerge from the room, the two of them frowning as they pause before me.

"What was that?" Jericho grabs me by the arm and pulls me to my feet.

"That's just Malachi showing his ass." I stagger up after him, teeth gritted as I brush the dirt off my uniform. A smear of blood blooms on my palms, and between the fresh bruises and the wounds from Faas, I have to will myself to remain calm.

Nazanin starts to pick at the dry bits stuck to my hair but then realizes what she's doing and backs away. "I'm guessing you two know each other," she says, folding her arms in front of her.

"Same village." I nod coolly. "And I may have stabbed him once before."

"Oh."

Neither Jericho nor Nazanin speaks again after that.

I'm still seething when we turn the corner, but the sight of the Lucis from yesterday's shooting drill stops me short.

"Royal heads, that's Lord Theodus Sol." Nazanin falls in at my right, mouth agape as she stares out at the Lucis too. "I knew I recognized him yesterday on the field."

Lord Sol stands alone at the entrance of the training center, his face hard and impassive, watching the steady stream of recruits pouring in and out of the hallway. While many of them make a show of bowing to the royal as they pass, I scoff low in my throat and keep my head held high.

"What's he doing here?" I mutter, more to myself than anyone else. "I thought the bloodlines rarely pay a visit to Fort Regulus."

They would much rather sit in the comfort of their bleeding court, drunk on power and yet completely useless in matters of war.

"I heard he's our division's internal adviser," Jericho tells us once we're on the move again. "He'll be working with Faas and reporting directly back to the queen. You know, boring military stuff."

"The military is only boring to those who haven't bled for it," I shoot back.

Lord Sol is just another sheltered brute with the blood of thousands on his hands.

Jaw clenched, I quicken my pace, but not before catching the royal's shadowy eyes for the briefest second. Then he's joined by the High Commander, and we only watch as the two of them disappear into one of the empty classrooms. With that, I shove my way out of the training center, say goodbye to Jericho and Nazanin, and head in the direction of the armory.

The domed building lies next to the airfield on the far side of the base, an ammunition ground with enough rifles to arm an entire nation. Soldiers mill about the long, winding rows and aisles, loading crates of explosives and firearms onto metal shelves stacked high to the ceiling. I'm barely through the steel overhead doors when the smell of gunpowder assaults my senses. I taste sulfur in the air.

My stomach churns, chased by a familiar pang of hunger that gnaws at me. I set my jaw, trying to ignore the ache as I march down one of the least crowded aisles leading to the back of the armory. When I turn the corner, Dane steps out in front of me. He leans up alongside the railings of a top shelf, one elbow propped against the metal rungs. His morning fatigues are long gone, replaced with a plain, fitted undershirt soaked through with sweat. A polished gun swings idly in his gloved hand, the magazine fully loaded.

"You know, I'd expect more discipline from someone barely keeping up with the squad." The look he gives me is the same one he wore back on the cliffs, calm, impassive. Yet despite his lackadaisical exterior, there's no denying the contempt in his voice.

I regard him with equal disdain, making sure to put some careful distance between us. Any closer and I might be tempted enough to grab the gun and shoot him in the foot with it.

"I was told Lieutenant Caspian would be here." My eyes sweep past him, scanning the open area for any indication of the lieutenant's presence. But unfortunately, Dane seems to be all alone.

"Caspian had business to attend to," he confirms with a light shrug.

"So let me guess, I'm stuck with you." I glare at him, my skin prickling at the thought of spending any more of my time with the squad leader. As if being forced to train with him, suffering his blows and scrutiny, isn't punishment enough.

"Trust me," Dane says, as though he can read my thoughts, "I'm the least of your problems." With a tilt of his chin, he gestures at the corner wall behind me. "Turn around."

I'm curious enough to do as he asks. Still, my teeth clench together as I whirl to see a large collection of rifles and handguns lining the length of the wall, all of them arranged in tight, orderly rows. A long wooden table sprawls a few feet across, littered with a colorful display of cleaning tools and ammunition trays.

Frowning, I glance over at Dane.

"You've been assigned to Basics" is all he tells me, as if that alone should mean something.

"And what is that, exactly?"

"Weapons cleaning." He strides over to the workstation and lays his gun off to the side, away from the rest of the clutter. His stained gloves come off next, and as he tugs on a clean pair, his gaze cuts to me. "You're to remove every rifle from the wall and strip all main parts for routine cleaning and polish. When you're finished with the reassembly, you'll have to restock the weapons and take full inventory. I expect it should take quite a few days to get through, which means you will report here every day, during mess, until the task is completed."

"You're joking." I blink up at him, but Dane only levels me with a stare. He makes no effort to respond. Instead, he turns his attention on the ammunition trays in front of him, emptying them of their contents. Bullets drop, one by one, and steel clinks as they pile on the table.

For a moment, all I can do is look on in disbelief. My eyes dart past him, to the number of firearms taking up every available stretch of wall space. There's a hundred or so rifles up there, with far more ammunition to sort through. Just the thought is enough to make my insides lurch. I'm no fool. For all his aloofness, even Dane knows it will take much more than a few days' work to complete a task this size. A challenge, more than anything. Especially when every hour I waste here is time that could be spent trying to find my way into Archives Hall. Worse, without the promise of mess, I'll have no choice but to suffer an entire week without food. Surely the commander must know it, too, which is why he's settled on this particular punishment. Another price of my failure.

"You should consider yourself lucky." Dane barely looks up as he speaks, rag in hand, wiping away at the bullets with trained efficiency.

"Is that so?" I roll my eyes and move closer to the other end of the workstation, meaning to leave him to his task and get on with mine. If I pace myself well enough, perhaps this torture will be over much sooner than I anticipate. Then I might still be able to salvage whatever time is left to focus on my own mission.

Finally, he raises his head. Though his expression doesn't change, a note of caution steels his next words. "A week in the armory is nothing compared to a night in Cliff Row," he says plainly. "And after your performance today, truth is, if Faas wanted, things could have gone much worse for you."

"I know what the commander's capable of," I snap back at him.

"Do you?" His eyes stray to the back of my hands, now flat against the edge of the table. I try not to wince as he scans the mess of open wounds and dried blood crusted over purple-bruised skin. Instead, I let my fists curl under the weight of his stare, chin raised when he dares to look my way again. As always, there is no flash of pity on the squad leader's face, and for once, I'm grateful for it.

"Right now, you're the weakest recruit on Faas's squad," he continues, "which makes you vulnerable, helpless, and at the mercy of a man who has none. What do you think he'll do to you once he no longer sees the value in keeping you around?"

My skin smarts at his bitter words, and beneath it, a dark plume of anger rises in me. I don't need Dane to lecture me on the commander's savagery. Not when I still feel the bite of the wooden stick on my bare knuckles. And even then, I know the scars are only a fraction of what the commander can do. After all, he's the same monster who had an innocent child killed on the first day, the one by whose order countless more have been gunned down. As much as I hate to admit it, the squad leader *is* right. There's a reason Faas Bakker was appointed the butcher of this damned slaughterhouse, and if I'm not careful, I may very well end up his next victim.

Though I don't say any of this to him, Dane reads my assent with little effort.

"You can't afford any more mistakes, Recruit," he offers as a final warning. "Do yourself a favor. Fall in line, *or else.*"

The implication is clear, the threat gleaming like a razor-sharp knife. For a moment, a tense silence passes between us as he gathers the clean bullets back into their trays. With the metal boxes stacked neatly in his hands, he circles the workstation, turns the corner, and disappears down the aisle without so much as a glance.

In his absence, the adrenaline in me withers to nothing, replaced by a sense of unease that sets my nerves on edge. I lean forward, elbows propped on the table, breathing deeply to steady my racing heart. Thrice now, the squad leader has managed to make me feel as though I am too weak and unruly to survive, a brittle doll days away from being torn apart.

Well, he's wrong.

The commander may leave scars and bruises on my skin; he may even keep me starved until I am weak and bloated. But neither he nor Dane will break me.

I won't let them.

With that spark of determination burning inside me, I straighten up and turn toward the weapons wall, eager to get moving. I can't decide where to begin, so I settle on the small section of firearms mounted at the far end. I'm halfway there when I spot an officer's uniform jacket draped on one of the wall hooks. The backpack hanging next to it is oddly familiar, and as I get closer, I can see the letters *D.G.* stitched into the tan-brown leather in threads of gold.

Dane Gray.

My pulse gives a sudden throb as I take in the squad leader's personal belongings, my eyes roving over each item in turn. A pair of knives, glinting from the mouth of his pack. The same army cap he wore at yesterday's combat training. Then there's his uniform jacket. . . .

Any recruit charged with burglary and larceny will be subject to life imprisonment.

Fall in line, or else.

Yet, I can't help myself when a plan emerges out of nowhere, a tease much too close to ignore. For a long moment, I linger on the spot, mulling it over despite the deal I made with Jericho and Nazanin last night. If this works, then there's a chance I won't have any need for the two thieves at all—or the map inside the lieutenant's office, for that matter. No reason to scale a den full of sharp-fanged leopards and risk getting mauled to death by those savage beasts. In fact, I might even manage to trick the security cameras, enough to sneak past them without getting caught. My mind spins as I search the plan for visible cracks, anything that might pose a real threat. When I find none, a smile turns my lips.

Because even though the squad leader didn't mean to, he's just handed me everything I need to break into Archives Hall on my own.

After hours of weapons cleaning and simulation drills on the training field, I sit still on my bunk, clad in Dane's oversize jacket. His military hat is pressed low over my eyes, its wide straps adjusted to fit my head. Dressed in the squad leader's uniform—now folded and tucked in all the right places—I look like another one of these Lucis soldiers. It's almost sickening. But for the promise of the truth, I'll gladly take the form of these monsters.

Around me, the entire barracks stirs in a deep slumber, the broken rhythm of snores rippling from the cots nearby. Night has fallen, and curfew has long since begun. Which only means there's a swarm of armed officers guarding every building and hallway as if their very lives depended on it. But I have the darkness outside these barracks on my side. A darkness so consuming, even the world becomes a shadow of itself.

I tuck the pair of stolen knives into my belt, sucking in a deep, shaky breath as I set my gaze on the closed door. It's been several minutes since Izara sluggishly dragged her way to the bath chamber. The girl could return any second, and when she does, I can't let her discover me here, certainly not in the Lucis' attire. A curious witness is all it would take to ruin my entire plan.

I brace up when Miriam starts to mumble about in her sleep. Across from her, Nazanin rouses onto her side to face me, and my chest tightens as I wonder if I've somehow alerted her. She only lets out a faint whimper, her eyes screwed shut. I don't miss the slight drool smeared across her cheek as she rolls over once more with lazy abandon.

In the stillness that follows, I loosen a quiet exhale.

I should leave now, before any of these girls catch me. But as the minutes tick by, a knot of fear coils in my stomach. So many things could go wrong tonight. For one, I could get caught before I even make it out of the barracks. I expect the security post will be crawling with guards this time of night, too many round-bellied men whose lecherous gazes seem to track every female recruit at every turn. The threat of what they could do to me if I'm caught is almost enough to weaken my already wavering resolve.

Then there's the distance between the barracks and Archives Hall to consider. Walking that far in the bleeding darkness, with nothing but a pair of knives to defend myself, is dangerous—and quite possibly stupid. My mind goes back to the deserter from last night, the second recruit who dared to escape, only to be mauled. His dying screams are a cold echo in my head. What will happen to me if any of the guards on patrol realize I'm not an officer?

My pulse races with all the possible outcomes, each one more frightening than the last. The plan that once appeared flawless in my head now taunts me with all the ways I could fail. Yet, despite the fear and panic clawing at my heart, I shake my arms loose, heave another breath, and rise slowly to my feet. I cross the room in long, muted strides, gaze darting ever so quickly as I crack the door open an inch.

A row of crystal globes bathes the empty hallway, casting slants of dim yellow light along the bare stone walls. The security post is just past this long stretch of corridor, a small wooden shack cut into the wall, next to the wrought iron gates.

The hallway is an eerie shadow, and I wait for the first sound of movement. When I'm certain there isn't a single guard on the prowl, I take a wary step forward, away from the safety of my sleeping quarters, and into the waiting darkness of the corridor.

This is it. I inhale, gathering all the courage I can muster. *No turning back now.*

My pace is swift, my wide eyes sweeping back and forth as I reach a bend in the hallway. I press against the wall, listening for the faint voices of the guards, but the only sounds in the hall are my muffled footsteps and the echo of my pounding pulse. The security cameras are present, though, a vigilant dot in the corner walls, watching from above. I tug on the hat, pulling it low enough to hide my features, and keep my face buried. The guards can't capture what they can't see, and from this view, any of those fools could easily mistake me for a common officer. Still, I set my gaze ahead and keep my senses alert as I approach the post.

A sudden urge *taps, taps, taps* up my spine, the icy finger of dread. I shiver against it.

Something isn't right.

Sure enough, the security post looks abandoned. Yet, a torchlight rolls down its small steps, discarded, as if someone only just dropped it moments ago. If the guard is on patrol, why would he leave his torch behind? If he isn't, then where is he?

A draft brushes against my nape, and my stomach twists in horror. I whip my head around, expecting to find the shadowy figure of a guard behind me.

I'm alone.

Not trusting the silence and the desolate hallway, I scurry toward the front metal gates rising just a few feet away. They loom closer with every passing second, and my heartbeat doubles as I close the distance.

I can make it.

I can make—

A scream reverberates behind the walls of the bath chamber to my right.

It echoes deep in my chest.

Then it cuts off abruptly.

EIGHTEEN

The scream is a familiar darkness. I've felt its choking hands before, back on the foothills, while I cowered beneath the weight of a Nightwalker. It is the same one I heard my first night on the base—a deep, mangled cry that tore through the walls of my sleeping quarters.

In the village, it was the Nightwalkers we had to fear. Here, the guards are just as monstrous.

The scream erupts once more. Without thinking, I shove through the door of the bath chamber. I have no plan, no idea what awaits me on the other side. Still, I charge forward, the two stolen knives drawn in my hands.

Inside, a row of private stalls spill across the back wall, each one marked by a fence of metal partition. All are dark and empty, except for the stall tucked into the farthest corner of the chamber, angled away from the rest.

"No one can hear you, girl." The guard's voice echoes from the shadows, followed by a broken whimper.

"Please—"

"Shut up!" he growls, striking the girl so hard, her screams shatter every part of my senses.

I'm back on the foothills, writhing under the Nightwalker's touch. His fingers push past my lips. His hand roams freely, tugging at my waist beads.

I haven't had a dark skin before.

I knew what he planned to do to me then, and I know what the guard is planning to do now.

My blood runs cold. A bitter, poisonous rage, born from the pain and shame and guilt I've felt since that horrible night, pours through me. I sprint past the stalls, recoiling in horror at the sight of the guard's burly frame hovering over a trembling body.

With a grunt, I stab the knives into his back, twisting the blades as far as they will go. Warm blood gushes from the wound, streaking down my arms. The guard lets out a strangled cry and topples back against the partition wall. That's when I see the thick coils of black hair. The deep dark skin now marred with cuts and bruises. Nausea churns in the pit of my stomach as I stare down at Izara Makinde's sprawled form. Her swollen eyes, the vicious marks all over her arms. Her fatigues hang in torn, loose shreds, and blood trickles down her nose, pooling in the hollows of her neck. Her sobs echo in the dark, empty space. They slice through me, leaving me paralyzed.

The guard moans. I drop next to Izara, hoping to get her up before he regains consciousness. But he's too quick. He latches onto my braids and yanks me backward, flinging me across the chamber. My head knocks against the white tiles set into the walls. Pain lances through my skull, a sharp ache spreading up my bones. Sluggishly, I touch the back of my head, wincing at the smear of blood on my fingers.

"You stupid bitch!" The guard's roar thunders above the ringing in my ears. His eyes bore into mine, blazing with dangerous fury. A chill hurtles up my spine as he descends on me. I try to spin out of his grasp, but his large hand closes around my neck, pressing me against the wall. I grit my teeth, clawing uselessly at his fingers.

"Do you have any idea what you've done?" He tugs me up by my throat, dangling me a few feet off the ground like a fish caught on a hook. The spiced, earthy smell of taba still lingers on his breath. My feet scramble for purchase as I squirm in his grasp. His grip tightens, claws squeezing until my vision goes black and I'm choking for air. "Now you can both die together."

Stars burst before my eyes. I can't see, can't breathe, my rapid gasps the only sounds to rend the air.

Still, my lips part. The words slur over one another. "The only one dying here tonight is you."

His fist collides with my jaw, and blood sprays from my mouth. The pain awakens something within, a beast too wild for me to tame. This time, I don't try to cage it. I set it loose.

A familiar clamor rattles in my skull as àse explodes to life inside me. Like dry kindling catching fire, my entire body ignites. I shudder in the hands of the guard, the tremors growing as thick curls of smoke gather around me, a gray fog shrouding me in its warm embrace. When it clears, my arms are engulfed in flames, the red sparks licking hungrily at my skin. It clings desperately to me, a loyal servant promising to obey, to do my bidding if I allow it.

"Sc-Scion." With a gasp, the guard flings me across the chamber. He blinks furiously, his gaze locked on me as he scrambles for his gun.

I recognize the terror in his eyes. It is the same one the Night-walker wore moments before I turned him to ash. The sight thrills a darkness within. Now he will know how it feels to be afraid. To be constantly surrounded by fear, forced to live in a world of murderous creatures ready to persecute us at will.

Àse drowns me in its warmth, burying me in a flood of heat. My heartbeat thrums at a frenzied pace as the magic gathers inside, dark and vehement, a vicious storm that ravages every inch of my being. I bare my teeth and unleash my wrath on the guard. There is no sympathy in me when I throw out my hands, knocking him off his feet with a swirling ball of fire.

He releases a sharp cry, limbs twitching as he crashes against the tiled walls. Blood splatters from the gaping hole burned right through his belly, its metallic tang heavy in the air. But I'm not finished with him, not yet.

The guard lurches forward, his groans a weak, gurgling sound. Even on the edge of death, I want him to hurt more. *Feel* the torment the Nightwalker awoke in me after that night, *feel* the horror Izara must have suffered beneath his wretched weight. I want to break this monster apart, destroy every last shred of his being. I want him to know how it feels to be reduced to nothing.

Despite his wide, bloodshot eyes, I move toward him with the weight of a fury still begging to be freed. Another blast of fire consumes his splayed form, the flames sprouting like gnarled roots beneath his charred skin.

This time, when the guard crumbles to ash before me, I do not scream. I do not run.

All I can do is breathe as the rush of àse overwhelms my senses, dulling me to the magnitude of what I've done. Then the buzz starts to fade, leaving behind a wave of exhaustion.

I crash to the ground, shivering as heat slowly ebbs beneath my skin, freeing me from its hold.

Izara's sobs pierce the air, snapping me back to reality. I ignore the pain burrowing into my muscles, ignore the ache sitting heavy in my head, and rush to her side.

She's managed to prop herself up, leaning with her back against the partition, arms wrapped tightly around herself. Her entire body trembles as tears roll down her swollen cheeks.

"Hey." I crouch low and try to reach for her hand.

"Don't." She cringes away quickly, shrinking into the small space behind the latrine. "Don't touch me, please."

The pain in her voice wrings me apart. Even though the guard is dead, I feel the same anger and rage snap through me like a whip. The girl before me isn't the same recruit I met two days ago, the fierce soldier who killed a boy with nothing but her bare knuckles. She withers into a frail shell, every whisper of strength in her bones gone, diminished. I realize then why the guard handpicked her. It's what weak men do—try to break a strong woman.

"It's all right," I murmur, allowing her the space she needs. "I won't hurt you. You're safe, I promise."

"He—he grabbed me," she whimpers, "dragged me inside. I tried—tried to fight him off. But I couldn't. I couldn't."

More tears well in Izara's brown eyes, clinging to her lashes. *I tried to fight him off, but I couldn't.* The words are a knife in my chest. How many girls have whispered the same? How many have screamed and fought and bled in this very chamber without someone there to help them, to stop *him*? That bitter understanding crawls up my throat, leaving a sour taste on my tongue. It's not fair. It's not fair.

Gingerly, she raises a finger to her face, shuddering as she traces a path down her neck. I have no doubt she can still feel the hands of the devil on her skin. Painful brands that become scars. Scars that might heal and fade. Others that will remain long after. My own wounds are still fresh on my mind, a prison I cannot escape.

Though I know nothing of Izara, I feel the urge to help her. I had no one to turn to after my attack, and I've borne the crushing weight of my silence ever since. There's no reason Izara should have to suffer like I did.

When I was a child, Mama always taught me to fight for those too weak to raise their fists. Scream for those too afraid to find their voice. And stand for those too tired to rise on their feet. Izara must know she will get through this. No matter how long it takes, she will survive.

"He tried to break you," I say, working to keep my voice soft, but steady. "He tried to take away your strength, your power. But you are still standing, Izara. You are still strong. And you . . . you are unbroken."

She glances up at me, her face pulled into a frown. "How do you know that?"

For a moment, I don't know how to respond, caught in the memory of the night I arrived home from the foothills. Back then, I'd felt so much shame, wondering just how much of what took place was my fault. It was why I failed to tell Baba the truth. Why I chose to keep the horror to myself. But what happened that night was no fault of mine. I didn't do anything wrong. And I refuse to bear the burden of that shame any longer.

I am greater than my fears.

A deep breath rattles in my chest as I gather enough courage to speak.

"I know what it feels like to be robbed of something so precious to you. To feel helpless, broken, like you are not in control of your own body. These people—they thrive on taking power. Over our minds, our bodies, our emotions. They think because we are girls, that we are something to be preyed upon. They are wrong. We are not helpless; we are not broken. Despite what scars they leave behind, our bodies are our own. Everything we feel, everything we are, belongs to us and us alone. Yes, we are girls, but we are not prey. Tonight, *we* are alive."

When I finish, Izara and I stare at each other for a long time. She heaves a breath, slowly pushing life and strength back into her lungs. This time, when I reach for her hands, she doesn't pull away. Instead, she laces her fingers with mine and squeezes tightly.

I have no idea how long we sit there, wedged into a corner inside the stall, our hands clasped together in comfortable silence. Across the chamber, clumps of ash drift onto the ground, a layer of soot streaking the pearly white tiles.

"You're a Scion." Izara's wary eyes search my face.

I startle at her words, and my heart lurches at the realization that I've exposed myself yet again to a stranger. The secret I've kept for fifteen years now lies in the hands of another recruit, someone who could easily turn me in to the commanders and summon the pardon clause. That sends a flurry of panic through me. Because if Izara chooses to report me, she gets to return to her village. The pardon clause would free her from this hell. A gift even I might have a hard time passing up if I was in her position.

I've handed the girl a rope. Now my pulse races as I wait for her to hang me with it.

But instead of stringing me up, she cuts me loose.

"Don't be afraid," she murmurs as she untangles her fingers from mine. "I won't tell."

She shifts slowly, straightening her limbs in front of her. A ragged breath hisses through her teeth. I watch her all the while, my brows furrowed. "Why?"

"Because—" Izara glances at the door quickly, as if worried her next words might fall on the wrong ears. Then she mumbles, so low I almost don't hear her, "My twin sister is a Scion, just like you."

It's the last thing I expected her to say, and my mouth drops open. "You're . . . you're Yoruba?"

"Descended from Yemoja," she answers. "But Amiyah is the only one in the family to inherit the Orisha's magic."

Silence falls over us for a long moment as I try to imagine Izara's twin sister in my head. *Amiyah, a descendant of Yemoja. The ancient goddess of the sea.* Another Scion living in hiding, surviving in a world we're told isn't meant for us. I wonder to what lengths she must have gone to keep her identity a secret, how much her family must have sacrificed to shield themselves from the Lucis' brutality.

"I never thought I'd meet another Yoruba," I mutter at last, "especially here."

Izara turns to look at me, and her lips curve with the shadow of a smile. "There may only be a few of us," she says, "less and less every day, but we are out there, Sloane."

For the next hour, Izara and I clean the guard's blood off the bath chamber's floor, wiping away traces of tonight's horror. Now as his remains swirl in the murky waters of the latrine, I lift up a silent prayer to Olodumarè.

No one must ever discover what we've done tonight.

Both our lives depend on it.

NINETEEN

In the morning, the tower bells echo, and a deep, startling voice blares overhead.

"All Storm Squad recruits report to the training hall immediately."

My mind flashes to the memory of the night guard, and my whole body tenses as images of his burnt corpse come rushing back. Last night, when Izara and I scrubbed the floors clean and disposed of his ashes, it seemed the worst was behind us. Somehow, against all odds, we'd managed to survive the nightmare without getting caught. A miracle, if nothing else.

Now, as I weave through the halls of the training center, I can't ignore the questions trailing close behind. What if Faas knows? Is there a chance another guard, perhaps even one of the security cameras, caught us rushing out of the bath chamber last night? By gods, am I seconds away from being exposed? Dread coils in my stomach as I approach the grand doors of the training hall, my pulse stuttering at the thought of what I could be walking into. With a shaky breath, I shove the heavy wooden doors open.

As usual, it seems I'm the last of the recruits to arrive. At least Dane and the commanders are nowhere to be seen. In their absence, the squad murmurs freely, quiet conversations buzzing between some of the recruits. I'm not surprised to find Malachi at the center of the chatter, flanked by two rather short and stocky boys whose names I haven't bothered to learn. Every few seconds or so, Malachi's hand drifts to the new bullet chain draped around his long neck, a reward from Faas after his performance on the cliffs yesterday. He wears the ammunition proudly, his grin wide and wicked, with a new kind of swagger to match. Watching him is unsettling enough, and perhaps it's because, unlike me, Malachi looks to have found his place on the squad so easily.

I turn from him, and my gaze cuts to Jericho and Nazanin, who are busy whispering to each other, oblivious to much else. Judging by their measured voices and close proximity, I'm almost certain they're plotting their next move into the lieutenant's office. I should join them, lend myself to their schemes, especially after my own failure from last night. But one look across the room, and all of that flees my mind at once.

Only Izara stands apart from the crowd, silent and distant, a world away from the noise bustling around her. She hardly slept all night, too disturbed by the nightmares and lingering pains. Even now, I don't doubt what thoughts are holding her captive, chaining her to the memory of what she endured. The bruises on her face are still visible, though she's tried to hide the scars on her neck behind a raised collar. Just the sight of it makes me ache, and bitterness sours my tongue as I slowly make my way to her. Whatever happens today, I don't regret burning that guard to death last night. It's what he deserved. And I certainly hope his soul is suffering in òrun iná, the eternal hell that awaits monsters like him.

Izara glances up at me as I settle in next to her. She shifts uncomfortably, adjusting the collar of her uniform.

Even though the last thing I want to do is remind her of last night's horror, I clear my throat and force the words out. "How are you?"

A twitch in her jaw. "I'm fine" is all she says.

I can only nod, noting her unease. This isn't a conversation she wishes to have, and I don't blame her. Our shared memory says a lot more than we ever could.

She angles her body and regards me for a moment, her brown eyes full of questions. "You don't think there's a chance the commanders found out about . . . last night, do you?"

It's the same thought I've wrestled with since the bells rang. Yet without Faas or Caspian present, we have no way of knowing exactly why they've called this assembly, not yet.

Before I can respond, the screen tucked into the corner of the room crackles to life, and a young, fair-skinned woman with brown ringlets of hair materializes above us.

"This just in," the news anchor says. "We're coming to you live from King's Isle, where last night, an assassination attempt took place inside Castlemore."

Her voice carries through the training hall, punctuated only by the low hum that thrums among every recruit, all of us asking the same question: Is the queen dead?

The thought of an assassination attempt being carried out on Olympia seems like an impossible victory, especially in a fortified palace like Castlemore. Still, a quick sensation trills up my spine, and my heartbeat hammers as I wait for confirmation.

"Fortunately, Queen Olympia and the royal bloodlines are safe. No casualties have been reported."

The news, unpleasant as it is, burns its way down my throat. Up on the screen, the broadcast continues as the news anchor glances at the papers laid out before her, scanning each detail with unblinking eyes.

"Certain aspects of the palace security breach are still pending, but at this time, we can confirm that the underground terrorist group known as the Blades has been linked to the attack. This morning, three suspects were arrested following a raid at one of the rebel hideouts, and charges have been made under the authority of Her Royal Highness." At that, the woman's voice catches. She clears her throat, pauses, then continues. "As many of you know, the Blades have been previously tied to several other attacks on the bloodlines, including the Crown Conspiracy, which saw the assassination of King Conan Ascellus in 330 PME."

More murmurs from the squad ripple in the air. Even I can't help but furrow my brows. Though it isn't my first time hearing about the sudden death of the king, I had no idea that bastard was assassinated by his own people. Prior to today, none of us knew anything about the Blades or the existence of such an organization inside the walls of Avalon. To most people, the capital island is a paradise, an enclave away from the pain and suffering that plague the rest of us in Nagea. If the Blades truly exist, how have they managed to survive this long?

"Very little is known about this terror group," the news anchor says. "But today's raid is another major victory for the Avalon Defense Forces. Now we take you to Castlemore, where Queen Olympia is expected to address the capital."

A second later, the Lucis bloodlines appear on-screen, and my insides churn at the sight of them. Lord Sol is there too, and though the internal adviser's presence is familiar enough, something about his strange demeanor makes me wary all the same. Still, the bloodlines look terribly majestic from above, all thirteen of them seated and robed in their white-and-gold-damask capes, like a cluster of blazing stars plucked from the heavens.

But even stars die, don't they?

The training hall falls deathly quiet, and every single recruit stands frozen as if the queen herself has physically manifested inside the room.

From her place on the throne, Olympia Turais's eyes blaze, betraying no signs of fear despite almost being killed mere hours ago. In fact, the queen looks as if she's just carried out an assassination of her own, draped in a crimson aso-òkè so rich, it clings to her skin like blood. Today, she wears no crown of rubies on her head. Instead, a damask gèlè sits intricately over her raven curls, black pearls and red diamonds glinting from the woven headpiece. In my mind, I imagine clawing pieces of the Yoruba attire off her wretched body, and a flare of heat scorches beneath my skin. I dig my nails into my palms, forcing down my àse and the terrible pain that follows.

"Last night, a group of rogue assassins broke into my home." Olympia's voice pierces through the screen, so sharp my chest lurches as she speaks. "They came for me, and they failed. Today, you will bear witness to the execution of these cowards. The Lucis will not tolerate any crimes of treason. Not on our own soil."

The angle of the video shifts, revealing three men kneeling in chains across the throne room. Their faces are hidden beneath the black hoods thrown over their heads. A wall of masked soldiers stands firmly behind, the barrels of their rifles pressed against the suspects' skulls. Olympia gives the firing squad a slight nod. A loud boom bounces off the walls of the training hall as the shots ring out, each one a deep, violent echo. The assassins tumble forward, their blood pooling slowly across the white marble floor.

A sudden chill seeps into the room, and gooseflesh prickles my bare arms. I've never witnessed the Lucis execute one of their own before, and the public display only serves as a reminder of the monarchy's cruelty.

When the queen rises to her feet, her glare burns right through the screen, a savage thing that makes my blood pound.

"Let this be a lesson to those of you affiliated with this terrorist group," she says, gathering her long, sweeping gown behind her. "If you are a traitor to the throne, if you are found conspiring against the crown, rest assured, I will find you. And I will kill you."

The video fades, and Olympia and the rest of the bloodlines disappear from sight, leaving us to mull over her final threat. I don't doubt the queen means every word. After all, you can never underestimate the power of a crazy bitch.

Long after the broadcast ends, silence hangs over us like a scythe, felled only by the slamming of doors. Faas barges into the training hall, flanked by Dane and Caspian. All at once, the squad snaps to attention, our boots pounding against the hard concrete as the three of them coast to a stop a few feet away.

"By now, you must be wondering why we've called you here." As always, the commander's presence casts a dark shadow, his voice cutting like the sharp edge of a newly forged blade.

The panic I felt when I first entered the training hall jolts through me again. I don't understand. I was certain the commander gathered us here to watch the assassins' public execution on display. If Faas's assembly has nothing to do with the bloodlines' broadcast, then why are we here?

Izara glances at me out of the corners of her eyes. I meet her gaze for a brief moment, and I know we're both thinking the same thing. My breath catches in my throat the longer I'm forced to stare up at Faas, waiting for him to speak.

He says nothing for a while. Finally, when he does, his words ring out across the training hall, and my heart practically stops.

"As part of your training, each of you will be required to participate in two separate Cleansings before deployment," Faas announces. "Your first mission begins now. Wheels up in five minutes."

It's the last thing I expected, and my entire body goes numb.

Despite the safety belts holding me in place, I struggle to sit still inside the massive airship. Izara takes up the space next to me, her hands tight around the grip of her assault rifle. My own weapon rests between my legs, a grim reminder of the operation ahead of us. One by one, the other recruits settle into the empty chairs lining the arched walls, while the commanders, Dane, and a dozen more soldiers cluster along the tail end of the ship's cabin.

The mood inside the airship is somber, tinged with an undercurrent of unease. I keep my face pressed to the glass, watching the world fall far below us. Outside the window, carpets of thick, white clouds drift across the sky, the freshly oiled wings of the airship gleaming as they slice right through. Three days after being forced to fly in one of these giant metal birds, I didn't expect to be trapped inside another so soon. Now even the constant hum of engines does little to distract from the impossible mission we've been tasked to carry out.

A Cleansing. The never-ending genocide of every Scion and Yoruba caught living in Nagea. The last Cleansing that took place in Agbajé was only twelve days ago. That afternoon, as the bells pealed a warning signal of the soldiers' arrival, Baba bolted the front door as quickly as he could, and we took shelter in my bedchamber. He held me in his arms as soldiers stormed the village, our eyes closed in prayer as their boots thundered past our hut. The horror lasted several hours, until we could no longer hear the frightening echo of gunfire, until Baba was certain the soldiers weren't there for me.

He was right.

As we learned later that night, it was an eight-year-old boy the army came for. When they found him with his mother, they gunned them both down in the middle of the square.

Now I'm the one moments away from invading a village, the one who must take another Scion's life even though it's the last thing I want to do.

A sharp ache stabs at my rib cage, as it has since the commander informed us about the mission. Teo's death is still a raw, gaping wound in my heart. I can't add another innocent life to my list of victims. I won't survive that kind of guilt.

After what feels like an eternity confined in such close proximity to Faas and his army, the airship swoops low, and the sudden drop wrenches me from my thoughts.

Sunlight streams through the cabin windows. I squint my eyes against the bright light as I glance out the curved pane of glass. Èkó Sea gleams like stardust below, and a scattering of seven islands spread out across the water, each one fringed by a braid of golden sand. These are the Èkó Islands, the ancient kingdom once ruled by Yemoja and her descendants—Scions who could bend the open waters to their will.

Like back in Ilé-Ifè, a bronze statue of the Orisha hovers above the sea, overlooking all seven islands. A shimmering blue aso-òkè wraps around Yemoja's curved form, and a tangle of blue and white translucent ìlèkè beads adorn the goddess's sculpted neck. A calabash of sacred river stones sits in the palms of her outstretched hands. The sight of the monument tugs at my memory, reminding me of days long gone, when Mama and I would journey here to the fishermen's islands, trading our cassava bushels for fresh catches of mackerel and catfish.

My gaze slides along the familiar shorelines before lingering on the seven gallows erected high above the seawater. Back in the institution, we learned about the fall of the Èkó Islands, the last of the sixteen Ancient Kingdoms to be conquered. On the day Èkó was invaded, there was no crackle of bombs, no hailstorm of bullets. Instead, Scion men and women were hanged from the gibbets, young children submerged underwater and left to drown. It is well known that the seabeds of Èkó are littered not with sunken vessels and buried treasures but with the bones of my ancestors and the faint echoes of their cries. Even now, as I stare at the long-forgotten gallows, I can almost see the ghosts of those who hung from those nooses centuries ago.

A cold shudder passes through me as the airship begins its descent on Eti-Osa, the largest of the seven isles. The village rises to greet us, a cloud of sand rippling down its shoreline. By the time we land, the fishermen's market is blanketed in a brown haze, the dust settling once the airship screeches to a halt and the whirring engines slow to a purr. We march down the low incline of the ramp, stopping when we reach the center of the square.

An eerie silence chokes Eti-Osa. The same market that bustles with artisans and fishermen and the cacophony of screaming hagglers now stands completely deserted. In the absence of its merchants, the square looks more like a graveyard, haunted by the shadow of a place I used to know.

A gust of wind sweeps in from the sea, sending a spray of salty mist across my face. The putrid smell of fish guts clings to the air, and some of the recruits wrinkle their noses against it. I barely react to the familiar odor, my eyes locked on Faas and the crowd of soldiers before us.

"Storm Squad, you are now in Eti-Osa." Though the commander doesn't yell, his voice echoes down the abandoned square.

A drop of sweat crawls down my back, and I try not to fidget with the rifle in my hands. Next to me, boots shuffle against the concrete as many of the recruits try but fail to keep still. A thread of nervous energy weaves through the squad, but the soldiers stand in stark contrast. Their postures are set and rigid, their muscles wound tight as they await the order to charge through the village. Their duty is to kill, and that is what they will do.

"We recently received intelligence that there are five Scions residing on this island." Faas's gaze flickers down the line of recruits. My jaw tightens when his eyes fall on me. "Jonah of Nineteen Eti-Osa village. Magda, Twenty-Five . . ."

As he lists out the names and addresses of each target, I try to imagine the faces of the people the commander has marked for death. People with life and magic thrumming through their veins. People like me. I don't know whether they are young or old, what lives they've lived—if they've barely lived at all. Jonah could be somebody's father, Magda a mother, perhaps even a sister. These people have done nothing to earn the Lucis' fear. Nothing to suffer their wrath. Yet, here we are, seconds away from killing them as if their lives do not matter.

As if they are nothing at all.

" . . . and finally, Semi of Forty-Eight Eti-Osa village," Faas says of the last Scion, and his expression hardens. "Your mission today is simple: locate the targets and bring them back to me. I don't care what tactics you use. Find them. Every last one of them. Eliminate anyone who stands in your way. But I want these scum alive. Move in, now!"

TWENTY

We race through the streets of Eti-Osa, our guns held high, the team leader barking out orders ahead of us. Since the start of the Cleansing, Faas has divided the squad into five teams, one for each target on his list. Nazanin is the only other recruit on my team, and we sprint side by side, catching up to the two soldiers leading our charge.

The team leader hastens us down the twisting alleyways of the village. Every curve and turn makes my pulse throb, and a sharp pressure rams against my chest as we approach Twenty-Five Eti-Osa village. Magda's hut squats along the edge of the street, a small dwelling made of sandstone and rusted metal roofing.

As expected, the door is bolted shut, the deep cracks beneath sealed off with a fresh plaster of clay. For a common thief, Magda's house might seem impenetrable. But with a single round of bullets, the team leader throws the door wide open, allowing us entry into the hut.

"We have you surrounded," he shouts as he moves through the living room, his gun raised. I try to mimic his movements, my wide eyes darting, finger trembling on the trigger. "If you attempt to run, you will be shot. Arms up. Come out quietly."

He doesn't wait for a response and sets his stony eyes on me and Nazanin.

"Sweep the hut," he orders, voice flat. "Grab anyone you see. If they put up a fight, kill them."

The other soldier bounds off in an instant, disappearing into the darkness of the hallway with Nazanin in tow. I should join them in their search, force Magda and her entire family out of whatever hiding place they've crawled into. I am a soldier now, and I know what is expected of me. I cannot show fear. I cannot run. Yet, I dash down a separate corridor that leads into the kitchen, knowing it's the last place anyone would choose to hide. My palms sweat, slick against the wooden countertop. I grip the edges until my knuckles crack and blood drains beneath the skin, wishing to gods I could escape the torment of today's mission. I don't want to be here.

A shrill cry shatters the silence, the noise raw and jagged like shards of broken glass. I jump at the sounds of tables crashing and bed frames rattling as they drag along the earthen floor. My breath catches in my throat as I rush back to the front room, pausing at the sight of a young girl kicking and screaming to escape the soldier's grasp. She looks about my age, no more than sixteen or seventeen, with midnight skin and long strands of threaded hair.

"Mama!" she cries, and I assume this must be Magda. "Let me go!"

She wrestles with the soldier, even managing a punch to his jaw despite her small frame. But the man is thrice her size, with a grip that tightens around her like iron cuffs. He handles her like a broken doll, his force brutish as he slams her to the ground before the team leader. When she lets out another scream, my heart plunges to my toes.

Stay down, I plead silently. *Don't resist.* But I know that if I were in Magda's position, I'd fight just as much as she's doing now. I'd rather die fighting than surrender only to be killed later.

"Magda!" Behind the soldier, Nazanin shoves an older couple out from the hallway, herding them toward the center of the room. At the sight of her daughter pinned to the ground, the gray-haired woman wrenches her arm free and lunges forward.

"On your knees!" The team leader aims his gun at her head. She freezes on the spot. "Get on your knees, now!"

She takes one lurching step backward and falls to the ground next to her husband.

"Officers, my daughter is not a Scion." Her voice trembles as she rubs her outstretched palms together. "We are not Yoruba. Please, I beg of you."

In her desperation, Magda's mother denies her heritage as easily as she breathes, cutting a divide between who she is and who she must be in order to live. It's a feeling I know too well, one that grew and festered into a deep loathing I struggled with for many years. I believed my magic was ugly, that my identity was a weapon. Believed I was something to be feared, hated and persecuted. I prayed to Olodumarè to take back his power, rid me of this terrible curse. Make me normal. Make me whole. Make me like *them*. Make me worthy of life.

Even now, years later, a small part of that hatred still simmers somewhere deep inside, bitter as poison and just as deadly. It's what makes the mother's denial so difficult to hear. Because despite the sorrow in her words and the pain laced into them, I know this is the only choice she has to save her family.

"Officers, we've done nothing wrong." Beside her, the husband shudders, his sobs racking through his bent body. "If you must kill anyone, kill me. Please, just let my daughter live."

"Silence." The team leader's eyes flash. After a moment's pause, he turns to his mate and gives the command. "Cuff her."

"No!"

Magda's mother leaps to her feet but drops just as quickly. I wince at the blood soaking through her flimsy blouse, the sudden pop of gunfire ringing in my ears. Magda lets out a bloodcurdling scream that sinks deep into my bones.

"Toyosi!" Her father staggers forward on his knees, terror blanching his face as he leans over his wife's corpse. He shakes every inch of her splayed form, his hands wet with her blood. This time, when the shot goes off, I press a hand to my mouth to stifle my gasp.

"No!" Magda thrashes on the ground, straining against the shackles closing around her bony wrists. "Papa, Mama!" Again and again, she yells out her parents' names, begs the gods to bring them back. But if the gods hear her, they don't answer. With one final, blistering scream, she surrenders herself to the soldiers.

Hot tears burn my eyes. For a moment, I stand frozen, staring in shock at the two bodies lying across from me, warm blood oozing from their wounds. Bile rises in my throat, and suddenly the hut is the last place I want to be. I stumble back a step, then another, and another, until I reach the doorway. The soldiers are too busy with Magda, so they don't notice when I flee the room, running into the alleyway behind the hut.

An open sewer stretches along the edge of the path, separating the huts from the patches of wilted cornfield beyond. I lower myself before it and empty out the contents of my stomach, coughing and heaving until there is nothing left. My brain whirls, the horror inside the hut replaying over and over in my head.

"Sloane?" I startle at Nazanin's sudden presence. She steps out of the shadow, her ashen face twisted into a frown. "Are you okay?"

I wipe the bile from my lips and force a nod, my throat too raw to speak.

"I couldn't stomach it either." Nazanin's voice is strained as she settles in next to me, our backs pressed against the stone walls.

Neither of us speaks, consumed by the tragedy of what has just happened. Guilt perches itself over my heart, a bird of prey swooping in for the kill. Magda's family is dead, and I'm just as responsible as the soldier who pulled the trigger. Their blood is on my hands. I wonder what Faas plans to do with the young Scion girl. Something tells me she will most likely end up in the confines of the Lucis' research center, tortured and experimented on like a rat dragged from the gutter. I hope she dies quickly. When she does, I hope Magda finds peace in òrun rere with her parents.

"Recruits, is there a problem?" The team leader seems to emerge out of nowhere, his footfalls light on the sand.

Nazanin and I straighten at once. "No, sir!"

He glances back and forth between us, searching our eyes for cracks, anything that might hint at our disloyalty to the Force. I try to remain still under his lingering gaze, ridding my face of all emotion. If the team leader should sense our pity for the dead, I already know who his next bullets will pierce. When he finds nothing, he nods his chin in Nazanin's direction.

"You, come with me," he says before turning to address me next. "And you, report to Forty-Eight Eti-Osa village immediately. You'll find a team already in place."

When I arrive at the address, the first thing I see are the bullet holes peppering the door. With a slight shove, the wooden frame shudders, swings off its hinges, and collapses onto the woven rushes. Clearly, Faas's men have already swept through this hut, their target already acquired. Still, I peer into the front room, listening for the soldiers' gruff voices or any sudden movement.

Save for my heavy breathing and the cashew tree rustling in the wind behind me, the hut is strangely quiet. I turn to leave, but something in the air shifts. Beyond the hallway, sandals brush against the earthen floor, so faint I almost don't hear. I draw my rifle and slip inside the hut, creeping slowly toward the source of the sound. If the soldiers are not here, who is?

Without the sunlight pouring through the doorway, darkness shrouds the entire corridor. I press forward, my heartbeat quickening as I approach a bedchamber at the end of the path.

Across the room, two bodies stand silhouetted in the shadows of a tall dresser, their wide, watery eyes flickering between my face and the weapon in my hands. A little boy, no more than eight years of age, scurries behind an old man, hands clutching the fabric of the elder's floor-length robe.

"We—we thought you were gone. Please, don't take my boy," the man croaks, veins jutting behind the deep wrinkles of his weathered skin. "Please," he whispers again, and I'm reminded of Baba and his gentle voice.

The familiar grooves of his face flash in my mind, giving way to the last memory I have of him. I shove it away before it can truly take hold and glance down at the boy still hiding behind the old man.

Forty-Eight Eti-Osa village.

"You're Semi," I whisper, remembering the names Faas listed back in the square. *And this must be his grandfather.*

The boy peeks out from behind the folds of the man's robe and nods slowly.

"He is just a child." His grandfather's voice takes on an urgent tone, his pleas desperate as tears streak down his cheeks. "He's all I have left. My daughter, please have mercy."

He wraps an arm around Semi's shoulder, hugging him close to his side. I don't know how he kept himself and the boy alive this long. If the bullet holes on the door are any indication, then Faas's men must have visited this hut already. How did they hide from the soldiers?

I look back and forth between the two of them, with their hands laced together, chests rising and falling as they await my next move. It would be too easy to turn around, leave, pretend I never saw them. They escaped death already; it'd be too cruel of me to drag them back to his gate. But what if I'm caught? Just because I got away with killing the guard last night doesn't mean I'll survive this time.

"I'm sorry, I can't—" I struggle to get the words out, a lump lodged in my throat. "They'll know—"

Footsteps echo over the rushes in the front room. Semi and his grandfather turn toward the door, their eyes frozen in sheer terror. Even I can't shake the ice in my bones as the steps grow closer and closer with each passing second.

"Recruit, target acquired?" A familiar voice rings outside the bedchamber. "Recruit?"

My heartbeat drums in my ears as I spring out of the room and down the corridor, coming to a stop before my team leader. Giant red welts track down the side of his tan face, battle scars he most likely earned from Magda before he delivered her to Faas. I only wish the girl had drawn more blood.

"Where's the rest of the team?" he asks, searching the darkness behind me.

"Hut's empty, sir." The lie rushes out at once, heavy as it rolls off my tongue. Even though I'm aware of the danger of what I'm doing and the doom that awaits me if I'm caught, I decide in that moment not to turn Semi and his grandfather in. I can't let them suffer like Magda and her family. I steel my nerves and try to sound convincing. "The team was gone by the time I arrived, but I'm certain they have the target."

He strides past me, craning his neck to see beyond the corridor. A growing dread winds its way through my limbs, its roots sinking deep into my bones. I force myself to remain still, a pillar against the brewing storm.

"Very well." The team leader whirls at last, his finger coming off the trigger. "Move out."

He brushes past me and heads for the door. When I'm sure he's gone, I rush back inside the bedchamber, gut wedged in my throat. With nowhere else to go, Semi and his grandfather have taken shelter behind the dresser, their bent shadows stretching across the floor.

"Hurry." I wave the both of them out of their poor hiding place. "You only have a few minutes before the soldiers double back."

My voice is harried, fingers trembling in front of me. Gods, what the hell am I doing? Once the team leader realizes the last target is still missing, he'll return for another sweep of the hut. Will he discover I lied to him?

Not if you succeed, my mind answers in a frantic whisper. *Not if you manage to save them both.*

I will. I have to.

Steeling myself, I guide them toward the door. "Come, come."

"Oh! Bless you, child." The grandfather bows low, even though an elder his age should never thank me in such a way. I don't deserve his respect. I haven't earned it yet. "May Olodumarè bless you."

He drags Semi forward by his wrist, the two of them slipping past me into the corridor. A plan quickly forms in my head when we reach the front room. All I have to do is sneak them into one of the already ransacked huts. Since the soldiers have their target, they will have no reason to return there. Semi and his grandfather will be safe inside until Faas and his men evacuate the island. It is a flawed plan, a shaky one at best. With too many soldiers patrolling the streets of Eti-Osa, the odds are against us. But right now, this is all I have. It has to work.

A few feet ahead, Semi pitches forward and almost loses his footing. I reach out with my hand, grabbing his arm to steady him. The boy starts to shake, tremors reverberating through his body. Veins stand out beneath his deep, dark skin, and his pupils disappear entirely until only the whites of his eyes remain. He opens his mouth and words spill out.

> "Má se gbékèlé eni nàà tí ó pa ìyá a rè
> Ajagun tí wón dè, alàgbàá tu sílè
> Omo tí wón bí, bàbá gbà á là
> Bé è nípàse owó ò re ni omo èjè yó dìde
> Nígbàtí ejò funfun bá kú
> Tí òtá bá sì di èjè."

As Semi chants, my vision blurs. The world darkens around me, plunging me into a void of complete blackness. Shadows twist and morph before my eyes, faceless figures flitting and dancing like fireflies in the night.

A hand reaches out from the darkness, wrapping around my throat. Nails like iron claws dig into my neck, and a voice screams at me to let go. I release my grip on Semi's wrist. The darkness clears. I'm back inside the hut, fingers tracing up my throat, feeling for a hand that is no longer there. Heat blooms beneath my touch as magic races to my fingertips. My muscles strain as I fight back the surge of àse, pushing down against it. Pain lashes through my body like a whip, and I groan, fists clenched, waiting for the magic to wane.

When the last of the pain dulls, I bend forward with my hands on my knees, trying to catch my breath. At first, I don't understand what's happened. Shadows stir behind my eyes before they slowly start to fade away. That's when I see Semi sprawled on the ground, his body convulsing in a violent seizure.

"Semi, Semi!" His grandfather is on the floor beside him. He cradles the boy in his arms, tapping his cheeks gently until the spasms stop. Slowly, Semi peels his eyelids open. "Breathe, my boy. Breathe."

"You—you're a descendant of Orunmila," I stammer.

It's the only thing that makes sense, the only explanation my mind latches onto. The flitting shadows, Semi's chants spoken in the ancient Yoruba language. Though I've never witnessed an Ifá divination before, I'm almost certain what Semi received was a vision, a foretelling from Orunmila meant for me. Though why, I'm not sure.

"Please, don't hurt him," his grandfather croaks as I kneel next to the boy. "He meant no harm."

"What was it you saw?" I ask, staring down at Semi's sweat-soaked face. "The shadows—what were they?"

"He doesn't know. He has no idea what any of it means."

At that, the boy glances up at his grandfather. "I do, Baba."

His voice is so small, so pained, it trembles from the toll the divination took on him. His grandfather blinks, a deep crease between his gray brows.

"Orunmila wanted her to know."

"Know what?" I snap at them both, my patience wearing thin. "Tell me."

Semi's lips part. He pauses then, hesitant, scrutinizing my face with a certain wariness. His silence only makes me want to shake the message out of him. I don't have time for this. The longer we remain here, the more we're sitting ducks for the soldiers to find us. He looks up at his grandfather, and only when the man gives a nod does he start to speak.

"Trust not the one who killed their mother. The warrior they chained, the elder freed. The child they spawned, the father saved. Thus, by your hand shall the Blood Scion rise. When the pale viper dies, and foe turns to blood."

By the time he finishes, Semi and his grandfather are watching me expectantly. They wait for me to offer some kind of clarity to the divine message. I only meet them with a frown.

"What the hell does that mean?"

Semi shrugs. "I don't know."

He draws a ragged breath, forcing air back into his lungs. Already, he looks better than he did moments ago, the shivers no longer claiming his body.

For a moment, I allow myself to puzzle over his foretelling, searching my brain for some kind of interpretation, anything that might lend meaning to the words. But despite my best efforts, I come up empty. Perhaps next time, Orunmila should be more coherent with his prophecy. I drive the divination from my mind and jump to my feet. I don't have time for complicated riddles.

"Get up, both of you," I say, heading toward the door. "We've already run out of time."

They scramble behind me as I poke my head out of the hut, searching for soldiers that may be roaming the streets. In the distance, I hear the echo of boots stomping the ground, the only indication that Faas's men are well on their way.

"They're coming, so we have to hurry," I urge them both. "Stay close. Whatever happens, don't stop."

We cross the street and duck into an alleyway around the corner. I race up ahead, with Semi and his grandfather no more than two feet behind, following my orders without question. Sweat breaks out over my skin as I sprint up and down the meandering paths, making sure to keep a good distance between us and the soldiers pouring into the streets. Recruits march down the crossing in front of us, their guns deftly drawn. We flatten our backs against the stone walls and hold our breath. A knot tightens in my chest when I catch sight of Izara's round face, Jericho's lanky frame, even Malachi's unkempt bun. It seems Faas has dispatched the entire squad to join in the soldiers' search. All for an eight-year-old boy whose only crime is that he exists.

Once the last of the recruits shuffles away, I point to the crossing. Semi grabs his grandfather's hand, and we bolt forward. Magda's house is just across the street, the familiar metal roofing coming into view. My pulse thunders with each step, and a tiny bud of hope blooms inside me. By gods, we're so close.

I can get them there. I can save them.

The second we clear out of the alleyway into the street, Faas appears in front of me, flanked by Dane and Caspian. I halt in my tracks, my heart a drumbeat away from cracking as more soldiers and recruits creep out of the shadows of the huts.

A trap, my mind screams. I led us into a trap.

"Baba!" Semi flees behind his grandfather, using the man's robe to shield his eyes. He shakes so much on his feet, I wonder if he's on the verge of another divination.

"It's okay," his grandfather whispers, trying to soothe him even as death stares them right in the face. "I'm right here. I'm right here with you."

Despair sprouts at the fear in his voice, thorned and prickly, and I feel a deep, hollow ache where hope once bloomed. Around us, the soldiers form a tight ring, trapping us in a circle we can't escape. I watch them all, wishing to gods there was something more I could do, a way out of the mess I've gotten myself into.

But there isn't.

It's over. I failed Semi. I failed them both.

With eyes full of tears, I look back and forth between the familiar faces of my squad, but none of them meet my gaze for their own sake. Only Dane glances briefly at me, though his expression betrays nothing but his usual hard glare.

"You thought you could help them escape, didn't you?" When Faas finally speaks, his voice hisses out like a snake's, dripping venom.

"I—didn't—"

I shrink back as if I can escape his wrath, but the commander snatches me by the collar and yanks me forward. His fist slams against my jaw, so hard I taste blood in my mouth. I stagger on my feet, the ground dipping beneath me, but Faas won't let me fall, my uniform bunched tightly in his hand.

He lowers his gaze, and my limbs tremble at the flash of fury in those two pits. "I have no room for Sympathizers on my squad."

When he raises his gun to my face, the air whooshes straight out of me. *This is it. He's going to kill me.* A familiar wave of terror overwhelms my body, a cold numbness that seeps into every fiber of my being.

Just as the commander's finger slides to the trigger, Dane cuts in front of him.

"Not yet," the squad leader says. For a moment, they hold each other's gazes, and an unspoken understanding seems to pass between them. "She'll serve as an example for the others."

Even before he draws his own weapon, I already know what he plans to do. After days of warning, Dane won't miss the opportunity to finally get rid of me himself.

You don't have what it takes to survive this place. Perhaps the bastard was right after all.

His ocean eyes lock on mine, and I stare into a dark, rippling tide as he brings the gun forward.

"I told you to fall in line," he murmurs so only I can hear.

The last thing I see is the butt of his gun striking my forehead.

Then I'm drowned in the deep darkness.

TWENTY-ONE

Back in Avalon, Faas orders the guards to tie me to the whipping post.

I kneel on the ground with my face pressed against the pole, the shackles around my wrists holding me in place. Tears spring down my cheeks, blurring the line of recruits spread out in front of me.

The whole squad stands across the training hall, shoulders set and backs straight as they await my fate. While most of them watch with naked terror, Malachi doesn't bother to hide his glee. He grins openly from his spot, his smile wild and ravenous when he meets my eyes. I heave a sob and jerk my gaze away.

Across from him, Caspian and Dane are present as well, two hulking shadows always at the commander's side. The memory of the squad leader striking me with the butt of his gun is still sharp in my mind, a pain that won't soon fade. But I don't have the luxury of being bitter, not now, not with Faas seconds away from a decision.

"Today, Recruit Shade was caught attempting to help one of the targets escape." The commander's deep voice carries in the suffocating silence of the training hall.

The disgust in his words drags me back to Eti-Osa and the echoing sound of gunfire. Semi's screams rise above the din, the terror in his eyes seared into my memory forever. I couldn't save him then, and I can't save myself now.

A tremor rolls through me as Faas bounds forward, closing the distance between us in two quick strides.

"This recruit has not only betrayed the Force," he says. "She's also betrayed her squad. So I leave her punishment in your hands."

Behind him, two guards distribute coiled wires to each of the recruits, a thin menace of steel that gleams with a promise of the pain to come.

By gods. He's forcing the squad to whip me to death, a fate worse than a bullet to the head. This way, the commander gets to watch me suffer before I die. In that moment, my gaze cuts to the squad leader. This is exactly what he wanted, the public display of torture he advocated for.

She'll serve as an example for the others.

Fear cleaves my heart in two. I yank hard on my chains, jerking back against the pole. No matter how much I fight, the wretched thing doesn't budge. The cuffs tighten around my wrists. I can't escape this.

"Thirty lashes to start," Faas growls, and the air catches in my throat. "Let's go."

The squad rushes forward, circling like a pack of wild hyenas ready to devour me. Even though I can't see the faces of the recruits, I don't miss the sudden rise and fall of their chests, the slight tremble of their fingers. They stand on shaky limbs, each one afraid to make the first move.

"Now!" Faas's voice thunders through the room, matching the quick, broken rhythm of my heartbeat.

I shut my eyes and suck in a deep breath.

Thirty lashes. I try to steel myself. *It will be quick. For Mama. Survive for Mama.*

Malachi is the first to raise his whip. When it lands on my back, pain explodes down my spine. I release a mad, guttural scream, writhing as a second wire snakes from one side of my rib to the other. My whole body shudders, convulsing against the pole. The whips crack down, one after another, two at a time, all eight at once.

"This is what happens when you show mercy to the enemy." Faas's voice is merely a ripple in the maelstrom of pain. "I will not tolerate any Sympathizers on my squad. Keep going. No one stops until I say so."

Steel tears away at my flesh, cutting deeper toward my bones.

Blood splatters, the metallic scent heavy on the air. I hear nothing but my own screams as àse sears beneath my skin and magic scorches my insides. The familiar clamor makes my head spin, a roaring buzz that threatens to split me apart as great tongues of fire snap and crackle through my veins. Every thread of magic I've fought to keep from unraveling rips free inside me. I am a doll with seams barely stitched together, now coming undone. With a sharp cry, I pull inward, using the last of my strength to tamp down my àse before it flares into something more, something greater beyond my feeble control. Instead, the ache in my body multiplies, sharpening with every hard bite of steel wire.

Light bursts across my vision. My mind goes dark. I see everything and nothing at once. Suddenly I'm begging for death, pleading for the gods to take me away, take me now.

I want to die.

Mama, I want to die.

TWENTY-TWO

When I open my eyes, the first thing I see is a shadow hovering over me. My whole body burns as if it's been set on fire, every inch of skin scraped raw from steel. I can't see the scars, but I feel the giant mess of welts on my back, searing deep into my spine.

I blink in and out of existence, and for a moment, I wonder if this is how it must feel to die. If I'm dead, then I hope my soul finds rest in òrun rere. I hope Olodumarè can rid me of my sins, cleanse me free of the blood that stains my hands, and welcome me into the peace of the afterlife.

"Sloane?"

A low murmur pulls me away from the void and brings me back to my senses. With as much strength as I can muster, I force my lids open. Slowly, the room materializes around me, and the shadow takes form. I find Izara perched on the edge of my bunk, staring at me with wide, weary eyes.

"What happened?" The words come out in a ragged whisper, hissed through clenched teeth.

The pain eats away at my mind, making it impossible to think beyond the memory of steel wire ripping apart my flesh. I don't know how I ended up back in the barracks, how much time has passed. A few hours—perhaps a day or two. Izara is quick to fill in the gaps.

"The guards left you in the hallway a few hours ago," she says. "I carried you inside and tried to clean you up with some bitter leaves I found growing behind the building."

The earthy smell still lingers in the air, and a blur of images squeezes through the fog in my mind. I see Izara leaning over me, rubbing the green leaves between her deft hands. I hear the echo of my own screams as she kneads the crushed herbs along my back, letting the extract seep into my wounds. Izara's pleas rise above my cries, begging for me to remain still, take the pain, stay alive.

"Thank you," I manage, because without her, there's a chance I'd be dead.

With a nod, she squeezes a bloody rag into the bucket of water at her feet. "The scars should heal fine. But the burns . . ." Her gaze slides up my outstretched arm, and her voice trails off.

I glance down to see what's caught her attention, wincing at the row of bloodred blisters pocking my arms. The memory of àse scorching my skin makes me shiver.

These weren't caused by steel, I realize, and a jolt of horror goes through me. These are burns, painful brands forged by my own fire.

"You're suppressing it, aren't you?" Izara looks at me, a knowing expression on her face. "Amiyah used to cough up buckets of water whenever she tried. It'll only get worse."

"I know, but without the iyerosun tea—"

"You have no way of pushing your magic down," she says softly. "And there are no more herbs left in your system."

I swallow around the bitter lump in my throat. In truth, the three days without Baba's àgbo have left me at the mercy of my àse. The pain is constant now, each day worse than the last, an excruciating torment I feel deep in my marrow. But even that seems small compared with the agony of being burned from the inside out, knowing there's nothing I can do to save myself.

I examine the blisters on my arms once more, the flesh around them too swollen to touch. Is this what I have to look forward to in the coming weeks? Thick welts and raw brands marring my skin as àse consumes me from within?

Now more than ever, I wish there was a way I could get to Baba. He would know what to do. He could save me from this pain. But my grandfather is a world away from me, a lifeline much too far to reach.

A long dreadful moment passes before Izara speaks again.

"Perhaps you could try harnessing it." The words rush past her lips. "Amiyah spent her whole life hiding her àse, just like you. Mama was afraid of what would happen if the guards found out. But I saw what it was doing to her. Suppressing magic takes a toll. Amiyah would be dead if she hadn't learned to harness her àse." Judging by the hope shining in her eyes, I can tell where this is going. "You could do the same. I . . . I can help you."

Though I'm sure she means well, I shake my head all the same. "If we get caught, they'll kill us both."

After today, Faas will have every reason to keep a closer eye on me, and I know better than to underestimate the commander again. Not when he already thinks I'm a Scion Sympathizer. Faas Bakker may have thought me weak and unworthy of his squad before, but if he suspects any more defiance, I know that bastard won't hesitate to kill me. Whatever happens, I can't drag Izara into my mess. I don't want her blood on my hands.

But the girl only pushes on. "You risked your life to save mine," she whispers, and at the reminder of last night's horror she traces a finger over the day-old bruises on her neck, massaging their rough edges. "Consider this my thank-you."

For a moment, I try to imagine what it would feel like to rid myself of the pain that comes from always pushing my àse down. In the ten years since it manifested, I never learned what it means to truly embrace this magic, to embrace myself. To feel whole for once, and not broken. It would be too easy to accept Izara's offer, but trapped behind these walls, surrounded by monsters with enough bullets to tear me apart, the threat of being discovered is just too great.

"It's too risky," I mutter into my blood-soaked mattress.

Beside me, Izara heaves a sigh. "I know you're afraid," she says, "but you can't put out an inferno by hiding the flame, Sloane. Without control, without resolve, you will be destroyed."

Her voice is low and heavy, the warning clear as day. It's all I can do to remain quiet, jaw tight, shutting my mind against her words. Izara may not understand what's at stake, but I do. I have no choice. I must bear these scars if it means living to see another day.

In my silence, Izara runs a wet rag across the floor, wiping away the small puddle that's gathered there. Fresh blood drips between her fingers as she gives the cloth a good wring, before tossing it next to the bucket full of dark brown water. She seems oddly at ease as she cleans through the mess, and I wonder how many times she must have done the same for her sister. Dimly, I'm reminded of myself and Luna. The many nights I spent huddled next to her in the bath chamber, scrubbing at the splotches of red blood, begging the gods for a miracle to save my best friend. Though our scars are not the same, I feel the pain just as deeply.

"Hey," Izara murmurs when she's done, glancing up at me once more. "I'm sorry if it seems like I'm pushing you. I guess after seeing what Amiyah went through, I can't imagine another Scion suffering just as much, or worse."

I shake my head, brushing off the apology with a pained but rather genuine smile. "It's fine," I assure her, "and you're right. It's just . . . well, I wish so many things were different."

She nods slowly, her solemn eyes locked with mine in shared understanding. I shift beneath her gaze, trying to sink into the comfort of the care she's provided, but my wounds are far too raw to feel anything but sudden bouts of pain and nausea.

I'm still struggling for a better resting position when Izara quietly asks, "What do you remember about the night your magic awakened?"

I look up to see her still staring, watching me, her thick, full brows drawn into a deep furrow.

"Why do you ask?" I blink back at her, ignoring the flash of old, shameful memories that make my skin crawl. Still, Malachi's screams ring in my ears, shrill and piercing, another cage of torment I cannot escape.

As if sensing my unease, Izara lays her hand against mine in a gentle gesture.

"What I meant was," she corrects herself, "was there a ceremony of any kind? A scarification ritual performed by your mother, perhaps?"

Confused, I meet her with a frown of my own. "I don't understand—"

"The Ancient Kingdoms called it àmì-orí," she tells me in a low, careful tone. "The marking of the head."

She pauses then, searching my face for a flicker of recognition, and it occurs to me that this is perhaps a tradition I should already know. Some ancient rite of passage taught to every Scion child. For me, it's yet another reminder of everything the Lucis robbed me of.

When I don't respond, Izara leans forward, her ringed fingers light on my scalp.

"In the past, long before the invasion," she says as she parts the dull lines between my braids, "every Scion of age would gather at the shrine, and deep incisions were cut into their scalp to anchor their àse to their blood deity." Finally, she pulls away and settles onto her knees, her attention turned back to me. "Incisions *you* don't seem to have."

"Why? What good is it supposed to do?"

"Because our ancestors believed àse can only be harnessed in a spiritual balance," she goes on to explain. "The same energy that flows through you, flows through the ancestors, to the Orishas, and all the way to Olodumarè. They called it odò àtòrunwá. *The divine current.* But that balance is made possible only when a Scion's magic is anchored to their blood deity. Without it, àse remains unbound. Wild and untamed. A magic too difficult to control, much less suppress."

It's like peering through a hole in the dirt, one deep enough to glimpse the bones of a culture buried far, far beneath. Cracked and brittle as they are, with their mottled edges and staccato rattle, in that moment, I am a child again, standing beneath the awnings of a guava tree, piling the remains of my spirituality close to me. As always, the knowledge of it wounds deeply; of course it does. Because if Izara's words are true, if magic was this *thing* that needed to be leashed, then it means I've lived the past fifteen years fighting a battle I was never going to win.

"How do you know so much about this?" I ask her, hoping to stanch the bitterness that bleeds through me.

"Mama." With that, Izara's expression turns grave. "As terrified as she was, àmì-orí was the only ritual she agreed to do. Not that she had much of a choice. There was a lake that sat behind our hut, and Amiyah and I used to spend hours swimming in it when we were little. On the night her magic manifested, Mama and I found her drowned at the bottom of the lake, which had been completely dried up."

For a second, she looks barely able to keep herself together, though she tries to mask it with a quick, shuddering breath. Even I can't hide the tremor of shock that passes through me. I'm no stranger to the dark underbelly of what it means to be a Scion, to possess this much magic and be at the mercy of a power far beyond my control. My own awakening branded me a murderer and left me with far too many scars to count. Despite the horror of what Amiyah went through, it's a small comfort to know she never has to suffer that kind of guilt.

Across from me, Izara clears her throat. "That was the night Mama marked her," she continues, and a tiny bit of warmth returns to her eyes. "Anchoring Amiyah's àse to Yemoja was the only way she knew to keep her alive. It calmed her magic for a little while, helped ease her pain, and I think it can do the same for you."

This time, I swallow any hesitation lingering on my tongue, allowing myself a moment to truly mull over her latest offer. Izara is right; I know she is. The burns on my arms are proof of that. Without the balm of Baba's herbs, I can no longer afford to walk this path alone. Not if I want to survive the rest of my days here.

"I should warn you, though," Izara adds, as if she can already sense my decision. "It's only temporary. Without proper training, the spiritual anchor could weaken and break. So you'd still have to learn to harness your àse. But this—this could buy you some time."

"How much time?"

"Enough to get through the next week or two."

A week isn't much, but even a few days of respite is better than nothing. "And this ritual," I say, "you really think you can perform it? *Here?*"

Izara touches a hand to the white-tipped bullet dangling from her neck and heaves a breath. The nod she gives me is true and certain, her conviction even more so.

"I know what we have to do."

The anticipation of it rolls through me, and a spark of hope kindles in the pit of my stomach. For the first time in my life, I dare to let it blaze freely.

Then a rapid tap comes to the door. Without warning, two figures dart inside the quarters, shutting the door just as quickly behind them.

Izara and I both jump, startled by Jericho's and Nazanin's sudden presence. The boy shouldn't be here and he knows it. Especially when the barracks officer explicitly forbade us from visiting any unassigned quarters. Yet, despite all the trouble he could find himself in, it's as though it's impossible for these two to be apart. I almost roll my eyes.

Izara draws a thin blanket over my arms, covering the blisters to avoid prying questions. The shifting motion sends a stab of pain through my entire body. I bite back the scream clawing up my throat, releasing slow, steadying breaths instead.

When the shock passes, my gaze flickers from Nazanin to Jericho. "What are you doing here?"

While I do not hold my squad responsible for what the commander forced them to do, the punishment I suffered at their hands is a horror I won't soon forget. A memory I know will haunt me for some time to come.

"We thought you might be hungry." Nazanin shoves a hand into the pocket of her uniform and removes a crushed slice of meat pie wrapped in clear plastic.

Though it's only been a day since Faas suspended my rations, I feel the deep, hollow ache of hunger, and my belly rumbles at the sight of the doughy pastry. Thankfully, only Izara is close enough to hear.

Across the room, Jericho's gaze slides over me, warm brown eyes fixed on my welts. His expression seems pained as he takes in the ghastly bruises, and when he catches my eye, he offers a sad smile.

"It was Naz's idea," he adds, lowering himself onto her bunk.

That draws a frown from me. "I thought you hated strays."

Nazanin only shrugs. "Sometimes I enjoy feeding them."

I regard the girl for a brief moment, unsure what to make of her. I've kept the same friends my whole life. Now, tossed into a world full of strangers, I struggle to read the people around me. Two days ago, Nazanin made it clear we were simply allies on a shared mission, nothing more. Then earlier today, she barely spoke a word to me behind Magda's hut, the two of us caught in a storm of terror we couldn't escape. Now she's risking the commander's wrath to bring me food?

I don't understand. But before I can press her further, Izara shifts, making her presence known.

"How did you get the food?" She studies the pie in Nazanin's hands with open curiosity. "The mess is closed."

"We stole it." Jericho doesn't even bother to lie as he leans back on the cot, arms spread out above his head.

"Aren't you afraid of getting caught?" Izara sounds genuinely intrigued.

I don't blame her. It takes guts to steal from the mess after hours, especially with so many guards on patrol. But after last night's stakeout, I'd expect nothing less from these two. Either Jericho and Nazanin are experts at their craft or they must be plain stupid.

"We're very good at what we do." Nazanin's smile is wide and just as smug as she is, but it's enough to make Izara chuckle.

It's my first time hearing her laugh, the dimples deepening in her cheeks. It doesn't last long, but the sight loosens an ache in my chest, plucking away a thread of my pain. Then she glances at my back and rises to her feet, the small bucket swaying in her hand.

"I'll go get a fresh pail for your wounds," she says, crossing the room swiftly.

Just as Izara reaches the door, Jericho straightens back up. "Would you—uh—like some help?"

"Sure," she murmurs, and the two of them exit the room together.

When the door shuts behind them, Nazanin takes up Izara's old spot, settling down at my side. The meat pie is still in her hands, but I can barely move my head, let alone lift a finger. So I gawk at the food, wishing to gods there was enough magic to somehow will it inside my mouth.

As if Nazanin can read my thought, she unwraps the plastic sheet and holds the pastry up to my lips. I open my mouth to take a bite, but pause, glancing at her freckled face.

"It's not poisoned, if that's what you're thinking." She chews off a piece of the pie and moans for extra measure. "See?"

I roll my eyes before sinking my teeth into the snack. The flakes melt on my tongue, chunks of seasoned meat and sweet potatoes filling my mouth. I close my eyes, savoring the taste far longer than a person should. Truly, a tremendous change from the starvation I've had to endure since yesterday. I devour the pie in three big bites, my stomach growling long after I'm done.

"Thank you," I mumble to Nazanin, grateful I won't have to go to bed hungry and in pain yet again.

A hush falls over us as she brushes the crumbs off my bloodstained sheets. As I stare at her, she raises her chin and returns my gaze. Her eyes narrow into something bitter and at once aching.

"When I was six, I was caught trying to steal from a merchant in the marketplace." She fidgets with her hands, dark eyes searching the lines of her palms. "I'd been starving for a week. I didn't see the officers patrolling the market that day. Two of them grabbed me before I could run, and they began to whip me. Again and again and again. I still have the scars to show for it."

A weight presses against my chest at the thought of a little girl suffering the same agony I did, forced to brave the cold bite of steel wire as it tears apart her skin. I don't know how Nazanin survived that kind of pain so young, but I think I am beginning to understand why she's here with me tonight.

"I don't have a problem with you, you know?" When I arch my brow, a small smile pulls at her full lips, a crack in her usual sly exterior. "It's just . . ." She struggles for the right thing to say, pausing once to collect herself. "Getting inside Archives Hall is very important—to Jericho. Nothing can go wrong."

I weigh the conflict warring on her face, gauging it, trying to read between her words. Finally, it dawns on me.

"You want something from there, too, don't you?"

The sudden tick in her jaw is a betrayal. Quietly, Nazanin twirls the plastic sheet between her fingers, and the longer it takes for her to respond, the more certain I am of my suspicion.

"I never knew my family." Her tone is hoarse and fragile, allowing me a peek at the girl behind the mask. "Back in Shaaré, my parents were black market traders. I was seven months old when the market was raided and they were both killed."

It's the last thing I expected to hear, and it sends a ripple of sadness through me. After all, I, too, know what it feels like to lose a parent to a black market raid, a pain we share. One that seems to have festered inside us for many years. But even though the Lucis took my father, at least I had Mama and Baba to turn to. Both were there for me when I was growing up, taking pieces of my heart and offering me all of theirs in return. Nazanin, like many other children in Nagea, were never given that chance. Instead, the Lucis ripped away her family and made her an orphan before she could even learn to crawl.

"I'm sorry" is all I can manage, gulping down the ache in my throat.

Nazanin nods. "They took my brothers, too," she whispers softly. "One was shipped off to the Itakpe mines, the other to the Gbomosho plantations. I spent years searching for a way to get them out, and . . . and I think I finally found one."

"How?"

With a turn of her head, she casts a glance sideways, toward the closed door. When she looks to me again, her eyes sharpen, taking on a hard edge. "There's a file inside Archives Hall containing a list of every major trade route between the Lucis and the free nations. If I can get it to the Black Wolf—"

"Who the hell is that?"

"Leader of the largest smuggling ring in Shaaré." She frowns, as though this is information I should already know. "She controls an underground network of weapons trafficking across Nagea. Anyway, I made a few runs for her in the past, whenever I needed to make a quick keddi. Now she's promised to help free my brothers if I bring her that file."

I've never heard anything about the Black Wolf or a smuggling organization this size running anywhere in Nagea. Even small, local smugglers like my father were a threat to the Lucis, and the monarchy is always quick to execute anyone caught. If the commanders should discover the truth about Nazanin's involvement, or her plans to steal the Lucis' trade routes from Archives Hall, certainly, she will be marked a traitor and dragged before the firing squad like the assassins from today's broadcast. But, for the promise of her brothers' freedom,

Nazanin will risk everything, even her own life, to get her family back. I know what determination looks like, and as I stare at her, I see that same ember burning wild in her brown eyes.

Still, so much of her plot seems ill-conceived, and I can't help but puzzle over the details in my head, trying to make sense of it.

"Even if you manage to get the file," I say to her, "how do you plan on returning to Shaaré?"

She inhales sharply and sits back on the thin foam of my cot, her head rested against the wall. "You heard what Faas said this morning. We have one more mission to carry out before deployment. The day of the second Cleansing, I'm—"

"You're going to desert." And just like that, the last piece of her scheme falls in place. I release a breath, eyeing her with quiet understanding, my own plans to escape to Ilè-Orisha lurking in the corners of my mind. "Does Jericho know?"

At that, she purses her lips, paling a little before me. "No, not yet. Not until he has to."

Again, her quick gaze darts to the door. I realize then she's checking to make sure Jericho hasn't returned yet. I don't know why she's chosen to keep this a secret from him. Perhaps she fears what the boy she loves might do with the truth. Whatever the reason, it's enough to set Nazanin on edge, her nerves fraying at the seams.

It's a feeling I know too well, having gone through the same with Teo. I can only hope Nazanin and Jericho are promised a fate better than the cursed one that took my heart.

"Hey." Despite my pain, I slide a hand over hers, drawing her attention away from the door. She glances down at the sudden gesture. When her eyes fall on me, her expression changes, softening into something delicate. It hurts too much to smile, but I force one onto my cracked lips anyway. "We're getting inside that damned hall, and—I think I might know a way."

Slowly, the color returns to her face, and she grins. "I'm listening."

"A Lucis disguise." I hold her gaze across the bed, one brow raised. "The guards' uniforms should serve us well, don't you think?"

I don't bother to share any details of last night's failed attempt. None of it matters now, not to Nazanin anyway. She's clever enough to follow the trail, picking her way through the specifics of what I'm proposing.

She nods once, her smile sharp and gleaming against the white of her teeth. "Looks like we're going to need some extra uniforms."

TWENTY-THREE

It takes ten days for my wounds to heal. The pain never truly fades, though, and every day, I train through the agony, careful not to draw attention to myself.

The squad is only as strong as its weakest soldier, Faas yells after whipping a male recruit for failing to complete the morning's Physical. He locks another in solitary confinement for five brutal days, without food or daylight, when the boy is caught stealing from the armory. Even Culture and Theory starts to eat away at our minds, as the lieutenant forces us to watch endless footage of Shadow Rebels in captivity.

We sit very, very still in the dim light of the classroom, with Caspian pacing between the rows, a loaded gun in his gloved hand, all of us watching as mutilated bodies of young men and women flash across the black screen. Prisoners hung from the ceiling by the skin of their toes, bled out like gutted swine. Repeated stabbings and drownings during interrogation. Torture after torture, the lieutenant forces us to chant *Edictus.*

By flesh and by bone, I will raise death unto them who dare defy the will of the throne,

In this, I will not fail. . . .

Though my insides scream, I don't dare fumble my words. Not this time. Not even when a young Rebel is bound and beaten for hours on end, every inch of her fingernails pried off with a pair of hot pincers.

Like the rest of my squad, I try to appear dutiful through it all. Unfazed by the Lucis' cruelty. Obedient and willing. Their docile little soldier.

Even when the training drills force my scars open, all I can do is hide my grief and pray no one notices the blood dripping onto the concrete floors. On those nights, I lie awake in bed, writhing as pain stabs through the gashes on my back.

When I do fall sleep, my nightmares are plagued by faces of the dead. They've become my family. I see so much of them, their absence wounds just as much as their presence does.

Some nights, Magda lies on the rushes inside her hut, guts spilled by my own rifle. Other nights, Semi traps me in an endless vision, chaining me to the twisting shadows of his prophecy. Faceless figures slither and coil around me like a bed of black mambas, their voices a hiss in the choking darkness.

Trust not the one who killed their mother. The warrior they chained, the elder freed. The child they spawned, the father saved. Thus, by your hand shall the Blood Scion rise. When the pale viper dies, and foe turns to blood.

The chant clings to the edges of my mind, shoving me deeper into the captivity of Semi's vision. I buy my freedom with two bullets. One for the boy, and another for myself.

Worse are the nights I spend with Teo, the two of us seated at the top of our village's half-pipe. Our wooden wheelies roll with abandon down the ramp, colliding when they reach the bottom. Neither of us moves to retrieve them. Teo's head rests on my shoulder, his heart thudding weakly in my hands. I carved it out. I know because the dagger still lies in the small space between us. Now his blood runs freely between my fingers, a metallic current cutting a twisted trail down my arms.

I startle awake, drenched in a puddle of sweat. *An illusion*, I breathe into the night. An apparition come to torment me. Then I glance down at my hands and see they are still stained a deep crimson.

I can't tell what's real and what isn't anymore. Am I a soldier or a child? Am I guilty? Am I innocent? I don't know. I don't know. I don't know.

So I stop sleeping.

Despite my stiff limbs, pounding pulse, and bloodshot eyes, I convince myself the exhaustion isn't so bad. The mission to Archives Hall provides enough distraction. Though, as it turns out, stealing three sets of the guards' uniforms is far more difficult than any of us anticipated. Especially with the wave of officers constantly patrolling the grounds at every hour. Even with Nazanin's and Jericho's best efforts, our progress has been painfully slow.

At least preparations for the àmì-orí come a bit easier, and it doesn't take long before Izara tells me we have everything we need to begin the ritual.

Tonight, I lie facedown on a stack of wooden crates, locked inside a bath stall, as she works a razor through my hair. The cornrows Luna braided before I left Agbajé have since been taken out. Now the fine teeth of the blade scrape along my scalp, quick rasps of metal against skin, severing each wiry strand from its root.

Outside, the curfew bell tolls, and guards parade the dark corridors of the barracks, their booted steps echoing ever so slightly beyond the bath chamber. If any of them should discover Izara here with me tonight, I don't want to imagine what punishment Faas would inflict on us both. The scars on my back still ache with the ghost of steel wire, despite the fresh poultice of bitter leaves smeared over the scabby flesh. Now, with the scarification ritual a few minutes away, all I can do is focus on the night ahead, reminding myself that I made the right decision.

Izara's presence brings me much-needed comfort, even as she drags the blade farther down my nape in quiet concentration. She kneels with her back against the partition wall, ignoring the droplets of water seeping through her fatigues from the nozzle overhead. Her practiced hands move in perfect, sweeping arcs.

In all my years, not once have I ever cut my hair so low, let alone considered the thought of going bald. But as she told me all week, it's the only way the ritual can be performed. Part of me wants to ask what Orisha came up with that rule. But I don't argue. If a few inches of hair is all that stands between me and relief from my àse, it's a small price I am willing to pay.

Above me, Izara sets the razor on the wooden edge of the crates. I fight the urge to run my hand over the bare skin, breath catching when I feel the soothing warmth of hot water on my head. With a bowl in one hand and a damp cloth in the other, she cleanses me of all spiritual impurities, scrubbing away anything that might prevent the anchoring of my àse. She's much too careful with me, her touch featherlight as she rinses me off and pats my head dry with a clean rag.

I open my eyes, blinking hard until my vision slowly adjusts. Izara leans back on the tiled floor across from me, her brown skin glowing like pearls in the darkness. For a moment, she regards me with a tilt of her chin, examining her own handiwork. Then, bending forward, she combs through the items on the ground, fishing for the broken mirror she borrowed from Nazanin earlier that evening.

Her gaze is warm and steady as she holds the shard to my face. "What do you think?"

I gape at my own reflection, pausing at the sight of the girl staring back at me. I am frail and starkly bruised, with bones too jutted from starvation and skin a deep, cruel purple. Yet, beneath the maze of scars, a new spark of ember gleams in my eyes, twisting my features into something both feral and fiercely alive.

I grin for the first time in weeks. "Thank you."

Izara smiles, too, as she lowers herself onto the already cramped floor, legs folded and tucked underneath. Two wooden bowls sit in front of her, one filled with a tiny bit of water, the other dry and empty. At least a dozen shell casings are strewn messily at her feet, along with a pair of rusted pincers lying dully in the dark. Even though I know Nazanin had a hand in where most of these came from, I'm still not sure what Izara plans to do with them.

She unclasps the thin silver chain around her neck, letting the bullet pendant fall between her legs. Her hand strays to the tool next, fingers tight around the metal handle as she locks a shell casing between its jaws.

"What are you doing?" I frown over her bent form.

"I need to extract enough iyerosun powder for the ritual," she murmurs, almost to herself.

I open my mouth to ask how exactly she plans to do this. Last I knew, the iyerosun Baba brewed into my tea was found only on the black market. And even then, it was nearly impossible to obtain.

"There's a reason Faas gave this to me our first day here." Izara speaks before I do. Her breath rattles out, a low hissing sound, as she grips the bullet in one hand and slips the shell casing over it. "Do you remember what he said to me after that training?"

I watch her in silence, thinking back to the body of the boy lying on the ground of the training hall. There's no denying the fierce pride that burned in Faas's eyes that day. Izara had killed another recruit. She'd done what the rest of us couldn't, and for that, her reward was a shiny white-tipped bullet. A destructive little weapon to feed her violence.

"I believe you'll find use for it on the Sahl." I echo the commander's words, though I'm still not sure I understand what she's getting at.

Izara nods from her place on the floor. "That's because ammunition of this kind is meant to be used against the Shadow Rebels," she tells me, working the pincers back and forth with such steely-eyed focus. "They're meant for Scions."

The bullet snaps off a moment later. Satisfied, Izara sets it aside. She tilts the casing just enough to dump the gunpowder into the water bowl. Almost immediately, fine grains of white powder swirl to the surface, crystallizing as they separate from the rest of the black liquid.

There's only one substance I know that does that when mixed

with water. My eyes widen the second I realize what I'm staring at.

"Is that—"

"Iyerosun." Finally, Izara glances up at me. At the look of confusion on my face, she starts on an explanation. "During the invasion, once the Lucis saw that the Ancient Kingdoms depended on the powder to nurture their fields and heal their sick, they burned down every Irosun tree across Nagea."

Of course. The story is familiar enough. I've heard it many times from Baba before, especially on days he struggled to find a smidgen of the powder in Agbajé.

"Then the Lucis later discovered that iyerosun, when laced with gunpowder, can be used to suppress a Scion's magic long enough to kill them. So they planted new trees." Izara sneers as she scrapes the pale crystals into a dry bowl. "Now barrels of iyerosun are harvested at the Gbomosho plantations every day, packed into these white-tipped bullets, and shipped off to the Sahl army."

My stomach churns at the implication. Though truly, I shouldn't be surprised. After all, I know, just as well as Izara does, that the Lucis' history is steeped in taking what was once sacred to our people and turning it into a weapon meant to destroy us.

Izara grinds the crystals between her fingers, crumbling each pellet into the familiar bone-white dust. Then her brown eyes lock on mine, dark and determined. "Are you ready?"

I tense before her, my nerves suddenly uneasy as I linger on the razor in her hand. Though a smaller threat compared with the horror of steel wire tearing at my flesh, I know it won't hurt any less.

Six incisions. That's what Izara said a few days ago, when I pressed her for more details about the àmì-orí ritual. *Six sacred markings for every magic born of Shango's odù.*

A constellation of scriptures stretching down my head like claws.

But if I can survive thirty lashes of searing pain, certainly I can survive this too. So despite the tightness in my chest, I nod once, releasing a long, hard breath. Izara bunches a clean towel in her hands and offers it to me.

"Now close your eyes and hold still." Her voice drops to a whisper as she shifts closer on her knees. She balances the bowl on the crates and lays one hand on the back of my neck, gripping gently. "Remember, no matter what happens, you cannot scream."

I do as she instructs, sinking my teeth into the fibers of the towel. With my forehead pressed into the wood, I brace myself for the full weight of the razor on my head. In that moment, my heartbeat stills. When I exhale, it is with a quick, silent prayer to Olodumarè.

"*Ìbàre Olorun tó kárí ayé,*" Izara begins to chant, molding the ancient Yoruba language into an incantation I do not understand. "*Ìbàre Shango, alágbára mímó. Mo ké pè yín gégé bí elérìí ìgbékalè yí—*"

Before I get a chance to ask her how she learned the forbidden tongue, the blade slices into my head. It burrows deep as Izara drags the metal along the flesh of my scalp. I gnash my teeth deeper into the fabric, every gasp a gurgling rattle in my throat as if I'm being drowned in a river of pain. It ripples over my skin in bitter waves, threatening to pull me underwater, into an endless muck of darkness and shadows.

"*Jakuta tí ń'se ìtósónà kádàrá àwon omo rè—*"

The razor scrapes from the top of my head down to my nape, tearing and ripping and burning its way into my skull. But there is something different about this pain, something ancient and twisted and alive, like the gnarled roots of a tree, writhing deeper and deeper into the ground. As it spreads, a chill sprouts up my bones.

This is worse than steel wire is all I can think as I shudder violently in Izara's grasp. Her ringed fingers dig into my neck in an effort to try to hold me down, keep me steady. But everything in me only screams, *Enough, stop, no more.*

I was wrong. I cannot take this pain. Not after all I've suffered these past weeks. I can't do this. I can't.

Blood gushes down my face. A warm, slick thing. It pools in the already-stained surface of the crates.

"Fi odù re hàn lára omobìrin yí—"

Izara's chants surge, her unfamiliar words weaving a tapestry of ancient scriptures into my head. Though I don't see them, I feel the jagged slants and curves of Shango's odù, each one a blooming bud beneath a soil of pain.

"Jàde wá nípasè ara omobìrin yí
Kún Sìlónù pèlu àse mímó re—"

Every incision drags me further and further beneath the rushing tide. My body pulses at a feverish rhythm as magic leeches away at the fragile pieces of my sanity. And still, still, Izara's lilting voice dances in my head. Her torturous hands carve centuries of a sacred history into my blood. When the sixth marking splits up my crown, I drown in the flood of my own fire. It chars my mind. Leaves ashes in its wake. I feel far away, leaden, a burning pyre sinking to the bottom of a dark river.

"Shango, Orisha iná
di agbára omoyín mú
Tun inú rè
Jé kí ó lè gbó ìlù àtòrunwá yín
Oba ńlá, gbó igbe wa."

Izara's incantations are a light in the dark. Then the gentle press of a hand closes around me, a familiar coolness that pulls me back to the surface. With a gasp, I force my lids open, body stiff and aching, eyes swimming with tears. Thick globs of saliva bubble in my mouth as I spit out the sopping wet towel. The crates beneath me are drenched in a mess of blood and sweat. Above me, Izara dabs iyerosun into my markings. The ache in my bones starts to ebb. The shudders cease. Magic that once ripped through me now threads itself back together, mending the broken fragments of my mind, until I am whole once again.

"Jé kí ó lè gbó ìlù àtòrunwá yín
Oba ńlá, gbó igbe wa."

A buzz thrums in my head as iyerosun crystallizes with my blood. I can feel the powder seeping inside, furling and unfurling through every fiber and every nerve. A liquid ember to set ablaze even the darkest parts of my being. When it explodes into my veins, bright whorls of àse spark to life beneath my skin, pulsing at my fingertips. I wince at the sight, as if expecting the rush of magic to brand, blister, leave more scars. But unlike the raw needles of fire that once stabbed through my body in rapid bursts, this time, my àse moves like a river. A calm and tranquil stream, with molten tendrils of reds and oranges that blaze from the purest of whites to the most brilliant blues. The glowing swirls are like nothing I've ever seen. And in that moment, all I can do is stare at the spirals of magic winding from my head down to my toes.

"Odò àtòrunwá," I murmur, breathless with understanding.

The divine current. It's what Izara called it. A spiritual balance between the past and the future, between gods and Scions, between all that is supreme and transcendent in òrun and the most tangible and mundane of ayé. An endless, flowing conduit of energy that binds me to Shango and Olodumarè and every ancestor that came before me.

"Can you hear it?" Sweat pours down Izara's face as she crashes back against the partition wall. Her quick, shallow breaths are a mirror of my own. Still, her wide eyes search mine with such intensity, they almost seem to burn. "Can you hear the drums?"

As àse courses through me, bathing me in a soothing comfort of warmth unlike any I've felt my entire life, my head rings with a familiar clamor. It reverberates in my skull, only this time, another sound swells beneath. It beats like a drum, pulses like a heartbeat. A deep rumble as ancient and vibrant as the roll of thunder itself.

I look to Izara incredulously. "What is that?"

"Àse," she says, and a true, joyful grin spreads across her face. "Every Orisha owns a magic sound. If you can hear Shango's drums, then it means the ritual worked."

I can. By gods, I can. The drums pound at a wild rhythm, and as it climbs, magic dances deeper and deeper in my veins.

"All this time, and I thought it was just noise," I whisper.

That same inaudible din has always been there, rattling away in my skull every time my àse surged. But I never knew where the sound came from or what it was. Yet, the noise grew so fervently, it became my very own warning bell. The bellow of a beast awakening.

But I was wrong, so wrong. Because there is nothing monstrous about this magic at all, nothing vile and corrupt like what the Lucis wanted me to believe. And to think I spent so long denying myself a sound as achingly pure and free as this.

I can't fight the tears that spring to my eyes, or the lump that sits heavy in my throat. To have lived fifteen years, stumbling through the dark shadows of myself, without a glimmer of light to see me through. Until today. Until now.

Until Izara.

"That is the sound of your magic, Sloane." Her voice floats around me, a soft, welcoming chime. "It's yours. Now listen."

And that is exactly what I do.

TWENTY-FOUR

When I sleep, I do not dream. For the first time in weeks, there are no ghosts, no illusions, not even the clawing whispers of a darkness that had slowly begun to plague my mind. Even my aches and pains seem to vanish overnight, leaving only a sudden rush of energy in their wake.

Out on the training field, I sprawl in the grass alongside the rest of my squad, our guns aimed at the row of target dummies lined up across the firing range. Lieutenant Caspian paces back and forth between us, rifle raised to his shoulder, with Lord Sol a silent shadow at his heels. The internal adviser has been making his rounds all week, tracking our progress during training and taking detailed reports with him back to the queen. Even though he hasn't said a word since his arrival on the field, his royal presence speaks volume. As always, the military is on the hunt for its weakest link, another frail fledgling for them to prey on. But I have survived nearly two weeks of torture with nothing but the sheer force of my own will, and not even the adviser's close proximity fazes me now.

Instead, I tighten my grip on the rifle, fingers steady on the trigger as I realign my sights. A loaded bandolier lies in the dirt next to me, feeding heavy rounds into the weapon's chamber in rapid succession. At the lieutenant's command, gunfire ripples in the still morning air. One by one, our dummies crash to the ground with a resounding thud.

It's my fifth drop of the day so far, an improvement after weeks of failed shots and near misfires. Caspian, especially, seems to take notice. At the sight of the bullet hole burned into another one of my target's skulls, the lieutenant gives me a rare nod. A slight gesture, but it stirs a familiar kind of sensation deep within. It is the same resolve

I've felt since my àmì-orí ritual, a gathering of strength, untethered and free. Every ounce of energy once poured into suppressing the force of my àse crackles through me now. I grasp onto it with equal fervor, bending it to my will for the duration of the training.

"Hey, great job out there." Jericho claps me on the shoulder as we make our way down the field an hour later. Several paces ahead, Nazanin and Izara trudge along, their rucksacks swinging heavily on their backs.

I nod my thanks, body buzzing with adrenaline left behind from the drill. Eleven drops in a single session isn't much, but it might just be enough to claw my way up from the bottom of the ranks. I'm tired of having a target on my back. Tired of the commander's wicked threat of steel wire, the squad leader's fixation on causing me pain, even Malachi's pointed jeers every time he's around. I will no longer be made a victim, not by any of them.

In that moment, Nazanin and Izara spin on their heels, walking backward with small, measured steps.

"It's the hair, isn't it?" Nazanin's face breaks into a grin. "Shaved the whole thing off; now here you are acting all brand-new."

"Like some kind of gun-wielding warrior bitch," Izara adds.

The three of them chuckle low, and even I can't help but snort.

"All right, enough of that." I shove past them lightly, my face flushing at their compliments. "Culture and Theory awaits, lest you'd all like to spend the night—"

"Counting bodies in Cliff Row." They grind out the rest of the lieutenant's promised threat, groaning as we take the short walk down to the training center.

We reach the front steps of the building with minutes to spare. Izara is the first to depart, something about coordinating tonight's formation drill with Faas before class.

"Commander's pet," Nazanin teases.

In response, Izara flips her the finger just as she disappears into the hallway. We burst into laughter, a warm, hearty sound I've barely heard since our arrival on this godsforsaken base. Jericho throws back his head, and Nazanin's eyes crinkle at the edges as they laugh with wild, reckless abandon, because they know, just as much as I do, that in these moments, joy like this is much too fleeting.

I'm still smiling when Nazanin cuts in front of me, her gaze sweeping past the cluster of soldiers smoking taba in the shade nearby.

"You should come by the barracks later, during mess," she whispers, and something in her demeanor changes.

"Why?"

Already, I'm frowning at the thought of having to miss today's ration, especially after nearly two weeks of starvation. With Basics finally over at the armory, the meager bowl of garri and groundnuts served by the Lucis cook is all I've looked forward to. In truth, I'm not sure I can survive another day guzzling down buckets of water to sate my hunger. What the hell could be more important than food?

When Jericho speaks next, his voice low and careful, I have my answer.

"There's something you have to see."

Jericho's cryptic words hum in my head as I rush past the front gates of the empty barracks. After nearly two weeks of attempting to steal the guards' uniforms, our failures have begun to feel like defeat. Without the cover of a disguise to conceal our identities, the security cameras remain a nuisance to overcome. Another obstacle in our mission to breaking into Archives Hall.

But now . . . if those very words mean what I think they mean, there's a possibility Jericho and Nazanin succeeded. And what a break-through that would be, to know uncovering the truth about Mama no longer seems impossible.

My heart thuds faster and faster with each step. Though hunger churns deep in my stomach, I set a brisk pace, making sure to stay far, far away from the security post and the guards' line of sight. Any recruit caught lingering about the barracks during mess hours certainly risks facing their wrath or more.

I reach a familiar bend in the hallway and scurry the short distance down to my quarters. I've only just entered the room when Nazanin grabs my arm and drags me inside, nudging the door closed behind her.

"What took you so long?" she asks, climbing back into her bunk, next to Jericho.

He sprawls with his legs against the wall, a half-eaten suya stick in his hand.

Almost immediately, my stomach groans at the sight of it. I'm grateful when Jericho tosses one wrapped skewer my way, which I catch with quick, nimble fingers.

"Where did you get this?" I tear off the wrapper, and within seconds, I've already bitten through half the suya meat. The peppery spice spills onto my tongue, a familiar comfort food that reminds me of home, of Mama.

"You didn't think we'd let you starve, did you?" Nazanin smiles as she reaches for the bag at the foot of her bunk. "Here, check it out."

With the suya stick now licked clean, I snatch the bag from her, anticipation pulsing through me as I rip through the dark plastic.

"You did it," I breathe, grinning at the guards' stolen uniforms bunched inside.

"It wasn't easy," Nazanin admits, "and they're really old. But they'll do just fine."

I nod in agreement. I can barely even tell the difference between these and the current ones. Except for the musty smell that lingers in the folds of the fabrics, the odor terribly rancid and just as potent.

I wrinkle my nose. "Why does it smell like someone died in these?"

"Because someone probably did." Jericho gives me a mischievous smile, his teeth flashing. "There's bloodstains on them too, if you really want to know."

"I didn't, but thanks." I hurl the uniforms at him, laughing as they drape over his face.

"Hey!" He chuckles as he gathers the uniforms into one solid piece and shoves it right under Nazanin's bunk.

"Will you two quit playing around so we can finalize this plan?" She throws a jab at Jericho's shoulder. "Mess is almost over, and we can't be caught in here."

I wipe at my eyes and perch on the edge of the bed. "Okay, okay. Where are we with the layout of the training center?"

Jericho riffles through his rucksack, pulling out the rough sketch he began working on last night. With one outstretched hand, he offers it to me.

For a moment, I squint at the crooked lines and distorted patterns of shapes scrawled along the length of the paper, trying to discern the outline. Clearly, drawing isn't Jericho's strongest suit. "What exactly am I looking at?"

"See, I told you it was terrible." Nazanin doesn't bother to stifle her giggles.

"I'm a thief, not an artist," Jericho retorts.

When they both look to me for my thoughts, I keep things neutral with a light shrug. "It's not *that* bad."

Nazanin only rolls her eyes. "Don't lie to him."

"Look," Jericho says as he takes the sketch from me and rests it in the middle of the bed. "Here's the northern entrance"—he points to a smudge on the paper—"and that is the leopards' den attached next to it." Then he dives into the plan, walking me through every detail as thoroughly as he can. "We know we have to scale the den to get inside the building. There's a stairwell leading up to the main level, which is divided into four wings: north, south, east, and west. The lieutenant's office is at the far end of the west wing—"

"So we head toward the training hall," I cut him off. "Caspian's office is just down the corridor."

"No." He shakes his head. "Better to go through the south wing. Head down to the gun range, just past the storage room, then cut across to the west."

"Why? That's the longest route."

"It's also the safest," he says. "There are five security posts between the north wing and the west." He stabs his finger along each spot, poking light holes into the sketch as he does. "Each post will have at least two guards on duty. That's ten officers we risk running into if we go that route. Even in disguise, we shouldn't draw too much attention."

In that, he's right. The soldiers' uniforms might help us blend in with ease, but the last thing we need is for the guards to make us out. If a longer route keeps us out of their grasp, so be it.

"Now, what's the catch?" My eyes flit back and forth between Jericho and Nazanin. So far, everything about the plan seems too easy, and after everything it took to get here, I know better than to trust such a simple process.

Sure enough, Nazanin heaves a sigh, her shoulders drooping. "There's a security camera right outside Caspian's office," she mumbles finally. "Top-left corner of the door. We have to blind it."

I frown. "How the hell are we supposed to do that?"

Jericho tosses me a small, rounded ball coated in black paint. "Paint pellet," he says as I rotate the ball between my fingers. "The Lucis use them to mark target dummies. If I can shoot it at the camera, I can blind it long enough for us to break in and steal the map."

"Oh."

I remain silent for a long minute, mulling over every single detail of the plan now. There's no doubt in my mind that Jericho is a great shooter. After all, I've seen him work his slingshot a few times, never once missing a target. But the camera won't be an easy hit, and without a blind, our plan will fail.

"Exactly how many of these pellet things do we have?" I ask him.

Nazanin juts out her chin at the ball. "Just that one," she says. "So whatever we do, we *have* to make it count."

I draw a shaky breath, my eyes on Jericho. "Do you really think you can hit it?"

Even when I know there are no guarantees, I just need to hear him say it aloud, if only to release a bit of the tension already knotting up my shoulders.

But the boy just shrugs. "I guess we'll find out."

It's not the answer I'm looking for, but it's the best he can give.

Next to him, Nazanin flashes me a small smile, the corners of her mouth tugging slightly. "The day is ours," she adds in an attempt to reassure me.

"The day is ours," Jericho repeats too.

It isn't the first time I've heard the mantra shared between them. Strange words that should mean nothing to me, but I echo them all the same.

The day is ours. Though it brings me no comfort, I try to hold on to the fact that, in this moment, at least we finally have everything we need to break into Archives Hall.

Now, with our plan complete, all we can do is bide our time and wait.

TWENTY-FIVE

A half hour later, the afternoon bells ring out, and I return to the training center for Combat. Inside one of the practice rooms, Dane cuts a vicious shadow across the floor, already dressed in combat fatigues. It's been eleven full days since I last saw the squad leader, and his very presence sets my nerves on a wire's edge. Even now, I can't forget the memory of him knocking me unconscious with his gun, a brute force that still draws a wince from me. The coward has certainly managed to avoid me since, letting me work at my task alone on days I reported to the armory for basic duty.

Dane fixes his terrible gaze on me as I stride into the room, sharp eyes roving over my form from head to toe. Though he lingers on my bald head the most, I don't flinch under the intensity of his stare. A day after my scarification ritual, the ancient scriptures of Shango's odù have since faded into dull markings, indiscernible now even to prying eyes. So I cross to the other side of the room, chin raised, determined not to take any notice of him. The sooner we get through today's training, the better off I'll be.

"You look . . . alive," he says, watching me undo the buttons of my uniform jacket.

I find the nearest wall hook and hang my belongings before coming to a stop in front of him.

"I'm not easily broken, Reaper," I practically snarl. In that moment, whatever burst of energy I've felt all morning quickly gives way to something else. A flush of anger that churns earnestly in the pit of my stomach.

The audacity of him to even talk to me after what he's done. Not only did Dane strike me back in Eti-Osa, it was he who urged Faas to have me whipped.

She'll serve as an example for the others.

I don't know why the squad leader thought I deserved that kind of pain. But my hatred for him has only grown tenfold since, barely simmering beneath the surface.

"Good to know you haven't lost that fire."

"Oh, believe me. I haven't."

He cocks his brow in response. A challenge, always a challenge.

I sneer at him and back off slowly, taking my stance a few feet away. Just as well, too, because a steady plume of àse worms its way through me, accompanied by the faint echo of Shango's drums. As the heat stirs along, my limbs tighten on instinct, as if expecting a familiar wave of pain to roll over me. It never comes.

Though it's only been a day, I'm still not used to the temporary reprieve my àmì-orí ritual provides. But I'm grateful for it all the same.

Now without my magic to distract, I turn my focus on the fight ahead. The last time I sparred with the squad leader, he nearly humiliated me. Fought me as though every blow were a call, and the longer I failed to answer, the less worthy I became.

Having me whipped was a calculated move. A cruel test with an even more vicious intent. To see just how far he could push me, exactly what it would take to break me. But Dane failed.

For eleven days, I've wanted nothing more than to show him that.

Shoulders squared and fists raised, I take my first step toward him. For a moment, Dane watches my every move, the intensity rippling in his eyes as he works a black strip of cloth around his palm. I tilt my head, brow raised in a challenge of my own. Only then does he roll up his sleeves, crack his long fingers, and take his stance.

He nods once, and the fight begins.

This time, I don't make the first move. Instead, I root myself to the mats, limbs centered and steady, bracing myself for his attack. Let him come to me.

When he bounds forward, a wicked chill careens down my spine.

He lunges at me with brutal speed, his blow swift and precise. Despite the sudden jolt of pain, I raise my elbow against the force of his punch. Shift on my heels and drive my fist into his ribs. For a second, I think I hear the faintest hint of a grunt as Dane lurches backward from the impact, but he recovers far too quickly.

"Good" is all he says as he once again rights himself into a proper stance.

I clench my teeth against the taunt loose on my tongue, hating the way my chest squeezes around his approval. I know more than to believe a Lucis like him. He's a liar, and any praise from him is nothing more than a trick, as if a single word is all he thinks I need to let my guard down. Well, it won't work. Not this time.

"Shut up," I snarl, "and fight me."

A tick in his jaw. A slight turn of his lips. "As you wish."

He pounces forward then, his cold gaze never leaving mine. One swing, and I'm struggling to keep up with Dane's assault. Though neither of us speaks again, I certainly hear him in the sheer might of his strikes. There is a feral talent to his footwork. A broken yet precise rhythm that allows him to move fluidly, like a bleeding panther prowling for prey. Just when I think I have his technique figured out, the bastard switches form right before my eyes.

With quick speed, I throw a left hook. He weaves, dodges too easily. A slight feint with his right hand and Dane fires a fast jab of his own. I'm too slow to duck. A horrible pain explodes across my face. I stagger under the full weight of his shot, eyes watering, a hollow sound buzzing in my head.

The small, sudden shift in my balance is all Dane needs to seize control of this fight. Once again, I find myself at the mercy of his blows. Blood rushes to my ears as he charges at me, again and again and again. His punches are harsh, and with each failure, the squad leader shows less and less mercy.

I pace around him now, breath seizing, trying in vain to land a swing. It doesn't matter how hard I fight, how fast I lunge; every attempt is futile, and a growing pressure bubbles inside my chest. I hate how he makes me feel so incompetent during these fights. So pathetically small and useless, like a cornered animal with nothing to defend herself.

I hate him. *I hate him.*

When a final blow knocks me to the ground, I gnash my teeth against the pain streaking up my spine. Though the scars on my back have long since healed, a dull ache still blooms from the wound, enough to make me wince.

Dane crouches next to me, his narrowed eyes hard from the fight. I set my jaw as I peel myself off the mats, anticipating another one of his taunts. Instead, he puts a hand on my arm, his fingers closing around my biceps. I flinch at the sudden contact.

"Don't you dare touch me." I slap away his grip and rise to my feet, pushing my palms against the cushioned floor for support.

Even without his touch, my skin burns with the ghost of his hand, and sickness crawls to the pit of my stomach. Let him grab me like that again. Swear to gods I'll burn off every last one of his bleeding fingers.

He takes a step backward, hands raised in silent surrender. "Is it your back?" he asks, watching me carefully.

My lips curl into a scowl. "What the hell do you care?"

A breath loosens out of him. "Contrary to what you might think, I do care about the well-being of my squad."

"Is that why you had me whipped?" I hiss in his face. "You take pleasure in watching me suffer, Reaper?"

"There are far better things to derive pleasure from," Dane says bluntly. "Not that."

I don't bother to hide my disgust. He must think this is some kind of joke, but I'm not laughing. Only a twisted brute would find humor in my pain. I know what horror I've been through these past eleven days. The ache, the tears, the scars that bleed with every tiny motion.

With a scoff, I shove past him, desperate to leave the practice room behind. If I have to spend another minute in close proximity to Dane, I fear what I might do to him. I've had enough of the squad leader for one day. But just as I get within a foot, Dane grips my arm and spins me around. I yank my limb free, imagining, for one single moment, what he would look like without his ten fingers. A shiver of heat teases its presence beneath my skin. The drums thud at a tempting beat.

"Yes, I had you whipped," Dane says sharply. "But I also saved your life. Do you think Faas had any intention of letting you walk after what you did?"

Semi. Guilt eats its way through me, a parasite gnawing away at my insides.

"You're not the first recruit to spare a Scion's life. But you *are* the first to live through it."

He stares down at me, his eyes neither cold nor hard. For once, I see a sliver of the boy in him as he tries to make me understand why he did what he did.

"I suppose I should thank you for my scars, then?" I cross my arms over my chest.

Despite what the squad leader says, I don't believe him. Not when I'll always have these thick ridges marring my back, a reminder of the hurt he caused. His empty words mean nothing to me.

Across from me, Dane's gaze hardens. He leans even closer, a familiar steel winding its way into his features. "You think it was easy convincing Faas not to kill you right there?" He speaks low, the words cold on his tongue. "You have no idea what I had to do—"

My heartbeat quickens at that. A dizzying rush of blood pounds in my ears.

"How dare you compare your suffering to mine?" I spit back at him. "What the hell did you lose? A day's worth of food? A night's rest? There are children in Nagea dying every hour, so I hope you're not looking for pity, because you won't find it here."

"Look, I understand what it's like—"

"Understand *what*? What it's like to be a child growing up in the slums? How can you understand a struggle you've never lived? You come from a life of privilege. A life that affords you the freedom to do whatever you wish. Kill whomever you want—"

"I am still a soldier," he retorts. "Sworn to serve, just like you."

"Oh, but we are not the same, are we?" The expression on my face is cold, ruthless and mocking. "You chose this life. I wasn't given a choice. No one's ever forced a gun to your hands and made you pull the trigger on your friends. When you go to bed at night, you never have to worry whether or not a Nightwalker will invade your home, kill your family, and rape your sisters."

Every word, every spoken truth, drags me back to my old life in Agbajé, tugging at a parade of painful memories. The more I remember, the harder it becomes to hide the quiver in my voice. Tears well in my eyes, born from old fears and new terrors.

"You people—you treat us like we are not human. You replace our smiles with blood, our hearts with bullets. You destroy our innocence and our beings. And when you no longer have any use for us, you feed us to the earth." My eyes narrow with intent. I weave my own thread of steel into my voice. "Tell me, Reaper. Is there someone out there who wants you dead? Or are you just another hand amongst many pulling the trigger?"

By the time I'm done, I'm trembling all over, flashes of rage coursing through my entire body. My àse responds with equal fervor, an invisible current of liquid fire threading through me, begging to be freed. With a newfound ease, I curl my fists around the magic until it ebbs away, dousing the spark before it flares into something more.

Dane stiffens in front of me, glints of his own anger burning green in his eyes. Despite the threat of what we both could do, I remain firm, without an ounce of fear or regret.

"We're done here," he rumbles low before heading straight for the door.

"That's what I thought," I yell at his retreating form. My breath rattles out in quick, shallow huffs, pushing against the walls of my chest.

When Dane reaches the door, his hand tightens around the knob. Just before he twists it open, he turns around. I cross my arms and raise an eyebrow at him, daring. I chose not to burn off his damned fingers, but it doesn't mean I can't ruin him with my words.

"You know, I've seen so many like you come in and out of this base," he says slowly, meeting my eyes. "Some don't get to leave at all. I can't change your fate. I can't undraft you. But I can help you survive, if you let me. I'm not the enemy. I'm only doing my job."

He runs a hand over his shaved head, grumbles to himself. When he barks out a laugh, I frown at his strange display of emotion, the most I've ever seen from him.

"What the hell's so funny?"

After a long pause, he sighs, moves his hand away from the door, and bounds forward. "Faas will have my head for telling you this, but Phase One of your training begins tonight. They're sending you to the Wild."

"Irúnmolè Forest?" My eyes widen. "That's—impossible."

I still remember the day Mama told me about the legend of the sacred forest. *The spirits of our ancestors are angry*, she'd said after much prodding on my part. According to Mama, in the ancient days, Irúnmolè was the burial place of the ancestors. Every year, during a pilgrimage known as the Egungun Festival, every Yoruba across Nagea would flock to our ancestral temple in Ijesha to pay homage to the dead. But all of that ended once the Lucis invaded. Sacrifices to the ancestors were abolished, the dead were forgotten, and in their anger, they cursed those sacred grounds.

Never go beyond the edge of the forest, Mama warned. I've lived by those words ever since, and they've kept me safe. Until now.

Dane stops a foot away from me. I still before him, brows furrowed, searching his face for anything that might disprove his words. When I find nothing, a cold weight settles in my stomach, heavy as stone.

By gods.

"No one survives it," I whisper, if only to myself.

"Few do," Dane murmurs.

"How?" What do the Lucis know that many of us don't?

"Kill or be killed," he says, and for a moment, I do not understand. But the longer he stares at me, those terrible words start to take on a new meaning. "Once you cross that border, the only way out is to spill blood. Faas knows it, which is why it's become a mandatory part of the training."

A blood sacrifice. I shake my head, stomach lurching in disbelief. In the early days, back when our shrines still stood, people often made sacrifices and animal offerings to the gods to appease them. Through ebo and ètùtù, Olodumarè would bless us and forgive our sins. But the gods never craved human blood. Why would the ancestors demand such a thing?

My mind whirls with too many questions. I glare up at Dane, studying the sharp lines of his face. As much as I don't want to believe him, what reason would the squad leader have to lie about this?

"Why are you helping me?" My voice is small, hoarse with the dread lodged thickly in my throat.

"Because it's my job." He shrugs, his answer surprisingly gentle. Then a muscle snaps in his temple. He's a soldier once again.

"Things can get very *strange* in there," Dane tells me, and I swallow hard. "Don't trust what you see, or hear, even if it seems familiar. Remember what you're there for. Do not hesitate. Good luck."

Tonight, Izara leads the evening formation alongside Faas, with the rest of us standing at attention, ready to obey her every command. Given her rank on the squad, it's no surprise she's become the commander's top recruit, and her new position as formation leader is a firm reminder of that.

At 2000h, when Faas finally dismisses us, I find Izara, Nazanin, and Jericho back in the barracks and relay the news to them. We're cramped together inside one of the storage rooms, huddled next to two tall dressers crammed with cleaning tools and supplies, hidden away from possible eavesdroppers. Our faces are still damp with sweat, chests heaving in an effort to steady our breathing. Exhaustion drags at my limbs, but the knowledge of what Dane told me and what the commanders are planning chase away any fatigue I might feel.

"Are you sure those were his exact words?" Nazanin asks for the third time since I dragged them inside the stale, fume-filled room. She stands between Jericho and Izara, voice faint, the braids woven into her hair now undone.

"They're sending us into the Wild." I look them dead in the eyes. "Tonight."

"Gods," Izara says under her breath.

She kicks at one of the dressers so hard it wobbles on loose wooden legs. Beside her, Jericho slumps against the back wall, a rush of air whistling past his lips.

We watch each other in silence for a long moment, a curtain of dread settling over us all. The possibility that we could be dead in a few hours is too difficult to ignore. Even now, part of me still wants to believe there's a chance Dane could be wrong, that the commanders wouldn't be so evil as to sacrifice so many of us for the sake of training. Then I remember it was Faas who had nearly two hundred children killed during the first assessment. Faas who ordered a Cleansing on Eti-Osa and forced us to watch as innocent lives were gunned down.

That bastard certainly won't hesitate to spill more blood, especially if it means weeding out the weakest link.

"They could have sent us anywhere else," Nazanin hisses through gritted teeth. She paces back and forth in the small space, her face cut into a deep frown. "Hell, I'd even take my chances at Mandrill Valley. Anything but that bloody forest. Why would the commander do this?"

"Because this is a killing hunt." Finally, Jericho straightens. "And we all know that murdering fiend won't miss an opportunity to pit us against each other. This is just another excuse to satisfy his bloodlust."

It's the first time he's spoken since we entered the storage room, and his words are somber enough.

Nazanin pauses in her step. The same terror she once wore in the alleyway behind Magda's hut flashes in her eyes now. "Do we really have to do this? *Again?*"

Neither of us can ever forget what happened that day on that island. Yet, something tells me it's nothing compared with the horror that awaits us inside Irúnmolè Forest.

"We don't have a choice," I murmur, a bitter, harrowing truth that sinks deep into my bones.

"Then we get in there and we hunt." Izara's voice hardens, her face grim with a familiar determination as she stares between the three of us. "If this is what the commanders want, then we fight with whatever we've got. No matter what, we don't stop fighting until we get out."

Quietly, we nod along, trying to mirror her steely resolve. But the second the curfew bell tolls, the air tenses around us, tinged with a lingering sense of unease. After all, none of us truly know what's to come tonight, whether or not we have what it takes to make it out of that forest alive. Yet, despite the veil of fear blanketing me now, I draw on my own will, latching onto it with quick, desperate fingers.

As the noise continues to reverberate around us, we exchange a final look. Then Jericho reaches for Nazanin's hand. Together, they shuffle toward the door, fingers clasped tightly, squeezing as they go. *For strength. For hope. For what may very well be the last time.*

The storage door cracks open a little. While Jericho pokes his head out, Nazanin hesitates, glancing over her shoulder at me and Izara.

"We can do this," she says with a pained smile.

I can only nod, my jaw tightening.

"Good luck," Izara whispers for us both.

When the door finally closes behind them, I take a shuddering breath and turn toward her. She stands with her back against the dresser, fingers tracing the wooden face. Something tells me there's more she wants to say. It's why we're both still here, even with curfew moments away. Though her strange, troubled expression gives me pause.

"What is it?"

She sighs as I join her on the other side of the dresser. "The ancestors won't make it easy for you to get out." Izara angles her body toward me. "Irúnmolè is no place for a Scion."

"Irúnmolè is no place for anyone," I murmur, and it's the truth. Just because the Lucis found a way to escape the spirit world once before doesn't mean we should go tussling in a forest full of angry creatures. Yet again, these idiots have managed to mess with a spirituality they know nothing of, except this time, it is with our lives at risk.

In my head, I curse at them as a sudden burst of anger comes over me. It's far more useful than fear.

"I blame Olympia and the bloodlines for this," I hiss aloud, scuffing at the stone floor with the heel of my boots. "I swear those monsters are everything that's wrong about this world."

"Forget the bloodlines," she says. "The ancestors are far more furious with Scions for the role they played in the ruin of the Ancient Kingdoms. They haven't forgotten, and they do not forgive."

That draws a frown from me. "Because of the Egungun Festival?"

She shakes her head slowly, eyes darkening as she speaks. "It's more than that. You know about the creation myth. You know it was Scions who ruled the kingdoms long after the gods departed. Scions who swore to uphold the duties of our land, swore to protect the sacredness of the ancestral place. But they failed. Now, because of them, the ancestors suffer every day, their spirits forever trapped between worlds. They know no peace, Sloane. This sacrifice, the deaths, they are only the consequence of a centuries-long failure, and the ancestors won't stop until Nagea is once again restored."

It's not what I expected to hear, and the shock of it jolts through me, keeping me silent for a minute or so. Even with what little knowledge I have of Irúnmolè, I always imagined the ancestors were our allies. Spirit elders we beseeched for guidance and blessings long before the Lucis arrived. Now I'm to believe they are my enemies, determined to punish me for the failures of the past? It doesn't make sense.

Yet, the longer I search Izara's face, something about the pain twisting her features pushes away any doubt I might have.

In that moment, despite what I don't yet understand, a new terrible realization crashes over me. "You think I'm not coming back, don't you?"

As soon as the words leave my mouth, bile rises in my throat. It takes great effort to force it back down, and I wince as I do.

"I don't know. I wish I did, but I don't." Beside me, Izara lowers her gaze, the veins on her head standing out sharply. "I do know the ancestors will come for you, and when they do, you have to be ready." She glances back at me then, her voice quivering around the next words. "Tonight you're not just the hunter, Sloane. Tonight you're also the hunted."

For the rest of the night, Izara's words linger in my head, the warning in them too impossible to ignore. It keeps me awake far into the dead hours, and I can only listen as Nazanin and Izara stir every so often in their own bunks.

If what she told me is true, there's an even greater chance I won't survive Irúnmolè Forest at all. Not with a world full of vengeful spirits hell-bent on taking my life. How in gods' names am I supposed to defend myself against the wrath of some centuries-old ancestors?

Just the thought chills my blood, sending cold shivers across my body. With trembling hands, I pull the blankets tightly over my form, allowing myself to sink under the sheets, as though I could possibly disappear somewhere no one will find me.

I crave an escape. Someplace without war, without the Lucis and the ancestors and the constant never-ending threat of death. Now more than ever, I crave rest.

I don't know when I drift off to sleep, but when I do, my nightmares welcome me in a restless embrace. I surrender myself to their haunting whispers, their grasping hands and sinking claws. They scratch and tear at every inch of my humanity, burrowing and—

Cre-e-eak.

With a gasp, I bolt awake. There's someone else in here.

Sweat trails down my face as I reach underneath my pillow for the pair of knives I stole from Dane back in the armory. Before I can grab them, two large silhouettes descend on me, their grips closing like manacles around my limbs.

I open my mouth to scream.

A bag is shoved over my head.

TWENTY-SIX

I wake in a clearing, with the sun blazing overhead, scorching the carpet of wilted grass at my feet. A dull ache lingers in my bones as I squint against the brilliant shards of light, trying to clear the fog from my head. My muscles are too heavy. Whatever the soldiers did to me back in the barracks must have knocked me out long enough for them to dump me here. My gaze shifts around, searching for Izara and Nazanin and any of the other familiar faces from my squad.

I'm all alone.

I stagger up slowly, swaying on stiff limbs. Across from me, a row of crumbling columns stretches down the length of the clearing, ruins of the Ijesha ancestral temple that once stood here centuries ago. Massive stands of iroko trees rise behind the ivory pillars, their branches bent outward like long, crooked fingers. A tremor careens down my spine when I realize where I am.

Irúnmolè Forest.

Dane was right. The commanders have tossed us into the Wild. By now, I imagine hundreds of other recruits waking up in various clearings, all of us staring into the haze of a sacred forest that might be our doom. Wherever Nazanin, Izara, and Jericho are, I hope to gods my friends are prepared enough, alert and ready for what's to come. More than anything else, I hope to gods we can make it out alive.

But no one survives Irúnmolè. It's what I've been told my whole life, a warning so many of us grew up on. Yet if everything the squad leader says is true, then surviving the forest means hunting down other recruits to kill. Spilling enough blood to buy my way out.

Once again, I must sacrifice others to save myself, trade their lives for my own freedom. But if Izara's words are any indication, then surely the recruits and I are not the only ones on the hunt today. The ancestors are on the prowl as well, and right now, their thirst for vengeance against all Scions is a threat I cannot ignore.

My heart gallops with the knowledge of what I have to do, and dread kindles a wildfire inside me.

Something stirs at my back. I glance over my shoulder to see a pair of Lucis officers far across the field. Together, they stand outside the door of a waiting airship, faces grim behind their glass helmets, rifles loaded and ready in their hands. These must be the two brutes who brought me here. Though neither of them moves a limb, I understand their presence well enough. Now that we're back in Nagea, the idea of escaping is a tempting possibility. If I even attempt to run, refuse this nightmare of a phase, I'm sure they've been given the order to kill me.

It would be too easy to do the same to them. There is enough rage brewing inside me, enough anger to want to turn my àse on them first. Burn them both to ash without any thought. But before I can reach for the familiar spark of fire, I catch sight of the shiny white orbs fitted to the wings of the airship. Even from this distance, the security cameras tick back and forth, capturing all they can with an inhuman focus. Of course.

To kill these bastards now would only mean death. And not just for me, but Baba and Luna as well. Because if I were to succeed, the Lucis would surely come for them, and more than my own, I can't put their lives at risk. I clench and unclench my fists, sneering as the opportunity to strike passes me by.

As always, there is no escaping this.

With nowhere else to turn, I inch forward, my legs quivering with every step. The forest path yawns open like the jaw of a feral beast, luring me closer into the belly of a waiting darkness. Heaving a breath, I slink past the tall undergrowth tugging at my hands with leafy arms and allow myself to be swallowed by the thick forest.

The warm air is heavy with the smell of wet wood, almost making it hard to breathe.

Then I hear it.

The whisper of my name, brushing against the hairs on my skin like a sudden breeze. Fear leaks through my pores. I whirl on my feet, searching for the opening I came through just moments ago. But there is no trace of the narrow path behind me. Instead, I'm surrounded by a world of towering iroko trees, giant boughs twisting and arching overhead, blocking any sign of sunlight. Darkness bleeds through the forest like inky-black blood, and the only source of light comes from the beds of fireflies twinkling along the underbrush like emerald stars. If I didn't know better, I might find them beautiful.

When a lone firefly buzzes close to my face, I swat it away, flicking it out of my line of vision. In response, the swarm rushes toward me, gathering like a nest of killer bees. I back away as fast as I can, but they cling to my skin, crawling up my neck, burrowing into my flesh. A scream tears from my lungs as I fall to the ground, crying for help, slapping desperately at their fluttering wings. The screams die on my lips as the horde of fireflies pours into my mouth, choking as they crawl down my throat.

I can't breathe. I can't see. I can't—

My eyes fly open. I'm lying in the bushes with my face pressed into the dirt. My whole body trembles, my breathing ragged as I scratch away at my skin. But there are no fireflies surrounding me, every touch of them gone as if they were never here.

It wasn't real, I tell myself, trying to wrap my brain around the horrible illusion. *It wasn't real.*

With a gasp, I push up onto my feet, ignoring the shiver creeping along my spine. A dry breeze rustles my fatigues, carrying with it the faint cries of a newborn child. The sobbing grows louder, multiplying as I slink down the snaking terrain. I reach the bend only to find a pair of young children walking up ahead, grass mats stacked on top of their heads.

For a moment, I pause at the sight, wondering how the kids ended up inside Irúnmolè Forest. They're much too young to be here.

"Hey!" I call after them, rushing to catch up. I can't get them out, but perhaps I could tell them what to do. "Wait!"

They don't answer. In fact, I'm not even sure they can hear me. When they disappear into the trunk of a large iroko tree, vanishing right before my eyes, I realize these aren't ordinary children at all.

Spirits. My stomach plunges to my feet and I stumble backward, surprised by their sudden presence. Iwin, Ebora, and Egbére, I don't know. I've never actually seen an Irúnmolè before. I have no idea what they look like, but I never expected something so real, *so human.*

I'm still staring at the giant tree in utter disbelief when someone rams into me from behind, shoving me back into the dirt. At first, I think it's another spirit, and every muscle in my body tenses at once. A crushing weight presses down on me, followed by a hissing whisper.

"I'm sorry," a girl's voice says, wrapping a thin rope around my neck. "This is the only way."

Before I can fight her off, the recruit's grip tightens around the string. True terror rushes through my blood as the rope digs deeper into my throat. I claw at it, struggling to loosen the pressure around my neck. I can't breathe. Lost in the haze of pain, I can barely think about how she figured out what needed to be done to escape the forest. She yanks on the rope, jerking my head so hard, a thin slice of blood blooms around my neck. My mind spins, and my vision blurs at the edges. I'm gasping for air.

In that moment, my survival instincts take over. I twist back and forth beneath her weight, enough to weaken her balance. The second her grasp loosens around the rope, I push off against the ground with every bit of strength I can gather.

The girl topples off. I scramble to my knees, my heartbeat thundering deep in my chest. Her dirt-streaked face isn't one I'm familiar with, another recruit most likely from a different squad.

When she throws out her foot, kicking me in the gut, I double over in pain. She steals the chance to knock me back to the ground, pouncing on me like an alley cat on the prowl. Her bony fingers are around my throat again, squeezing the life out of me. I grit my teeth and reach deep into my mind, desperately trying to call my fire to life.

I feel nothing. Not the wild rhythm of Shango's drums in my head. Not even the token hum of àse in my blood. There is no trace of magic in my veins. It's gone, abandoning me at a time when I need it most. My pulse echoes in my ears, a low, uneven thrum that slows with each passing second.

I'm going to die.

Without the fire, my hands flail across the ground, searching for something, anything, to defend myself. One moment, my fingers close around a rock. In the next, I'm bashing the jagged stone against the girl's head. Even when her hands slide down my throat and she slips off my chest, I don't stop bashing. My rage spills out, a monster blinding me to the horror of what I'm doing. Blood splashes into my mouth. The tangy taste of iron coats my tongue, pulling me from a shadowy edge.

The recruit lies before me, her face mangled and crushed from the brutal force of the rock. Gasping, I toss the stone to the ground and scramble far, far away from her corpse. Bile churns in my gut, rising up my throat as blood pools around the girl's head. I fold over myself and retch until my stomach burns with the pain.

She wanted to kill you. A voice whispers in my head. *If you hadn't killed her, she would have succeeded.* But even my thoughts feel so wrong, a way for me to justify my own evil. Free myself from the guilt wrapping around me like a black shroud.

I glance at the body across from me, my hand heavy with the

weight of a rock that's no longer there. The memory is still too fresh on my mind, a terrible stain I can't erase. Still, my watery eyes dart back and forth, searching for my way out. With every passing second, I wait for the forest to disappear, wait for something to bring me back to the clearing. Dane said the only way out is to spill blood. I killed her. This is what the Lucis wanted. So why in gods' names am I still here?

If the girl's death isn't payment enough, how many must I kill to leave this wretched world behind?

My heart beats at a broken rhythm. Then a feverish warmth crawls over me, a sudden pressure that forces me to look up. High above my head, at least a hundred hissing creatures hang upside down from the boughs. Unlike the weeping children, there is something wrong about these spirit beings. Something nightmarish in the way their obsidian bodies seem to scorch and coalesce, each creature weaving in and out of the other as if made of molten liquid. They move in a black rivulet, winding downward on a cobweb of thin, dangling branches.

Drip by drip, fat droplets of moisture land on my shoulder. I let out a strangled cry as the heat of it melts off a chunk of my fatigues, blistering the skin underneath. With all my might, I jolt to my feet and fling myself across the dirt.

Tonight you're not just the hunter, Sloane. Tonight you're also the hunted.

A bitter chill burns through my belly as I realize the true purpose behind the creatures' attack. The ancestors have discovered a Scion in their midst. And in retaliation for them being trapped in this hell, they are coming for me.

Fighting against the pain spreading down my arm, I rise on weak limbs. My body smarts, fingers trembling as I rip a strip off my fatigues to bandage my wounds. Though a wave of dizziness hits me, I force myself down the winding path and set off in search of more recruits.

I am not a killer, but today, I must become something worse.

Even if it means hunting down the others, like a predator loose among prey.

It's the only chance I have of escaping this place.

The thought spurs me on at a frenzied pace. With the girl's rope in hand, I run and run and run until I come to a river curving along the forest floor. Even in the dark, the water glistens like black pearls, rippling ever so gently around the form of a woman knee-deep in its shallows. Across from her, a child crouches at the edge of the bank, a familiar glint in her eyes as water sloshes around her bare feet. When the woman splashes a handful in her face, the child lets out a giggle and scampers off on quick, tiny legs.

"Sloane, come on. These buckets won't move themselves, and—"

I still have to fill the rest.

The memory rushes to the surface of my mind, unbidden, as if willed on by someone else. Large wooden pails brimming with water from the Oba River. Mama's reaching hand as she calls for me to join her. The quiet hum of a lullaby on her lips.

Yes, yes. I remember. These are my most treasured moments. A trove of memories I've kept filed away these past two years, now blooming so fervently around me that I feel a deep, tightening ache in my chest.

I look to the woman in the river, *really* look at her. Long brown locks cascade down her face, but that isn't what leaves me wide-eyed and breathless.

"Mama?" I gasp at the scarf looped around her neck, the sunburst patterns a familiar sight.

She turns her head to me, hands on hips, and the warmth of a smile touches her golden eyes. "Get in here and help me with these, will you?"

Her voice wraps itself around me in a full embrace, a soothing comfort that dulls my aches and pains, kisses away the scars she left behind two years ago. In that moment, I forsake all else. The hunt, my escape, even the ancestors' wicked desire for revenge. They fall far, far away now, like plumes of feathers drifting on the wind. In their absence, an emotion takes flight in me, soaring higher and higher on mended wings.

My eyes are full of tears as I take my first step toward the river. The child moves with me, a shadow keeping an even pace at my side. Then she skips ahead, light and innocent and free, without grief nor guilt. And as she goes and goes and goes, all I can do is follow behind.

By the time I reach the bank, Mama is in front of me, so close, I can almost touch her. And I want—want to grab her tender hands in mine. Feel the soft caress of her fingers on my face. I want my mama so badly, I'd go wherever this memory takes me.

Her calloused hand reaches for mine. Before our fingers brush, I feel an odd, creeping sensation beneath my feet. Then a pained groan shudders out from the surrounding trees.

"Help me."

I whirl in the direction of the sound, searching through the deep dark of the forest. A choking stillness greets me, as though the air itself holds its breath. Unseen fingers claw at my nerves, made worse by the sensation now writhing up my legs.

I frown as I turn to Mama again, but the woman before me is someone—no, *something*—else entirely. A hissing cobra stands in her place, monstrous in length and impossibly black, with smooth patterned scales gleaming down its raised body.

Just the sight of it frees me from my daze. I scream out my terror. Fall to the dirt and scuttle backward, all crab-like and scrambling.

My mind spins, swings off its hinges, especially at the swarm of coiled cobras rippling across the forest floor, like—

Like a current.

It wasn't real. Not the river, not Mama. Not even that single, fleeting memory of her in my head. None of it was real.

The ancestors are fucking with me.

Preying on my vulnerability.

The realization is so startling, so achingly real, it numbs me all over. Then the serpent flares its hood and stretches its jaw. A thousand jagged fangs are bared to strike.

"Help me." The groan echoes once more.

I have no idea where the sound comes from, whom it belongs to. Just as the cobra barrels down on me, I flee.

I have to get out of here. Claw my way out of this grave before the ancestors bury me alive. As many times as they've succeeded in the past, I can't let them do the same to me.

Fight, Sloane. No matter what, don't ever stop fighting.

Determination pulses through my limbs as I tear through the stand of baobab trees, heart thudding, hauling myself faster and faster down the rock-strewn ground. In my haste, I don't see the log lying in the center of my path. Not until I stumble over it and go flying across the dirt, landing hard on my back. Only then do I notice the body of a boy sprawled next to me.

Sweat pours from his brown face, plastering his hair to his forehead. His limbs are contorted in all the wrong places, as if broken ten times too many. As I crawl over to him, my gaze moves to his stomach and the lump of raw flesh spilling from the hole in his gut. Blood gushes thickly down his torso, reddening his fatigues as it pools around him.

"Help me." The boy gasps, struggling to breathe, as he glances up at me. A look of pure pain flashes in his tear-soaked eyes.

For a moment, I can only stare at him in shock, wondering what kind of savage beast did this. But even I know there are too many recruits and spirits roaming this forest, all of us capable and just as monstrous.

I don't know what I'm doing, how best to help an already dying boy. Shakily, I lean over his body, my hands reaching out. Warm blood drips between my fingers now as I scoop his innards and try to stuff them back into the hole. There's too much, too much. The more I try, the more his blood splatters everywhere.

Something breaks inside me. When I look to him, it is through a fog of my own tears. "I—I can't—can't stop the bleeding."

A gurgling sound escapes his lips. "I know."

It's a cruel thing to leave a soul tipping on the edge of an abyss like this, forced to await an inevitable fate. And the longer I stare at the boy, I slowly start to realize what he means for me to do.

No. I shake my head. I can't, I can't. Even when the thought of freedom crawls to the back of my mind, a sick and insidious thing that only fills me with shame, I shove it far away.

"Please," the boy breathes, and my chest cleaves in two.

Without another word, I close my palm over his mouth and press the other to the bridge of his nose. A tremor passes through him when I begin to push and squeeze, making it impossible for him to breathe.

Teo's eyes bulge, then loll. I'm back inside the city dome, staring into his warm, chestnut face moments before the gun went off and a bullet sank into his skull. These hands have taken too many lives. These violent, murdering hands of mine.

Oh gods, oh gods, oh gods.

"I'm so sorry. I'm so sorry," I whisper through my tears as the boy shudders uncontrollably in my grasp, his body still fighting even when he no longer can. I shake with him, feeling the light go out of me as I tumble down, down, down, into a pool of endless darkness.

It takes one minute for him to die. I know because I count every harrowing second.

Finally, the shudders still. The boy goes limp.

I slump against the base of the tree and allow myself to cry. My sobs echo in the vast, lonely forest, and I wish more than anything the nightmare would end. I even welcome death now. Anything to take me away from the horror of this world, from the darkness quickly turning my soul to rot.

Let the ancestors come for me; let them bleed me dry. I will not fight them.

But the only demons that haunt me are the faces of the two recruits. My hands are stained with their blood, my mind a prisoner to their memory. I'd rather die than kill another one. I'd rather be lost to the earth than become the monster the Lucis want me to be.

I'm done. I swear I'm done.

I don't know how long I remain by the tree. An hour, perhaps two? It doesn't matter. Eventually footsteps echo up ahead. I spot what looks like the shadow of a boy, and like the wretch I am, my first thought is to attack. Before I can even stop myself, I'm on my feet, body burning, my fatigues torn to shreds. Yet, all I can think of are the ways to sneak up on this one.

This kill will free you. Whispers fill my mind, a poisonous snake come to tempt me. *This one is it.*

By gods, what is happening to me?

I edge forward, shadowed by the wide trunk of the iroko tree. The boy limps closer, unaware. I see my chance to lunge and I take it, knocking him to the ground.

For someone caught off guard, the recruit is rather quick. He slams the back of his head against my forehead, and I stumble backward, dazed with pain. In the moment it takes me to recover, the boy rolls away and jumps to his feet. I manage to find my footing and stagger up after him. That's when I see the rage shining in his cold brown eyes. The eyes of a devil I know too well.

Malachi.

"I knew I'd find you soon enough." He stares me down as if I'm the last obstacle between him and his freedom.

Of course I am. Something tells me he's mine as well. Everything that happened tonight has led us both to this very moment, a moment I don't doubt Malachi has craved for so long.

With my death, the boy will finally have his vengeance. With my death, Malachi will finally be free. But I'm not going down without a fight. Neither is he, I'm sure.

And now, without even a sliver of magic to defend myself with, this is a kill I must earn.

I glare at him and clench my jaw.

"You want to fight, let's fight."

TWENTY-SEVEN

It begins with a punch.

Malachi lunges at me, his eyes lit with a burning darkness. I dodge the first blow to my face. He swings at me again, and blood trickles from the cut above my eye. I stumble away, my vision fading in and out.

A sharp ache throbs in my skull. Despite the stabbing pain, I charge at Malachi and drive a right hook into his cheek. He staggers backward, almost losing his footing. With a grunt, he shoves into me, cornering me against the trunk of an iroko tree. His blows are heavy, each one a falling hammer on my head. When one lands on my cheek, I scream, my throat raw and burning. Crimson coats my face, smearing the bark of the giant tree. Malachi's eyes widen as my blood seeps into the wood and disappears completely. He stops punching when the iroko starts to swell, its roots stretching beneath the earth with a single taste.

The trees are alive, I realize, remembering the terrible wails of the children who vanished into them. I push the image away just as Malachi scrambles off me. With a clenched fist, I rush after him, delivering a blow to his jaw. Blood gathers between his lips. He flicks out his tongue like a snake and licks the blood away.

We circle one another, buzzing flies with broken wings, our breaths harried and sharp. Our names whisper in the wind. Even though we are alone, I feel the invisible weight of a thousand eyes upon us. Ghostly spectators come to watch two old enemies destroy each other in the shadows of a haunted forest. Malachi must feel it, too, because his gaze sweeps back and forth as he peers into the darkness.

His chest rises and falls in a frightening rhythm. Sweat leaks off his skin, soaking through his muddy fatigues. For a brief moment, Malachi's armor cracks, and I see him back when we were two scrawny kids performing stunts on a village pipe, competing for the glory of a wooden trophy. We've hated each other for so long, it's easy to forget we are only fifteen. Too young, too innocent, and far too fragile for these never-ending horrors that continue to plague our lives.

The words are out of my mouth before I can drag them back. "I know you're hurt—"

"Hurt?" Malachi's gaze hardens. "You killed the only family I ever knew. I was five when I had to learn to survive on my own. You took them away and left me with nothing."

A bitter dam of emotion floods me as the memory of the fire sears through my mind. The screams of the dead echo in my head. I see the faces of his parents behind the twisting flames.

Across from me, Malachi balls his fists. He dons a new armor, a shield against his own vulnerability. "The Lucis are not the evil ones here, Sloane. You are. You and every other Scion scum out there. I'll kill them all, starting with you. Everyone you know, everyone you care about—Baba, Luna—they will suffer the same fate. I'll make sure of it."

I wish he hadn't said that. The darkness surges inside me, a venom clawing at my senses, poisoning what little pity I felt for the boy a moment ago.

Blood rushes to my ears, dulling every sound around me as I charge at him. When I get within a foot, a flash of silver catches my eyes. I barely manage to twist out of the way before Malachi's knife scratches against my shoulder. I don't have time to wonder how he got his hands on the blade, its razor-sharp teeth gleaming with the threat of death. *My death.*

Malachi swings forward with the weapon aimed in my face. My heartbeat doubles as I spin and duck, trying to escape. I'm not fast enough and the devil is too quick. With a hard kick to the gut, he drops me into the dirt. When I scramble up on my feet, he strikes at me again. I land on my back. Malachi descends on me in the same moment, his weight heavy on my chest.

I look up into the eyes of a monster, fangs bared and muscles taut, as he tries to drive the knife into my heart. The sharp point of the blade pierces my fatigues and grazes the skin beneath.

He's going to kill me.

My whole body trembles. I bite back a cry. With all the strength I can muster, I bring my head forward, knocking my forehead against his own. A hot pain lances through my skull, and tears blur my vision. The blow is enough to throw Malachi off my chest. The knife slips from his grasp and clatters across the forest floor.

We dive after it, the both of us clawing our way through the dirt, kicking and scratching and tearing at each other. I struggle to reach the knife. My fingers barely scrape the wooden handle before Malachi snatches me by the leg and drags me back. With a grunt, I drive my boot into his face and pitch forward again. Just as my grip closes around the handle, Malachi pounces on me, his mouth twisted into a feral scream.

I cry out with him, thrusting the knife upward in the same moment. A sickening squelch echoes as steel finds flesh. The blade burrows into his neck.

Malachi gasps.

His terror-stricken eyes roll as he topples to the side, fingers quivering on the knife's handle. Blood gurgles from his lips, a crimson bud blooming in his mouth.

Breath sputters. His body goes limp.

When Malachi dies, I expect to feel victory, a swell of pride, but it never comes. Instead, I sink to the ground next to him, staring through a blur of tears as memories of our childhood flit before my eyes.

Visions of the village's half-pipe. The familiar spin of my wooden wheelie beneath my feet. Malachi's bright grin every time he landed a trick. Shahid and Teo off to the side, caught in their usual mindless banter, and Luna, giggling inside her helmet as she came gliding down the slope. I remember the faces of the other children, too, though Malachi stands out the most.

Golden skin and hazel eyes like fallen leaves. He was different back then, a brazen boy with a kind heart. But like everything else around me, I ruined him. Whatever future Malachi might have had, I took it away the night I killed his parents.

My breath rattles out, searing as it escapes my lungs. Slowly, I turn to Malachi, letting my fingers find his eyes.

I'm sorry I took them away. I'm sorry I left you with nothing. I'm sorry I never said I'm sorry.

With a few silent words of prayer, I pull his lids closed.

Suddenly a rush of howling wind gathers around me. It whips about my face so violently, cracks away at the crooked boughs overhead. Gnarled tree roots rise beneath the dirt, branched and thorny, with giant limbs that crawl and slither along the sodden earth. As they spread like cobwebs around me, each massive branch stretches higher and higher, morphing into a circle of shadowed beings as black as the night itself.

Tonight you're not just the hunter, Sloane. Tonight you're also the hunted.

After hours of torment and taunting, finally the ancestors have come to finish what Malachi started.

I look on in horror as strands of dark moss squirm and writhe where their skin should be, and a netting of jagged thorns drapes over their faces like veils. When their mouths open, revealing a bottomless pit of soil and roots, I start to scramble away.

But I can't move. I can barely even part my lips, every muscle in me held in place by invisible hands. Instead, I cower in the midst of a thousand spirits, all of them screaming my name until I hear everything and nothing at all.

Death. It won't be long now before he, too, arrives. I wonder how the ancestors will deliver me into his reaching grasp. Perhaps with my blood guzzled down their greedy throats, or my flesh torn raw between their spiked teeth? I do not understand the full magnitude of their fury, their deep desire to punish all Scions for the failures of the past. But if I could speak, I'd tell them killing me won't quench their savage thirst. It won't feed their lustful hunger for revenge. If I could speak, I'd tell the ancestors killing me won't grant them the one thing they desire most: peace.

After all, it failed to do the same for me.

Their chorus of cries rips through my being. For a brief, shuddering moment, I can only watch as one among them glides forward on skeletal legs. Swarms of fireflies flutter around her head like a crown, their buzzing wings and choking bodies all too familiar.

When the spirit gets within an inch of me, my limbs protest, fighting to move, stand, do anything to escape a fate I know is surely coming. But it seems all I can manage is a silent scream trapped in my throat.

The spirit's form contorts slowly, taking on the figure of a slender woman, with skin as deep and luminous as midnight, and eyes the pale milky glow of the moon.

"Is this better?" Her hissing voice thins the very breath in my lungs. Before I can muster enough sense to form a thought, a moss-covered hand strays to my face. Alive and worming, the strands wrap around my neck, a threatening noose.

"I am Alagba," she says, "spirit elder of this realm. When the Sleepless told me the descendant of an old enemy was in our domain, I knew I had to see for myself. You reek of your ancestor's blood."

Her words lash out, swift and cracking like a whip. I remain frozen in her magicked grasp, unable to comprehend anything beyond the terror and desperation now clouding my mind. Malachi's body still lies next to me, bathed in crimson, with the blood of two more recruits shaming my hands. Perhaps death is the only freedom I deserve after all I've done. But even on the edge of that ruin, I keep fighting because something in me won't allow me to give up easily.

"Save your strength," Alagba hisses. "As much as I'd love to kill you today, the gods have claimed your fate, and sadly, it doesn't end here. Not yet. So I'll only leave you with this."

She leans closer, and in those full, moonlit eyes, I glimpse the thousands of souls trapped inside her body at once. Their distant cries drift out of her, carrying on the wind as they scrape past my ears.

"Sixteen were they who poisoned this land. Sixteen were they who conquered the gods. A war that began with the greed of Sixteen will thus end with the sacrifice of Sixteen. But remember, Sixteen rose once before and Sixteen will rise once again. Your only path to freedom then lies in Sixteen corners."

My heartbeat thunders with the string of ancient riddles. But I don't get a chance to ask what any of it means as Alagba's pale eyes meet mine for another second.

"Make haste; they're coming." Her diadem of fireflies twinkle in the dark. And then she's gone, vanishing with the others like a stolen whisper.

The forest stills.

As if pulled from a terrible trance, my body jerks forward. The sudden movement sends me sprawling to the ground, and wet soil clumps between my lips. My mouth opens, choking down quick gasps of air as my senses slowly return. Still, my gaze darts around, wide and frantic, searching the space around me for signs of the ancestors.

I'm alone.

Across from me, branches coil and unfurl like wooden serpents, splitting at the roots to reveal a long, winding trail. I can't blink back the tears, but I heave a sigh at the familiar footpath stretching before me. I rise quickly, limbs aching and heavy, as I hobble past Malachi's body.

I don't know why Alagba chose to let me go free, or what plans she and the gods have in store for me. But in this moment, nothing matters but the sunlight pouring through the thick canopy in warm arcing rays, illuminating the path beyond.

With one final glance at the corpse behind me, I step slowly into freedom.

TWENTY-EIGHT

The sun has fallen behind the horizon by the time we reach Fort Regulus. As the airship rolls to a stop, I remain very, very still, rooted between the two Lucis officers who plucked me from Irúnmolè Forest hours ago. As we wait for the familiar groan of the ramp door, the minutes seem to pass in an endless cycle, a void of ticking seconds and shadowed voices. Metal grinding against metal. The purr of an engine. Fractures of my own consciousness. It stretches on and on, cracked and wispy, a loosely spun gossamer. In the hours since I emerged from Irúnmolè, even time holds little meaning.

The officers leave me at the front gates of the barracks without so much as a word. To them, I'm just another recruit who completed the first phase. They don't care about the lives I took or the blood on my hands. They don't care about the tears in my eyes or the screams buried in my throat. To them, I'm just another survivor to be delivered to the base.

I move down the hall slowly, with the ghosts of the recruits trailing not too far behind. I killed them, and so now they haunt me. The first girl calls me a savage for how I chose to take her life. Her face is still mangled and her eyes are two hollow pits, crushed under the weight of a rock. I nod through her curses of an empty life, a doomed soul, finding brief solace only with the second recruit, though he doesn't linger long. But Malachi is the worst of all.

Even in death, the boy promises a lifetime of vengeance. *You will never know freedom, Sloane. You will always remain burdened by your guilt, and it is that guilt that will kill you someday.*

Somehow, I walk into a solid wall dressed in gray fatigues, and it is that collision that rids me of my ghosts and pulls me from the edge of an abyss. Strong hands grip my arms to steady me. When I look up,

Dane is standing before me, green eyes boring into mine beneath the hood raised over his head.

"You're here." He frees my arms, but without his support, my legs wobble. Before they give out, I push my back against the stone walls of the hall. Dane joins me there. After the day I've had, I can't find the strength to send the squad leader away. Perhaps because with him around, I don't have to listen to the whispers of my ghosts.

"All it took was three kills," I tell him, needing to confess my sins to anyone who will listen.

For a long moment, he only stares at the ground, and the silence stretching between us offers no comfort. This close to him, though, I can hear the rising beat of his heart, drowned only by the heavy pounding of my own. With a tip of his chin, he turns his face to me.

"Sometimes, the things we don't want to do are exactly what needs to be done," he says, as if that alone will wash away the guilt.

Is that what I'm searching for? Someone to tell me I had no choice? A way to ease my shame? I shake my head. I don't deserve such reprieve.

An aching weight presses down on me, making my knees buckle. I slide down the wall and force myself to the ground. The concrete floor is cold to touch, chasing away some of the heat beneath my skin. Since I left Irúnmolè, I've felt the gentle surge of àse coursing through my veins, the return of a fire that was smothered inside a twisted forest. Now a familiar warmth spreads down my spine as Shango's drums thud at a steady rhythm in my head. How odd, that I find myself embracing it.

Once again, Dane joins me, easing himself down slowly. He's rather tall, and his long limbs almost take up the breadth of the hallway. He props them up, tucking his knees close to his chest. I don't know why he stays, but his presence is strangely comforting. I don't want to be alone right now.

"The recruits you killed," he murmurs, "do you think they would have done the same to you if they had the chance?"

I can still feel his gaze on me, watching carefully, but I don't have the courage to meet his eyes. So I glance down at my palms, at the lines etched into the folds of my skin, as if the answers I seek are within those markings, waiting to be read.

"Surviving the base comes at a price," Dane continues, his meaning clear. "It's okay to question the morality of your actions. To know you're no longer the person you were before you came here. This life, this world, it changes you."

Tears spring to my eyes, prickling hot as they threaten to spill. I blink them away, my jaw clenched. "I killed so many today. I am a murderer."

It's like poking a hole in a dam, and questions flood the depths of my mind. How many more recruits, Scions, and Yorubas will I have to kill to save my head? How much more will I lose for the sake of survival? In the end, what will become of me?

I wrestle with the last question the most, fighting back an answer I already know in my heart, unable to accept the painful truth. A truth I wish for the world I could change. A future I wish I could avoid.

But you can't unmake a monster. You just can't.

"You are a fighter." Dane's voice cuts through my tangled thoughts, burrowing deep in my head. "Be careful not to lose your mind to the guilt. I've seen it replace the will to survive."

Finally, I twist my body and glance up at him. The hood of his sweater hangs at his shoulders now, revealing his full face, the sharp angles of his jawline. His eyes are warm and gentle, gentler than I've ever seen them in the two weeks we've trained together. For a second, I allow myself to stare into them, and it's almost easy to forget who he is and all he's done. But Dane is a soldier, not a boy. One bound by duty to kill people like me. The squad leader may have warned me about Irúnmolè Forest, but he's also the same soldier who had me whipped. The same soldier who hurt me. The same soldier who would execute me if he knew my truth.

I force a shaky breath and settle back against the wall. Those kind eyes do not belong on Reapers like him.

"You don't owe me your sympathy," I mutter. "You don't know me."

"No," he replies. "But I remember how I felt coming out of the Wild many years ago. I killed four soldiers that day. I was ten."

Ten. My heart slams against my ribs at the image of a young innocent boy wandering through the Irúnmolè Forest alone, searching for other children like himself to kill. I'm too numb for words.

"They won't make it easy for you to remember who you are." Dane's eyes shine with the ghost of his own past. "They want you to remember *them.* They want you to remember the Phases. And worst of all, they want you to remember the monster they've made of you."

When he rises, I think he's ready to leave. Instead, he stoops low in front of me, his broad frame casting a shadow over my head. He opens his hand to me. A round, white-tipped bullet glints in his outstretched palm, looped to a braid of silver metal.

"This is for you," he says before draping Faas's bullet chain around my neck.

The weight of the ammunition presses against my collarbone, and my hand shakes as I run my fingers along the smooth steel. A prize for my kills, a symbol of who I'm becoming. A weapon forged to destroy other Scions like myself. My chest tightens at the irony.

"You have to decide what matters most: your humanity or your survival," Dane adds, and I swallow around the lump lodged in my throat. As much as I hate to admit it, I know the squad leader is right. "I'm sorry, Sloane. But you can't have both."

It's the first time he's said my name. For a brief, fleeting moment, the sound of it shakes something loose inside me. I raise my head slowly, locking eyes with him. A faint energy ripples in the ocean, an unfamiliar force fighting to break the surface. Before I can even place it, the strange thing is gone, replaced by an emptiness left behind from his words.

Dane leaves me standing outside my door. I watch him stroll away, and only when he disappears around the bend do I enter my shared quarters. Sleep would be merciful right now, but the sight of Izara sitting on her own bunk pushes all thoughts of rest away.

Her fatigues hang loose, grass-stained and torn, with splotches of red-and-purple bruises darkening her face. She looks as haggard as I feel, wrecked from the day's horror. But she's here. She's alive.

A knot unravels in my stomach. Up until this moment, I never realized how worried I was about her, wondering whether she'd make it out of Irúnmolè Forest, and if I'd ever see her again.

Izara must have thought the same, too, because when she meets my eyes, a long sigh of relief escapes us both.

"How?" she whispers, searching my face for some kind of explanation.

I shouldn't be here, and we both know it. Yet somehow, the ancestors chose to keep me alive when, in truth, they should have killed me like they did every other Scion who stumbled into their fold. I still don't know why they let me go. But the forest, with all of its horrors, is the last place I want to return to right now. Though I doubt I'll ever truly leave that place behind.

A slight shrug is all I can give to Izara, and I hope it's answer enough.

With a kick, I slam the door closed and move to sit beside her. The two bullets around her neck clang as she shifts, angling her body toward me. Her fists curl around the end of a bloody wooden shank. I stare at the weapon knowingly, imagining whose blood stains its tip, how many recruits Izara took out with it, how much of herself she gave up in her fight to get out.

"Miriam's dead," she says of the fourth girl on our squad. "The barracks officer came to clean out her dresser half an hour ago."

I glance at the corner of the room and, sure enough, one of the shared drawers has been thrown wide open, emptied of all its contents.

Even though I barely spoke a word to Miriam while she was around, news of her death still sends a jolt through me. Especially with the knowledge that Izara was the one to take her life. My gaze slides up to her then, settling on the blood-crusted bruises on her face. "Are you all right?"

She grinds her jaw, nods once. "We got out. We survived. It's all that matters."

It sounds like a prayer. If only it were that easy.

"Every single one of those deaths is a step closer to freedom, Sloane." Izara senses my unease, and her voice sharpens, unwavering in her conviction. "Sometimes, you have to walk in the dark before you can see the light. We did what needed to be done."

Her words are prickly thorns, stabbing at my chest.

"H-how can you even say that?" When I look into her eyes, I expect to see the pain she's trying to bury away. Instead, I see flashes of the girl who killed a recruit our first day here on the base. Cold, unfeeling, a ruthless soldier in the making. But I refuse to believe she's any of those things. Not the girl who nursed me back to life after my whipping. The same girl who gave me an anchor to latch onto when my àse threatened to pull me under.

"Those recruits were like us. Children who are now dead because we killed them. Don't you feel any remorse?"

I watch her all the while, but not even a flicker of emotion crosses Izara's face. A bitter taste gathers in my mouth. Her grip tightens around the shank as she grapples with her words, unable to push them out.

For a while, the silence persists, until finally, she whispers, "I'm dying, Sloane."

"What?" I blink up at her, stunned by the news.

"I'm dying," she repeats, and her expression darkens into something grim. "I was born with a blood disease. My parents are herbalists, but neither of them knew what it was. Not at first. Not until I started having these horrible pains that would sometimes last for weeks. I spent my whole life visiting every other herbalist in my village, and they all said the same thing. There's no cure for what I have. Not in Nagea, at least."

She exhales slowly, a long, hissing breath that makes my heart ache. *A blood disease.* It's the last thing I expected, and it sounds somber to my ears. Back in Agbajé, I saw many children die from ailments the village herbalist just couldn't cure. Most of us in Nagea can't afford the luxury of skilled physicians or proper medicine, and must rely only on bitter concoctions and home-brewed remedies to relieve our symptoms. If there are no herbs that can save Izara, then what? The truth of it burns, and heat spreads across my face.

"I'm so sorry, Izara," I manage, the words sticking in my throat. But I know no amount of sympathy will ever be enough.

I run my gaze over her small, willowy frame. The sickly flush of yellow tinging her dark skin. Izara is one of the strongest on the squad, the only recruit I know with two bullets now on her chain. All this time, I never would have guessed she was this ill, let alone dying. How has she managed to train through the pain? What is Izara fighting and killing for when she doesn't have to?

"You shouldn't be here." My sadness is bone-deep.

But Izara just shakes her head. "I'm exactly where I need to be," she says, tossing the shank on the ground. "There's something I came here to do."

She casts a glance at the locked door, making sure we're still alone. Then with her legs folded underneath, she adjusts her weight on the bed. I shift on the foam to mirror her pose.

"What I'm about to tell you never leaves this room." She turns to look at me head-on, eyes flashing. "I told you about my sister. How she's . . . like you?"

I nod.

"I was never drafted," she whispers. "My sister was, but I took her place."

The weight of her admission slams into me, shocking me more than anything else. "Why would you do that?"

"Because she's my blood, and I'd do anything to protect her. She couldn't survive this world, but I can."

Her voice softens as she speaks. It's obvious how deeply Izara cares for her twin sister, enough to sacrifice her own freedom to keep the Scion girl away from Avalon. A difficult, impossible choice. But I understand why she did it. After all, it's the same reason I couldn't flee with Teo, not if it meant putting Baba's and Luna's lives at risk. I'd do anything to protect my family, protect the ones I love, and Izara is no different.

Izara . . . My eyes widen when the realization sweeps over me. If Izara was the one drafted, then it means the person standing before me is—

"Amiyah?" I gasp.

She offers a small, kind smile. "Amiyah Kehinde Makinde, yes."

Kehinde. Her true Yoruba name. I think it means second-born, recalling what little Mama told me of the Yoruba tradition. If she is Kehinde, then her sister must be Taiwo, the first of the twins.

"Nice to meet you, Amiyah." I extend a hand to her, my lips pulling with the shadow of a smile. "I'm Sloane Folashadé."

I haven't spoken my real name aloud in so long, it almost sounds foreign on my tongue. Still, a true grin spreads up Amiyah's face as she takes my hand in hers.

"So what now?" I sigh a moment later, slumping back against the wall.

"I have a plan." Amiyah shifts a little closer to me until we're resting side by side. "Once we get to the Sahl, I'm going to find Ilè-Orisha."

"You're going to desert?" I stop just short of saying *too.*

Her ringed fingers tremble in her lap, and she clasps her hands tightly together. "No herbalist in Egba can cure me, but a descendant of Obaluaye can."

"The Orisha of sickness and healing," I breathe.

Of course. An ordinary herbalist might not be able to save Amiyah, but the right Scion could heal her blood disease and keep her from dying. With magic, Amiyah could survive. And where else would one find a descendant of Obaluaye if not in Ilè-Orisha with the Shadow Rebels?

Like a puzzle, every piece of her plan starts to fall into place. Her decision to come to Avalon in place of her sister. Her unflinching strength during training. Even the guilt she won't allow herself to feel—it's all for one purpose: to save herself from the jaws of death.

"This plan is all I have," she murmurs next to me. "It's what drives me, what keeps me going despite all the madness." At that, I glance at her, meeting narrowed eyes. "You think I'm remorseless, but you're wrong. I know what guilt feels like. Every day we spend behind these walls, I feel its grip tightening around me. But guilt doesn't save, Sloane. It only festers and grows until it leaves you dead. And I don't want to die."

When her voice cracks, I chide myself for having judged her in the first place. Who am I to question someone else's emotion? I know the guilt she speaks of. I've felt its choking grasp since the moment I pulled that trigger on Teo. I can't fault Amiyah for trying to free herself from that burden. I only wish I were strong enough to do the same.

I reach for her hand, squeezing a little. *I'm sorry. I was wrong about you.* She returns the gesture in kind, her grip tightening around mine.

"How do you plan on getting to Ilè-Orisha?"

"I don't know." She shrugs, but a steely determination hardens her face. "They say only those who are destined to find Ilè-Orisha do. Well, I make my own destiny, and I won't rest until I find it."

Slowly, I lift a hand to my neck, running my fingers along the beaded choker Baba gave me the night before I left Agbajé. *This will lead you to Ilè-Orisha*, he said in the flickering light of our table lantern. Baba also warned me never to reveal the map carved into the cowrie shells to a single soul. But Amiyah isn't a Lucis officer. She's Yoruba like me, one who's offered me nothing but care and kindness since I first met her. She's a friend.

I inhale a deep breath and loosen the strings of the choker, letting it slide off my neck.

"I think I can help with that," I say, squeezing the cowrie shells between my fingers before turning it over to her.

For a moment, she holds the choker up to her face, brows pinched as she examines the intricate carvings spread across the shells. When she realizes what she's really staring at, her jaw drops.

"Gods above." Her eyes snap to me. "Is this what I think it is?"

"A map to Ilè-Orisha."

"H-how did you get this?"

"It belonged to my grandmother." My voice is low. "Baba gave it to me before I left. Said he wanted me to escape to Ilè-Orisha. Find some kind of peace."

The memory of that night comes to mind, the sorrow woven on my grandfather's face still too familiar. Just the reminder makes me ache. As painful as it is to accept I'll never see Baba again, I made a promise to him, and it's one I intend to keep. But whatever future awaits me out there on the Sahl, perhaps I don't have to face it alone.

"You can come with me," I offer gently, tilting my head toward her. "We can flee together."

"Are you serious?"

I nod, smiling as tears pool in Amiyah's eyes. I have no doubt she would have done everything she could to find Ilè-Orisha on her own. At least now, she has a fighting chance. When she starts to cry, I draw her closer to me, wrapping my arms around her shoulders. She hugs fiercely.

"My gods. This is really happening."

Her voice brims with so much hope. It spills into me, warming my insides, filling me with a renewed burst of energy. With that, I exhale slowly, releasing some of the burden that's weighed over me since I left Irúnmolè Forest.

We can do this, I tell myself, feeling lighter than I've felt in days. Two more weeks, and Amiyah and I can escape to Ilè-Orisha together.

When we both pull away, her easy laughter bounces off the walls of our quarters, contagious enough that even I start to chuckle. Then the bells echo in the hallway, and she springs to her feet. Before I can ask what she's doing, she's already tugging me off the bed and dragging me toward the door.

"Come on. We're late," she calls over her shoulder.

"Where are we going?"

"You'll see."

She starts off into the hallway, light and quick in her steps, with me stumbling after her, trying to keep up. She takes me up several flights of stairs hidden behind an unassuming door, ignoring my protests and the endless deluge of questions.

When we finally reach the top of the stairwell, Amiyah shoves the door open, revealing a wide rooftop terrace overlooking the vast Atali Ocean.

"What are we doing—" I glance out to see Nazanin and Jericho leaning over the ledge, their bodies pressed against each other as they stare out at the moonlit waters. At the familiar sight of them, the same relief I felt with Amiyah earlier pulses through me, and I sigh low in my throat.

Then the door slams shut, causing them both to whirl.

"Sloane!" Nazanin pries herself away from Jericho and rushes forward, arms swinging around my neck in a tight embrace. I fold my limbs around her, squeezing her back in turn. We've come a long way, she and I. From comrades in training to allies trading jabs over a shared mission. Our relationship certainly took a turn the day she fed me after my whipping. Now I couldn't imagine another day here without the comfort of her friendship.

Jericho and Amiyah join in, and we remain that way for a very long time, the four of us wrapped in a cocoon of warmth that folds itself weightlessly around me.

We're alive, their touch says. *We got out.*

Their sudden display of emotion breaks my resolve, and tears swim in my eyes. When we finally untangle ourselves, there are stupid, crooked smiles pasted on our wet faces.

I wipe my eyes and heave a breath, gulping deeply as I walk over to the ledge. Despite the warm night, a cool ocean breeze brushes against my bare arms, and gooseflesh rises on my skin. The moon pouts low on the horizon, an orb of glowing crimson kissing the rippling tide. The sight is a rare beauty amid so much ugliness, a small glimmer of light in the surrounding darkness.

"It's peaceful up here," I murmur as Amiyah falls in next to me. Nazanin and Jericho take up the space to my left, arms wrapped around each other's waists in an intimate show of affection.

"I figured we could use it as a meeting spot," Jericho says. "I've been watching for movement. No one ever comes up here."

I nod along, feeling a strange sense of calm settle over me. The terrace looks nothing like Agbajé, but it reminds me so much of home, of the days Teo and I spent perched on the rooftop of his hut, tossing our hopes and dreams back and forth like two practiced jugglers. Though those days are long gone, perhaps whatever solace I found in those simple moments, I could find the same here too.

"What's that?" Amiyah snaps me out of my thoughts, her gaze fixed on the thousands of lanterns floating down a faraway beach.

"The Lucis are celebrating First Bright," Jericho replies.

Festival of the First Light, I think, recalling my old lessons from the institution. A celebration to honor the day the Lucis arrived in Nagea from the dark ruins of the old world, marking the beginning of their post migration era.

My chest tightens as I watch the lanterns bob idly along the beach. I don't know what unnerves me more—that the festival is also a celebration of the Lucis' invasion of the Ancient Kingdoms, or that while we were busy fighting for our lives inside Irúnmolè Forest, these monsters had the gall to throw a bleeding party.

"I heard the guards talking about the queen's masked ball happening at Castlemore tonight," Jericho shakes his head. "They won't shut up about it."

In spite of my anger, the first seedling of a plan blooms in front of me, a tiny bud that quickly starts to sprout. I close my eyes and run it over, trying to smooth out its rough petals.

After a moment, I jerk my chin toward him. "Who's going to be at the ball?"

He shrugs. "Everyone, I'm assuming."

The guards. Since First Bright is a major holiday for the Lucis, chances are many of the officers will be required to attend the festival. Which means—they might cut corners, perhaps even get sloppy. A rush of adrenaline jolts through me, making me as buoyant as the lanterns riding the ocean waves. It's exactly the opportunity we've been waiting for, one well-timed shot to break into Archives Hall with little interference.

"It's time." I round on Jericho and Nazanin, forcing us all into a small circle.

"Time for what?" Amiyah's gaze flits back and forth among the three of us, a deep furrow in her brows. I almost forgot she knows nothing of our mission, or the plans we've spent the past week setting in place. But with all the truths already spilled tonight, what's one more? It might as well be a night of many reveals.

"You're not the only one who came here on a mission," I start, glancing at the others before I continue. When Jericho and Nazanin nod their approval, I tell Amiyah everything—about Mama's disappearance, Jericho's imprisoned parents, even the Book of Records. Everything except Nazanin's secret dealings with the Black Wolf. Judging by the sharp nails she digs into my side, it's obvious she's yet to share her own plans with Jericho. "All we need is the tunnel map inside Caspian's office," I finish in a rush, "and tonight might be the perfect time to steal it."

Amiyah bites down on her lip. When her eyes meet mine again, an offer already sparks in them. "I want to help."

"I can't ask you to do that." I fold my arms across my chest, overcome by the sudden urge to protect her. Even if the base might be crawling with fewer guards tonight, that doesn't make it any safer. Amiyah's already sacrificed enough. It'd be cruel of me to ask more of her.

"You're not asking. I'm offering." Her gaze flies to Nazanin and Jericho, as if expecting them to back her up. "You guys are going to need more eyes on the ground," she presses. But thankfully, neither of them takes the bait.

"Sloane's right." When Nazanin finally speaks, her voice is sharp, all matter-of-fact. "We all have a stake in this. You don't. If anything goes wrong, you don't deserve to suffer the consequences. Besides, someone has to live to tell this epic tale."

That lightens the mood a little. Even Amiyah breathes a long sigh now, conceding at last.

"Fine." She looks to each of us once more, but her eyes linger on me the most as she whispers, "Stay alive, will you?"

"Always." I wink at her before turning to face Jericho and Nazanin. The corners of their mouths lift, curving into twin smiles.

I grin back at them. "Let's go make some good trouble."

TWENTY-NINE

There is only one rule to scaling a leopards' den:

Whatever you do, don't fall.

It's those words that ring in my ears as I clamber up the side railings of the fence, fingers locked around the metal bars, booted feet grasping for footholds. Across from me, Jericho and Nazanin scuttle along like two spiders in perfect harmony, gaining momentum despite the leopards prowling not too far below. At least five of them stalk the grounds of the den, with two more sprawled beneath the jackalberry tree, their pale blue eyes winking in the deep shadows.

The guards take the leopards out on patrol every night.

That was what Jericho said weeks ago, at the start of this bleeding mission. It's what we planned for. But none of us could have anticipated that most of the guards would attend the queen's ball, leaving the beasts to remain in their cages for the night.

Now just the sight of them makes my stomach churn. In that moment, an image of the second deserter comes rushing back. The ghost of his screams echo in my head as I recall how the beasts tore at every inch of his limbs. I shudder at the memory, body burning, as though I can feel the leopards' teeth sinking into my own flesh, grinding bones and tendons between their jaws.

For a heartbeat, I press my body against the cold metal, pinned like a dead fly to the fence, too frozen to move a muscle. The night air that was warm only an hour ago now bites against my skin, seeping through the guards' stolen uniform. But not even the sudden chill can distract me from my fears, especially not with death lurking ten feet below.

A slight jerk of the railings forces me to glance up, head raised to the two dark silhouettes hovering high above me.

"Hurry," Nazanin hisses before she and Jericho haul themselves over to the other side of the fence.

I don't know how they managed to make it to the top so quickly, but it's all I can do to swallow my terror, draw a deep breath, and force my feet upward.

I quicken my pace, both palms so terribly slick against the rungs that it takes every effort to maintain my balance against the fence. Though my body teeters in the wind, I latch onto the metal with desperate fingers, hoisting my full weight over the railings once I reach the edge.

"You all right?" Jericho asks as I land in next to him.

I only manage a nod before we launch right back into action. The descent is much easier, our movement nimble and brisk as we scale down to the narrow footpath connecting the northern entrance to the den. It takes all of one minute to cover the rest of the distance, and we leap off the fence when we're low enough to the ground.

I gulp down air as my boots once again hit the packed earth. Now that I'm back on solid ground, a dogged sense of conviction sweeps through me, accompanied by a momentary burst of relief. It vanishes the instant a pair of leopards lunge forward on the other side of the den, their piercing eyes fixed intently on us. We scurry away in time, every hair on my neck standing taut. Even with the fence cutting a divide between us, their bared fangs and ferocious snarls are enough to send us bolting for the door.

The northern entrance remains unbarred and unguarded, allowing us to slip into the training center undetected. Without any officers or surveillance in place, it's a mad dash up the stairs, our boots slapping against the concrete as we race the whole flight to the main level.

The hallways are familiar now, long stretches of gray concrete barely illuminated by the globe lights overhead. I set a rapid pace, with Jericho and Nazanin on either side, our silhouettes stretching along the painted walls as we dart toward the southern wing.

With the First Bright ball well underway, the guards are few and scattered tonight, just as expected. A few officers idle in their posts, their boisterous laughter booming down the empty corridors. We keep to the shadows, hedging along a narrow bend, careful not to meander too close to their slurring voices. Even with so few of them around, the guards are still armed. While the lot might already be drunk on palm wine and taba, it doesn't mean they've forgotten how to shoot.

A tremor ticks up my spine as I try to imagine what our doom would look like if any of these men should catch us. Faas would certainly be the first to hear of this, and I doubt the commander would spare my life this time around. Though an ache tightens in my chest, I exhale quickly, hoping to expel a bit of my fear as we hasten farther down the hallway.

At least our stolen uniforms provide enough disguise against the cameras' leering gazes, allowing us to look the part should the security feed pick us up. The stiff fabric hangs loosely on my body, the bloodstains smeared along the sleeves far too much to ignore. But the dim lights serve us well, making the dark smudges difficult enough to notice.

Soon we're heading away from the gun range, cutting straight into the west wing. Here, the training hall looms off to the side, its familiar grounds long deserted. A buzz of energy rolls through me as we creep past it, inching closer and closer to Caspian's office. Now with the tunnels' map so close within our reach, I turn my prayers on the camera right outside the lieutenant's office. One paint pellet is all we have for a single, well-aimed shot. One I pray will be forceful enough to blind the camera to our presence.

If Jericho succeeds tonight, we'll finally have everything we need to break into Archives Hall. In a few minutes, I could finally learn the truth about Mama.

My heart thumps as we turn the corner and the lieutenant's door rises into view. A wide plank of mahogany inlaid with small glass panels, and a round, white orb peering overhead.

"Are you ready?" I glance sideways at Jericho.

In response, he fits the black pellet to his slingshot with a deftly trained hand, the strings pulled back and taut. A low breath gusts out of him as he trains his eyes on the angled camera, his lanky frame straight and rigid. He looks every bit the sharpshooter he is.

In the seconds it takes him to home in on his target, Nazanin and I huddle closely behind him, our fingers wound together in silent prayer.

Another huff of breath and Jericho loosens the strings, sending the pellet hurtling forward at a dizzying speed. A coat of black paint splatters across the lens of the camera, and the device gives a low whine.

I allow myself a moment's laughter, smiling a little as Nazanin presses a kiss to Jericho's face. Then, with no time left to waste, I rush toward the office door and push down on the brass handle. No matter how hard I try, the bleeding thing remains shut.

Nazanin nudges me off to the side and leans forward, examining the keyhole. She pulls a pin free from her braids and shoves it inside, twisting the thin metal around.

"I hear footsteps," I whisper, and my gaze flicks to the hallway to our left. Two uniformed silhouettes stretch out into thin lines as they approach the bend. The officers' drunken voices float past my ears, growing louder and louder with each passing second.

"Hurry, Naz," Jericho adds.

"I got it. I got it."

Something clicks. This time, when she yanks on the handle, it budges without effort.

The door wrenches open with a slight push.

"Get in!" I shove them both inside, shutting the door seconds before the guards round the curve.

Their footfalls echo out in the hallway, heavy on the concrete floor. We remain still, careful not to make a sound until their steps fade into the distance.

For an instant, darkness presses in on us, sliced only by the moon-light streaming through the small square window to my right. Jericho flips a switch in the wall, and the globes set in the ceiling wink to life. Warm, yellow light pours into the small chamber.

The office itself is pretty unremarkable, splashed in dull gray paint, with a row of shelving units drilled into the wall. A hefty box-shaped device squats atop Caspian's desk, and stacks of colorful paper spill in disarray across the wooden surface. Despite his unmatched shooting skills, it seems the lieutenant is a rather messy man.

"There's the map." Jericho gestures at a brown wooden board hung on a wall across the room.

Of the dozens of papers pinned to the plank, the map is the only parchment that catches my attention. Nazanin and I run toward it, but she reaches the board first, snatching the map before I do. Her eyes dance back and forth as she scans the intricate grids winding up and down the paper. Judging by the frown on her face, she has no idea what any of the lines mean. She gives up soon enough and turns the map over to me.

My stomach flutters as I grip its creased edges, surveying the different routes and entry points. "My gods, the tunnels lead everywhere."

In fact, it seems all of Fort Regulus may have been built on these underground passages, each channel worming its way from the squad quarters, past the training center, into Archives Hall, the research facility, and the soldiers' barracks beyond.

"Do you see an entrance nearby?" Beside me, Nazanin squints at the large parchment in my hands.

My gaze flits down the paper until I find the tunnel grids connecting the training center to Archives Hall. There are over five entrances in the northern side of this building alone, but Caspian's office is in the west wing.

With one finger on the map, I trace the grids sideways, not blinking until I find exactly what I'm looking for.

"There." I stab my finger at the entry point.

"So where to?" she asks, looking up at me.

"Lower level." With a breath, I fold the map into a small square. "I know where it is."

Across from us, Jericho leans over the lieutenant's desk, scattering the already messy pile about before pulling a torchlight out from one of its cabinets. It flickers on with a click, its light dim but there. Sufficient enough to see us through the tunnels.

Jericho straightens up. "Let's get out of here."

Already, he's at the door, the torchlight swinging in one hand. With his other hand rested on the handle, he presses his left ear against the wood, listening, making sure there are no guards lurking outside. When he's certain the hallway is clear, he flips the switch and plunges us back into darkness.

Gingerly, he pries the door open. A burst of cool air greets us as we rush out of the lieutenant's office, the map tucked safely in my pocket.

My turn now.

The tunnels are an altar of the dead. A rubble of skulls litters the hard-packed earth, crumbling bones and thin vertebrae strewn across the old, sodden ground. Even the bare stone walls are lined with corpses, a monstrous display of fright-eyed faces frozen beneath a slab of concrete and rot.

I nearly stumble at the sight of them, legs wobbling as I struggle to stay on my feet. Despite the darkness that bleeds through the tunnels, my wide eyes travel down the endless row of bodies until I can barely see through my own tears.

Until I can barely move.

Nazanin is the first to step forward, her hands tracing the deep grooves in the wall. "Are these—"

"Scions." Jericho nods, tracking each corpse with the dim light of the torch. "Looks like they were buried alive."

Hearing it aloud doesn't lessen the blow, and my chest squeezes as though the very breath has been knocked out of me.

By gods, these aren't tunnels at all. No, these are graves.

A mass grave of my people.

It stretches far, far beyond, into the branching pathways and deepest burrows. Severed heads and limbs worked into every pillar and ruined column, like some kind of hidden treasure for generations of Lucis to soon discover. An underground trophy to be venerated forever.

"This is absolutely heinous," Nazanin whispers, and my àse ripples out in agreement.

A current of heat courses through me faster than it has since the àmì-orí ritual. The sensation is so sudden that, for a moment, I can hardly keep a firm grasp on the swirls of magic weaving beneath my skin. Just as the heat leaks out to the surface, I clench my fists against the fire, forcing it back down.

When the sensation lifts, I harden myself against the emotions tugging at my heart, driving away any ounce of attachment to the corpses. For all that must be done tonight, I cannot allow myself to sink into my pain. Not this time.

Focus on Mama, I remind myself. *Focus on what lies ahead.*

Breathing low, I turn to Jericho and pluck the torch out of his grasp, letting the yellow light illuminate the curving maze beyond.

"Let's keep moving," I say, stalking off down one of the trails.

The air inside the tunnels is damp and cool, the ground wet and moldy beneath my feet. Murky water oozes from the cracks in the earth and soaks right through my boots, drenching my socks. Nazanin groans as we wade through a shallow seepage. The puddles splish and splash against our knees as we scuttle past.

Back on dry land, I bring the map up to my face, the parchment rustling as I track the tunnel paths splitting every which way. There are many trails zigzagging toward Archives Hall, some more meandrous than others.

"This one." I settle on the least winding path, and we sprint toward it at a relentless pace.

We reach a fork in the tunnel, only to arrive at a dead end minutes later. Another branch, and the stone ceilings are nearly caved in. Even when we turn a different corner, try to clear the debris from our path, the narrowed walls press in on all sides, making it impossible to squeeze through the fallen wreckage.

"It's a jungle down here," Jericho says, his voice echoing as we come to a halt at another open fork.

I scour the map again, wheezing as I follow its complex web of routes and entry points for the third time. Certainly, without this as a guide, we would never make it out of here.

Sweat rolls down my back, and a light sheen glistens on both Nazanin's and Jericho's faces. I know the promise I made to them. They've fulfilled their end of the bargain, and it's my turn to do the same. But after several minutes of scrabbling about, trying to navigate one accessible trail without a dead end, we shuffle in the same spot like wayward insects caught in a spider's web.

Gods, it feels like we've gone everywhere and nowhere at all.

With wide, frantic eyes, I home in on the parchment in my hands, paying closer attention to the tunnel lines. Even the ones that veer off in different directions. It's possible many of these tunnels are nothing but collapsed concrete and stones now, but at least one of them must be functional still.

I just have to find it.

One tunnel in particular runs parallel to our current trail, a long pathway that splits off toward a trio of buildings—including Archives Hall.

Limbs burning, I set off toward it. Nazanin and Jericho fall in behind me, boots echoing, as I force us down what I pray will be our final route. Silence hangs over us for a long while, the three of us focused on the path ahead. Every so often, I pause to return to the map, making sure we're still on the right track. The deeper we go, the more I slowly allow myself to be reassured by the wending terrain. If this branch remains untouched, we should be approaching Archives Hall any minute.

For the first time since the start of the mission, dread pools in my gut. A dull pressure builds in my chest as I turn my thoughts inward: on Mama, on the information soon to be within my grasp. After two years of endless searching, of village gossips that sparked Luna's illness and a deep ostracism that left me and Baba poor and starved, I will finally uncover the truth about what happened the night Mama disappeared.

Yet, what if after everything we've done tonight, we still can't get inside the Archives?

What if the truth about Mama is far worse than I imagined?

My pulse races with each horrible thought, made worse by the exhaustion now dragging at my legs. I exhale slowly and push forward, grip tightening around the torchlight.

In my mind, I build a cage around my fears, shoving them in one doubt at a time. I lock up every single thought of failure. I can't allow myself to feel any of it. Not right now.

A spark of adrenaline ignites inside me as we continue down the path, until every step slowly brings with it a sense of surety. Everything I came here for now lies on the other side of these stone walls. I refuse to let myself believe otherwise.

My pace slows when we come to a makeshift stairwell at the bottom of the tunnel. Stone slabs spread over a set of iron rods poking out from the wall, ascending upward in a steep fashion. There, at the top of the stairs, an iron door looms, its frame bent inward, a layer of rust eating away at its forgotten hinges. The door looks old and weathered from years of disuse, with a thick coating of cobwebs sheathing much of its bolts and latches. Certainly, the kind of abandoned door that would lead straight into Archives Hall.

"Is this it?"

"Are we here?"

Together, Nazanin and Jericho search my face for an answer, a glimmer of hope shining in their eyes.

An ember of it sparks in me, too, as I bound up the stairs, with the two of them at my heels. My heart gallops in my chest once we reach the landing at the top. With a quick, steadying hand, I scrape the cobwebs off the door's handle, wrench every bolt and latch loose, and yank downward with added force.

The door groans back slowly, and warm light spills from a long hallway made of polished marble, its towering walls framed with gilded paintings and lifelike murals of the royal bloodlines. If I squint hard enough, I can make out every bleeding face of the Founding Lucis within that canvas, their terrible features so intricately cut, as though frozen in time.

Even without me peering at the map, the pristine floors and Heritage Wall are enough to give away the building's sole purpose.

By gods.

Finally, I look between Jericho's and Nazanin's waiting expressions, at the shadow of a smile now tugging at the corners of their lips.

I can't help but offer a smile of my own, the words falling like a song on my tongue.

"The day is ours."

THIRTY

We burst into the long, empty corridors of Archives Hall, fueled by a wild rush of hope and adrenaline. There are no security posts in sight, not a single officer to keep us on our toes, save for the dozen or so cameras turned toward the open chamber looming close ahead.

The Archives Room. My heart hammers against my ribs as we draw nearer to its sliding glass doors. With the security cameras watching every inch of the entrance from above, there's no way one of them won't pick us up. Even in our stolen uniforms, we can't escape the eyes of a dozen cameras upon us. I'm sure it's why the Lucis haven't bothered to place any patrolling officers in here. The second we cross those borders, it's only a matter of time until the alarm goes off.

The threat shadows our every move, an unavoidable risk, and still, we push forward. We've come too far, sacrificed too much, not to see this through.

Just before we step into the cameras' line of sight, Jericho stops midstride. He tilts his face toward me and Nazanin.

"Three minutes," he whispers, urgent now. "We split up. Search for anything with the word *Record* in it. Whoever finds the book first, alert the others."

I nod along with Nazanin, my nerves twitching with energy. It pours through me as I dare to take my first step toward the sliding doors. Another, and we're well within visible range. Jericho and Nazanin charge into the room first, darting in different directions.

No turning back now. Drawing on my own courage, I rush in after them, letting the door slide shut behind me.

Inside the room, elaborate walls of towering shelves are arranged in rows across the smooth linoleum floor. Volumes of leather-bound books, ancient tomes, and printed records spill down the length of the chamber. Between them, columns of steel and concrete dot every aisle, twisting upward into a glass-roofed ceiling decorated with stained frescoes.

Three minutes.

My boots slap against the tiles as I sprint toward the aisle at the far end of the chamber. I've never seen a library before; nothing like this exists in Agbajé. Even our ancient Yoruba texts are forbidden, most of them burned and destroyed to keep us from learning the truth behind our own history. It's exactly what the Lucis want. If we don't know who we are, where we come from, we can never begin to understand what we're capable of.

Blood pounds in my ears as I turn into the aisle, expecting to find more rows of shelved files like the others. Instead, framed pictures spread behind thick panes of glass, each one hung in an orderly manner along the unblemished walls. A parade of Lucis soldiers rolls out before me, uniformed men and women with battle-hardened eyes and lips set in a grim line. I'm not surprised to find Olympia in their midst, a general among soldiers, her picture hung high above the rest.

These are the faces of the decorated monsters who fought on the Sahl, soldiers who have slaughtered and buried thousands of my kind in the name of power.

It's all I can do not to send the frames crashing to the floor, teeth clenched as I tear myself away from the bleeding display.

Two minutes.

Hurry, Sloane.

I weave in and out of the aisles, my gaze tracking the labels carved into the bottom of the shelves: from *Scion War Diaries* and *Personnel Records of the First War* to the section labeled *Service Files.* My heartbeat quickens the farther I go, searching every corner for a miracle in a book. Still, I find nothing on the *Book of Records.*

Gods, what if the records aren't here? What if this is just another horrible dead end?

Now, with less than two minutes left, my body trembles with restless unease. Just as I slip into a different aisle, a birdsong trills from the other side of the chamber.

A signal.

My limbs are moving already, taking me in the direction of the noise. I cross the room in quick strides, reaching the middle aisle in a matter of seconds.

Down the lane, Nazanin crouches on the ground next to Jericho, her arms wrapped around his bent shoulders. I pause in my step, frowning as his quiet sobs echo in the stillness of the Archives Room. At first, I don't understand. Until I see the bound book lying in the space between them, its pages spread apart.

Weeks ago, Jericho told me his parents had been arrested during an uprising in Shaaré. Finding out whether they were still alive was all he wanted, the hope he held on to. Judging by the tears in his eyes, I can only assume the answer. His muffled cries send a ripple of sadness through me as I halt in front of him and Nazanin.

She stares up at me through a cloud of her own tears, her shoulders heaving. "They didn't even make it through the night," she chokes out.

The ache tightens in my chest. "I'm so sorry, Jericho."

In response, he grabs the Book of Records with tentative hands and turns the hefty tome over to me.

"Go ahead." The words quiver on his lips. "I know you need answers too."

My grip is weak, my fingers barely catching as I take the book from him and step off to the side. We're only a minute away from our agreed departure, but I can't force myself to begin the search.

What if what I discover inside these pages is far worse than I ever imagined?

My thoughts spiral. Panic crawls up my throat, making it harder for me to breathe. With all the resolve I can muster, I fill my lungs with air and crack the Book of Records open.

Forty seconds.

It takes a little of that to flip through the pages, chasing down the long list of names arranged in ordered letters. On every page, the full names of the victims run parallel to their current status. The prominent ones even have pictures of their faces stamped into the left corner of the page, along with detailed comments on their crimes, all of them completed by the signing Lucis officer.

Every page bleeds a new list, hundreds and hundreds of new names. But as my fingers linger on where *Adeline Shade* should be, it's soon replaced by the name of another unfamiliar victim.

"It—it's not here," I stammer, my gaze sweeping over the records again and again and again. Still, I find nothing.

"What do you mean?" Across the floor, Nazanin turns her wet eyes on me.

"Her name," I whisper. "It's not here."

Twenty seconds.

My thoughts are so scrambled, frantic and deceiving, that for one frightening moment, I start to wonder if perhaps I was wrong. Perhaps the Nightwalkers had nothing to do with Mama's disappearance after all. Perhaps she and Felipe . . .

But even that thought seems so wrong and muddled. I know these monsters are responsible for what happened to Mama. I know it.

But if she isn't in the records, then where the hell is she?

"Did she go by a different name?" Nazanin swipes at her face as she and Jericho rise to their feet. "A maiden name, maybe?"

There's no way she could have known her suggestion would dredge up far more than I'm prepared for. But the realization comes so suddenly that a tremor runs down my spine, raising gooseflesh on my skin.

With trembling hands, I flip all the way back to the beginning, turning the pages as fast as they'll go.

Ten seconds.

One final toss and—there. Cut into a corner of the page, I pause at the image of a face so familiar, I'd recognize it even in the bleeding darkness.

Brown locks sweep down her angular face, golden eyes shining just as they did moments before she left the hut that night.

Mama?

A buzz rolls through me at the sight of her. Though the woman in the image looks everything like my mother, she dons the Lucis' full military attire, fists clenched over her heart in proper salute. *What is this?* Who *is this?* My mind races as I try to understand, but the longer I stare, the more questions spring like thorns in my head.

Full name: Adelina Folashadé

Alias: Lieutenant Margery North, CR-254-389-64

Comments: See Service Files for Information Pertaining to This Military Personnel

The report below the image offers no solace, and this time, the unanswered questions are much, much worse. Especially as the name next to the alias jumps out at me.

Who the hell is Margery North? What connection does this soldier have to Mama?

The alarm blares overhead, frantic and loud, our only warning bell that the security cameras have picked us up. The guards are coming for us, and I can only imagine more will join them in time. Already, Nazanin and Jericho are on the move, their hands wound together, dragging each other forward.

"Sloane!" Nazanin shouts several paces up ahead. "We have to go!"

She's waving me forward, gesturing wildly with all the desperation she feels. I should scramble after them, leave the Archives behind. Head back to the tunnels, straight to the barracks. Return to safety.

It's what we agreed on. But I can barely move, rooted in place, the Book of Records clutched tightly in my grasp.

After two years of searching, two years of digging grave after grave for buried scraps of the truth, finally, *finally*, I found something. But as the name Margery North echoes in my head, I know it's only a tiny piece of a puzzle I've yet to solve.

I can't leave. Not now, not when there's still far more to uncover.

Whoever Mama is, *was*, I have to know.

The echoing screech of the alarm continues as Nazanin breaks away from Jericho and rushes over to me.

"What the hell are you doing?" She huffs, breathless with fear.

"I can't leave," I tell her quietly. "The truth about Mama's still in here, and I have to find it."

"Sloane, if you stay, the guards will find you." Her voice is an urgent plea.

When she glances past Jericho to the sliding doors, I do the same. After a second or so, our eyes meet, and I know we both share a similar thought. Any moment now, an army of uniformed officers will come pouring into that empty hallway, guns blaring and ready to kill.

We're sitting ducks the longer we remain here, our chances of escaping dwindling with every passing second.

"Did you get it?" I ask Nazanin instead. "Did you get the trade routes?"

That was her mission. It's why she's here. The Lucis' confidential file that she plans to use to buy her brothers' freedom.

She nods grimly, knowing what I'm really trying to say.

I reach for her hands then and clasp them between mine. "You understand I've waited two years for this moment," I say with conviction. "I have to see it through, Naz. No matter what."

She remains quiet for another second or so, but in the end, she gives my hands a gentle squeeze, her features softening. "You do what you have to do, and do it fast," she whispers. "The day is yours."

Though something tightens in my chest, I nod, steeling myself. "Keep to the path," I instruct her. "Turn left at the fork. Take the third branch down, and it should lead you to the barracks. Take care of Jericho, and stay safe."

She flings her arms around my shoulders, pulling me into a crushing embrace. "Good luck, Sloane."

And then she's off, racing out of the Archives Room with Jericho at her side. When I'm sure they're gone, my eyes dart to the information beneath Mama's image, reading through the details once more.

See Service Files for Information Pertaining to This Military Personnel.

Yes, yes. I remember racing past the *Service Files* section only several minutes ago, one of the last two aisles just beyond the Lucis' wall of pictures. With a burst of determination, I commit the lieutenant's identification numbers to memory and tear off in a frenzy. I keep a breakneck pace as I round the corner aisle, almost tripping over my own feet. Now that the guards are on their way, I must act quickly, swiftly.

I don't have much time.

It takes all of one minute to locate the labeled section, sifting through the stack of folders tucked into the shelves in perfect rows. Each folder bears a series of identification numbers on its cover, the Lucis winged-torch crest stamped right beneath, along with the word *Confidential* branded in bloodred ink.

My heart slaps against my rib cage as I push one folder into the next, searching until I find the exact numbers. My breath catches, body tensing, as I pry the folder off the shelf.

For a brief instant, I grip it with both hands, too numb to do anything but stare at the name scrawled across the face in solid letters.

Lieutenant Margery North.

CR-254-389-64.

Clammy fingers leave damp marks along the edges of the cover.

Go ahead, I urge myself. *Open it.*

I do.

It's as though I'm staring through a parade of Mama's—*no,*

Lieutenant Margery North's—old life. An array of official files spill into my palms, birth certificates and medical records. Service forms and identification tags—all of them telling the story of a little girl once named Adelina Folashadé, who stole into Avalon with her younger sister when she was only five years old. Together, they'd escaped a routine Cleansing in Oyo and took on the false identities of Margery North and Cecily North. Two sisters who would go on to become fearsome warriors among the ranks of Lucis soldiers.

By gods. My body trembles as my gaze winds down the printed pages, trying to absorb as much as my brain will allow. I never even knew Mama had much of a family, let alone a younger sister whose death they forged, all so she could escape to Ilè-Orisha.

Every new detail is like poison on my tongue, choking and burning as it forces its way down my throat.

It's right there, right there.

Adelina Folashadé is Margery North.

Margery North is Adelina Folashadé.

Yoruba born and Lucis raised. Mama lived thirteen years of her life here, on these very grounds. A soldier who fought her way to glory, to status, collecting ribbons and medallions for her famed brutality.

Mama was a soldier, just like me.

Oh gods, oh gods.

Bile chokes the back of my throat when I see the image of Mama standing next to Olympia and the rest of their unit, looking every bit the soldiers they are. To know that Mama once stood in the presence of the queen, as comrades, allies, is a bitter lump to swallow.

But the records and certificates in the next pile are far more difficult to read, branding me with the worst of all truths. Like the day Mama was captured by Olympia for the conspiracy to assassinate King Ascellus and the royal bloodlines. Like the grotesque details of the torture she suffered while she was locked in Cliff Row, barely surviving as they mutilated every inch of her skin, marking her like the traitor they believed she was.

I don't know how Mama managed to escape Cliff Row after her capture, but she did. And it was in that brief period in time that *Adeline Shade* was spawned. Another shadow born of both Margery and Adelina's past.

Hers is a life I know, a life I grew up around.

A life I believed was the only one Mama led.

But I was wrong, so wrong.

And she was, too. She had to have been if she believed she could eke out the rest of her days in the shadows of a dusty village, away from the shackles of the Lucis. Away from Olympia.

April 18, 340 PME—Lieutenant Margery North was captured and killed by Nightwalkers on the Agbajé foothills under the order of Queen Olympia Turais.

The words parade before my eyes again and again, and a hollow feeling settles in my stomach, cold as stone.

There it is, at the bottom of the death certificate, the truth about what really happened that night.

Captured and killed by Nightwalkers.

Even though I knew those monsters had a hand in Mama's disappearance, the confirmation is still a dagger to my chest, cutting deep, jagged wounds. Everything I came here for, everything I killed and fought for, is right here in my hands.

Mama is dead.

The Lucis killed her.

Olympia murdered her.

She did not betray her family. Her memory is a blessing, not a curse. The villagers were wrong. They were wrong. They were wrong.

They were wrong.

Baba and I are free of shame.

With one hand on my chest, I fold over and gasp for air.

I can't breathe. Nor can I fight the pain as it radiates from within, tugging and squeezing and wrenching at the corners of my heart. Hot, angry tears track down my face, and through the blur, I glimpse the life Mama once lived. Before the Lucis ripped through her world and tore it all apart.

Adelina Folashadé. Margery North. Adeline Shade.

They made her a refugee, a child soldier, a murderer, a deserter.

And then—

And then they killed her. The voice reverberates in my head as darkness bleeds through the core of my being. *They took her from me.*

They took her.

My rage is a violent storm, a gathering of heat and fire swirling like a tempest inside me. It lashes against my spiritual anchor, a fiery battle of wills.

It shouldn't feel like this. Not after the àmì-orí ritual.

Yet, as the pain ravages my senses, Shango's drums thunder in my head, pounding at a wild, fervent rhythm. It doesn't matter how hard I try, I can't fight the terrible wave of heat breaking over me.

When flames burst to life on my fingers, licking at the edges of the folder, I toss the papers to the ground and stomp on them until they're nothing but ash. Still, àse stabs through me with the terror of a thousand needles burrowing deep into my skin. My body burns, hot and feverish, as magic crashes through my veins. It scalds my throat, throbs behind the back of my eyes until my vision starts to spot. Fresh tears fall and sizzle on my cheeks.

No, no, no.

Not tonight, not yet. Amiyah said I'd have more time.

But after only two days of reprieve, every effort to push back against my magic now drags throbbing blisters across my skin. I cry out in agony, claw at my stolen uniform, ripping fabric away from skin as the fire threatens to burn me from within.

I see it in the tendrils of àse dragging flaming claws across my flesh. The drums crash into a violent thunder in my head. With outstretched hands, I grasp at my skull, trying to force out the clamor, willing the world to right itself once more. But lost in the haze of fear and pain and shame and guilt, my àse bursts.

I scream.

I don't know the moment my spiritual anchor breaks. But I feel it.

Pain. It comes over me like a rolling sickness, pulling me in and out of consciousness. One minute I'm hunched on the ground, panting hard. The next, a shaft of blinding light stretches beneath my closed lids, red and white and impossibly bright, threatening to consume me. I feel it in my blood, in my bones, scorching and blistering away until I am made raw and hollow.

Until I am nothing at all.

When I open my eyes again, I expect to find my entire being ripped apart, skin sloughed off, reduced to a withering husk. But though my spirit is charred and broken, I am still whole.

I lie there, hot and trembling, my breath a broken gurgle, unable to tear my eyes from the fire now eating away at the tunnels' map, burning every inch of the parchment to ash. The flakes scatter into the air; soot settles onto my face.

Still, I watch as more flames slither across the floor like red serpents, twisting and dancing up the wooden tower to my right. With a shudder, the shelves collapse to the ground, sending giant waves of dust rippling through the hall. The books cascade onto the floor, each one a clattering burning mess.

With the full weight of the fire now forced out of me, my senses return slowly. Somehow, I manage to stagger to my feet, gasping at the spreading flames. Red and orange dots flicker at the edge of my vision. Torrents of fire leap from shelf to shelf, aisle to aisle, devouring everything in its path.

Gods, I never wanted this. But as the back shelves topple to the ground, spilling over in a cloud of fire and ash, I force my limbs into a sprint, stumbling over myself as I try to flee from the chaos. Deep gray smoke billows upward to the ceiling. Shards of glass rain down from above.

My heartbeat pounds with every step I take. But I've only just made it to the sliding doors when I bump into two solid figures, the impact sending me to the ground.

"Sloane!" Grabbing both my hands, Nazanin and Jericho haul me back up on my feet. Though Jericho's eyes are still heavy and red, he seems better than he was moments ago.

"Are you okay?" he asks. "We heard a noise and came back." At the sound of glass still clattering to the ground, he glances past my head. "What the hell is that?"

I can barely force the words out, my chest heaving with every ragged, hollow gasp.

Nazanin's eyes widen, and she lets out a horrible scream. "Fire!"

The alarm is still blaring, the flames barreling forward at a terrifying speed. Blood rushes to my head as we push through the door in the same moment a shattering boom erupts behind us.

Archives Hall explodes in a roaring blaze. The blast picks us up off our feet, throwing us across the hallway.

At first, I hear nothing but the loud ringing in my ears.

Then another alarm carries, and the first silhouettes of the guards appear at the far end of the hall.

Through the choking haze of fire and smoke, I find Nazanin's and Jericho's bloodied faces.

I mouth the word *Run*.

THIRTY-ONE

We race through the familiar underpass with the guards at our backs, their booted feet pounding against the hard-packed earth. Overhead, the alarm blares. The choking smell of fire and ash permeates the tunnel air. Smoke clogs my nostrils and lungs. Archives Hall is burning, and I'm the one who lit the match. The flames still crackle behind my eyelids, blackening the wooden shelves, lapping at the leather-bound books. They surge higher and higher, orange fingers clawing at the glass-roofed ceiling.

My heart thunders as I sprint down the curving passage with Jericho and Nazanin at my side. They match my strides, their heavy breathing an echo in my ears. Blood stains their ruined fatigues, and soot clings heavily to their skin. But worst of all is the fear clouding their eyes, a cold mirror of my own.

We made it inside the Archives without getting caught. And we would have made it out if I hadn't unleashed that fire. Gods, if I'd just left as planned, perhaps we would already be back in the barracks, the three of us tucked away in our bunks, formulating the next steps in our plans. But that was before I learned the Lucis are the ones who took Mama from me. Now pain grips me in a tight embrace as the name Margery North echoes over and over in my head, searing a path into my memory.

Mama is dead. She's really gone.

I thought uncovering the truth about her disappearance would set me free, slowly begin to heal the wounds she left behind two years ago. Finding the truth would rid Luna of her illness and make things right for Baba in the village. It would lessen my grief. The truth would fade my scars. But all it's done is poke more holes at my heart and fill it with a burning vengeance.

I swear to gods I'll destroy everything the Lucis ever built.

They killed Mama, and for that, I'll rain fire on their precious island.

Despite the tears blurring my vision, I push my limbs forward, weaving us in and out of the twisting trail. Skulls and bones crunch underfoot, but it isn't the dead that need saving now.

Keep to the path. Turn left at the fork. Take the third branch down, and it should lead you to the barracks. I repeat the same directions I gave Nazanin only moments ago, tracking a mental route in my mind even without the map as a guide. Behind us, guards scream out orders, their voices rumbling off the cracked stone walls. The ground shudders and heavy tremors rattle the domed ceiling, sending light pebbles over our heads.

My stomach clenches as more and more guards pour into the tunnels, the air hot and heavy with their presence. Judging by the chorus of barked commands, every bleeding soldier has been dispatched to the tunnels tonight. I try not to think about how many of them the commander must have called away from the celebration, or what any of these men will do if we should get captured. I try not to remember the sting of steel wire ripping away at my flesh. No matter what, I can't let the guards find us down here.

Up ahead, the tunnel forks, splitting into four—not three—narrow routes. Beads of sweat drip down my back as we slide to a sudden halt.

"Which way?" Nazanin hisses, her breath coming in short, ragged pants.

My gaze darts back and forth between each path, unsure how to proceed. This part of the tunnel is unfamiliar, and with the map lost to the Archives Hall fire, I—I just don't know.

"Sloane, which way?" Nazanin's voice quivers in warning.

Footsteps echo. The guards are closing in, and I have no idea how to get us back to the barracks. My heart beats louder with each passing second.

By gods. We're not going to make it out.

Think, Sloane. In my head, I picture the map, tracking the grid lines and entry points across the parchment. The barracks is just around one of these narrow bends. I know it is. But—which one?

The air shifts. A deep growl rumbles through the tunnels. I whirl on shaky limbs, only to find a pair of pale blue eyes glowing in the darkness. The hairs on the back of my neck rise as I stare into the face of a Nagean leopard. The Lucis' highly trained beasts. The fearsome thing snarls, baring sharp fangs.

We scream.

Then we're off, bolting down one of the unfamiliar pathways. I can only hope to gods this winds all the way back to the barracks. I can only hope there isn't a dead end up ahead. The leopard's menacing roar cuts a violent shiver down my spine.

I glance backward, expecting to find Jericho and Nazanin chasing my every step. Instead of my friends, the beast hurtles forward at a maddening pace, so close that I lose my footing and tumble to the ground.

Get up, get up, get up!

The leopard prowls low when it gets within an inch of me.

I only crawl backward with my hands.

It flicks a long, spiny tongue over yellowed fangs, readying to pounce.

The buzz of magic is still in me, eating at my senses. With the spiritual anchor now broken, àse streaks hungrily through my veins, fighting for release. This time, I reach for it, grasping with quick, desperate fervor.

The beast leaps through the air and lunges forward. Its razor-sharp claws scratch through my fatigues, carving ragged lines into my thighs. Hot flashing pain cracks through me like a whip. I cry out as a blast of fire shoots from my hands, wrapping itself around the beast in thick shrouds of flames. The leopard releases a terrifying howl, loud enough to make the earth shudder beneath me.

It speeds off in a burning frenzy, as if it can outrun the fire gorging away at its skin. My breath scalds in my throat, drowned by the heavy sounds of footfalls and screaming guards. The flaming beast has alerted them to my presence. Now their booted steps grow louder as they descend upon me.

Out of desperation, out of fear, I reach into my mind once more, latching onto the remnants of àse surging beneath my skin. The swell of magic overwhelms, but for the second time that night, I grip it like a bleeding lifeline. Every vein in my body thrums with heat, every bone and every fiber a kindled match.

The guards are close, *too close*.

With a feral scream, I let go. An inferno ignites in front of me, a wall of flames that twists upwards, licking at the cracked stones overhead. The beauty of a fire is that it knows no bounds, and neither does mine. It spills forward, racing down the tunnels at a frightening speed. On the other side of the blazing wall, the guards scream, their boots stomping the ground as they try to flee the chaos. But this is a fire they can't outrun. The stench of cooked flesh wafts up my nostrils. Strangled screams ring in my ears. They are the wails of the dying.

For a moment, I remain on the floor, gasping as flashes of blinding pain writhe through me. It would be too easy to lie there in the dirt, wait for the guards or another snarling beast to find me. Wait for the earth to pull me under.

I'm tired.

Then two distant shouts blare out from a separate section of the tunnels, shrill and piercing and shockingly familiar. I jolt at the sound of Nazanin's and Jericho's cries, the horror caught in their voices, accompanied by the violent outburst of the guards' assault.

"We've got them! We've got them!"

Terror rakes its icy claws over my skin as I stagger to my feet, trembling all over. Jericho's and Nazanin's faces burst into my mind, and even from this distance, I picture them tackled to the ground, bodies buried into the dirt. Two beaten shadows beneath the crushing weight of the guards' boots.

Oh gods, oh gods, oh gods.

I should go back for them. Jericho and Nazanin returned for me earlier, and I should do the same for them. But as their screams fill every branch of the tunnels and more and more guards close in on my friends, I'm only seized by my own unwavering sense of survival.

It is the same selfishness that led me to kill Teo back inside the city dome, sacrificing the life of the boy I loved instead of my own. It is that same selfishness that drove me to commit multiple murders in one single day. The same one that cost Malachi his life and freed me from the clutches of Irúnmolè.

Time and time again, I choose to live in my own inhumanity, knowing what the cost will be.

Tonight is no different.

I can't fight the tears coursing down my cheeks as I turn away from my friends and their broken cries, abandoning them to the full wrath of the guards and the commanders.

I'm no hero. I'm only doing what I have to do.

The sobs heave in my chest, and tightness chokes my throat as I edge down the bend. I still don't know where this tunnel path leads. I plod along anyway.

There, tucked away in the darkness, a silhouetted figure looms, watching with familiar green eyes.

My whole body freezes as he steps out of the shadows.

Dane.

THIRTY-TWO

Back in the barracks, Dane paces up and down a cold, unfamiliar room, his long limbs only taking him so far each time. His black fatigues cling to his sweat-soaked skin, and a layer of soot smears the right side of his face.

I blink at him, still shaken from what happened inside the tunnels tonight. My fatigues are worse than his, ragged and torn, barely hanging on by a thread. Blood drips from the long gash in my thigh, staining the ground at my feet. I should bandage my wounds, wash the grime off my skin, but Dane's presence keeps me rooted in place—a silent threat.

He hasn't spoken a word to me since he led me away from the tunnels and the guards pressing in. Not since he watched me command an inferno and discovered my Scion identity. The memory of him standing there, stone-faced and deathly still, flashes through my mind. A feverish heat spreads through my body, both from the fresh bruises on my skin and the remnants of àse searing beneath. Without an anchor to keep my magic in place, the burn stabs like a needle threading through the patchwork of my veins. Yet, despite the pain, I set my jaw and glance at Dane, waiting for him to speak.

Instead, silence hangs over us, a large boulder pressing down on me until I can no longer withstand another second of it.

"Say something." I can't hide the quiver in my voice.

He stops pacing and spins around to face me. The same hard expression he wore in the shadows returns to his eyes. "You're a Scion."

He can barely force the words out, stumbling over them with pained effort. I doubt Dane's ever spoken to a Scion a day in his life. Soldiers like him are trained to let their guns do the talking.

"Is this the part where you take me to Faas? Or do you just kill me here?"

I look around the room he's locked us into, an empty prison on the building's highest floor. There are no bunks in sight, no worn-down dressers stuffed with army fatigues and the recruits' charcoal uniforms. He's chosen to keep me away from my quarters on purpose, away from the other recruits and their curious, prying eyes.

In that moment, I can't help but think that if Dane were to kill me now, this would certainly be the place to do it. No one would think to look for me up here.

The same instinct that drove me to my feet in the tunnels returns. I glance at the door, imagining all the possible ways I could escape, save myself from this cage. But one look back at Dane and I know there is no way out.

He remains quiet, muscles twitching in his hard-set jaw. My heart gallops in my chest the longer I hold his gaze, wondering if Dane is about to doom me to the same fate as Jericho and Nazanin.

My friends were captured tonight, and it's all my fault. I'm the one who chose to remain in the Archives far longer than I should have. I compromised the entire mission and endangered their lives. And yet, they returned for me when they could have fled to safety. They came back, and I failed to save them when they needed me most. No, I abandoned them. Ignored their desperate pleas and left them to suffer the guards alone.

What kind of person does that?

A selfish wretch, that's who.

My stomach plummets at the bitter truth. Now that the guards have them, it won't be long now before they're interrogated, subjected to worse torture than I can even imagine. The commander will blame them for the Archives Hall fire. He'll want to know how they got into the tunnels, how many others were involved. He'll torment them for answers, and when the bastard's finally had enough, he'll toss them into Cliff Row to be tried and executed later.

Will Jericho and Nazanin talk? Will they give me away to Faas? Perhaps they already have, and the guards are well on their way to me. Perhaps I'm moments away from being locked in a prison cell of my own. For all of my betrayal, Olodumarè knows I don't deserve their silence and protection.

Certainly not after tonight.

An image of the two of them suffering behind bars flashes through my mind, bringing with it a swell of pain and guilt. I'm not sure how much time Nazanin and Jericho have left, but now, with my own survival teetering on a knife's edge, it's all I can do to glance up at the squad leader again.

Even if my friends don't expose me, Dane could.

Once, the squad leader had me nearly whipped to death when he thought I was a Scion Sympathizer. Now that he knows what I am, will he have me killed the way he's killed others before me?

"If you needed a way inside Archives Hall, you should have come to me." His voice is so small, I almost don't hear him. "You should have told me."

"Tell *you*?" I glare up at him. "Tell you what, exactly? That I'm a Scion? That the only reason I'm here is to find out the truth about my missing mother?" An ache flares deep in my chest at the mention of her. The memory of the file inside Archives Hall is still too fresh. But I don't want to be reminded of any of it, not right now. I dig blood-crusted nails into my palms, allowing the pain to overwhelm instead. "In case you've forgotten, you're a soldier, Dane. One whose duty is to kill people like me."

He shakes his head, as though those words are too painful for him to hear. "You burned down an entire building. Do you have any idea how many soldiers died tonight?"

"How dare you stand there and talk about the dead." My lips curl into a bitter sneer. "How many Shadow Rebels have *you* gunned down? A hundred? A thousand? How much of my people's blood stains your bleeding hands?"

When he leans forward, a shiver creeps down my spine, but I force myself to remain still.

"Do you even have any idea what it's like on the Sahl?" His voice is ice, his face a brewing storm. "The terror of watching your friends speared to death, tumbling through bodies cut open with machetes, and praying your next breath won't be your last. The Shadow Rebels have maimed countless child soldiers who—"

"Child soldiers your queen forced onto the front lines! Children your commanders armed with assault rifles instead of books!"

A rush of anger explodes inside me. It coaxes my àse to the surface, and a current of heat ripples in the small space between us. The intensity of the warmth settles over us like a hot breath. It constricts at my lungs, just as a sheen of sweat breaks out across Dane's brow. I inhale quickly, sucking in enough air to steady myself. When I'm finally able to speak again, my words come out in a hoarse whisper.

"My people didn't start this war. Yours did. They took our lands, massacred us, destroyed our culture and our identity. If the Shadow Rebels are fighting today, it is to reclaim what the Lucis stole centuries ago."

"There would be no war if Scions hadn't drowned Nero Regulus's parents," Dane manages, and I sense the unease in him.

I force out a little laugh, though his false beliefs hold no humor. "Is that what the colonizers taught you at your stupid institution?"

He straightens before me, his broad shoulders firmly set. "It's our world's history, Sloane."

I almost slap him across his face. Instead, I ball my hands into fists, clenching them at my sides.

"History and myths are two very different things," I hiss low. "Let's not confuse them."

My feet move of their own accord as I back away slowly, fighting off the sting under my skin. A bitter distance grows between us, and I let it. If I have to stand so close to Dane, I fear what I might do to him. I was wrong to think I could let my guard down around this boy, wrong to even consider befriending a soldier like him. Avalon made Dane, and the Force raised him. I see it so clearly now.

"Was the massacre of the first settlers a myth too?" He pushes on. "Hundreds of thousands of old-world survivors, all of them wiped out by a deadly plague."

Like Faas, like that viper bitch of a queen, Dane spews his own twisted history, reciting the same ignorance he's been taught. Of course, he won't tell the whole story. They never do.

He shifts, as if wanting to move a little closer. But then he thinks better of it and draws back an inch, returning to his previous position with solemn eyes.

"I've witnessed the bloodlines' cruelty," he mutters, almost to himself. "I know they rule with oppressive hands. I've also seen what Scions are capable of, how much destruction they can wield. How do you defend yourself against that kind of magic when you have none? How do you fight absolute power?"

"Ask your queen," I snarl between my teeth. "She's the one responsible for this genocide."

My lips tremble when I think about Mama and the days she spent as a soldier inside these walls, fighting alongside Olympia, forced to serve a monarchy that thrives on oppressing our people, burying us in the earth one bullet at a time. *They'd sooner destroy you for fear of what they do not understand.*

"Gods, you people—you hate us so much, but we didn't ask to be born with magic. The gods blessed us with it. You fear us for what we cannot change, fear us because we are different and powerful. Yet, we are the ones dying by the thousands every day. The ones living in hiding, forced to suppress our magic, even as it destroys us from the inside. Do you know what it's like to push that much power down?"

When the storm of emotion breaks, my voice cracks. Tears prick at my eyes. I blink them away, biting the insides of my cheeks to keep from crying. Not here. Not in front of him. I will not put my strength on display for a weak boy. Instead, I roll up the sleeves of my uniform and stretch out my arms, revealing the rows of fresh blisters and old scars.

"These are my burns." I thrust my arms in his face. "This is the pain every Scion must suffer in order to survive in your world. So tell me, how do we defend ourselves against your fear? How do we fight your absolute ignorance?"

His gaze lingers on the bruises, tracking every blister with a tick of his jaw. When he glances up at me, something strange glints behind his eyes. Sadness, pity—whatever it is, I don't care.

"I'm so stupid," I tell him, "stupid to think you could be different from Faas and Caspian and every other bleeding machine trapped behind these godsforsaken walls. But I know now you're just like them. People like you could never understand what it feels like to be forced to hide who you are."

The words scorch as they leave my mouth, and a charred taste lingers on my tongue. Despite the tremor pulsing through my body, I push my limbs forward, bridging the chasm I built between us moments ago. My heart thrums in my ears as I peer up at him, searching his familiar face.

"You've seen what I am," I murmur. "Are you afraid of me, Dane? Am I the scum your commanders say I am? If you believe this, then arrest me now. Take me to Faas. Or better yet, do your job, Reaper, and kill me yourself."

The next moments pass, with the two of us standing there, hearts beating at a fevered rhythm, fighting the urge to do what we know must be done.

With a single word, Dane could wrap me in chains, drag me off to his commander, and take away my freedom.

With a single flame, I could set him on fire, reduce him to ash, and keep my freedom a little longer.

Killing him should be easy. After all, the boy means nothing to me. Yet, I find myself reining back my àse, yanking on it even as it begs to be freed.

It seems Dane also keeps himself on a tight leash.

My whole body is braced for his killing blow.

Instead, he leaves me there, wide-eyed and staring, as he turns and stalks out of the room.

His muttered response barely reaches my ears. "I can't."

THIRTY-THREE

For one week, Dane avoids me. For one week, I remain alive.

Despite all the horrible things he said, his last words linger, a growing echo in my head. After days spent mulling over them, I've yet to decipher what they truly mean.

Is Dane sparing me? Why?

Time and time again, I ask myself the same question, unable to make sense of it. The thought of him choosing to keep me alive, saving me from the commander's wrath, is an impossible wish. After all, Dane is a soldier, a boy with too many of my people's blood on his hands. He won't risk his duty to protect a Scion like me. He has no reason to.

Yet every day, I wait for an arrest that never comes. By the sixth day, I start to wonder what kind of mind games the squad leader is playing. If this is a trick, I never get a chance to ask because there is no sign of him anywhere. Strange that I find myself hoping to catch a glimpse of him, listening for his voice, but no matter how much I will him to appear, it seems Dane's somehow vanished into thin air.

"Officer Gray has been sent on a mission to the Sahl," Lieutenant Caspian tells us the next morning during Culture and Theory. The rifle across his back sways as he marches up and down the classroom aisle, spreading more propaganda about the Shadow Rebels' ambush beyond the front lines.

Though I try not to think about why Dane's gone to the desert front, or what he might be doing out there, his sudden absence coaxes an unfamiliar emotion out of me. Whatever it is flits away too quickly. I hate it all the same, and I hate Dane even more for it.

Hours after my afternoon session with the new combat instructor, I make my way up to the rooftop, where Amiyah already waits for me along the terrace's ledge. She keeps her gaze steady on the horizon, her warm face glowing as it catches the golden light of the sunset. It's getting late now, and I imagine she has been here a little while. But with the new strict measures the commander imposed following the Archives Hall fire, the entire base has been under constant surveillance. At least a dozen guards patrol the hallways of the barracks at every hour, with hordes more crawling about the grounds like ants. Even the security cameras track us everywhere we go, forcing me and Amiyah to find new ways to maneuver around them.

With a huff, I pull back the shawl wrapped around my head and fall in next to her. The ocean wind drifts in, a cool, salty breeze that rustles her thick coils and raises gooseflesh along my bare arms. I slip my hands into the sleeves of my uniform jacket, tugging the coat tighter around myself as Amiyah glances sidelong at me.

"It's strange," she murmurs, "being up here without Nazanin and Jericho."

I can only nod, my stomach clenched as a familiar pang of guilt wrenches through me. It's been one week since the Archives Hall mission and my friends were captured in the underground tunnels. Every night since, I've woken up to Jericho's and Nazanin's panicked voices in my head, but it's the thought of them suffering in Cliff Row that haunts me the most. With their execution looming close, I've racked my brain for days, trying to come up with something, anything, to save my friends from the ruin I brought upon them. But Cliff Row is just as impenetrable as every other fortress on this bleeding island, if not more. I could never break into a place like that.

It's impossible.

"I never should have abandoned them." I set my jaw, grinding the pain between my teeth. "I should have gone back for them."

If Nazanin and Jericho should die today, their blood will be on my hands.

Amiyah just shakes her head. "If you did, you would have been caught too." Her eyes bore into me, but there's sadness in them even as she speaks. "They knew the risk, Sloane, and you have far too much to lose."

The words are familiar. It's the same warning she's given me all week, since the moment I told her what happened inside the Archives. It lingers in the air even now, a reminder of the threat that hangs over me should the Lucis discover the truth behind my connection to Margery North.

All these years, and I never once knew Mama was a soldier here, let alone a high-ranking officer of the crown. The image of her standing there alongside Olympia and the rest of their unit still stabs at my mind. A brand seared into my memory forever.

I want to believe the woman who raised me is nothing like the soldier in that picture. Yet, when I think of Mama now, I see the thick ridges of scars that snaked down her back, the dark bruises and cuts that marred her entire body. I was seven when she taught me to sharpen a dagger with a whetstone until it gleamed, showed me the most effective way to grip the hilt for a proper thrust, and cautioned me never to leave the hut without a blade or two. Behind all of her warmth, she always did possess an air of steely ferocity, even then. All from a life I never knew she lived. A past rife with blood and violence.

I don't know why she and Baba hid the truth from me. Whatever the reason, I suppose it doesn't matter now.

"How long do you think Officer Gray will be gone?" Amiyah interrupts my thoughts, a note of concern in her voice.

I feel just as uncertain as she does about the squad leader's absence, not knowing what he'll do once he returns from the desert front. Dane is the only other person here who knows the truth about my identity. And while he may have spared me that night, I find it hard to believe he'd do it again. At the thought, a familiar pressure clamps down on my chest, making me wince.

Next to me, Amiyah narrows her eyes into a scowl as she echoes what I already know. "You never should have allowed him to leave that room."

But right as she may be, I can't dwell on my mistakes. Not now. Not when the ones who killed Mama have yet to pay for what they've done.

"Believe me," I say, "there's a long list of people I want dead."

The same spark of fury that was kindled that night still burns hot in my heart, a cobra feeding on my pain and heartache, leaving me with only a cruel hunger for revenge. More than anything, I want to hurt Olympia and the bloodlines for what they've done, for all the lives they've stolen from me. I want to make these monsters bleed.

"You're out for revenge, aren't you?" Amiyah regards me as though she can hear the dark thoughts hissing in my head.

A bitter ache churns in the pit of my stomach, but I don't bother denying it. "I'm not leaving this island without making the royals pay."

She frowns, her unease palpable. "How do you plan to do that?"

"I'm working on it," I tell her, and I really am.

The thought of taking down the monarchy is all that's kept me sane this past week, my only path to redemption. When I shut my eyes, it's easy to imagine all the ways I could destroy them. Rip these savages apart and burn down the crown once and for all. An assassination of the bloodlines is the only plot I've latched onto. But with the monarchy stowed away in King's Isle, carrying it out seems almost impossible. The royal island lies on the other side of the capital city, a fortress far removed from the rest of Avalon. Still, that doesn't stop me from mulling over the possibility again and again, searching for some kind of weakness in the Lucis stronghold.

There's a crack in there somewhere. I just have to find it.

After a moment's silence, Amiyah angles her body away from the ocean, turning to look at me fully. Despite the weight of her stare, I lock my gaze forward, refusing to meet her eyes.

"I know your desire for revenge," she says slowly. "I know you want vengeance for what the royals did, but you can't afford to be reckless about this, Sloane. Not now."

"A minute ago, you were fine with me killing Dane," I mutter, fists clenched tightly against the ledge.

"Dane isn't the one in charge," she shoots back. "He's just a cog in the machine. But going after Olympia, the bloodlines? That's a suicide mission. Look around you. We're surrounded by *their* army, *their* Force. Thousands of soldiers who will readily gun you down before they let you get within any proximity of their queen. You won't survive it."

I scoff low. "So, what, you're asking me to do nothing?"

"I'm asking you to stay alive." With a breath, she takes my hand and squeezes it between her ringed fingers, her touch warm and full of meaning. "Survive this last week of training with me, and we can escape to Ilè-Orisha as planned. Finding sanctuary with the Shadow Rebels is our only hope, more than anything else. It's all we've been fighting for since we came here. It's freedom, Sloane."

"I don't want that freedom," I hiss, yanking my hand free. "Not if it means the bloodlines will continue to remain in power. These bastards have taken everything from me. Mama, my father, my friends—all of them gone because of these savages. While they sit there on their bleeding thrones, we're forced to murder and destroy to defend their damned army." The words tremble out of me, bitter and sharp and jagged, a razor blade cutting into an already open wound. "Every day, we shed pieces of ourselves, our humanity, just to prop up a monarchy whose very hands are stained with the blood of *our* people. No, no. I don't want freedom." I grit my teeth, turning to face her now. "I want justice. I want to see the fear in Olympia's eyes as she's forced to watch everything she loves go up in flames, everyone she holds dear crumble to ash. Then I want to kill her."

The thought sends a flare of heat through me, scarlet threads of fire weaving along my veins. Since the very moment my spiritual anchor broke, I've felt every buzz of àse in my blood, a burning sensation so forceful it leaves branded scars across my skin. Amiyah tells me I can always reanchor it by training my magic, learning how to properly harness my àse. But with the eyes of the Lucis everywhere we go, I can only bite my lip against the terrible pain, knees buckling as I wait for the rush of heat to ebb.

Amiyah remains quiet for some time. A long beat of silence stretches between us, filled only by the crackle of tension in the air. Overhead, the sky darkens, leaving a haze of purple bruises across the horizon. An hour left to curfew. By now, Amiyah and I should already be heading back down. Evening formation drills will begin soon enough, and I don't want to think of what Faas will do if we're the last to arrive at the training field. But neither of us moves.

I know what she wants me to say—that my threats are idle words, born only from fresh pain and anger, with little spark to truly catch fire. But to admit as much to Amiyah would be a lie. So I do nothing but watch as a long-tailed nightjar swoops low over the ocean, leafy brown wings gliding along the giant waves.

When Amiyah finally speaks again, her voice is a pleading whisper. "Have you even stopped to consider what would happen if you fail?"

No, I haven't. But that's the problem with vengeance, isn't it? It births such a ravenous beast within you that not even the risk of failure is enough to sate its cravings.

"What about me?" she asks, eyes shining. "Has it ever crossed your stubborn mind that if you choose to go down this path, then I'll have to walk it with you?"

I don't doubt that at all. We've been saving each other this past month, and the thought of walking away now feels too strange for us both, a realization too startling to grasp. Truth is it would be too easy to drag Amiyah along this path with me. But I know, deep down, how far it goes. I know exactly where this road leads. And I can't, *I won't,* ask her to make that kind of sacrifice.

I don't want to die, she told me back then.

"Whatever happens next week will be mine to face and mine alone," I force out. "This isn't your fight, Amiyah."

"It doesn't have to be yours either, Sloane. We were forced into this army a month ago, but we don't have to be soldiers anymore. In Ilè-Orisha, we can be children again. We can be free."

My face burns when she reaches for my hand once more. Warm fingers entwine with mine, gripping and squeezing tight. Jaw clenched, I steel my nerves and pull away quickly.

"I think it was you who was meant to find Ilè-Orisha all along."

"Sloane—"

"You came here to find a cure for yourself, and I made a promise to you that I would help." Without hesitation, my hands are around my neck, tugging at the strings of my cowrie shell necklace. "Here, take this." She frowns when I drop the choker into her outstretched palm, closing her long, shaky fingers around it. "Get to the Sahl, find the Shadow Rebels' fortress, and demand one of Obaluaye's descendants heal you. After everything we've been through, at least one of us deserves to find peace."

Amiyah shakes her head, eyes darkening with tears she refuses to shed. "I can't believe you're going to do this."

Despite the ache slowly chipping away at my resolve, I nod with unwavering surety. "It's the only way to make things right." *I need to do this.*

In that moment, Amiyah nods too. Though she smiles at me a little, something like determination hardens her expression.

"Then you know what you have to do," she says quietly. "Since the bloodlines won't come to you, you have to go to them. Right now, there's only one possible way to get to King's Isle."

I stare back at her, my brow raised. "How?"

"Faas's bullets." She sighs.

My gaze drops to the pair of white-tipped ammunition strung to her neck, and like a creature born from the depths of my mind, the commander's bleeding face crawls into my head. Faas stands just as he did our first day here on the base, cold and brutish in his military ensemble, his deep voice echoing in the darkness around me.

The first amongst you to earn three bullets from me will have the honor of visiting Castlemore to meet the queen and the royal bloodlines before deployment.

Back then, I cringed away from the reward, scoffed at the few recruits who marveled at the idea. Now I can't help but dwell on the opportunity myself, my heart hammering as I weigh every possible aspect of the plan. A royal gathering of this kind would certainly ensure that all the bloodlines are present in one room, Olympia included.

By gods, is this it?

I let the scenario play out in my head, and the more I linger on it, it becomes easier and easier to convince myself of the plan. That close to Olympia and her royal lords, I could kill them all. I know I could.

"If you're going to rise against their army, then you have to train, Sloane." I don't miss the firm warning in Amiyah's voice. "And not just in combat. If you're going to have any chance of surviving this, you need to learn to harness your àse. You can't avoid it any longer."

In that, she's right. If this is to work, I must finally learn to control this magic. Learn to wield it into a weapon powerful enough to destroy the force of the Lucis army. The monarchy may have their bombs and bullets, but what I have is far greater than any weapon in their arsenal. What I have is Shango's fire coursing through my veins, a fire that has always demanded to be freed. Instead, I built a cage around it, afraid of what might happen should the Lucis discover the truth. I kept it shackled and buried too long, as though it were a beast that needed to be tamed. Treat something like a monster, and it will certainly learn to become a monster. So of course, I suffered for it, collecting scars and brands that have only multiplied since my spiritual anchor broke.

But why should I deny myself the strength of a god whose wrath could easily burn this wretched world to ash?

No more.

I won't make that mistake again. I won't cower in the face of fear.

So despite everything Amiyah and I both stand to lose, I look to the one person I trust to teach me how to truly summon my àse at will.

"Okay," I whisper at last.

"Okay." She heaves a breath. "We start tonight."

In the distance, the bells echo from the soldiers' tower, a familiar peal that carries on for some time. Then the world stills around us.

Time to go.

Amiyah and I move as quickly as we can, draping the shawls over our heads, shielding our faces from view. We cross the terrace in two long strides, but just as we reach the door, she pauses, one hand gripping the rusted handle.

"Sloane?"

"What?"

She glances back at me and smiles. A true, feral smile. Something like pride burns fiercely in her eyes. "When you reach King's Isle," she says, "do what infernos do. Spread the flame, Folashadé. Let them burn."

THIRTY-FOUR

I arrive at the training center in the early hours, when the sun's rays are still grasping for purchase of the sky. The familiar hallways are a quiet tomb, and the first rousing notes of reveille won't be heard for another bell or two, allowing me enough time to train on my own.

Inside one of the practice rooms, I work my nerves into a heavy bag dangling from the chain overhead. I have only one week of training left, with only one round of ammunition to my name. If I am going to make it to King's Isle, I need to figure out a way to earn two of the commander's remaining bullets, and soon. It will be difficult, a challenge more than anything. But certainly not impossible.

Sweat drips down my back, soaking through my already damp fatigues. With every kick, the tension in my muscles fades, replaced by a pounding rush of adrenaline. Though my limbs burn, I pivot on my left foot and swing out with my right leg, striking the bag with greater effort. My ragged breath echoes, the only sound in the otherwise empty room. I adjust my gloves and settle into a proper stance, readying myself for another round.

"You should try adding more power on your foot."

I whirl to the oddly soft voice. A lean figure emerges from the doorway of the practice room. He's a tall brute of a man, with piercing brown eyes, bone-bald head, and skin the rich brown color of iroko wood. The sight of the Lucis is so shockingly familiar that my hands fall to my sides. I drop my neck into a stiff, sudden bow.

"Lord Sol."

His name trembles on my lips. After weeks of catching shadows of the internal adviser at every training drill across the base, Lord Theodus Sol is the last person I expect to see standing here this early. And now, without his white-and-gold damask cape, the royal's clothing seems so plain for someone of such high nobility. Yet, his very presence still sets my teeth on edge.

"My apologies, Ms. Shade," Theodus says, taking a small step forward. "I didn't mean to startle you."

My stomach lurches at the sound of my name in his mouth, and all I can do is stare at him, wide-eyed. "You—you know who I am?"

Of course he does. His position as internal adviser would allow him access to such information. Yet, when the brute moves closer, his footfalls silent on the concrete floor, I stumble back a step, my gaze fixed on him.

"Sloane Folashadé," he finally answers when he gets within an inch of me. "Daughter of Isaiah and Adelina Folashadé, born April 18, 327 PME, in the Nagean village of Agbajé."

His words strike me like a blow, and my entire body freezes as if doused with a bucket of ice.

By gods. He knows.

How? How the hell did he find out? Did Dane tell him? Has the squad leader chosen to expose my true identity after all?

My pulse races until I'm seized by a strong, sudden urge to flee the room. I shift uneasily on my feet, eyes darting to the exit behind the bald man. There are no uniformed officers pouring through the doorway, not yet at least. But even if I try to run, where will I go? I'm trapped on this bleeding island with no chance of escaping. Àse throbs beneath my skin, ready to ignite if need be. For one brief, terrifying second, I consider letting its molten force loose.

Theodus must sense my turmoil because he raises his palm in a single gesture and immediately adds, "You have no reason to fear me, Sloane. Believe me, I do not wish to turn you in."

My heartbeat is an echoing thunder in my ears, so loud I wonder if the royal can hear it. *He's lying,* my mind warns. A man like him would never save my life. Not willingly, not unless he wants something in return.

"Why?" I regard him with a look of suspicion.

"The very first time I saw you was two years ago." Across from me, Theodus presses a hand to the bag, his eyes closed as if recalling a distant memory. Something flickers across his face, a strange emotion I cannot place. With a sigh, he peels his eyes open. "You appeared like a swirl in the wind and disappeared just as quickly. Swift enough that I couldn't grasp anything beyond your pain. Your desperation was true, though for what, I didn't know. It didn't matter how hard I attempted to understand. I simply couldn't. So I tried to get you out of my head. Not all divinations are meant to be read, and perhaps this was one."

Divination. A chill creeps over my skin, and my eyes snap up to his. "You're . . . a Scion?"

He winces, but manages a quick, solemn nod. "A descendant of Orunmila."

For a moment, confusion clouds my mind as I search the royal for traces of a lie, a dark humor of some sort. I flinch when I find nothing.

"That's impossible," I choke out.

"Is it?" His smile is dark, a twisted mask to hide the sadness beneath. "When my father, the late Lord General Elijah Sol, married a woman from a Nagean village years ago, he had no way of knowing she would be his downfall." He speaks slowly, pacing as he does. "My father had married a Scion, and in doing so, endangered the rest of the royal bloodlines. When Ascellus later discovered this, he stripped the entire Sol line of their nobility." His voice wavers as he comes to a stop in front of me. "I was four when I was made to watch my mother die."

Though he tries to hide them, the tears in his eyes are hard to blink away. Even though I don't want to believe anything Theodus says, the torment tugging at his face makes it all too real. Lucis or not, Scion or not, no child should ever have to suffer that kind of pain.

"The king wanted me dead, too," he says with a hint of bitterness in his tone. "That is, until he learned of my magic. You see, Ascellus thought he could manipulate my gift for his own gain, so rather than kill me, he raised me as a prisoner in his court. For thirty-four years, I became the Lucis' greatest weapon against the Shadow Rebels."

As his last words sink in, a wave of terror crashes through me. I gasp as the revelation sears down my throat, leaving a burning ache in my chest.

"By gods, you've been helping them," I whisper numbly.

The endless massacre on the Sahl, the never-ending Cleansing across Nagea . . . the horror slowly starts to make sense. The Lucis have found a way to fight magic with magic.

Now, images of Faas's wretched lists flash across my vision, each one filled with too many names, Scions' and Yorubas' alike. The commander's always known where to go, who to hunt. Every bleeding time, that bastard's claimed victory over so many innocent lives. All along, I thought it was because of the pardon clause, but how much of it was aided by Theodus's visions?

Mama. My chest tightens, and I can't help but wonder whether Theodus was responsible for her capture as well.

"Did you know?" I whisper. "Did you know about *her*?"

"Your mother? I knew she, too, had her plans for the bloodlines," he admits. "I saw this long before she set her mind to it. For a while, her triumph seemed certain. And just as well, I did everything I could to keep the attention away from her. Hid every divination concerning her from Ascellus. Believe me, Adelina's capture came as a surprise. Even for me."

I nod bitterly, trying to force down the pain. Gods, our magic was meant to save us, to protect us. Yet, it's the very thing the Lucis have exploited, another piece of culture to be stolen and used as a weapon. With Theodus on their side, we never stood a chance.

Nausea churns in me as I glance back at the seer. This time, he refuses to hold my gaze, his jaw tightening as he stares straight ahead, looking at nothing and perhaps everything at once.

"You judge me," he says after a moment of silence, "but you and I, we are alike in many ways."

My first thought is to tell him that I'm nothing like him, that I could never turn my magic against my own kind. Then I remember the blood on my hands, the parade of ghosts that have become my nightly companions. No Scion or Yoruba has ever been burned by my fire, but I've certainly turned my bullets on some of them.

"Children of war are born from war, Sloane. And we are, both of us, a legacy of this ruined world." Finally, Theodus's stern gaze cuts to mine. "When Ascellus spared my life all those years ago, he not only kept me captive; he condemned me to a lifetime of guilt. To know you and you alone are responsible for the genocide of your people is a torment I could never escape. From the moment you set foot inside that city dome, you've borne the same pain and guilt."

I swallow hard. He's right. Guilt is a tyrant I cannot escape, caging me in a prison of my own making. It's been almost a month since I was forced to take Teo's life, and the memory of what happened inside that chamber still makes me horribly sick.

Theodus whirls, shuffling away slowly. Without thought, I follow. We reach the other end of the practice room, where a large mirror takes up the entire breadth of the concrete wall. Theodus stands before it, examining his own reflection for a moment. I watch him all the while, my breath echoing in the fallen silence. The man in the mirror is no longer the Lucis I saw when I first arrived on the base. His face is too drawn, his cheekbones too sunken, with dark shadows dulling his eyes and skin. He wears a noose instead of a crown. He is a Lucis royal in name only, a Scion by blood, and a prisoner in every sense.

"For so long, I believed the horror would never end," he says, cutting through my thoughts. "Hope was a slave man's key. I had none. Then you came along." He studies me in the mirror, a subtle smile warming his gaunt features. "So forceful were you, I kept awake through the nights. But it wasn't until the night of the fire, the night Archives Hall burned, that the divination truly formed. The truth you discovered inside that chamber wasn't what you'd hoped for, but it was one that set you on a path of vengeance. Vengeance against those who took your mother from you." He turns, and the look on his face sends a tremor through me. "I've seen your rage, Sloane. I know where it leads."

My pulse quickens. Now that Theodus knows what I'm planning, will he hand me over to the Lucis? After all, he is still Olympia's seer, one bound by duty to thwart any imminent attack on the royal bloodlines. Yet, when I force myself to stare up at him, I frown at the hope shining, unbridled, in his eyes.

"I know you think this is a fight for revenge." His voice is low but firm. "Truly, it is a fight for freedom, Sloane. For our people. For every child who no longer has to face the doom of conscription. For the little girl who traded her freedom for family. For the friends you've lost, and the ones awaiting execution in the shadows of a prison cell."

Jericho and Nazanin. My heart seizes, haunted by the guilt I've felt since the moment I abandoned them inside those tunnels. It's the worst thing I could have done, a regret I'll live with for the rest of my life. But if there's even a sliver of a chance that I could still save them, a way to right my wrongs, I have to take it.

"You really think I can free them?" I ask, looking desperately at the seer.

Theodus leans close, and the expression on his face changes, replaced by grim determination. "Sloane, you can free us all."

Fire burns in his eyes. Steel hardens his voice.

"There will be no peace as long as the Lucis continue to rule. So long as the monarchy still stands, we will always remain buried in the mud. It's why I let Ascellus die when the Blades came for him. It is for the same reason I've chosen not to warn the bloodlines of your impending *visit*."

Something in his gaze heats my blood, fanning the flame already burning inside me.

"What exactly are you saying?" My pulse pounds in my ears.

"Whether or not you find victory in your mission is a darkness I can't see beyond," he admits. "But if Olodumarè should shine favor upon you, if you should succeed where so many have failed, then you, my dear, could be the fire that sets this world ablaze."

Àse crackles in my veins the more Theodus speaks. But it's his final words that sear into my mind long after he leaves.

"When the legends of heroes are told," he says, "they won't just remember you, Sloane Folashadé. They will fear your name."

The rest of the day goes by in a blur of simulation drills, close combat, and hours of strategy and tactics in desert warfare. With deployment only a week away, Faas shifts the focus of our training, so most of the day is spent honing our knowledge of advanced artillery, aircraft, and the harsh, changing terrain of the Sahl. Though I try my best to remain alert, vigilant, my mind wanders back to Theodus and the mission to King's Isle.

That night, I lie awake in my bunk and wait for sleep to find me. It never does. Instead, I end up staring at the cracked ceiling of my quarters as Amiyah snores a few feet away.

The conversation with the seer is still a lingering buzz in my head. While I've only just met him, I believe everything Theodus told me. After all, he's just like me. Another Scion trapped beneath the weight of a monarchy, abused and chained, a pawn to prolong its reign. The bloodlines thought they could mold him, turn everything they hate into a weapon only they can wield. It's the worst kind of savagery, but I expect nothing less from these bastards. Too bad the gods have other plans.

You can free us all. Those were Theodus's words, born from the divinations Orunmila himself has shown to him. Long ago, I asked Mama if the gods would ever return, to fight for us, take back everything the Lucis stole. Now I know the gods are truly here. They guide my path. With them at my side, freedom will be ours in a week.

It's past midnight when a knock comes on my door. Amiyah stirs in her sleep, but not enough to wake as I edge closer toward the door, unaware of what awaits me on the other side.

An army of guards? The commanders? My hand quivers as I turn the handle a little, cracking the door open an inch.

Instead, I'm staring up at a familiar silhouette, keen green eyes alight in the shadows of the hallway.

"Dane?" My heart knocks against my ribs at the sight of him. On instinct, I turn my gaze on the corridor, peering uneasily into the darkness. Still, there are no soldiers or commanders at the ready. Breathing low, I glance up at him, my brows furrowed. "What are you doing here?"

In the week since I last saw the squad leader, he's grown a faint stubble, the sparse cluster of hair dotting his jawline. When he looks down at me, a strange shadow stirs behind his expression. Whatever he's been through this past week has left a visible strain on him.

"Do you want to get out of here?" he murmurs, his dark features searching mine.

I frown, silently aware of my thudding pulse. "It's past curfew."

"So?"

I hold his gaze, unsure. Yet, something in his eyes tugs at my curiosity, beckoning to me. After one week of his absence, even beneath all of my hatred, I'm ashamed of how much I desire his presence. At the thought, my chest gives a slight lurch, a traitorous admission I'm quick to dismiss. Besides, I know I won't fall asleep tonight, not with

Theodus's words still parading in the depths of my mind. My nerves are a twitching mess, and I've already run through everything the seer said too many times to count. Perhaps I could use this distraction, even if it comes in the form of Dane.

I draw a shaky breath and grab my uniform jacket. "Lead the way."

THIRTY-FIVE

"The cliffs?"

Moonbeams fall upon the jagged rocks, casting bright stripes across the dull gray stones. On the other side, ocean waves slap against the high bluffs, the salty breeze cool on my bare skin. The last time I was up on these hills, I traversed a chasm with nothing but a thick cord of rope gripped between my fingers. Even though it was almost a month ago, the memory of the first Physical still sets my teeth on edge.

"It's my favorite spot on the base," Dane says softly.

He brushes past me and starts up the slope. I gulp down a few breaths before climbing up after him, my legs trembling the farther up we go, until we're standing seventy feet above the churning waters. Starlight shimmers off the waves. From this height, they look like fireflies in the night, sprinkled silvers to illuminate the vast ocean beyond.

"I can see why," I murmur. Now that I'm not dangling helplessly in the air, seconds away from plummeting to my death, I look on in mesmerized wonder.

Dane settles down on the ledge and rubs his hands along his thin fatigues. "When I'm up here, I feel like I'm worlds away from everything happening down there."

His words hang in the space between us, thick and heavy with meaning. With a sigh, I lower myself beside him, my palms flat against the cool surface. Together, we turn our gazes outward, staring at nothingness with a calmness unlike any I've felt in a long time.

Next to me, Dane's chest rises and falls at a steady pace, small wisps of breath pushing past his lips. Whatever shadows lurked behind his gaze back in the squad quarters are long gone, replaced by a peaceful stare that thaws his cold features. In the week since he's been away,

I've amassed more than a dozen questions in my head. Now that he's here, mere inches from me, I can't bring myself to ask any of them. My nerves keep me mute, and I wait for him to speak instead.

"When I was growing up, my parents traveled a lot." His voice is low as he stares out at the horizon. "Every time they returned home with stories of their adventures, I remember thinking: One day, I'm going to do the same. See the world beyond these walls."

"Where would you go?" I ask, glancing sidelong at him.

"There's a faraway island my parents often spoke of," he says. "Satafri. They came across it during one of their expeditions, just below the southern ruins of the continent. My father said it was unlike anything he'd ever seen. The mountains, waterfalls, and coastlines. He said the sunsets of Satafri were like a festival of colors that went on every night."

There's warmth in his words as he speaks, enough to draw me in, filling my imagination of the distant land with light and wonder and freedom. A far cry from the darkness and ruin that is Fort Regulus.

"Sounds like a dream," I whisper when he finishes.

He nods once, his jaw working slightly.

"Perhaps it's not too late." Truth is, if Dane wanted, he could leave Avalon behind. Unlike many of us, he could pick up and begin a different life someplace anew.

He tucks his knees up to his chest and shrugs. "In another life, maybe."

Though his tone remains casual, his face is heavy with sadness so achingly familiar it gives me pause. Especially because growing up, I felt the same, knowing what I dreamed as a child would never be my future.

My fingers close around a smooth pebble. I toss it off the cliff into the waiting darkness. "When I was little, all I wanted was to become a wooden-wheeler champion."

"What?" Dane tilts his head and looks at me fully. A small smile pulls at the corners of his mouth. In spite of myself, I linger on the curve of his lips a little too long. When he notices me staring, I glance away, teasing another pebble between my fingers.

"I had it all planned out," I continue. "When I turned eighteen, I'd compete in the continental games and be the first female to win the wooden trophy."

"Are you that good?" I meet his gaze again, only to find him still watching, waiting.

I nod with all the conviction I feel whenever I get a chance to speak about wooden wheeling. "I'm the best."

His smile turns into a full grin that splits his face, and easy laughter escapes him. Even I can't help but chuckle, releasing a bit of the tension in my body. Moonlight dances across his brown skin, and for a moment, we regard one another, a strange energy surging between us. It crackles in the air, clawing at the heat flaring through my body. My chest lurches in response, made worse by the fire ablaze in Dane's eyes. If I stare any longer, I fear it might consume me. So I turn to the ocean, glance at my hands, all so I won't have to look at his face. After what feels like an eternity, I clear my throat and return my attention to him.

"Uh, I heard you were sent on a mission to the Sahl," I say too quickly. "How was it?"

Though he tries to mask it, his expression hardens. Now it's his turn to pick at the pebbles around him, scratching each one against the rocky surface beneath us.

"They wanted me to help train a new crop of prisoners from the free nations," he mutters, keeping his head bowed.

My brows pull into a frown. "I had no idea the Draft extended to the free nations."

"Not officially." Reluctantly, Dane lifts his chin and looks up at me, his features tightening. "Most of the prisoners are Nageans who were caught fleeing into their territories. The free nations are bound by treaty to turn them over to the army. They're then sent to the Sahl to serve for life."

"I see." A bitter knowledge sweeps through me when I think about Teo and the freedom he believed he could have in Naine. If what Dane tells me is true, then there's a chance Teo would have ended up back on the Sahl anyway, fighting the same war he tried to run from. If only I'd known what I know now before he fled. Perhaps we could have done so many things differently.

Beside me, Dane stirs. His eyes narrow, and a long silence passes between us as he traces faint strokes in the ground. He repeats the lines over and over, as if trying to lose himself in the distraction of it. Beneath his fatigues, muscles strain in his arms, cut by a row of fresh scars, all of them most likely earned while he was away. The swollen red ridges stand out starkly against his skin, oddly familiar in their pattern. Even in the darkness, I realize then what it is I'm looking at. *Burns.*

At first, I don't understand—until he starts to speak.

"The night I arrived on the Sahl, I was leading a small unit on a routine patrol when we were ambushed by insurgents. Scions."

A sudden chill settles into my bones. *The Shadow Rebels did that to him?*

"At least fourteen of them," he says. "The Shadowlands beyond the front lines are constantly ravaged by dust storms, so none of us saw them coming. We were surrounded. If they'd wanted, they could easily have done worse. The prisoners were untrained and poorly equipped, and most would rather die than take down the Shadow Rebels. They weren't like the rest of the child soldiers. They weren't broken, hardened. So it came down to me to defend the unit. It was the first time in years I looked Death in the face and thought, it has come for me."

"How did you escape?"

"A woman." His voice is jagged, betraying his nerves. "She must have been their commander. Shaved head and golden-eyed. She said they were only there for the prisoners, and if I released them, no further harm would come to me. I've been a soldier for twelve years, and in all those years, I've only spared a life once." He pauses long enough to give me a knowing look. "My duty is to kill. Eliminate all enemy targets. In that moment, knowing what the Rebels wanted, I should have shot the prisoners before they could get their hands on them. Even if it meant dying. It's what the Force expects from me. Blood and valor to the very end.

"Yet, when I drew my rifle at all six of them, I knew I couldn't pull the trigger. Not because I believed the woman when she said she'd spare my life. In fact, I was certain I was a dead man the second I lowered my weapon. But I couldn't pull the trigger because when I looked at the faces staring back at me, I didn't see the enemy. I saw terrified men and women, innocent boys and girls. I saw a shadow of who I was before I became *this*."

"So you let them go."

"*They* let me go." He runs a hand over his face and releases a breath. "Those Rebels—they had every reason to kill me. The burns are nothing compared to what they could have done. Yet, once they got what they came for, they turned around and vanished into the storm. I don't know why they did what they did. The devil knows I didn't deserve their mercy."

"Is that why you haven't turned me in yet?" I finally ask the one question I've been too afraid to ask him. "They spared your life, and now you feel compelled to do the same?"

For a second, he peers at me, then back to the lines in the ground. "I never planned to turn you in," he mumbles. "It's why I deleted footage of that night from the training center's security feed."

His response isn't at all what I expected. "You did what?"

"When your friends were captured inside the tunnels, I knew Faas would want to see the surveillance tapes. Once that happens, he'd figure out there's a third recruit involved. Then it would only be a matter of time before you're caught." He leans back a little and his fatigues pull slightly, enough to reveal his bare torso. I swallow around the knot in my throat, realizing yet again, how horribly close I came to losing everything. "I took care of it, though," Dane adds, "so you have nothing to worry about."

Even when I know it's the truth, part of me still refuses to believe.

By gods. If that footage had fallen into the commander's hands, there's a chance I'd be locked up in Cliff Row right now, awaiting execution alongside Jericho and Nazanin. But for whatever reason, Dane is sparing me from that terrible fate.

"Why?" I blurt out. "Why are you protecting me?"

"I could ask you the same." His eyes narrow. "I'm the only one around here who knows who you are and what you did. Yet, that night inside the barracks, you chose to let me walk when you could have killed me."

He doesn't break his stare as he lets the words linger. Though he waits for a response, I remain quiet, remembering the night he caught me inside the tunnels, the heated exchange that followed after. The sight of him standing there, cruel and resolute in his attempt to justify the Lucis' brutality, felt like the worst kind of betrayal. I could have killed him then if I'd wanted.

You never should have allowed him to leave that room.

Knowing what he was capable of, to let him walk away felt like a weakness. And perhaps, deep down, that's what it was. Because somewhere along the way, whatever resentment I once felt toward the squad leader has morphed into something else, something different.

I should hate Dane Gray for all he is, but I don't. I don't.

I'm not foolish enough to admit as much to him, though. I know vulnerability in the hands of a soldier is a weapon easily exploited.

"I could still do it, you know?" A lie. But I drag my gaze over him anyway, the intent clear.

"I know." He says nothing for some time, his fingers curled around the blades of grass stuck in a crevice in the ledge. "Look, I never wanted to be a soldier, Sloane," he tells me as he yanks away at the weeds. "I never wanted to be responsible for the death of so many Scions and Yorubas. Years ago, I was forced to make a choice: survival or humanity. I chose survival, not just for myself, but for someone who mattered most to me. It was the only choice I thought could save her."

"Who?"

The wind whispers around us as I await his reply. He breathes heavily, and veins branch out on his forehead, each one a hard web across his temple. When he stares up at me, his expression is carefully guarded, a mask to hide the truth that lies beneath.

"My sister," he murmurs at last, letting his disguise fall. "Ara."

He has a sister. The shock of that knowledge jolts through me. Before tonight, I never gave much thought to the squad leader or what life he'd led beyond the walls of Fort Regulus. To me, he was always a soldier, never a boy.

"What happened to her?" I ask him. "Where is she?"

"Imprisoned in Cliff Row."

My eyes widen. It's the last thing I ever thought he would say, and it only raises more questions in my mind. "Why?"

He looks over his shoulder, scanning the darkness until he's certain we're truly alone. Then he turns his attention back to me.

"You've heard about the Crown Conspiracy? How King Ascellus died?"

"He was assassinated by the Blades," I reply, even as Theodus's haunting words echo. *It's why I let Ascellus die.*

Dane takes a deep breath. "Ascellus was murdered by my parents."

"What?" I blink, taken aback.

"I was six at the time." His words tumble out in a rush. "I had no idea my parents were involved with the Blades. Not until the night of the assassination. Somehow, Ara knew. She barely managed to push me down the escape tunnels before the soldiers arrived. They tortured her for hours until Olympia gave the order to burn down the house and take her to Cliff Row."

With each detail, he peels back layers and layers of his painful past, breathing light into the darkness swirling around him. Now the longer I stare, the easier it becomes to imagine the life he lived before the attack, before his parents were killed and his sister was taken. He was a boy once, a child with a family to call his own. Until the Lucis ripped his world apart and turned him into a killer, a Reaper. I wonder now who Dane might have been if his parents were still alive and his sister far from Cliff Row. Whatever future he was destined to live is long gone, replaced with a life of endless war.

"How did you make it out of the tunnels alive?"

"The Blades found me a few days later and brought me underground. But with Ara stuck in prison, I knew I had to do something. So with the help of the Blades, my identity was erased from the Avalon database and I was enrolled in the Force. That was the day I became Dane Gray."

A flood of emotion fills his eyes as his last words echo, a haunting buzz in my ears. My pulse races when I realize what he's really trying to say.

"What is your real name?" I ask softly.

"Omari," he whispers so low, I barely hear him. "Omari Wells."

For a moment, I sit there, at a loss for words. Though slivers of moonlight cast his face into shadows, it's the first time I'm seeing him for who he truly is: a lone boy aching for his lost family, searching, desperately, for an anchor to cling to in the maelstrom of a brutal world.

"So all of this . . . it's all for your sister?"

"Ara's only in that hellhole because she chose to save my life instead of her own."

"What happened that night wasn't your fault," I murmur. "You were only a child. You both were."

Even in the darkness, I glimpse the grief that weighs him down, a heavy stone propped against his tense shoulders. Before I can stop myself, I reach out with a hand, closing my palm around his clenched fist. He trembles beneath my touch, fingers splayed at the sudden gesture. But he doesn't pull away.

"You're not like them, you know?"

At that, Omari's jaw tightens. "A few good deeds don't unmake a monster, Sloane."

"No, they don't. But people like Faas and Olympia, they fight and kill for power, for greed. Their strength comes from keeping Nagea divided. Not like you. Not like so many others fighting for family, for hope and change and freedom. That is what separates a monster from a hero. You are no monster, Omari."

He's quiet for some time, long enough for me to sense what thoughts are plaguing his silence. After many years of being raised to kill, maim, and destroy, the boy he sees in the mirror is no hero, but a creation of the Force's savagery. *Real monsters are not born*, he told me once. We *are made*.

I understand now what he meant by those words, why the squad leader is the way he is.

Without thought, he winds his fingers between mine, his thumb pressed gently enough against the back of my hand. A rush of warmth spreads through me. Then it's my turn to flex my fingers, nerves twitching ever so slightly. A small, unexpected comfort, that is all. After all, we've both lost our hearts to the Lucis, and we both bear the pain of that loss every day. An open wound that never stops bleeding.

When he angles his body toward me, I'm keenly aware of how close we've gotten, the hairbreadth of space that separates us now.

"Why can't the Blades help Ara?" I unclasp my hand from his own and draw back a little.

Something seems to register on his face, and he does the same, pulling himself back into place.

"They are," he says with a strained voice. "But Ara wasn't the only one who was taken after the Crown Conspiracy. Many members of the Blades lost their families that night. They want retribution, and they think assassinating the bloodlines is the only way. Except every attempt they've made since Ascellus has failed."

I keep still as he speaks, trying to make sense of it all. The first time I heard about the Blades was weeks ago, when the attack on Olympia and the royals was broadcasted. Back then, I had no idea how far the monarchy's hatred spread, how many of our lives had been crushed under their oppressive feet. If the Blades are determined to bring down the bloodlines, then perhaps they only need the right opportunity to strike again.

A plan unfurls in my head. I puzzle over it, running through the details of my original mission. Though the strategy in place is a solid one, an alliance with the underground rebel group would ensure that every aspect of the attack is well executed. With more highly trained soldiers at my disposal, I wouldn't have to fight the monarchy and her army on my own. An advantage, one that could possibly lead to an even greater victory.

You can free us all, Theodus said hours ago. I wonder if the seer saw this, too, the tentative path my mission would take and to whom it would lead me.

In the starlight, Omari's eyes gleam. I glance up at him, searching his face for anything that might reveal where his loyalties lie. Before tonight, I'd always considered the squad leader an enemy, a soldier who would easily kill me if he discovered who I was. Yet, despite what he knows, Omari is choosing to keep me alive. Because while the squad leader may fight for the Force, his true allegiance remains with the Blades—and even more so, his sister.

Now more than ever, I want to believe he'll do anything to free her from Cliff Row. Even if it means committing treason.

I draw a breath and choose my next words carefully. "What if there was another attempt?"

Omari's face falls on me, a furrow in his brows. "What are you talking about?"

"The night I broke into Archives Hall . . ." My voice wavers as the picture of Mama standing next to the queen and the rest of their unit comes to mind. "That was the night I learned the truth about my mother and why Olympia had her killed."

"Who was she?"

"A lieutenant—here in Avalon. She went by the name Margery North." This sends a flash of recognition across his face, and a low breath gusts out of him. "Did you know her?"

He nods in return. "We studied her back at the institution. They called her the Scythe of Nagea."

An image of the file I found in Archives Hall materializes in my head, every piece of Mama's—*no, Margery North's*—personal records spilling before my eyes. Her birth certificate, medical records, military service forms—all proof of a life she lived here before. The life of a soldier she was forced into.

Bile climbs up the back of my throat. I force it down as I wrap my arms around my legs, hugging both knees close to my chest. Though I keep my eyes straight ahead, I can feel the weight of Omari's gaze on me.

"It's strange," I mutter, "to know my mother once fought for the same people I was raised to fear."

Next to me, Omari shakes his head. "Margery North was one of the greatest lieutenants to ever walk these grounds, and yes, she fought for a cause, but it was never to protect the crown or the bloodlines.

Even when she was locked away in Cliff Row, there were rumors—"

"What kind of rumors?" I ask, turning to him.

"That she'd gotten really close to a fellow prisoner," he tells me. "Someone even the bloodlines were afraid of."

"Who?"

"Lord General Elijah Sol."

I frown at that. "Theodus's—I mean, Lord Sol's father?"

Earlier, when the seer told me of his past, I vaguely recall him mentioning something about his father as well. A Lucis lord who was imprisoned for marrying a Scion woman. The man's betrayal had not only left Theodus without a mother; it cost him his freedom too. If what Omari tells me is true, what possible alliance could Mama have forged with Theodus's father?

Omari is quick to explain what he learned at the institution. "Both Margery North and Elijah Sol were set to be executed on the same day. But the night before their execution, a fire burned through half of the cellblocks in Cliff Row, and both were presumed dead among the casualties. At first, Olympia wasn't convinced. She believed it was all a ruse orchestrated by the two of them in an attempt to escape. Following the investigation, though, there was enough evidence to conclude that the bodies found in the fire were those of the lieutenant and the general. That was until two years ago, when Olympia received intelligence that Margery North had been sighted in a village in Nagea, and—"

"The queen finally had her executed." A bitter ache throbs in my chest, made worse by the realization that despite all Mama did to escape this wretched life, somehow, it still caught up to her. Against Olympia, she never stood a chance.

When the tears start to collect, I dig nails into flesh, letting the pain overwhelm instead. I will not weep for my loss tonight. Not while the bloodlines are still alive, tucked away in the safety of their precious island.

"I'm sorry," Omari whispers.

"Don't be." I harden my heart against the grief, replacing it with a spark of dark, seething anger. It claws at the àse in my blood, and a rush of heat ripples beneath my skin as I bring myself to face Omari. "I'm going to avenge her." My voice is sharp and steely. "I'm going to kill the royals. And I think the Blades would be very interested in my plan."

He gives me a look of deep concern. "Sloane, listen. I've sat through many assassination plots against the bloodlines. None of them ever worked out as planned because Olympia always sees them coming. The monarchy is heavily protected. It's just going to be another suicide mission."

I can't help but bristle. "You don't know that."

"I know Faas, and that bastard will defend Olympia to his last breath."

"Then I'll kill him too." I level him with a glare. "I'm not afraid of Faas. Not anymore."

"Even if it means losing your life?"

Omari watches me a minute longer, searching for a flicker of uncertainty, of doubt. But after all I've been through in the past month, I feel everything but. *I am greater than my fears.* Now more than ever, I clutch those words tightly to my heart. It's all I need to destroy the royal bloodlines in a few days.

"You know, my grandfather used to say only the dead have truly earned the right to do nothing. As long as you live and walk this earth, you must make a mark. The bloodlines have taken so much from me and my people. Enough is enough. Those monsters are not invincible, Omari. They can be hurt. They can be killed. All I ask is you bring me to the Blades, and everything we've fought and killed for can finally be ours. Ara can finally be free."

At that, a cloud of emotion sweeps across his face, a desperation born of our shared pain.

"If we were to do this," he says after a long moment, "if we were to assassinate them, how exactly do you plan to get to King's Isle?"

"It's simple." I tap a finger on the white-tipped bullet, remembering the day he draped the chain over my neck. His focus drops to the ammunition resting against my collarbone, and in that instant, he seems to understand what I'm trying to say.

"The recruits' visit to Castlemore." His eyes shine as he stares up at me.

"It's the perfect opportunity to strike."

He brushes a hand along his jawline, mulling over the plan. "And the bullets? You've only got a week of training left, and two more rounds to earn. You're running out of time."

In the dark, his words echo, the question in them lingering between us. After a month spent training with the squad leader, I know what he's really asking me. How far am I willing to go? How much of myself am I ready to sacrifice for this mission?

Once, he told me to survive this place, I must become a monster. *Humanity or survival?* Back then, I wasn't so sure. Now I am.

"I know what I have to do," I tell him with all the conviction I can muster.

He doesn't speak for a while, weighing the risk in his head. If the Lucis should ever discover what we're planning, Omari and I will be tried and executed for treason. All he has to do is say no and walk away. Turn me in to the commanders. But we've both suffered terribly at the hands of the Lucis, lost too much to a monarchy that insists on dooming us to a life of ruin. More than that, Olympia took away the only family Omari has left, and he wants her to pay just as much as I do.

Finally, he draws a ragged breath.

"Okay." He nods, and his voice takes on a knife's edge. "If at the end of all this, you're the one chosen for King's Isle, then I'll bring the Blades to you. You have my word."

I know what determination looks like, and when we lock eyes, I see a shadow of my own resolve in him. After all, we are, both of us, two weapons carving out a bloody path to freedom.

Freedom for his sister.

Freedom for my people.

Omari's eyes linger on mine for another second or so. Then he shoves a hand into his pocket, pulling something out.

"I—uh—was going to give this to you before deployment, but . . ." His voice trails off as he puts his hand out in front of me. The rare gold medallion he wears during training now winks in the folds of his palm.

Without thinking, I reach for the delicate piece of jewelry, letting the thin chain dangle between my fingers. The medallion itself is made of real Ganne gold, a remarkable round nagi coin with some kind of insignia carved into it. Taking a closer look, I realize it's a symbol of two flaming crossed blades, with the words *Humanity Always* engraved in a smooth arc below.

"What is this?" I glance back up to see Omari staring, watching me with those familiar kind eyes.

"It belonged to my mother, back when she was a member of the Blades." Warmth seeps into his voice as he speaks. "When I joined the Force, I kept it with me as a reminder of who I was and what I was fighting for. But as the years passed, I lost sight of that."

This life, this world, it changes you, he told me once.

"And you think I have as well."

"No, I think you've fought hard against an institution that was built to break children like you. But unlike the rest of us, you survived. There's a strength in you that's both terrifying and rare. I saw it that day inside the city dome. I also saw you struggling to hold on to it as training went on. I know what you've been through this past month, Sloane. How much of yourself you've sacrificed for this world. I just want you to remember that your humanity is worth fighting for.

No matter what happens next, don't lose sight of *that*."

Shadows dance across his face. But beneath them, a force of vulnerability splashes to the surface, causing deep ripples in the ocean. I've never heard Omari speak this way before. Never knew he spared a moment's thought on me. I am terrifying and rare. He is consuming and raw. And in this moment, we are, both of us, made and unmade.

With a brush of my finger, I trace the words on the medallion slowly, my heart twisting around them. *Humanity Always.* After everything I've done to get here, everyone I've killed, I don't know if I could ever return to who I was before I stepped foot in Avalon. My innocence died the moment I pulled a trigger, and nothing I do can ever bring it back. It's a small comfort, though, to know once the royals are dead, no child will ever have to sacrifice pieces of themselves to this world again. In a few days, the Draft will end for good. I try to latch onto that now, a lifeline more than anything else.

"Thank you," I murmur to Omari.

A muscle ticks in his jaw as he leans forward. "May I?"

When he takes the chain from my trembling hands, I turn my back slowly to him. His fingers brush against my nape, every slight graze of his nails enough to raise the hairs on my skin. With a click, Omari clasps the metal in place. A low breath loosens in his chest, a sudden heat in the air that makes me shudder, all gooseflesh and flushed skin.

The medallion lies just below my collarbone, a few inches above the bullet chain. It seems fitting in a way that I would wear both. One, to represent my life as a child soldier, the brutality of the training I've endured this past month, trading lives for the glory of ammunition. The other, a reminder of all I've lost, and what little humanity I hope to regain, if any at all.

I curl my clammy fingers around the gold coin, squeezing just a little, before turning back to the boy in front of me. There's a familiarity to his presence that draws me in, a fragile web that was woven since the very moment he whispered my name. Perhaps even longer than I know. Omari is everything I should hate, and I am everything he should kill. Yet as he watches me, a silent fire in the starlight, those thoughts fall far, far away.

I remain still for a moment, afraid of what I might do if I even dare to move a muscle. But what little restraint I have left slips off the second Omari drags a calloused finger along the slope of my jaw, a burning caress that trails downward until he finds the dip in my chin. He pauses there, his expression shadowed with a tangle of emotions. But I see the want in him too. So much want, I should pull away.

There is a chasm where my heart should be, an aching hole left behind after Teo's death. He tore it out of me when I took his life. I told him I didn't want it back, told him I'd be okay with that emptiness. And I was. I tried to be. Until now.

"Is it greedy to want something you can't have?" Omari asks, as though our thoughts tread the same selfish path.

Yes, yes, I want to say. But the dark spark alive in those eyes tugs something entirely different out of me.

"Not tonight" is all I murmur, and it's all he needed to hear.

Omari moves even closer, both hands on my thighs, sliding me toward him with purpose. Every touch is fire, more fire than the one I possess, searing the very skin on my body, licking away the thoughts in my head screaming *caution, caution, caution*, until nothing remains but a flame taunting me with both heat and desire.

Lost in his haze, I make a sudden, heady move of my own. Lift up slowly and plant myself on his outstretched legs. Even wrap these liquid limbs tightly around his waist. Our breaths echo in the silence, ragged and quick, broken only by the violent thud of our hearts. The feel of his chest against mine sends a flood of warmth down my spine. A heat so wild I feel too delirious with desire. And still, still, Omari lures me closer, one hand molten against the small of my back. My entire body thrums, hot and alive, every inch of muscle pulled taut.

Then his lips are on my own, and it's like drowning in a deep dark blaze.

I let him. I let Omari Wells consume me.

Far below, the ocean waves churn, lapping endlessly against the rocky outcrops. The breeze whispers like a lover around us, trails a naked finger along my skin. Despite the heat, I shiver against him. Snake my arms around his neck and curl inward, arching all of myself into his body. Omari kisses me hard, a deep and hungry kiss so defiant I can almost taste the challenge in it. My nerves spark to life with every deliberate caress of his fingers. He leaves carnal brushstrokes all over me. I feel too exposed, too raw, in his grasp. When he kisses his way down to the hollows of my neck, I forget to breathe, gasp for air. His mouth does wicked things, lips kindling a canvas already set to burn. And I want to. Gods, I want to. Heat claws its way out of the deepest parts of me, sending my pulse on a feverish errand.

One bite, and Omari sets me aflame.

A wild fire to cleave the darkness.

If only for a night.

THIRTY-SIX

The last days of training are not without their own horrors. I commit myself to the drills, Faas's grueling Physicals, even the brutal conditioning sessions that slowly begin to wear on my spirit.

Worst of all is the Kabba Cleansing, an unspeakable horror that will forever leave a stain on my hands. Though I may never find the words to speak of it, I did what I had to do.

Still, every memory of it turns me hollow with guilt, the deaths spinning in an endless, broken loop. I can still hear the screams of the dying, taste their blood on my tongue, see the bodies tumbling off the sides of the mountains like fallen rocks. I can still smell the rot of their burned flesh in the air. I can still feel the squelch of their torn limbs beneath my boots.

In the end, I know I will have to account for my sins. No savagery of that kind could go unjudged. In that, Olodumarè will bring me to justice.

But by gods, I did what I had to do.

I earned my bullet, and with it, I'm a step closer to destroying the royal bloodlines. It's what I'm fighting for, isn't it? The singular purpose that pushes me to constantly mold myself in the image of what the Lucis want.

A soldier, a killer, their reaper.

This is the path they've forged for me, the darkness I myself have chosen to walk.

All to be my people's hope. To be their sword and their shield and the one who saves us all. It doesn't matter what happens to me, how fraught and broken I become at the end of this. For the promise of freedom, I will sacrifice so much more to bring back the flame.

Soon, I feel myself start to fall apart, pieces of my humanity never to be made whole again.

In the night, I dream of a monster drenched in blood. When I wake, I see the same monster perched on my bunk, covered in nothing but ash and soot. With midnight skin and eyes like burning coals, she bares her teeth and tears my world apart with her claws.

You and I, she hisses at me. *It's always been you and I.*

She is my destiny after all.

Amiyah's and Omari's presence draws me from the edge of an abyss. With them by my side, I don't have to think about the ghosts that haunt my nights, the tears that fall from my lashes, the screams that burrow into my head. With them by my side, I don an armor, a shield against my own grief. Even as pieces of that armor begin to crack, leaving me bare and vulnerable, I cling tightly to my training sessions all the same. In the mornings, Amiyah pushes me to harness every source of my àse, grasping at different threads of emotion to coax my magic out of me. With Shango's drums beating in my head and the Orisha's fire swirling beneath my skin, I come to know what it truly means to embrace the warmth of a magic no longer buried. Then there are the nights Omari and I spend together, trading blows and kisses in the emptiness of a training room. Every punch he lands, I block with ease. Every kick, I dodge smoothly. He doesn't relent, though, always keeping me on my toes with the growing level of intensity.

Through it all, the commanders keep us starved, leaving only the brave to steal whatever rations they can from the mess after hours. Those who are foolish enough to get caught are killed on sight.

For the first time since we arrived on the base, recruits from varying squads are brought together and locked inside the training ground for two sleepless nights. Of course, the commanders warn that anyone who falls asleep can be killed by the other recruits, once again driving us to become savages around each other. Amiyah and I manage to survive only through quick thinking and shared effort. While I steal enough rations to fill our hungry bellies, she keeps watch for any guard on patrol duty. On nights when she drifts off to sleep, I stay awake, ready to fend off any recruit who dares look our way.

By the time the madness ends, Amiyah and I are the only two recruits left on Storm Squad, each with two bullets strung to our necks.

On the morning of our deployment, Grand Hall hums with the murmurs of four hundred child soldiers. Nearly half of what arrived on Fort Regulus a month ago.

Across the chamber, Faas stalks up the dais, his charcoal uniform pressed to a sharp crease. As always, the medals and ribbons across his uniform stand out in vivid colors, a shiny decoration of his cruelty. He's silhouetted by a long line of commanders from varying squads, with Lieutenant Caspian and Omari standing close behind.

"Recruits!" the High Commander booms, the black whorls on his face glinting as they catch the light. "Congratulations on the successful completion of your training."

A thunderous applause rolls through the crowd, with some of the recruits even shouting, "*Blood and valor to the very end!*"

I clench my jaw against the noise, knowing the great sacrifices it took to get here. We've killed so many—friends, families—and most of these recruits will only kill more once they arrive on the Sahl. We may have survived training, but we will forever remain chained to this life of death and ruin. A life without freedom. A life of war we can no longer avoid.

I can put an end to it, I think, and my conversations with Theodus and Omari come to mind. The Draft, the monarchy's reign of terror—everything will change once Olympia and the royal bloodlines are dead. I'll make sure of it.

Beside me, Amiyah stirs, her hand clasped firmly around mine. She stares straight ahead, her face scrunched in equal distaste, unnerved by the raucous energy of the hall. The beaded choker I gifted her last week lies flush at the base of her neck, a promise of what today means for us both. In a few hours, Amiyah will be on her way to the Sahl, a deployed soldier on the verge of deserting. I know what her heart desires most, the cure she so desperately needs to save herself. Now, with barely any time left between us, I squeeze the hands of the girl who's kept me anchored this past month, hoping to gods she makes it to Ilè-Orisha. After everything we've been through, I hope Amiyah finds the freedom she deserves.

"For those of you who remain, your journey as soldiers is just beginning," Faas says, his voice a deep, echoing rumble. "Today, you leave for the Sahl to join your fellow comrades in our fight against the Shadow Rebels. But before you embark on this next mission, the Force demands one final test from you. Phase Two of your training begins now."

Hours pass.

When the guard finally comes to retrieve me, I'm already dressed in battle uniform, ready to face whatever obstacle lies ahead. My heart pounds, and a burst of adrenaline winds through me as the guard leads me down the familiar hallways of the training center.

This is it. A chance to earn the third, final bullet. Make it to King's Isle. No matter what happens today, I cannot fail.

As we approach the entrance of the training hall, I wonder if Amiyah has gone through the phase already. I haven't seen her since we left Grand Hall and the guards ushered us inside our individual quarters. Wherever Amiyah is, I hope to gods she's alive.

I take a deep breath as the guard shoves the iron doors open. The moment we enter the training hall, I pause in my step. The chamber has been transformed into something else entirely—a sweeping arena with over a thousand Lucis soldiers spilling down rows of arching benches. A large steel cage looms in the center of the hall, curved iron bars shining ahead. My eyes travel down the crowded room, the pounding feet, the chaos of roaring voices. A shudder rattles along my spine as realization hits me.

This is a battle. The soldiers have come to see a fight, watch two recruits spill blood, scream for the death of the weaker warrior.

I should have known Faas would find a way to pit us against each other one last time. It's the first phase all over again—another test of survival. *Kill or be killed*. But I'm not the one dying today.

I shake the tension from my limbs, loosen the stiffness in my joints. The sea of bodies parts, offering me a wide, unobstructed view of the cage. My opponent stands with Caspian and Faas, thick coils of black hair pulled into a high bun. Her brown eyes dart across the arena, searching frantically, until they land on me.

She freezes at the exact same moment my body goes numb.

Amiyah.

For a second, I can barely move, my steps lurching even as the guard shoves me down the narrow path. The crowd's screams are an echo in my ears, their tugging hands a ghost on my skin. I fix my gaze on Amiyah's ashen face, the tremor raking through her body as the distance closes between us.

By gods. After all we've done to survive, this is what it comes down to? Once again, the Lucis have shoved me into a steel cage, and my key to freedom is to take a life. Amiyah's or mine. After today, one of us will be dead, the other broken for eternity. Either Amiyah won't get to find her cure, or I won't get a chance to kill the royals and end this war. We can't have both.

In a haze, I climb inside the cage and come to a stop before Amiyah and the two commanders.

"Recruits." Faas glares between the both of us. "This is a fight to the death. By the end of this match, only one of you will emerge from this cage alive. There are no weapons. You must rely only on the skills you've acquired this past month. Do not think. Do not hesitate. Kill or be killed."

Blood rushes to my ears as the commander's words echo in my head. I glance at Amiyah, wincing at the tears swimming in her eyes. A bitter rage kindles in my stomach as the commanders bound out of the cage. Haven't they taken enough from me? First Mama, then Teo. Now Amiyah? The pain is in me, sharp and jagged, a twisted knife in my heart.

"I should have seen this coming." Amiyah's voice quivers, mirroring my fear.

"I can't do this," I whisper through my own tears. "I won't do it."

"We don't have a choice," she spits out as Faas begins the countdown.

Nine—

I think about Teo, the friend whose life I took back inside the city dome. All because I didn't want to die. Because I wanted to uncover the truth about Mama, no matter the cost.

Seven—

His ghost still haunts me to this day. Not just him, but the ghosts of the other recruits I killed as well.

Four—

I can't add Amiyah to the parade. Not her. I can't kill innocent people anymore.

Two—

Perhaps it could be great. Death. A chance to leave this all behind. The suffering, the pain, the bloodshed. Quiet the horrors and take my monster with me before it grows to become the savage they've bred it—*me*—to be. With my death, I could spare Amiyah's life. With my death, I could end it all.

One.

"Fight, Sloane!" she screams as she charges toward me.

When she throws her first punch, all thoughts of death vanish from my mind. My survival instinct kicks in at once, and I block the blow with ease. Every maneuver I learned from Omari these past few days comes rushing back. My foot flies out. Before it connects with her stomach, Amiyah snatches my leg and shoves me backward. I lose my footing, and she drives into me again, slamming my back against the metal bars.

An explosion of pain spreads down my spine. I stifle a groan and swing hard, punching her in the ribs. For a second, she clutches her side, wincing from the sudden blow.

I hit her too hard. Guilt crawls into the pit of my stomach because I know the terrible pain she already suffers from her illness. But my guilt is lesser than my will to live.

So I fight.

The arena rumbles with the shouts of a thousand spectators as Amiyah and I dance across the cage. Her punch lands above my eye, cutting a gash across my brow. Blood trickles down my face. Despite the force of the blow, I lunge at her, hitting my friend square in the jaw. A scream erupts from her mouth. Blood and saliva spray onto the floor.

The shot claws at her rage, and I see the moment her mind goes dark. *Every single one of those deaths is a step closer to freedom*, she told me once. It's why she buried away her guilt, why she wouldn't allow herself to feel any remorse. The same ruthlessness I glimpsed within her that day flashes in her eyes now. Despite what she said last night, I know this is a battle Amiyah intends to win.

She charges forward, locking heads and limbs with me. When I see my opening, I jab my elbows into her arms, releasing us both from the wretched dance.

My pulse thunders as she sends a kick into my stomach. I double over, wheezing as air rushes from my lungs. She bounds forward, hoping to steal the moment to attack. Instead, I throw an uppercut into her chin and knock her back on her feet. With a second punch,

Amiyah crashes to the ground. Blood drips from her nose, pooling between her lips.

The sight makes me sick. I force down bile as Amiyah sweeps my feet out from under me. My head bangs against the concrete, and a terrible ache spears through my skull. The cage spins. I blink away the stars just as Amiyah pounces on me, raining punches down my face.

Blood coats me like a second skin. I scream out my terror.

I don't want to die. I don't want to die.

That deep, poisonous hunger to live, survive no matter the cost, taints my mind. I thrust my hips, throwing Amiyah off me. She struggles to latch on but pitches sideways instead. I roll over and scramble up on my feet. I don't wait for her to stand. My foot lands on her chest, and she goes flying across the cage. She coughs up blood. Another kick knocks her against the bars, making them rattle. I descend on her, my blows brutal as they fall on her head, her cheeks, her eyes. *Kill or be killed* howls in my mind, awakening a monstrous rage I never knew I possessed.

Outside the cage, the faces of the soldiers are a blur. They roar through the mayhem, their feet stomping against the concrete, iron bars clenched between their shaking fists. They crave the violence, as if every hit is a meal and Amiyah's blood will quench their thirsts.

My chest rises and falls in time with their savage cheers. In my fury, I don't notice when Amiyah stops fighting. I don't notice when she cowers under the weight of my blows, refusing to throw one of her own. She lies there like an empty shell, a bleeding, broken gazelle caught in the jaws of a hungry leopard. Every punch sprays my face with blood. Every punch wrenches a strangled cry from her throat.

I want to stop. I can't.

Something cracks. Blood gurgles from her mouth. She heaves a breath.

Still, I punch.

With a final blow, I kill my friend. I kill my hope, my strength, every single part of me I've clung to this past month. With that final blow, I kill myself.

Beneath me, Amiyah stares with wide, frozen eyes. I see pain in them too. Pain and suffering and death.

I killed her. The realization flings me off her chest. I land next to her body, shaking and trembling, my breath echoing in ragged gasps. Tears stream down my cheeks.

What have I done? Oh gods, what have I done?

"I'm so sorry." The words are a shocking whisper as guilt tears my being apart. "I'm so sorry."

Once, there was a girl who prayed for heroes, saviors of men to doom the monsters of her world. But that little girl is long gone.

I killed her.

I am a monster. I am one of them.

THIRTY-SEVEN

A wispy shadow grazes at the tips of my fingers, taunting close enough for me to grasp.

Death is here.

I want to seize it, wrap it around the calluses of my hand, hold on, and never let go.

I want to die. I deserve to die.

On the rooftop, I curl up against the ruined ledge and cry. My world swims in darkness, and in that void, I glimpse Mama's strength, Teo's hope, Amiyah's resolve. Everything I clung to, every flimsy thread of humanity that kept me anchored—they've taken from me. Now I'm left bleeding alone, with an emptiness as vast as the ocean beyond, knowing all too well what a monster the Lucis have made of me.

Children of war are born from war, Theodus told me once. What the seer failed to mention is that, in the end, we are also destroyed by war.

I stagger up slowly, a deep, hollow ache pulsing through my limbs. They tremble, threatening to give out, but I force myself to remain standing. Beyond the ledge, the ocean waves rise with the setting sun. By now, Olympia and the royals will be awaiting our arrival at Castlemore. I am the last recruit remaining on Storm Squad, and so I have earned my place among the ranks of broken children. Every drop of spilled blood, every innocent death, has led me to this very day. The day when the bloodlines finally answer for all the bloodshed they've caused, all the lives they've stolen from me.

Today, I will burn them all. Every last one of them.

For the first time since I left the training center, I am without tears. I am without pain.

I am nothing.

PART III

THE TREASON

Ìbèrè ogun là ń mò. Kò séni tí ó mo ìparí rè.
We only know the beginning of war.
No one knows how it ends.
—**PROVERB FROM THE ANCIENT KINGDOM OF KABBA**

THIRTY-EIGHT

An hour after Amiyah's death, I return to the barracks with three bullets to my name and one final mission on my mind. Omari waits for me inside my room, but he's not alone.

My gaze slides past the row of now-empty bunks to the silhouette of the soldier standing firm beside him. Lieutenant Caspian is dressed in a full military uniform embroidered with bright stripes and a row of gleaming medals. As always, a pair of black gloves shrouds his hands, and a long assault rifle cuts broadly across his back, held in place by a thin sling.

The lieutenant is the last person I'd expect to find in my quarters, and his sudden presence pricks at my skin like a hot knife. I linger at the door, my fingers tight around the handle as I glance back and forth between him and Omari.

"What's going on?"

"Shut the door, Ms. Shade," Caspian says, his voice deep.

As if sensing my unease, Omari crosses to me, his warm, familiar hand closing around my wrist. His touch is sorely gentle, yet when his fingers stray to my bloodied knuckles, I flinch at the memory of the steel cage and Amiyah's broken corpse. The images sear my insides. I taste bile on my tongue. When I look up, Omari is staring at me, jaw clenched as he grinds pain and pity between his teeth.

I'm sorry, those ocean eyes seem to say. I can only nod, a lump caught in my throat. With a reassuring squeeze, he pulls me forward. I step into the room slowly, ignoring the rapid thrum of my heartbeat as the door closes behind me.

When I get within a few feet of Caspian, I come to a halt and wrench Omari back a step.

"What is he doing here?" I murmur, searching his face for an answer.

"I promised I'd bring the Blades to you," Omari tells me. "Lieutenant Caspian is the league's second-in-command."

My eyes snap to the man across from me. "*He's* one of them?"

Caspian, who was there when Faas had me whipped. *Caspian*, who did nothing but watch while that bastard pitted us against each other. *Caspian*, who stood alongside the commander moments before I was forced to kill my friend. Every training, every wretched drill and phase and Cleansing, parades before my eyes, a bitter reminder of the suffering I've endured at the military's brutal hands. All I've lost and sacrificed because the commanders wish it so. Now I'm to believe this brute fights for change?

No. If this is who stands for the Blades, then I want nothing to do with them. I don't need a monster's strength to bring down a dozen other monsters.

I am a descendant of Shango, the god of heat and fire. I am a living inferno.

I am enough.

When I turn my glare on the lieutenant again, I hope he sees the flame burning in my eyes. The same one the military failed to snuff out.

"How can you live with yourself after everything you've done?" I hiss through gritted teeth. "I've heard the Blades fight for honor. Where is yours?"

Caspian shifts, boots scraping against the stone floor as he folds his arms in front of him. "For what it's worth, I'm sorry, Sloane," he offers without hesitation. "I know you have no reason to trust me, but Omari informed us of your plan, and you should know the Blades are prepared to join your mission. All we ask in return is that you lead us to Ilè-Orisha."

At the mention of the Shadow Rebels' fortress, I resist the urge to touch the cowrie shells around my neck. The beaded choker presses against the base of my throat now, an hour after I unstrung it from Amiyah's corpse.

Instead, my laughter echoes. A bitter, hollow ghost. "Why the hell would I do that?"

He looks to Omari briefly, exchanging a weighted glance only they understand. When he returns his gaze to me, I match his stance with a raised brow.

"Because," the lieutenant breathes, "it's what Margery North would have wanted."

"You told him?" I snarl, rounding on Omari.

"Not for the reasons you think," he answers quickly, and I note the plea in his next words. "Sloane, you might want to hear him out."

I hesitate. There's nothing the lieutenant could possibly say to make me change my mind. If the Shadow Rebels are alive today, it is only because the Lucis have yet to discover their hidden lair. I won't condemn my people to worse pain than they've already endured. Not for Omari, and especially not for the Blades.

I have the mind to tell Caspian where to shove whatever twisted story he's wrangled up in his head. That is, until the brute starts to speak.

"Eighteen years ago, when your mother founded the League of Blades, it was her mission to raise an army inside Avalon, one the royal bloodlines wouldn't see coming. The Blades would aid in her sister's rebellion, and with the Shadow Rebels as an ally, the Lucis wouldn't stand a chance."

"I don't believe you," I whisper, shaking my head. But even as the words slip out, a small part of me wonders if this is at all possible.

Is there a chance the lieutenant could be telling the truth? After all, Mama was a soldier here once. The record inside Archives Hall is confirmation enough. Both Theodus and Omari also told me Mama had a plan of her own to destroy the bloodlines. Even when she was locked away in Cliff Row, she never stopped plotting the monarchy's ruin and collapse. What better way to do so than by turning their own people and their bullets against them? Steel against steel. After all, the Lucis had weaponized everything that was ours and used it against us. It was only right to do the same to them.

Across the room, Caspian remains silent, a soldier's expression on his face, as he watches me chase after my thoughts until I've run them ragged.

"I was twelve when Margery recruited me," he murmurs, slowly tugging at the gloves covering his hands. "A common street kid whose parents had just been imprisoned for theft. But to further punish them for their crimes, King Ascellus also took something from me."

Since the day I met the lieutenant, I've often wondered what he hides beneath that thick layer of black leather. But now, as the whole thing starts to come off, I can't help but gasp at the intricate wiring of metal forged into his ten fingers.

Of course, the old king took his hands.

"If it weren't for Margery," Caspian says, flexing the metal tendons with practiced ease, "I wouldn't be here today. She taught me everything I know. And not just me, but others in the league as well." He glances up at me as he slips the gloves back on, once again shielding his metal hands from sight. "The Blades only exist today because of the strength and courage your mother showed when she was barely a year older than you are now."

The ease with which the lieutenant speaks about Mama is strange, and I can only watch as his demeanor changes before my eyes. I've never seen him like this—a human rather than the cold, ruthless savage I know him to be.

He fixes me with his quartz gaze, expectant, meaning for me to understand, to believe. Everything he's done, he did for the Blades. To protect them. To carry on Mama's legacy. But try as I might, I can't see beyond the assault rifle he forced into my hands, the target dummies sculpted in the likeness of my people, all of them pierced by his own bullets. Try as I might, I can't unmask the monster.

So with a deep, shuddering breath, I turn to the only thing left of this world that is still real, still true and achingly sure. The last piece of myself not yet broken. For all his flaws, Omari won't lie to me. Not with this.

"Did you know?" I ask slowly, looking into his eyes. "Is any of this true?"

He gives me a single nod. "Your mother was the one who recruited my parents. The Crown Conspiracy, the one that killed Ascellus and several other members of the royal families—that was in retaliation for what the king did to her."

My chest tightens at the realization. Mama's mission claimed too many lives, but it seems Omari is the one who suffered most. His parents are dead, with his sister on the brink of execution. Everyone Omari loves is gone, all because of Mama and her failure. The knowledge of it makes me wince. I can't repeat the same mistakes Mama made. I must find a way to right her wrongs, save Ara from the jaws of death.

No matter what happens today, I cannot fail.

"Everything you've been through this past month is exactly what your mother fought to avoid," Caspian says. My nerves twitch as he edges forward, but I keep my limbs still, toes curling inside my boots. "For more than three centuries, Scions and Yorubas have suffered under the bloodlines' oppressive hands. But there are also people within these walls, underneath these grounds, living in a constant state of fear. Lucis begging for freedom, just like you. Nagean or not, Scion or not, we are, all of us, prisoners of the crown." His words are firm and measured. I look up to meet the lieutenant's determined eyes. "Your mother knew this, and she died trying to change it. With you on our side, we have a chance to finish what she started."

"Why Ilè-Orisha?" I press him, trying to understand, trying to believe. "Once Olympia and the royals are dead, the Scion War ends. What other reason would you have to find the Shadow Rebels?"

"Just because you take down those monsters doesn't mean others won't rise in their place. We live in a world where even the most powerful are controlled by invisible hands, Sloane. Even if you succeed in your mission today, the war is far from over."

Silence descends as the lieutenant and I stare at each other for a long moment. I can see the truth plain as day in his face, yet it isn't enough to convince me. Lieutenant Caspian has always been there, always Faas's right-hand man. And as Baba once told me, you are the monster you keep.

Beside me, Omari takes my hand. I let him guide me away, his touch tender on my skin. When we finally stop in the corner of the room, he pulls me into him. Strong arms wrap me in a cocoon I wish could shield me from all my horrors.

"I don't trust him," I breathe into his chest.

"Then trust me," he whispers, the quick, panicked rhythm of his heartbeat keeping time with my own.

Though he won't admit it, I know Omari is just as afraid as I am. Today's mission could be the beginning of our freedom or the one that dooms us all. But we both know failure isn't an option. Not when there are so many lives at stake.

"Even if everything he says is true, you think someone like him would agree to free Jericho and Nazanin when this is all over?" I push back. "He and Faas are the ones who locked them there in the first place. He won't release them, Omari, and I will not leave my friends to die in Cliff Row."

My voice quivers around the memory of the night Jericho and Nazanin were captured in the tunnels, hollowed out by that same familiar guilt. I failed them once before, and I will not do the same to them again.

Sloane, you can free us all.

Now more than ever, I have to believe in Theodus's words. If nothing else, I have to believe the seer's divination cannot be wrong.

Omari plants a kiss on my shaved head, then another on my forehead, before drawing back a step. I drop my gaze to the floor in the same moment.

"Look at me," he says, and, with a gentle press of his thumb, he tips my chin back up, forcing me to meet his eyes. "When this is all over, I promise I'll be the one to free them. Not him. Me."

At the flicker of hesitation still visible on my face, he lowers his fingers over mine once more, squeezing with every word.

"I wouldn't have brought Caspian to you if I didn't think this could work. A week ago, when you told me the bloodlines are not invincible, that they could be hurt, I believed you. Today, I need you to believe me when I tell you the Blades won't betray you. These are my people, Sloane. They can be yours, too, if you let them."

His ocean eyes beseech mine, a silent plea in them. *Trust me.* If he had said those exact words a month ago, I would have scoffed in his face. If I dared enough, perhaps I might even have spat at his feet. But the soldier I met a month ago isn't the same person I've come to know now. A broken boy, a lost soul, shackled to a life he can't escape, all to save a sister who traded her freedom for his. After everything we've done to get here, I can't deny him the freedom I promised him.

I believed you. Now it's my turn to do the same.

Trust me.

With one final look at Omari's gleaming eyes, I whirl around to face Caspian. He looks up in the same moment, his hands clasped tightly behind him.

"Once the mission is complete, I will take you to Ilè-Orisha," I say, kindling enough fire to my voice. "But make no mistake, Lieutenant. I am no longer the girl from the village. I will not lie on my back and be trampled on. If this is some kind of game and I find out you're using me, I will kill you."

"Fair enough."

It's the first time I've seen the lieutenant smile. I hate how much it suits him.

A knock sounds at the door, and the three of us startle on our feet.

"Officer Shade, it's time," the familiar voice of the barracks officer echoes on the other side of the wooden frame.

I tighten my jaw against the new title. Hours ago, the woman would have addressed me as *Recruit*. But I am a soldier now. An officer of the crown. After today, I won't have to answer to either ever again.

Àse runs freely in my veins, and I let a spark of fire loose in my palms. Omari's and Caspian's eyes widen at the twisting flames. The heat surges, but I close my fists around it, putting out the fire—for now.

At the door, I look over my shoulder and address the two of them. "You know what you have to do."

THIRTY-NINE

Castlemore was built to burn. With its white stone walls, ornate arches, and gold filigree columns, Olympia's royal home is a lavish mess begging to be set aflame. The grand residence sits atop a sloping hill overlooking the rest of the royal court. Sunlight glimmers off the row of marble houses and proud turrets, each one bearing the banner of a different bloodline. Despite the lush terraces and gold-trimmed fountains, I can barely bring myself to stare at them too long. I could never see the beauty of a place ruled by ugly hands.

After an hour-long journey from Fort Regulus, we arrive on King's Isle, the crown land of Avalon. In the afternoon heat, the government towers shimmer like ice sculptures behind the royal court, with touches of Ganne gold worked into the domed canopies of other administrative buildings.

As our wheeled wagon climbs higher up the hill, the recruits seated next to me snap their heads in attention, spellbound by the jewel of a city dazzling before their eyes. Murraya hedges trimmed into the different shapes of the bloodlines' heraldic animals adorn the sidewalks of the asphalt road. Mussaenda flowers bloom like blush ornaments along the median strip. A parade of civilians stops to watch the procession of black transports heading toward Castlemore. Though some of the Lucis are clothed in suited garments, others don an array of vibrant Yoruba attires. Burly men drowning in fancy, overflowing agbadas. Women squeezed into the latest ankara trends, their skin caked with camwood powder to protect against the blazing sun. Even from behind the tinted glass windows, they look like a swarm of rain bugs crawled up from the dirt.

With a scowl, I turn my glare away from the sight. It's a reminder of why I'm here and what today means.

Finally, we reach the top of the hill. The palace's gilded gates swing open, and the wheeled wagon rolls onto the paved grounds. Barrel-shaped columns arrange themselves beyond the palatial courtyard. At the center, a three-headed snake fountain coils and slithers as it sprays jets of water into a swirling emerald pool. The Turais banner flutters high above the serpentine structure, the motto *Strike with Venom* gleaming like bared fangs.

Any other day, the threat in those words would be enough to poke at my resolve. But today is different. Today, Olympia Turais isn't the one striking.

I am.

The wagon coasts to a stop before the palace entrance. I jump out, joining the current of recruits from varying squads as they trail behind a pair of uniformed officers. We trudge up the courtyard steps into a domed foyer with stained glass ceiling and elaborate wall frescoes. Servants mill about the winding corridors, but it is the armed guards my eyes linger on, silhouetted against every corner of the palace halls. I lose count after about thirty, and their presence soon casts a dark shadow on the mission at hand.

I dig my nails into my palms as dread slowly sinks in, a stone heavy in my chest. Last night, when I worked through the plan again with Omari, it sounded impressive enough, a well-disguised ploy the royals wouldn't even see coming. Without Theodus to warn them of the attack, I was convinced nothing could go wrong. The bloodlines had made another error in keeping the seer alive, in thinking they could turn him against his own people. They thought Theodus would be their greatest weapon, not knowing he'd be the one to doom them all. With him and the Blades on my side, the plan seemed certain. Now, with so many guards patrolling the palace grounds, I find myself questioning everything, imagining all the different ways I could fail.

We turn a corner, and the officers lead us down a hallway lined with large portraits and ancient relics. My feet slow as I take in the ceremonial vessels locked behind glass alongside brass armlets and sacred bronze heads—all of them stolen from the Ancient Kingdoms during the invasion. These are my people's history. Ceramic sculptures and ivory plaques. By gods, these are our artifacts. Yet these thieves have the gall to put them on display as a symbol of their triumph. Their spoils of war.

I clench and unclench my fists as my gaze travels down the entire length of the wall, my heart seizing at the horrible images depicted in those bleeding portraits. These bastards have stolen from us, looted from us, raped and destroyed every last piece of our culture. And yet—yet, we are the ones they call savages. We are the ones deemed too unworthy to live.

It's all I can do to tamp down my fear, replacing it with a familiar spark of fury. I will make these monsters pay for everything. I will make them suffer just as they've done to my people.

Today, I will reclaim every piece of culture the Lucis have stolen from me.

The two officers leave us in a large waiting chamber. I can barely sit still as recruits are ushered into the throne room one at a time. Omari told me this would happen. He said Olympia and the royals often granted private audience to each recruit, to make us feel like we are *something* after a month of being broken into *nothing*.

The horror ends today.

There will be no more children for the Lucis to corrupt. No more children for them to use, abuse, and destroy.

For the next few hours, I fall into a tense, restless state, so I pace back and forth in the now empty space. A while later, when the door cracks wide open, a female officer stands in the doorway, catching me off guard.

"Officer Shade." She gestures at me with a wave. "They are ready for you."

My stomach lurches as I follow the officer down a separate

corridor leading to the throne room. *This is it.* My mind races with each step up the tiled marble floors. Àse hums through my veins in response, ribbons of fire winding up and down my arms in a blaze of colors. I draw more of the heat into my skin until there's nothing visible, a weapon close enough to wield when the time comes.

We march up a small flight of stairs, where the tall, arching doors of the throne room loom. The two guards at the entrance pull the doors open, allowing us entry inside the grand chamber. The walls of the throne room are painted a brilliant white, just as I saw in Olympia's broadcast when I first arrived on the base. Even the marbles set in the ground are gleaming pearls, well polished enough to glimpse my twisted reflection along their smooth surface. Dressed in the official charcoal uniform of the military, the girl staring back at me isn't someone I recognize. A soldier, a child, a Scion, a killer. I am a traitor to my kind, a murderer of friend and foe. I am broken. I am lost. I am sin and forgiveness.

Across the room, gilded thrones form a graceful row on a dais, each one claimed by a Lucis lord. This time, the only one missing from the lot is Theodus, and just as well, too, for what is surely about to take place in here tonight.

As always, the royals drown in their customary white-and-gold damask capes, their sharp, pointed eyes scanning my face like those of vultures waiting to devour prey. More than two dozen masked sentries rise behind them like a spiked wall, with Faas a hulking shadow at the queen's side.

I know Faas, and that bastard will defend Olympia to his last breath, Omari said some nights ago. Though the commander is the last person I expect to see, I know not even his presence will unravel today's mission. If the commander wishes to die alongside his queen, so be it.

Halfway through the chamber, the female officer presses a hand to my shoulder, halting my steps.

I grind my teeth as I dip my head into a low bow. "My lords. Your Highness."

"What is your name, soldier?" Olympia speaks in a rich, satiny tone.

For once, the queen's outfit matches the Lucis' official white-and-gold colors, draped in a diamond-studded aso-òkè that wraps around her petite form in delicate pleats.

Never in my life would I have expected to be standing this close to the royal bloodlines, and the small distance between us makes my skin prickle. Once again, a coil of dread winds its way around my chest, gripping tight.

This is it. My heartbeat roars in my ears. *There is no going back now.*

I draw a sharp intake of breath and force steel and fire into my voice.

"I am Sloane Folashadé—"

A surprised murmur spreads among the bloodlines, the first ripple in a disturbed ocean.

"Daughter of Adelina Folashadé—"

Olympia's eyes flash in recognition. Behind her, the sentries' bullets click into place.

"Or as most of you know her—Lieutenant Margery North."

Two dozen soldiers draw their rifles, their barrels aimed directly at me. With great speed, they press inward, forming a tight circle, enough to block all twelve royals from sight. *From my line of attack.* I'm not surprised when Faas breaks through the ring, cold fury set in his gaze as he bounds forward. The last time I saw that same madness in his eyes was back in Eti-Osa, when he trapped me in a ring of soldiers much like this one. That day, he'd forced the squad to whip me nearly to death. Today, despite the threat of what the commander could do, I don't shrink away from his brutish grasp. Whatever power the bastard still thinks he has over me, he's about to watch it crumble before his eyes.

"I always knew there was something different about you," he growls.

When his blow lands on my jaw, a harsh ring echoes in my ears. The ache is sharp and hot, reverberating through my skull as blood pools in my mouth.

I laugh through the pain and spit crimson in his face. "You're still the same monster I met a month ago, Commander."

The color drains from him as he wipes the spittle away. "I should have killed you back in Eti-Osa," he hisses low. "I won't make the same mistake again."

We lock eyes for one heated moment. I don't doubt the commander means every word. Dimly, I wonder if he knew Mama, if their paths crossed at all while she trained in Fort Regulus. I wonder who Faas was before he became the monster he is today. Another child broken by war, forged into a weapon, unleashed upon other children to repeat the same vicious cycle. Whatever humanity he once had died with him a long time ago.

With a sudden jerk, he releases me and looks past my shoulder. His mouth twitches slightly, betraying a shadow of satisfaction. When the stomping of boots echoes behind me, I know why.

As the troop of soldiers pours into the throne room, Faas steps away, returning to his post at Olympia's side. Like the queen's sentries, the soldiers' faces are hidden behind dark helmets, heavy guns drawn deftly in their hands.

The firing squad.

I recognize the synchronized rhythm of their movements, the swiftness with which they take a life. I swallow a deep, mighty breath as I examine the long row of soldiers. They form a line a few yards away, waiting for the queen's order.

Any moment now. I harden my nerves and straighten my shoulders, turning my attention to the bloodlines.

"A living relative of Margery North." Olympia's voice is a finely honed blade, sharp enough to cut. "If I knew poor Margery mothered a child, I would have granted you an audience long ago, dear."

Audience. She says the word so plainly, though we both know what she really means. If the Lucis knew Mama had a family to her name, they would have come for me and Baba and killed us. Olympia, especially, would have made sure of it. I have no knowledge of what transpired between her and Mama back when they were both soldiers training together at Fort Regulus, but whatever it is seems to have left the queen vulnerable, even after all these years. I see it in the way she peers at me, her face darkening as if she's seen a ghost. Despite the rage sparking in her eyes, her cold mask cracks a little, undercut by a shadow of fear.

Olympia may have succeeded in killing Mama, but the queen isn't without her own wounds. Others do not see it, but I do. The viper bleeds too.

She tilts her head to the side, one elbow on the armrest of her throne in a false attempt to maintain a calm, royal demeanor.

"Tell me," she taunts, "have you come here to find out how your wretched mother died? Or perhaps it is to avenge her?"

My whole body shakes, hands trembling as the fire in me begs for release. Instead, I curl my fists inward, tightening my rein on my àse a little longer. *Not yet.*

"I suppose I have the Force to thank for your brazenness." The queen leans back in her seat. "But it seems whatever training you received this past month has also made you foolish—foolish enough to think you could march into my home with only a name to defend yourself. Your mother did the same once, and like you, she, too, failed. Now here you are, soon to meet the same fate she met on those foothills years ago." She edges forward, fangs bared in true form as she hisses, "I will bury you in the mud together."

"You can't bury what isn't dead." The fire in me spills over.

"Silence!" Up on the dais, Olympia sets her jaw, iron-clawed fingers flexed in front of her. The threat is plain. If I push her far enough, I know where those claws will pierce.

I should hold my tongue, remain docile. It's what they want. While they sit there on their iron thrones, spewing bigotry, protecting their privilege, I'm to remain on my knees, complacent in my anger. After centuries of oppression, of torment and pain and suffering, they dare judge me for my rage.

Silence. It's what they want. But Mama once told me, *When the world tries to silence you, do not go quiet. Scream, Sloane.*

Today, my words are a weapon, and I have every intention of using it.

With her voice in my head, urging me on, I take a bold, defiant step forward. Before me, the guards' hands stray to their rifles. Olympia's fists tighten around the armrests. I don't care. She's said enough. My turn now.

I stare up at the bloodlines with every last ounce of my resolve. "You call us monsters, yet you destroy the lives of innocent children, use us as pawns to fight your war—"

"The cost of war is heavy, dear," the queen says dryly.

"But you are not the ones paying them!" The words rip from my throat, ragged and trembling. "By gods, you say we are scum, yet you steal from us, dress like us, live and thrive on a land drenched with the blood of my people. How many children died for you to sit on that bleeding throne? How many Yorubas and Scions massacred to prolong your reign? And still—*still*, killing us isn't enough. It will never be enough."

The ache in my chest is constant, a sharp, stabbing pain that flares as the ghost of Amiyah moves before my eyes. She's trailed by Teo and Magda and Semi and every last one of my kills. Yorubas and Scions, innocent boys and girls—all of them bled dry for the glory of a dozen tyrants. *No more.*

Though tears stain my cheeks, I force another step forward until

I'm face-to-face with the tide of soldiers and the cold threat of their gun barrels.

"Know this," I sneer in their faces. "Despite how many of us you continue to kill, how many child soldiers you pluck from their villages every year, the Shadow Rebels won't stop fighting. Yorubas and Scions across Nagea won't stop rising." My heart thrashes against my rib cage as I stare beyond the soldiers' shield, meeting the queen's icy glare. "I have seen your fate, Olympia, and it is not victorious."

She swoops down from her throne and pushes through the circle of soldiers in a quick, menacing blur. *Come closer. I dare you.*

Her grip is around my neck, iron claws digging into my throat, enough to pierce the skin, enough to draw blood. Pain blooms from her touch. I blink fresh new tears from my eyes. Her choking hands are familiar, and for a brief, hazy moment, I'm reminded of Semi and his vague divination. Flitting shadows dance in my memory. Hands of darkness wrap around my throat.

Trust not the one who killed their mother. The warrior they chained, the elder freed. The child they spawned, the father saved. Thus, by your hand shall the Blood Scion rise. When the pale viper dies, and foe turns to blood.

Is this what Semi glimpsed in his vision? Is Olympia the pale viper fated to die? Am I the Blood Scion?

I gasp in the queen's grasp, struggling to breathe, struggling to speak.

"I will have you know your entire existence, and that of those rats, is a tragedy waiting to be written," she growls, her voice dripping venom.

The pain twists my rage, my anger, my fear, into something greater than me, into words stronger than any. My blood pounds in my ears. I grit my teeth and say, "So long as it's written in your blood."

She squeezes harder. "If Margery North herself couldn't kill me, what makes you think you can?"

For as long as I've known the queen, she has been nothing but cold. But even cold things burn. With enough heat and just the right amount of fire, cold things can be broken too. And as long as I still draw breath, I will break her.

Àse buzzes impatiently through my veins, fighting to break free. I've held my leash on it for too long. I will no longer deny my magic the freedom it craves. Not anymore.

"Because—" I lift a hand to my throat and press my palm flat against the queen's grip. "My mother wasn't a Scion. I am."

The fire races, tearing through flesh and bone in its path to reach my hand. When the first current of heat jumps into Olympia's skin, her eyes widen. The flames burn right through, leaving a bloody handprint against her alabaster skin. She yanks her hand free and releases a horrible scream.

"Kill her! Kill her now!"

A breath gusts out of me as the firing squad draws its weapons.

Gunfire crackles through the throne room.

FORTY

Olympia's guards are the first to fall. Bullets slice through the air, the roar of gunfire echoing across the throne room. The sound reverberates in my chest, burrowing so deeply, I feel it in my bones. Behind me, members of the firing squad have taken off their black masks. Now one face stands out sharply among the wave of soldiers.

Caspian.

The lieutenant moves in a blur, swift and deadly as the round missiles he fires into the line of rushing guards. Even with his metal hands, his shots are well aimed, piercing flesh and bone, leaving a trail of bodies in his wake. Two flaming crossed blades gleam on his assault rifle—the symbol of the League of Blades. Every soldier on the squad bears the same fiery insignia on the barrel of their loaded weapons. I don't recognize any of their faces, but the precise formation with which they attack is familiar, well-timed. After all, this is *my* plan, *my* mission. Now that the Blades are here, the royal bloodlines don't stand a chance. Even with the army pouring into the room, the Lucis are still outnumbered.

My heartbeat howls in my ears as one of the guards protecting Lord Kaus catches a bullet to his neck. Blood sprays across the royal's face, and the pudgy man shrieks. He opens his mouth to scream again, but his wails cut off abruptly when another bullet sinks into his skull.

One down, eleven more to go.

Panic rips through the throne room. The cries of the royals rend the air as they scramble to escape the chaos. Hidden behind a blockade of guards, they crawl on all fours, scurrying toward the exit like rats fleeing a burning hole. The sight of them awakens the rage stirring in the pit of my stomach. I'll give these vermin something to run from.

A rush of adrenaline buzzes through me as Shango's drums rise to a frenzy inside my skull. I welcome the ancient sound as it washes over me. It rumbles like thunder deep within, every pulsating beat pushing magic and warmth into my veins. The current ripples beneath my skin, swirls of reds and blues that dance in a fluid, glowing wave. Àse tears through my core, alive and free, a flaming spark that ignites every part of my being.

The bloodlines are nearing the double doors now. Teeth bared, I reach for my fire with an ease I've never felt before.

Let them burn. Amiyah's voice echoes in my head.

And that is what I do.

With a scream, I send a cannonball of fire streaking across the room. When the flames hit the ground, they swell upward, surging into a thick wall that blocks any escape to the door. The first blast throws the guards to the ground, swallowing them in a roaring blaze. Bodies drop, brain matter exploding in a sickening mess of red and gray. An overwhelming stench of blood taints the air, a sharp copper tang that coats the back of my throat.

The screams of the dying fuel my fury, a beast with razor-sharp fangs and talons to tear through skin. So many will die today. The guards. The bloodlines. Faas. Olympia. This is what they deserve, the ruin they've brought upon themselves. They wanted me to be a monster. I will be the worst monster they ever created.

Gunfire chokes the air. The royal army darts in every direction, their bullets shuddering above my head. As the Lucis fight through the tangle of bodies, my àse roars in kind. Great spurts of fire, born from my fingertips, incinerate those foolish enough to cross my line of sight. Without hesitation, without remorse, I burn them all, spreading the flames wide enough so no one is spared.

Truly, I kindled this fire with the darkest parts of my being, so when it burns, they will feel my rage, feel my pain, feel the soldier they've created seething with the overwhelming desire to destroy every last one of them.

Flames twist across the marble floors, licking at the fallen corpses lying around me. Though the faces of the dead are scorched beyond recognition, I can still make out the Lucis' white-and-gold damask capes, a charred mess of embroidery and loose threads. Next to them, the royal army's soldiers kneel over themselves, coughing up blood as they slowly meet their death.

The throne room bursts aflame. Smoke and ash fog my vision, painting the walls of Castlemore in a dark, cloudy haze. Still, gunshots ring out across the burning chamber, a deep rumble that shakes the ground beneath my feet. Across from me, a hail of bullets tears a hole through a guard's stomach, dropping him in a pool of his own blood.

The Blades are still fighting; this is the battle they've prepared for their entire lives. The day when the monarchy falls and freedom rises in its place. With so many of the bloodlines dead, the freedom we fight for is so close that, for the first time, I can almost imagine a world without the royals, without child soldiers, without war. The world Teo once believed we could have. The world Mama died for. The world Amiyah dreamed of.

Now only one person stands in our way.

Finally, through a cloud of black smoke, I see her.

Olympia cowers behind Faas as the commander tries to usher her to safety. He sprays the room with an assault of bullets, dropping a few Blades who stand in his way. My wall of fire has fallen, giving them a chance to escape the throne room. Once they make it past those doors, any hope I have of killing Olympia disappears.

My heartbeat thuds, pushing against my rib cage as I draw on the remnants of àse in my blood. A bud of fire blooms to life on my hands. I race forward, the flames spitting and crackling with each step. My nerves scream, a fiery beast thrumming with magic and rage the closer I get to them.

I'm a few bodies away when Olympia's gaze lands on me. The same horror I saw on her face earlier bleeds through her now as she gestures wildly to the commander, screaming words in his face.

"Kill her! Shoot her!"

Faas turns his attention and weapon on me, aiming at my head. His eyes are coal black, betraying no signs of fear, as bullets click into place. Before they find release, I throw out my hands, knocking the commander off his feet with a jolting flame. I don't wait for him to rise, nor do I expect him to. Another blast tosses Faas against the wall. A weak groan escapes him. The fire tears through his uniform, exposing the charred skin beneath. Blood oozes from the commander's burns, leaving behind a red trail as he pitches forward, scrambling for his gun.

It would be too easy to kill him now, but a monster like Faas doesn't deserve a quick death. No, I want to make him suffer, make him pay for all he's done to me and every other child he's forced into this life of war.

With all the strength I can muster, I build a cage of inferno around the man who was once my commander, much like the one he shoved me and Amiyah into hours ago. This bastard watched as we did a wretched dance of death trapped behind steel bars. Now it's his turn.

Let him dance to his death.

Let him burn.

The flames wrap around him, hissing and sputtering as they devour every inch of his flesh. Faas howls in agony. I leave him to his fate and turn my wrath on Olympia.

Without her shield, the queen desperately fights to reach the doors. She dodges behind ashen bodies, shoves the last of her guards in the line of fire, all to protect herself. All to get to safety. Too bad she won't make it out.

Àse churns through my veins, a river of molten fire that races beneath my skin. In my palms, orange-red tongues lick at the shuddering air. I snuff them out with a quick flick of my wrists.

Mama raised the Blades to fight steel against steel. Olympia killed her for it. Now she'll know how it feels to die by the very weapon they buried Mama with.

I yank Faas's bullet chain from my neck and snatch a gun from one of the dead guards. One by one, I load each round into the chamber as I march toward Olympia. The moment she reaches the exit, I fire the first bullet at her leg, sending her to her knees.

That's for Teo.

She crawls along the blood-soaked floors, her body trembling as she lifts a hand to the door's handle. The next bullet sinks into her shoulder. She releases a guttural scream as she slumps forward.

For Amiyah.

Olympia glances up when I stop in front of her, her blue eyes cold even as she stares death in the face.

"You can't kill me," she growls. "I am still your queen!"

A plea. A cry for help.

But I have no compassion for my oppressor. I have no mercy left in me for this tyrant.

I am vengeful. I am merciless. And I do not care.

"This one's for Mama," I say, burying the third bullet into her skull.

Olympia's blood sprays everywhere, staining the floors a deep crimson. She falls backward, crashing against the doorframe. The door wrenches open under her weight, and her body thuds when it lands in the hallway. Even in death, Olympia looks terribly fragile, a broken doll with papery skin and hollow, empty eyes.

The pale viper is dead, and I killed her.

I killed the queen.

My limbs give out and I fall to my knees next to Olympia's body. For a moment, I can only stare at the blood leaking out of her bullet holes. My breath echoes in the silence of the corridor, fast and harried as I push air back into my lungs.

Across from me, the throne room is strangely quiet, the floors flooded with a procession of the dead. Thick flurries of ash drift overhead, coating the faces of the surviving Blades as they tend to their wounded men and women.

It's over. I gasp as the truth slowly sinks in.

The royal bloodlines are dead. All twelve of them. The monarchy has fallen at last. And from their ruin, my people will rise. Yorubas and Scions will once again know what it means to be free, to live. It's everything they never wanted us to be. Everything they took from us. Now the time has come to put ourselves back together. A million broken pieces to be made whole again.

I inhale slowly, and a blanket of warmth drapes over me. Then Caspian is at my side, his arm tightening around my shoulders as he pulls me away from Olympia's corpse. I let him drag me down the stone steps, but not before stealing another glance at the throne room. I just need to see it one last time to truly believe it is over.

I am alive. I am free.

Outside Castlemore, the sky bleeds crimson as the sun sets beyond the horizon. Plumes of black-gray smoke curl above our heads, billowing through the thick, hazy air. With the Blades charging ahead, and Caspian at my side, we race past the palace walls into the courtyard, our eyes darting, searching for an incoming army. Soon news of the royals' assassination will reach Fort Regulus, and every soldier on the base will flood these grounds. We'll be long gone by the time they arrive, well on our way to Ilè-Orisha. Now that the lieutenant has upheld his end of the bargain, it's my turn to do the same.

We've only reached the palace gates when I spot a known figure approaching from behind the gilded bars. Broad frame, full lips, and ocean eyes. It's all so familiar, and the sight of him is enough to set my heart galloping.

"Omari!"

In that moment, he glances out beyond the gates. Like a moth drawn to a flame, his gaze locks on me. Already, my feet are moving of their own accord, pushing me right into the arms of the boy I certainly hoped I'd see again. He swoops me into a crushing embrace, his hands trembling on my back.

"It's over," I breathe into his neck. "We did it."

A spark of heat pulses through me as his grip tightens around my waist, pressing me deeper into him. Though his hands still quiver, his touch is gentle, soothing, and desire blooms where his fingers trail. Perhaps it's the adrenaline still coursing through my veins, the knowledge that I somehow escaped death despite its cold grasp on me. For whatever reason, I feel emboldened enough to pull away from Omari and slowly press my lips to his.

At first, he hesitates. His body tenses against mine, and I taste the fear on his lips. I don't know why he's so afraid, especially when he has no reason to be. The bloodlines are dead. Ara can be saved, along with Jericho and Nazanin and every Yoruba and Scion across Nagea.

We won. It's over.

"Trust me." The same words he spoke to me earlier tremble on my mouth now. He searches my face for a moment, a hurricane of emotion sweeping behind his green eyes. Then he inches close. His fingers graze my chin, tilting it up, just a little. This time, when our lips brush, his restraint breaks. The kiss is hot and searing and demanding, a razor sharp enough to slice through me. With every taste, àse cuts deep into my core. The heat is more than I can control. It floods my veins, bathing me in swirls of light and color, pushing fire and life and freedom into my body. He kisses me like it's the only thing left to do in this new, free world. He kisses me tomorrow. He kisses me forever.

Then Omari's hands are around my neck, chasing the warmth away from my skin. No, not hands. This is something different, something cold and unfamiliar, a choking noose around my throat. When it clamps shut, I have my answer.

An iron collar. A round menace of steel now prickling hot at my throat. A sharp ache creeps into my body, the pain intensifying as Omari breaks away from me, the ghost of his kiss still lingering on my lips.

"What are you doing?" I gasp aloud.

Without his support, I crumple to the ground. The burn is unlike anything I've ever felt, worse even than my own fire as it rips through my being. Terror gnaws at my spine. A scream wells up in my throat. *What is this? What is happening to me?*

I lift my gaze to Omari, but the boy won't even look at me. He's only an inch away, and yet, we've never been further apart. My pulse roars as I claw at the locked collar. It smolders, too hot to touch.

This is no ordinary device, I realize with growing horror. Whatever this is, it's ancient, forged from magic, spelled by àse itself.

Àse. Out of desperation, I reach for my own magic, yanking on the familiar energy threading through my blood. But it doesn't come to me. No matter how hard I try, it doesn't answer my call. Instead, heat flares inside my veins, a trapped beast fighting to escape. I cry out as it leaves painful brands and scars across my body.

The world screams with me. For a second, I don't understand—until I see the wave of soldiers pouring out of the shadows, surrounding Caspian and the rest of the Blades. There's too many to fight, too many to gun down. The Blades are outnumbered, and there's nowhere to run.

No, no, no. It wasn't supposed to happen this way. We were free. By gods, we were free until Omari wrapped us back in chains.

The boy crouches low in front of me. Hands that once felt tender and warm on my skin now grip me with such force, sharp nails dig into my flesh.

"I don't understand," I choke out through my tears. "Why are you doing this?"

His ocean eyes are cold, colder than I've ever seen them before. This isn't the same boy whose taste still lingers on my tongue. Instead, a stranger stands in his place.

He leans close. When he opens his mouth, his words strike like tinder.

"For Ara."

FORTY-ONE

The shackles around my wrists rattle with force, yanked by two soldiers dragging me toward a palace I just escaped. More uniformed officers follow behind, a blockade of armed men ready to strike if I dare make a move. They push and prod, keeping me at a stumbling pace as we cross the grounds of Castlemore. The smoke swirls overhead, thick clouds of flame licking at the few remaining turrets still standing.

On instinct, I reach out to the twisting fire, desperate to feel the buzz of àse in my blood. The magic hums beneath, but once again, it doesn't answer. Instead, a burst of pain streaks through my entire body. Omari's collar sears around my neck. I hiss as tears sting my eyes, threatening to spill.

Even now, Omari's cold eyes flash in my mind. The ghost of his hands burns around my throat. *For Ara*, he said, moments before he handed me off to the soldiers. Try as I might, I can't bring myself to understand where his betrayal comes from. The royal bloodlines are dead, just as we planned. Ara and the rest of the Blades can be freed. It's the freedom he's always wanted, the cause he fought and killed for. I gave it to him, and he clamped a collar around my neck.

Trust me.

I wish I hadn't believed him when he whispered those words. I wish I hadn't allowed myself to be swept away by a soldier who hid his true nature behind empty kisses and a false heart.

An ache swells inside my chest as the officers lead me past the palace courtyard, shoving me toward a flat building behind the grand residence. Darkness bleeds from the narrow alleyway, and for a moment, I wonder if the officers have brought me to a torture chamber. Instead, when the door opens, I find a familiar figure standing in the middle of the room. Even with his back turned to me, I'd recognize his slightly bent frame anywhere, the raised birthmark at the nape of his neck.

"Baba!"

He whirls slowly, the tears already streaming down his face. The sight of him shatters the last of my resolve. I wrench myself away from the soldiers' grasps and run into my grandfather's arms.

He swoops me into a crushing embrace, and for a moment, we cling tightly to one another, for fear of what might happen if we let go. A month after being forced to say goodbye to Baba, I never thought I'd see him again. But here he is, alive and well, standing before me. *For now.* I don't know when I start to cry, but the sobs ache in my throat as I bury my head into his chest.

"I'm so sorry," I whisper, because now I understand why the soldiers have brought me here, why they've captured my grandfather too. "This is all my fault."

He kisses my shaved head, his tears leaking onto my skin as he pushes warmth and comfort into my body. "You did nothing wrong, Sloane."

Though his voice is gentle, Baba's pain is so achingly familiar, my stomach tightens around it. Then the officers are upon us. One of them grips my grandfather's arm, yanking him away from me.

"Let him go!" I lurch after them, but another officer jerks me backward. As the distance yawns between us, a chill races up my spine at the thought of losing Baba all over again because of what I've done. My breath catches as I address the line of soldiers surrounding me, begging anyone who will listen. "It's me you want. I did this. I killed the bloodlines. Please, just let him go."

"I'm afraid I can't do that, Sloane."

The voice floats out of nowhere, tinged with a surety that wasn't there the last time we spoke. I look up to find Theodus emerging from the shadows, his footsteps light against the concrete. Omari trails at his heels, making sure to keep his face straight ahead. After the nights we've had, the boy won't even meet my eyes. I can't help but frown at the sight of him and Theodus together, my mind grasping for an answer that doesn't yet make sense.

"Theodus?" He marches up a raised platform, lowering himself onto a plush throne inlaid with white velvet. I swallow hard, my throat suddenly parched. "Wh-what's going on?"

The seer fixes his brown eyes on Baba, and for the first time, I recognize something in them—something I can't yet place. A thin smile gleams on his face, the sharp edge of a twisted knife.

"Care to tell her, Elijah? Or shall I?"

Elijah? My gaze sweeps back and forth between him and Baba. The color drains from my grandfather's face when he locks eyes with Theodus. A strange darkness haunts them both.

"Tell me what?" I ask the two of them, my voice suddenly small. "Baba?"

Instead of my grandfather, it's Theodus who speaks. "My dear, I am your father."

His voice echoes in my ears, so loud it assaults my senses. Already I'm shaking my head, disparaging of his words.

"No," I whisper almost to myself, backing away slowly.

It's impossible.

"My father died the year I was born," I tell him, even as my voice wavers. "He was a black market trader. He hoarded steel and the Lucis—they killed him. They . . ." I trail off when my gaze cuts to my grandfather, pausing at the flicker of sadness behind his eyes. "Baba?" He dips his head, refusing to so much as look at me. "Baba, please say something."

"I'm sorry, Sloane," he mumbles at last. His words are enough to unravel my entire being.

A shiver catches me from the nape down to the skin of my toes. And still, I refuse to believe.

"You're wrong," I rush out. "You're lying."

"I have no use for lies," Theodus says, his tone a cold menace. "You were inside Archives Hall. You read the records on Margery North. Saw the death certificate issued when Olympia believed she'd perished in the Cliff Row fire. And yet, somehow, Adelina escaped. How?"

An image of Mama's file flashes in my mind, memories from the day I broke into the Archives and uncovered a truth that sent me down this path. A path I alone chose to walk. Because I believed it would lead to justice, to freedom. I was so wrong. But the records—*yes*, there were so many. Relics of a brutal life Mama once lived, bound in service to the Lucis until the day she became unbound.

There was enough evidence to conclude that the bodies found were those of the lieutenant and the general.

That's what Omari told me when he took me up to the cliffs that night. Now pieces of our conversation flutter around me, each one buzzing in my head until it's almost too loud to ignore.

Gods above.

"It was you." I turn to Baba, my limbs shaking as I force the words out. "You're Lord General Elijah Sol."

"The last true heir to the Sol bloodline," Theodus echoes from his place on the throne. "But that was before he betrayed his own kind by marrying a Scion and fathering her only child."

Yeye Celeste. Her name howls in my ears, haunted by the ghost of Baba's voice. *Celeste could see anything, predict anything. The future was hers to read, and she died for it.*

My stomach plunges with the realization, the tremors in my legs dragging me to the ground.

"You could have saved her," Theodus whispers, his eyes hardening as they shift to Baba. "You could have saved me. But you left us both to die."

There is true pain laced between his words, a deep sorrow I could never truly understand. Across from me, my grandfather moves his head back and forth, barely able to choke down his sobs. "I tried—I tried."

"No, Father. You ran. While I spent years in Ascellus's captivity, you chose freedom that wasn't yours. Freedom you didn't deserve." Disgust coats his next words like poison as his gaze flicks toward me. "He is a Lucis, Sloane," he says, and something shatters in me. "He is everything you hate in the monarchy."

Stop.

"A ruthless general who led his army on countless raids and Cleansings across Nagea."

Please, stop.

With a gasp, my chest caves inward. Folds itself around my heart. Bitter tears spill down my cheeks. *It's too much. Too much.* But Theodus only continues. With every wretched word, he strips my grandfather bare, exposing glimpses of a life I never knew he lived.

"Your *baba* is nothing more than a murderer of Yorubas and Scions," the seer tells me with a thin curve to his lips. "He is a bigot. The Death Bringer himself."

"Stop!" The scream rips through my throat as pain claws at fragile parts of my being. All my life, I've always known who Baba was. He was my grandfather, my friend, my salvation. A source of warmth and safety in this bleeding darkness. Now I'm to believe that this man—the one who raised me, the one who fed and clothed me, the only family I have left—I'm to believe he's one of *them*?

No. There has to be some kind of explanation, something, anything, to clear Baba of Theodus's lies. I have no reason to believe anything the seer tells me. Not anymore. Not after everything. My pulse thunders. Despite the harsh ringing in my ears, I push my fists into the cold concrete and raise my chin, glaring at him.

"No," I hiss again, baring teeth.

Theodus descends the platform, his dark eyes blazing as he bounds toward me. I scramble up on my feet and back away, but the soldier behind me tugs at my chains, forcing me in place. Theodus grabs my wrist and jerks me forward.

"What are you doing?" My breath slows when he pulls a small knife from his belt, the silver blade gleaming in the low light. "Let me go!" I struggle in his grasp, fighting to get away, but his grip only tightens around my wrist.

"Theodus!" I think I hear Baba yell as he brings the blade down on my arm, slicing upward.

A bolt of pain spears through me. I grit my teeth as the knife burrows deep into my skin and blood gushes from the wound. Theodus digs his fingers into it, wrenching a scream from my throat.

My vision blurs. Dark shadows unfurl at the edges of my mind until the room fades entirely.

For a moment, the darkness presses in, but unlike Semi's vision, it doesn't last long. When it lifts, shadows twist before me like black tendrils, morphing into two young figures—one as familiar as my own skin.

Mama stalks around a heavy bag inside one of the practice rooms of Fort Regulus, lithe and nimble, her keen eyes trained on the lanky boy at her side. Theodus tries to mimic her fluid movements, but he's no soldier, and he's far too clumsy. Yet, Mama laughs freely when one of his kicks misses and he topples over, pulling her down to the mats with him. Fire and desire dance in her eyes moments before Theodus kisses her. In his divination, their love breathes; it begets, births a new life—a child with fire in her eyes and magic in her blood.

In his divination, I see the truth. A burning truth I can no longer deny.

Once, my dreams were filled with faces, all of them molded in the image of what I thought my father would look like. I wanted very much to put a face to the name, to breathe life into a past I never lived, even if it was only in my dreams.

Now I know the man Mama and Baba created was a facade, a lie told to a little girl so hungry for answers that she believed every word. *I believed.* I wrapped my heart around the tale of Isaiah, the black market trader. Isaiah, the doting husband. Isaiah, the murdered father.

They took him from me, I cried, not knowing he never truly existed. The man I thought my father to be isn't in fact who he is.

Not Isaiah, but Theodus.

A Lucis. A Scion.

My father.

The earth sways beneath my feet as Theodus drags me through a parade of visions, chaining me to the fleeting horrors of his past.

My stomach churns when I see Baba seated among the row of royals, clad in his own white-and-gold damask cape. He looks nothing like the grandfather I've known my entire life, with distant eyes and dark, stone-set features. A Lucis lord in every sense. The shadows dissolve, transforming into an image of Baba holding his newborn son as Celeste croons a warm lullaby next to him. He possesses her magic of divination and Baba's fearless spirit, but it is their forbidden love that would come to brand the child most, like a permanent scar. Still, Theodus's arrival is a spark of light in the darkness of Baba's world, second only to the first time he laid eyes on his sweet Celeste.

Then the vision shifts, wrenching me forward through the years. When the tendrils take shape, Theodus is four, a fright-eyed boy chained to a leash, forced to watch the firing squad end his mother's life with a hail of bullets. His screams echo long after the memory vanishes, replaced by the endless years of abuse Theodus suffers at Ascellus's hands.

I see it all—the whipping, the deaths, frequent nights of torture and starvation. A brutality no child should ever have to endure.

Ascellus breaks him apart, and from his shattered pieces, the king forges himself a new weapon. A machine capable of turning against his own kind, even his own heart.

Mama.

The shadows teeter at the edge of my vision, furling and unfurling, hesitant to truly take shape. Then I see it. The Nightwalkers forcing Mama and Felipe onto their knees. The explosion of gunfire, shuddering through the darkness of the foothills. And Theodus—a shadow leaning over Mama's body, watching as she sputters out her last breath.

A tremor snakes through my being. I sink back to the floor, my limbs giving out from under me. But Theodus isn't finished with me yet. He kneads his fingers deeper into my wound, into my blood, ignoring my screams as his shadows weave themselves back together.

Omari materializes in the empty hallways of the training center, the hidden conversations between the seer and the soldier unspooling before my wet eyes. Then I'm thrust into the tunnels the night of the Archives Hall fire, watching the guards chase after Jericho and Nazanin until they've closed in on them. By gods, it was Theodus who led them straight into their hands, told the guards exactly where to go in order to capture my friends. No matter what I did that night, I was never meant to save them because it wasn't what the seer wanted. My stomach plummets at the knowledge.

Soon I'm the one standing next to Theodus, deep in an exchange that only just took place last week yet feels like a lifetime ago.

Sloane, you can free us all.

He told me so many lies, too much deceit I wish I could have seen right through. As the shadows stretch into a gossamer, Theodus's divination skitters forward, plunging me knee-deep into a red river, where Scion bodies float in waste, and a ruined man wears a crown made of their bones.

Through it all, Semi's chants ring over and over in my ears.

*Trust not the one who killed their mother. The warrior they chained,
the elder freed. The child they spawned, the father saved. Thus, by your
hand shall the Blood Scion rise. When the pale viper dies, and foe turns
to blood.*

The realization burns through me, searing up the walls of my
throat. With a scream, I rip myself away from Theodus's grasp. I
can't—I don't want to see any more of his grim future.

Slowly, the walls of the palace chamber rise around me. I gasp
from my place on the floor, my heart hammering too fast in my chest.
Tears course down my cheeks as I lift my face up to Theodus. It's as if
I'm looking into the eyes of someone else entirely. Theodus was four
when Yeye Celeste died. He betrayed Mama and Baba freed her. He is
my father in flesh and blood, a shadow of the man I've always longed
for. He is a devious liar, a broken marionette. A beast of prey on the
edge of a dark, twisted path.

"You're the Blood Scion," I choke out.

They say the truth will set you free. Yet, it's only tied shackles
around my wrists and dragged me back into captivity.

Theodus stares down at me for a brief moment, his hands clasped
behind his back. Then he turns toward the dais, leaving me alone and
shaking. Somehow, Baba's broken free of his soldier's restraint and
rushes forward, crouching low at my side. I can't erase the memory of
him seated and robed among the circle of other royals. Still, I don't
squirm away when he wraps his arms around my shoulders, pressing
me into him.

"Did you know that before a descendant of Orunmila can understand a divination, he must be well versed in the sacred practice of
Ifá?" Theodus says across the room. He sits on his false throne with a
king's ease, one leg resting languidly against the gilded arm. "Ascellus didn't know this when he spared my life. So of course, it came
as a shock when he later discovered I was useless to him. I thought
the king would kill me then. Surely, there was no reason to keep a

powerless Scion alive. But Ascellus was determined, and for years, I became a madman's experiment. Everything he did to coax my magic out of me failed. I glimpsed nothing but flitting shadows, faceless figures, broken prophecies.

"The king became convinced my failure was deliberate. *I was punishing him*, he said. Imagine. In his rage, he ordered a Cleansing. Scions who were found that day were brought to me. To kill. This would be the punishment for my defiance. He had no way of knowing that the very essence of àse was in a Scion's blood. That a single drop of it was potent enough to strengthen another Scion's magic. The Ancient Kingdoms called it èwò. A sacred taboo. Yet, without knowing, Ascellus had found a way to unlock my divination. From that day forth, I became known as the Blood Scion."

The title echoes, another future Semi saw that has now come to pass. If only I'd spent more time trying to understand the boy's divination when he first told it to me. Perhaps I could have seen right through Theodus's manipulation.

I glance down at my arm, where blood still oozes from the cut the seer left behind. I wonder how many Scions Theodus has bled out for a glimpse of the future. Too many, if the memories I saw are any indication. They flit before my eyes now, but only one lingers. I'm back on the foothills with Mama, watching the sadness brim in her eyes the moment she realizes it was Theodus who betrayed her. Horrible hands squeeze at my heart, threatening to break, to shatter completely.

"You lied to me," I whisper, looking up at him through a flood of tears. "You told me you had nothing to do with Mama's capture. Led me to believe killing the bloodlines was the right thing to do. You knew I wanted to avenge Mama, and you preyed on my weakness. But it was *you* all along."

It was always you.

"Adelina was fated to die," he answers softly, his expression devoid of emotion, of life. "Once she set her mind on liberating every Scion and Yoruba across Nagea, I knew I couldn't let her live. The future she dreamed of was one that could never be. I warned her there would be a price to pay. I told her what would happen if she kept fighting for a free Nagea. She didn't listen."

"She was fighting for *your* freedom! For our people's freedom. The same freedom you told me you believed in!"

My voice crackles with the rage I feel igniting inside me. It ravages my senses, clawing for release. I wish I could make him pay for what he's done. Theodus used me, and for that, I want to make him bleed.

"Scions of your kind are not meant to be free, my dear," Theodus says, taking my outburst in stride. He maintains his poised demeanor, but I know the devil is at his most calm when he's about to strike. "I've seen what you can become," he continues, "the great darkness born from your magic. If Scions are allowed to rule, if magic is allowed to thrive, it will bring nothing but destruction to us all."

"Gods, you sound just like them." I shake my head, seeing for the first time how badly damaged he is. Three decades of abuse and oppression can't be unlearned in a single day, if at all. Yet, hearing Theodus echo the same sentiments the Lucis have used to justify their evil leaves a bitter taste in my mouth. My stomach turns. "After everything they did to you, everything they took from you, you still remain bound to them."

His mask of indifference cracks, revealing a flicker of emotion beneath. He grips the arms of his throne with such force, the wood splinters.

"Prisoners are kept in chains," he sneers down at me, leaning forward. "Today, I broke free of my shackles. Now thanks to you, a descendant of the ancient Adenuga line will once again sit on the throne of Nagea."

"Celeste's final foretelling." Beside me, Baba's eyes widen as he glares at his son, his jaw agape.

My own mind buzzes, scrambling to piece it all together. How deep does this go? How many months, years, went into this kind of treachery?

Theodus only nods. "She said a child born of her own flesh and blood would once again rule this land. Said someday, I'd be king. That the world would kneel at my feet. And I'd be the one to usher in a new age. She was right."

A winner's pride glimmers in his eyes, and cold numbness settles deep in my bones. Without knowing, Celeste had planted a lust for power in her son, but that was before his humanity was plucked out by a savage king. It's the worst thing she could have done, because a boy without humanity is no human, but a monster. And Theodus might just be the most monstrous of us all. And I helped—I helped a vicious boy rise to his feet. Out of vengeance, out of rage, I got rid of the only thing standing between him and the throne. A stab of pain cuts across my chest.

Gods above, what have I done?

"The age of Scions is over," Theodus announces. "The gods have shown this to me. Starting tomorrow, I will cleanse Nagea of every trace of magic left in its blood."

"You're a madman," I growl at him as he rises from his throne. "A product of all that the Lucis sought to accomplish. You are no father of mine. And I feel sorry for you. Because now I see how badly Ascellus has broken you. You have no honor, no identity, no culture to call your own. You are a bastard, Theodus. And the gods will punish you for what you've done."

Tears prick my eyes knowing this is no one's fault but mine. I'm the puppet who allowed herself to be strung and pulled by invisible hands. Now Theodus will destroy everything I fought to save, everyone I killed the bloodlines to liberate.

"My gods only punish monsters," he says when he gets within an inch of me. "And today, you rid the world of a dozen demons. Now it's my turn to do the same."

He reaches for the collar around my neck, tugging it hard enough to test its clasp. Despite how hard he pulls, it doesn't budge. Theodus smirks, satisfied. In my desperation, I push against the restraint of the collar, searching for my magic. But like before, my skin only burns. A groan pushes past my lips.

"Don't bother," Theodus says above my head. "The more you force it, the more pain you feel."

"What is this?" I hiss, waiting for the blistering sensation to pass. "What have you done to me?"

"Osanyin's collar," he answers. "An ancient artifact believed to have been forged from the sacred staff of Osanyin himself." *The Orisha of magic and spells.* "It's meant to trap a Scion's àse inside their own body. Once it locks, the clasp can't be broken until the Scion dies."

Fear carves me up. Even without Olympia and the royals, I am still a prisoner. Only this time, my oppressor wields a magic of his own. His bigotry isn't born from fear, but from decades of self-hatred. Now that hatred will spill into all of Nagea, a parasite gnawing at whatever magic it can devour. If only I knew how to stop him. I freed the monster. How the hell do I get him back into his cage?

Despite my nerves and the grief of knowing what Theodus has planned, I straighten my spine and look up at him.

"I will spit on your grave," I snarl. "Mark my words."

He flashes me a feral grin. "My dear, you won't live to see the dawn."

Next to me, Baba tries to reach for his son with a trembling hand. "Theodus—"

"Goodbye, Father." He spits in his face, cutting a wide berth between them both. "May your spirit find rest in òrun rere."

With that, he gestures to his soldiers, giving them the order to begin the execution. Baba huddles closer to me, clutching my hands in his, whispering silent prayers to gods that were never his. But I suppose gods are gods and prayers are prayers, and sometimes, just believing is enough.

Theodus's wave of soldiers swells up against us, at least a dozen of them, all armed with loaded rifles taunting of a death to come. Behind their masked faces, I spot Omari on the far side of the room, trailing Theodus as the seer retreats to his platform for a better view. A sudden ache throbs in my chest at the sight of him. The question I've wanted to ask since he clamped the collar around my neck burns my lips. Before I can stop myself, my mouth opens.

"Reaper!" I yell after him. He whirls immediately, his brows pinched together. "Was any of it real?" I force out, hating the slight shiver in my voice. "Or were you just following orders?"

His jaw tightens and he swallows hard. "Theodus came to me," he admits. "He was the one who sent me to the tunnels the night of the fire. He told me whatever I found down there, I had to protect. Keeping you alive, getting you to King's Isle, was the only way I could save Ara."

When he caught me inside the tunnels that night, I expected Omari to drag me to the commanders. In the end, all he said was *I can't*. Now I understand why.

Omari used me, just like Theodus ordered him to. Every wretched kiss and every bleeding touch—it was all a ploy, a ruse to get closer to me, to shove me down this horrible path. I was a task, another mission for a soldier to complete.

"I was just a pawn," I say, more to myself than to him. "Something to be sacrificed."

A bloody means to a bloody end.

Nothing more.

My heart sinks into my toes and tears burn the back of my eyes. But gods help me, I won't shed another one. Not for him.

At the edge of my vision, I think I see him flinch. When I look closely, his shoulders are squared, his eyes like green pools of fire.

"We're soldiers," he tells me, as if that alone could justify what he's done. "This is the only life we know."

I'm no stranger to the weapons Omari wields and the talent with which he uses them to draw blood. I know what it's like to be at the mercy of the squad leader's brutal blows. After all, I trained with him for a month. But this—this has to be his deadliest weapon yet. I know because it's the only one to wound too deep. The only one to truly scar.

I nod slowly, trying not to wince at the pain winding through me. I am the one made of fire. Yet, I am the one who got burned.

"You're dead to me." I spit the words at him before settling back into Baba's arms.

"I know," Omari murmurs. He moves quickly, turning his body and his heart away from me.

The soldiers tower over my head, making it hard to see his retreating frame. Still, I hear the echo of his footsteps as he takes his place behind Theodus.

Next to me, Baba sobs into my chest, heavy tremors racking through his frail body. Drawing him close is so natural to me that I don't think twice before planting a kiss on his forehead. He glances up at me, and all I can do is stare into his watery brown eyes.

"I'm sorry," he whispers, his voice a quivering shadow. "I never wanted you to find out this way."

I shake my head even now, turning the truth over and over, struggling to wrap my mind around all of it. There's a reason Baba knew iyerosun was the only thing that could suppress my àse. Why he never spoke of his old life, burying the memories of Yeye Celeste and his son beneath a haze of grief and guilt. His is a past riddled with violence and bloodshed, darkness and death, and all the evil born from his very own hands. Because no matter how much I try to fight it, the truth is: my grandfather was a Lucis royal once, a warlord who lived his life slaughtering the very thing he claims to love. That single knowledge drags jagged wounds all over my body, but the pain and scars are a familiar thing to me now.

"You should have told me" is all I say to him.

He nods in the way only a broken man would. "I've lived with my ghosts for too long, I didn't know how to part with them—even for you." The sorrow woven into his voice pierces my heart, but this time, I will myself to remain still. "Believe me, Sloane. I had no idea who Adelina was when I met her inside Cliff Row all those years ago. I was resigned to my fate until I learned my son fathered her unborn child. I knew then I had to find a way to get you both out. I couldn't undo the mistakes of my past, but Adelina gave me a chance at a future I was never worthy of. And from the day you were born, I swore, *swore* to her that I would always protect you, always keep you safe. It was all she asked of me, and I failed. I failed and I'm sorry, Sloane."

His words rattle something deep inside me. A smothered fire, fighting to break free, to burn.

All my life, I fought against who I was, what I was capable of. I denied my identity and my magic because it was what the world demanded of me. Doing so kept me safe. It also made me hopeless and terribly afraid.

The soldiers form a line ahead of us, their guns raised in silent order. With a gasp, Baba nudges his head into my shoulder and shuts his eyes. Strangely, he looks serene in this moment, ready to welcome death if it should come for him. After years of living his life in hiding, tucked away in the shadows of a dusty village, perhaps this is the peace he craves.

But I am only a child—a child who's barely even lived at all. These bastards robbed me of my childhood, my innocence, and my humanity. They led me to believe I was a curse, an abomination, a plague to be rid of. They took my name and my culture. They stole my freedom and I fought back. With everything inside me, every last bit of strength I had, I took down twelve monsters. I escaped an oppressive world just to be chained to another. But I have tasted freedom, and by gods, I refuse to spit it out.

Despite what Theodus may think, I am not the queen. I am not easily broken.

No. I am a Scion. A warrior made of heart and fire.

I deserve to live. I deserve to survive.

After everything I've been through, I won't submit to death so easily.

Not today.

FORTY-TWO

The soldiers' countdown is familiar, plunging me into the depths of a dark abyss.

Osanyin's collar burns around my neck, keeping my àse far from my reach and out of my control. Despite its magical hold, I search for the fire I know exists deep inside my being. It is mine, after all. It belongs to me and I to it. No spell can keep it away.

It is mine.

Pain tears through my body in endless waves the more I push against the boundaries of the spell. It counters, threatening to burn me alive as a blaze of heat explodes inside me.

I scream.

Blisters swell on my arms, my chest, my back, scorching every inch of my skin. Beside me, Baba seizes my shoulders and yells my name, pleading for me to regain control. Though his touch is gentle, soothing, heavy clamor drowns out the sound of his voice. Fiery dots nibble at the edge of my vision. The world behind my closed lids is wrapped in twisting hues of red, a gathering inferno that seems to stretch on forever. My breath hitches as the air slowly begins to warm around me. Heat pulses into a feverish sensation that entices just as much as it overwhelms. I tremble on my knees, beads of sweat dripping down my skin. Fire crawls up my throat, burns a pathway across my tongue and past my lips. Words rip open inside me.

> *"Shango, Obakoso*
> *Orisha iná*
> *Mo jí èmí re ní wákàtí yìí*
> *Yá mi ní agbára re*
> *Kún mi pèlú àse re—"*

The chant is an ancient language, a Yoruba tongue I do not understand. But—I do. *I do understand.* Though unfamiliar words rush out of my mouth, the meaning is as vivid as the firestorm raging before my eyes. With each sacred praise, I summon the god of fire. I invoke the spirit of my blood deity. The chant thrums with a life of its own, growing into a frenzy that seems to shake the earth beneath my feet.

> "*Shango, mo pàse fún èmí apanirun re*
> *Tan iná ìbínú re kalè*
> *Jakuta, gbó igbe mi*
> *Jàde wá nípasè ara mi*
> *Shango, jà fún mi!*"

Like a single droplet of rain, the smallest wisp of heat curls through me. It doesn't scorch. It doesn't brand. This is no fire born of a spelled collar. This is my magic.

My fire.

My heart grasps desperately at it, reaching deeper until I feel the first surge of àse trickling back into my blood. The faint echo of Shango's drum pounds in my head. Tears spill down my cheeks as my deity's divine energy courses through my veins once more. When I latch onto it, I don't let go. Instead, I pull with all my strength, pouring my hope, my pain, my rage, into it.

Heat ripples in the air around me. I open my eyes to a world of fire. It gathers the line of soldiers in a blaze, spitting them out in a torrent of cinder and ash. Theodus's army has multiplied since I last laid eyes on it. The soldiers shoot heavy rounds of ammunition at me and Baba, but a shield of fire surrounds us both. Bullets singe and melt, unable to pierce the twisting flames.

I rise with the fury of a divine god. The shackles around my wrist glow a brilliant orange before dissolving into a silvery puddle at my feet. I lift a hand to the collar around my neck. Just as my fingers graze the curved steel, it shatters under my touch. A million stones slink across the floor, racing to rejoin, until the iron collar mends itself back together.

I spot Theodus across the room in the same moment. When he sees me, he doesn't flee like the bloodlines did. Instead, he charges forward with his army of soldiers, their onslaught of bullets peppering the air. A chaos of gunfire rings around me. But I am untouchable. I am divine.

I am Shango's fire.

Àse ravages my entire being. The surge of energy is too much, too potent, until I'm caught in a riptide of magic far beyond my own control. I collapse to my knees a few feet away from the soldiers, clawing at my body. My skin itches, my bones rattle, and blood gushes from my nose, my ears, my eyes.

I want to burn. I want to burn. I want to burn.

When the world erupts, there is no flame, no fire.

Only ash.

One by one, the soldiers bound forward, but they crumble before they reach me. Bullets rip apart, piece by piece, until steel turns to dust. The chamber walls do the same as wooden planks and concrete tear from the building structure. Overhead, the roof shingles cave inward, wide fissures revealing puffs of dark gray clouds streaked with infinite reds. Broken shards swirl around me like a black storm. The soldiers who come too close are reduced to cinder.

At the sight of their men falling, the few remaining soldiers flee Theodus's side. Even the seer has no choice but to run. His soot-covered face shines behind the smoke, true madness burning in his gaze as Omari drags him away from the ashen world.

I kneel in the face of so much carnage, the remnants of my àse still churning in my blood. It overwhelms my senses, dragging me in and out of my own mind, deeper, deeper, into a spiritual trance. My breath stutters. Glazed eyes roll into the back of my skull as magic wraps itself around my being, refusing to let go. Like a tidal wave, Shango's fire floods my veins. I see it in the tendrils of àse, swirling like a storm of molten fire beneath my skin.

When it breaks, I unleash.

King's Isle burns around me, the flames spreading far and wide, devouring an island built on the blood and bones of my people. The bloom of the explosion is blinding as concrete shudders, and rows upon rows of buildings erupt in shrouds of flame and smoke. An inferno to rain destruction on all that Theodus thinks he's won. If this is the path my father has chosen, I will raze the earth before I let him walk it.

"Let go." Baba's dark face flashes in the heat of the fire, a desperate plea in his voice.

I should listen to him. *Let go.* But I have lost too much to this world and the people who dwell in it. For all they've done to me, I want to make them pay. Omari and Theodus and each and every single one of their soldiers. Wherever they are, I want to make them bleed.

Spread the flame, Folashadé. Let them burn.

The fire weaves along my skin, hissing and crackling as it engulfs every inch of my form. It clothes my body in a fiery cloak, threads of embers writhing through me like silk.

"Sloane, LET GO!" Baba screams behind the haze, but I no longer hear him.

Across the room, a blur of figures bounds toward us through the shadows. I twist a ball of fire in my hands, ready to send a blast at any soldier who dares come too close. But as the silhouettes take shape, a familiar face rises into view.

Caspian.

The Blades.

In that moment, a loud drumming drags me back into the trance, an ancient rhythm that thunders in my ears.

Gba ara re sílè.

The voice rumbles from somewhere deep within. I don't know where it comes from, whom it belongs to. But the Yoruba language echoes and, like the chant, my mind translates it with ease.

Let go.

Fi agbára re pamó, omo mi. O ti pè èmí mi. Mo ti gbó igbe re. Gba ara re sílè.

Save your strength, my child. You have summoned my spirit, and I have answered. Let go.

Who are you? What is happening to me?

I search my mind for an answer, trying to make sense of what I don't yet understand. Even when I fight to free myself from the trance, the magic latches on with feral, burning teeth. In my head, I hear the wild dance of the drums, the clashing cymbal of my heart against my ribs.

It's too much. Too much.

My limbs convulse. My breathing slows. Hot, falling tears sear a brand into my cheeks.

"Who are you?" I scream the last of my strength into the inferno.

When the voice speaks again, a violent thunder slashes across the open skies. Thunderstones clatter into a heap at my feet.

Omo Orisha, rántí eni tí ò jé. Máse gbàgbé iná tí ń jó nínu ison re. Omo oba iná, rántí mi.

Daughter of Orisha, remember who you are. Don't you forget the fire running through your veins.

Daughter of a fiery king, remember me.

Another clap of thunder splits the heavens apart.

In his fire, I see the truth.

Shango.

ACKNOWLEDGMENTS

First and above all else, thank you, God, for letting me live out this dream. You've taught me what courage in the face of failure looks like, and for every milestone reached, I owe it all to you.

My husband, Matthew, who dared to ask one simple question ten years ago, not knowing how life changing it would be, thank you for being a constant throughout this journey. You are my best friend, my sounding board, the first critique partner on every project, my daily therapist and support system, and truly the most inspiring human in my world.

To my parents, thank you for giving me the world. Without your sacrifices, this dream never would have been possible. You taught me what it means to persevere, keep the faith, and never stop trying. Mama, I am nothing without your prayers. Papa, thank you for being my guiding light.

I have the best brother in the world, and so much of our childhood was me following in his footsteps. Michael, you are and always will be my role model, my inspiration behind rocking G-Unit to school on civvies day, and the root of all my horror movie nightmares. Watching you chase your life's goal inspired me to do the same, and I'm the proudest sister because I got to see you conquer medical school this year. The warmest thanks to my sister-in-law, Amilyn, for being one of the funniest, realest, dopest sisters I could ask for. We will always have the hours spent trying to learn Shoki the night before my traditional wedding.

My mother-in-law, Sharon, who has been one of the most supportive people in my corner, thank you for your enthusiasm and words of encouragement over the years. I'm forever grateful to have you in my world. I have too many aunties, uncles, cousins, nephews, and nieces to name, but my heartfelt appreciation to my extended family both near and far, as well as to my Danso in-laws. Thank you for the years of love and support.

Of course, I wouldn't be the woman I am today without these powerful queens in my life: Veronica, Tee, Danait, Alyssa, Drea, Rhona, Mel, Danielle, Lynnette, and Henrietta. In more ways than one, you've all been my inspirations and my infinite well of motivation. All my love to you ladies.

For the past eight years, I've dreamed about the moment I get to write this special thank-you to my favorite lil' man, Major. Truth is, this book would never have been completed without him, especially with the countless all-nighters he pulled with me year after year. You are such a light, buddy, and I am the luckiest to call you mine.

I've always been an avid reader, hungry for new adventures and new worlds I could escape into. *Things Fall Apart* by Chinua Achebe was the first book I read that grounded me in a world much like my own, the first book that birthed a curiosity in me about the power of stories, the magic of creating them, and it would later become the first book that influenced much of my own writing. I consider myself incredibly lucky to have had African literature to turn to when I was growing up, and my deepest admiration goes out to these legends and pioneers of stories who wove words that kindled a flame.

The Black literature class I took with Professor Andrea Davies and Yafet Tewelde in university was a pivotal point in my journey as both a Black woman and a Black author. Thank you both for shaping my understanding of Blackness and for the depth you brought to the reading of *Mama Day* and *The Book of Negroes*.

The road to publication can be such a strange, meandering experience, and I certainly never envisioned the path mine would take. In 2018, I was on my honeymoon when I queried *Blood Scion* with only the first five chapters to a handful of agents. I had no idea what the outcome would be, but somehow Victoria Marini saw something in those pages that made her want to help bring this book out into the world. Thank you so much for believing in this story; I'm forever grateful for all that you've done.

To Jenny Bent, the fiercest literary leader, maker of all dreams, and fellow real estate junkie—I cannot thank you enough for your support and unwavering belief in my stories, welcoming me into the TBA fold, and for being the standard in all things publishing. I'm honored to have you so fearlessly leading the charge on this journey.

Many authors have a bucket list of things they hope to one day achieve, and when I found out Debbie Deuble Hill and Alec Frankel wanted to represent *Blood Scion* for film, I hit that milestone. Thank you for helping me share my book with the movie industry. I couldn't have imagined a better duo to champion this story.

Publishing *Blood Scion* under the HarperCollins banner has always been a dream of mine, and I'm honored to have worked with so many brilliant minds to bring this book to life. My continued gratitude to Kristen Pettit, editor extraordinaire and plot wizard, who has understood the very heart of this story since the beginning and has been patient throughout the entire process. Thank you for pushing and guiding me along the way. Here's to spreading many more flames in book two. My biggest thanks as well to Clare Vaughn, whose editorial questions and first reader notes helped transform this manuscript into a worthy novel. My executive managing editor, Mark Rifkin, senior production editor, Shona McCarthy, and copyeditor, Sarah Chassé, for the genius that is their style sheet and for making every single line in this book what it is today. I'm in awe of you all. My production editor, Nicole Moreno, and proofreaders, Jaime Herbeck and Lana Barnes, gave this book the final touches it needed, and for that, I am deeply grateful.

Taj Francis is the magician behind *Blood Scion*'s epic cover and, without a doubt, one of the best artists in the game. Corina Lupp designed one hell of a jacket, and I'm so privileged to be able to say you both had a hand in the creation of this book. Many more thanks to Mitch Thorpe, my in-house publicist, the incredible teams in marketing and publicity, the entire HarperTeen family, and the creative gems behind Epic Reads—all of whom continue to work tirelessly behind the scenes to share *Blood Scion* with the world. To Megan Beatie, for finding new ways to get this book into more readers' hands. It's been an absolute joy having you on board this ship. Much admiration to Kadeen Griffiths—your early enthusiasm and support for this book means the world; and to Doris Allen, who not only introduced me to the haunting musical genius that is Jacob Banks but loved *Blood Scion* enough to devour it not once but twice. A big shout-out also goes to Lara T. Kareem, my sensitivity reader and fellow Naija queen, for getting the depth of this story in more ways than I could have ever asked for. Your sensitivity notes remain a treasure on my desk.

The year 2017 changed my life, and it's in part because of Pitch Wars. All my appreciation goes to Brenda Drake and the wonderful Pitch Wars committee for creating a mentorship program that has not only launched careers but fostered lifelong friendships.

To Claribel Ortega and Kat Cho, my Pitch Wars mentors and two of the most talented and inspiring people I know, you somehow managed to see through the chaos that was *Blood Scion*'s early draft and pushed me to take this story to a place far beyond my own imagination. Thank you so much for your support over the years. #Teamoji *for life*!

Without Pitch Wars, I never would have met my writing wife and one of my best friends, Alexandria Sturtz. You've been a pillar of support since the beginning, and I couldn't imagine going on this wild, crazy journey without you. Please keep feeding me more female characters who continue to smash the patriarchy, because Tally and Akiva still own my heart after all these years.

I'm so fortunate to have many incredibly talented writers in my circle, and Roseanne Brown definitely wears the crown as queen of fantasy romance. Rosie, I'm thankful for your friendship; humor; yes, the weirdness you leave in my DMs; and even more that you gave the world Malik, my perfect soft boi. Here's to more epic life and writing adventures and the holy oil that remains forever on deck.

Ciannon Smart and I started this wild ride together, and, in the years since, we've gone from sprint partners to critique partners to partners in crime. C, I'm so privileged to know you and to truly call you a friend and a sister. You are such a force in this industry and the world ain't even ready, but we won't spill that tea here. So I'll just thank you for being the goddess that you are and for the times we've broken our own damn record whenever we hop on a call. I think we're at four hours now, lord.

I feel truly blessed to have a circle of ladies in this community whose friendship also means the world: J. Elle, Louisa, Faridah, Abbey, Sarah, and one of my day one writing pals, Lindsey. Thank you for your unending support, the advice that never fails, and the magic you continue to create. To the Afro-Caribbean Avengers, the Toronto Crew, the Black Mermaids, the 22 Debuts, and my fellow 2017 Warriors—you lot are literally the most talented, brilliant people I've met in this industry, and I couldn't be more grateful for the years of support, enthusiasm, and much-needed motivation. Rooting for you all, always.

Many authors have paved the way for me to be where I am today, and my deepest gratitude goes to every single one of you for breaking down those doors and shattering those ceilings with your words. Shout-out to Dhonielle Clayton, the fiercest queen of all—thank you for continuing to inspire the rest of us. And to everyone who's helped me navigate this strange world of publishing, CPs, and industry pals alike; I'm only here because of your feedback, encouragement, mentorship, and invaluable insights.

A special thank-you goes out to every blogger, librarian, teacher, and bookseller who has somehow shown more love to this feisty little book than I could dream possible. I treasure the interactions, posts, messages, and every bit of attention you've given to *Blood Scion*.

And to you, fellow reader, thank you for welcoming Sloane into your world. Writing this book has been a decade-long journey of growth, healing, overcoming challenges, and finding myself. When I first met Sloane, she was loud and ferocious, a young girl full of life and courage and bravery—so much that I was very afraid to write her story in the beginning. But as it turned out, going on that journey with her ten years ago was the best thing I could have done for myself. Because through her, I discovered the power of my own voice, and, for that, this story will always have a special place in my heart.

I hope you love it just as much, and I hope Sloane's journey sparks all the fire in you, too.